Praise for Stephen Russell Payne

"Stephen Russell Payne has emerged as a new voice in Vermont's impressive pantheon of creative writers, and a powerful one. For years I've enjoyed his journalism and short fiction. Now, with his first novel, he has written a dramatic story of suspense, love, and redemption. *Cliff Walking* is written with clarity, passion, and great sympathy for, and understanding of, all aspects of human nature."

— HOWARD FRANK MOSHER
Award-winning author of *Points North*

"Peopled with characters that openly disdain the postcard Vermont, the stories of Stephen Russell Payne plumb the depths of rural hardship, farm life, and small dreams. Thanks to Payne's unerring eye for detail and ear for voice, these stories turn modest lives into treasure, by revealing the tenderness that makes them possible."

— STEPHEN KIERNAN
Award-winning author of *The Curiosity* and *The Baker's Secret*

"Stephen Russell Payne's short story collection, *Ties That Bind Us*, is a spectacular debut by a writer who knows his characters, the state of Vermont, and the frailties of human beings caught up in the mortal coil; he does it all with grace, depth, intimacy, and at times a sly sense of humor. I loved these stories."

— ERNEST HEBERT
Professor of English, Dartmouth College, author of the *Darby* series

---

"Stephen Russell Payne's short stories have shown him to be among New England's finest writers of regional fiction. His first novel, *Cliff Walking,* is an absorbing story, skillfully told. We believe in these characters and care about them. What Payne has given us isn't a plotless "literary" novel, but a warm and touching love story full of suspense and conflict, likely to have wide popular appeal. Payne is in top form."

— X. J. KENNEDY
Recipient of the Robert Frost Medal and the Jackson Poetry Prize

"Stephen Russell Payne's new short story collection, *Ties That Bind Us,* is a terrific piece of work. Payne is a 4th generation Vermonter and knows his kinsmen well. His stories bring to life—not in the voice of an omniscient narrator—but in the voices of those living them, Vermont's hardscrabble past. Payne leads us into an earlier Vermont, replete with durable characters, both in their own lives and in our memory."

— BILL SCHUBART
Author of *Panhead* and *Lila and Theron*

"No one writes with as much passion and insight about northern Vermont as Stephen Russell Payne. With the meticulousness of a surgeon, and the lyricism of a poet, Payne captures the tenacity and honesty of the denizens of the Green Mountain State's small towns and villages. Reading Payne is like a visit from a good old friend. His tales are always infused with equal measures of humor, wisdom, and love."

— JENNIFER FINNY BOYLAN
Best-selling author of *She's Not There*

"Stephen Payne's new collection of stories, *Ties That Bind Us,* takes us far off the interstates, ski slopes, and upscale bed-and-breakfasts and microbreweries to the backroads, backwoods, and half-abandoned former mill towns of a Vermont most visitors to the Green Mountain State don't know exists. His wonderfully independent-minded characters are the very last of a breed whose like will not be seen again. These stories, written with clear-eyed affection, gentle humor, and great expertise, remind me of *Country of the Pointed Firs.* They are a loving exploration of a unique but vanishing place and its noble people, who know better than anyone that their way of life is fading fast."

— HOWARD FRANK MOSHER
Award-winning author of *A Stranger in the Kingdom*

"*Riding My Guitar* is the entertaining story of a true Vermont original. Rick Norcross's amazing journey has taken him throughout the U.S. and to Europe, but at heart he remains a friendly, modest and very talented Vermonter. In telling this story of the irrepressible Norcross, Stephen Payne also gives us a vivid picture of rural Vermont in the 1950s and '60s. It's a fun read!"

— TOM SLAYTON
Editor emeritus, *Vermont Life Magazine*

LIFE ON A CLIFF

ALSO BY STEPHEN RUSSELL PAYNE

Boston, Vermont — First Poems of Stephen Russell Payne
Cliff Walking — A Novel
Riding My Guitar — The Rick Norcross Story
Ties That Bind Us — A Collection of Vermont Short Stories.

LIFE ON A CLIFF

A NOVEL

STEPHEN RUSSELL PAYNE

CEDAR LEDGE PUBLISHING

Life on a Cliff
First Edition, August 2018

Text copyright © 2018 by Stephen Russell Payne
Author photo by Natalie Stultz
Cover and interior design by Winslow Colwell/Wren Song Design

The text of this publication was set in Adobe Caslon.

Published in the United States by Cedar Ledge Publishing
St. Albans, Vermont 05478

ISBN: 978-1-7322599-0-4
Library of Congress Control Number: 2018908290

Printed in the United States of America

For information, permissions, and appearances, please visit
www.StephenRussellPayne.com or Facebook at Stephen Russell Payne.

To my beloved family,
Marietta, Christopher, and Meghan,
and my brother, Uncle John.

And in memory of my parents,
Louise McGill and Russell Sturdee Payne.
They always said, "You can do anything you set your mind to,"
and I believed them.

There's a silence that falls
in the midst of a storm,
as the elements wait and decide,
to unleash their forces on
mortals like me,
or to move on and let us survive

—from "Fire" by David Mallett

CHAPTER ONE

WELL BEFORE SUNRISE, FRANCIS WAS AWAKENED BY KATE'S thrashing in the bed, so he got up and sat in the eastern window-well next to his grandmother's blown-glass whaling lamp. He nudged the metal-framed window open enough that a thin stream of cool sea air entered the bedroom. Watching over Kate lying twisted in the sheets, he wished he could take away her demons, give her all the comfort she needed and deserved. But times were hard, and after the trauma of the trial, they had lost the softness they'd found with each other, the urge to lovingly touch whenever they were in each other's presence. He missed that, in part because it symbolized what was so different with Kate from his marriage to Rachael. Kate went deeper inside him and in ways he'd never experienced before. He wanted to get that back.

Francis thought about Stringer sleeping downstairs, this beautiful kid living in his house. Francis wanted nothing more than for them all to enjoy being a normal family. Or at least something resembling normal, which he'd come to realize none of them had ever experienced. It was hard for Francis to admit, but he, too, had changed over the winter, become less open, more guarded and reclusive, similar to how he'd been after Rachael died and before he met Kate and Stringer. Francis wanted to love Kate unconditionally, something he'd never gotten from his father but had desperately wanted. Even now, he was hesitant—or scared—to commit to it.

Kate struggled to get away from Leland, who was on top of her, jamming her wrists into the coils of the mattress. She twisted her head back and forth trying to avoid his breath, which was laced with cigarettes and cheap whiskey.

"No!" she yelled, twisting back and forth, trying to escape his grip. Despite her legs being partially bound, she was at least able to knee him.

"It's okay."

"Leave me alone!"

"Kate, it's—"

"Get off me, you pig!"

Exhausted from years of fighting for her life, Kate's arms and legs lost their strength. As her muscles relaxed, to her surprise, she realized no one was actually holding her down. She was free.

"Kate, you're having another nightmare."

She cautiously opened her eyes, saw Francis sitting on the edge of the bed. He gently pulled on a twisted sheet, unwinding it from her legs.

Kate swept several matted strands of long, sweaty hair from her face and pushed herself back against the headboard. A sharp headache pounded between her temples, like she had a bad hangover. Perhaps she did, of the emotional kind.

"Another Leland dream?"

Kate nodded. "They're awful." She pulled her knees tight to her chest.

"It seems like you're purging him from your system."

"Yeah, like shit out of a sewer pipe." Kate took a drink of water from a glass on the bedside table. "That peckerhead's still torturing me, and he's been dead since last fall."

Francis put his hand gently on her forearm. "It takes a long time to get over years of abuse. It doesn't fade away easily."

"I know, but I'm sick of feeling crazy." She pointed at her head. "And it's not just Leland that's got the squirrels going up here."

"Perhaps you should get together with Ginny. She *is* your sponsor."

Kate rubbed her eyes. "I know, but she'll be pissed with me. I haven't gone to a meeting in a while."

"They do seem to help you. Besides, you're still in pretty early recovery."

"It's been almost a year. You'd think I'd have my act together by now."

"It's been quite a year. It's a wonder you survived."

She stared at the disheveled bedclothes.

"Kate, I want to help you in any way I can."

"I know."

Kate felt a tangle of emotions struggling between her mind and heart. Francis was such a good man, but she really didn't get him, so staid and controlled. She looked at him inquisitively. "Don't you ever lose it? Just go crazy with everything that's happened?"

He nodded. "Inside I do, but I try not to show it."

"Well, it makes me crazier that you seem so together all the time."

"I'm not, really."

"Well could you at least act a little crazy sometimes?"

"I'll try, but you didn't know my father. If he even heard me walking in the hallway of our house he chastised me."

"And I had a crazy mother who was loose as a goose."

Francis leaned forward and kissed Kate's forehead.

Kate shook her head. "You must wonder what you've gotten yourself into with me."

"It has crossed my mind a time or two." He smiled. "Fleetingly, though."

"You must be crazy, too."

"Well, I am an artist."

Francis got up and started down the stairs. "I'll make coffee and meet you out on the lawn."

After Francis disappeared, Kate tucked her head against her knees. She was far from having her shit together. This new life was better than anything she'd known, except being with a 'perfect' guy was driving her nuts, even more so as she was trying to deal with conflicted feelings on her own. She knew from experience that wouldn't go well. Though she dreaded it, she had to call Ginny.

By the time Francis had made coffee, he found Kate sitting outside at the edge of the cliff, wrapped in his field coat. She stared out over a relatively placid sea, the morning sky painted a dozen shades of red, pink, and orange—delicate brush strokes underlying wispy strands of cirrus clouds. The fresh sunlight illuminated Kate's profile. She looked radiant. Despite their recent discord, Francis was quite sure he had found his soulmate, though it had been through the most unimaginable circumstances. And though he had felt thoroughly in love with her in the months after they met, he was aware that the intense chaos that followed had caused him to pull back from her emotionally.

Carrying two steaming cups of coffee, Francis joined Kate on the bluff. She kept her gaze on the ocean.

"What's wrong?" he asked.

Kate began rocking back and forth. "I hate it when you ask that. A lot's wrong, Francis. I have my life back—a good life—but I'm not sure what to do with it. This is all foreign to me, like I'm wearing clothes that don't fit."

Francis leaned back on the grass. "I know things were crazy during the trial, but I hoped by now you would feel more at home."

There was a long silence. Then, knowing they could usually talk about Stringer without getting into a fight, Francis changed the subject. "I'm glad Stringer started that part-time job on Ginny's boat. It's tough work, but if he could try and pull Delbert Ready out of the raging Atlantic, he can handle a bunch of lobster traps."

"We'll see. It's not the lobsters I'm worried about. Shelly said Ginny's got some rough guys on her boat. Maybe too rough for Stringer's good."

Francis took a swallow of coffee, the hot liquid warming him from the inside. "I know lobstermen are a rugged bunch, but I don't think Ginny would let him go out with anyone who's dangerous."

"She'd better not." Kate looked at Francis. "I'm concerned about String. He's become distant, hardly talks to me. And that new girl… Of all the chicks he could've met, he's interested in some lowlife named Sam."

Francis perked up. "I hadn't heard about her. The last thing String said to me was he wanted to get out of here and go back to California. You can see it in his paintings."

"That was before he met Sam."

"I see. Quite a change, as he's obviously been angry with the way he was treated around Leland's death. He's been through an awful lot, more than I could have withstood at his age."

"You went through your own hard times."

"Yes, but nothing like he has. Anyway, what do you know about this girl?"

"She's an orphan from Biddeford, some mill town on the south coast. Her guardian's a guy named Nelson, works on Ginny's boat. The nicer one of the guys, but he drinks a lot. Shelly knows him, told her this Sam kid is tough, been passed around a lot since she was sent up from Massachusetts a few years ago: foster homes, neglect, abuse, same old shit. She's supposed to play the guitar real well but gets high a lot. Anyway, you know I worry about Stringer drinking and getting into drugs. Genetics aren't exactly on his side."

"Is he really sweet on this girl?"

"They just met a couple weeks ago, but a fire's been lit. Shelly says she's a 'street beauty,' whatever that is. She said Sam's playing over at a place called the Mill Pub Saturday night. I'm going to check her out."

"I've heard that's a rough place. I don't know if I'd go over there."

Kate turned and stared at Francis. "Are you kidding me? If that's all I need to do to check out my kid's girl, I'm going."

"I meant neither of you should go." Francis did not want to start the day off fighting. He looked toward the horizon where the sun had risen above a couple of lobster boats working among the islands. The bright colors underlying the clouds had faded to pastels and were melding into daylight. "Maybe the job on the boat will give Stringer a new focus, a way to work out his aggressions. Plus, he likes being on the water."

"He is excited about doing something new, and he's painting up a storm. He's even got some art dealer interested in him." Kate paused. "I think String's okay. It's me that's the problem. I feel restless and irritable, and when I have these dreams, they fill me with fear again, like it used to be before we left California."

Francis reached out to touch her hand. "I'm sorry."

Kate withdrew. "Please stop saying you're sorry. It's not your fault. You're not responsible for everything." She got up. "Anyway, this guy Richard, the art dealer, is coming by this morning to talk about String's work."

"I didn't know." Francis was taken aback.

"He called yesterday while you were at the gallery."

Francis stood. "Where's he from?"

"New York, but he has a camp up here somewhere."

"Shouldn't I look into him for you? I have contacts."

"I know, but String and I need to do some things for ourselves. I'll talk to you about it, but I've got to meet him early 'cause I'm working the lunch shift."

"Why don't you quit working at that place?"

"I need to be able to support Stringer and me."

"Not really."

"Yes, I do. And don't talk down to me." She started walking toward the bungalow.

"Sorry. I mean, I didn't intend it to come out like that. I hate to see you work so hard in a place like The Claw, especially for Jake."

"He's just an old fool. Plus, he was the only one who took a chance and gave me a job when we got here."

Francis took a step toward her, softened his voice. "I just want you to have something better. You've suffered enough. I'm happy to support both of you."

Kate moved away. "Please stop pampering me, Francis. I feel like a kept woman."

"You know that's not my intent. I actually thought you'd be basically on your own, running the gallery by now. You could, if you wanted to."

Kate was steaming. "I'm not Rachael."

"No, you're not."

Kate's face tightened. "What's that supposed to mean?"

"I didn't—"

"Never mind." Kate pushed her fingers through her hair, letting it fall haphazardly over her shoulders. "Look, I appreciate what you've done for me, for us, but I can't do this perfect-life thing right now. I feel like I can't breathe. It's making me crazy. Crazier."

Francis was confused but knew when to quit. "I'll leave you alone then." He stepped toward the house. "I'm going for a walk and then to Portland to do a few errands. I'll be back late afternoon. Don't forget we have dinner at the yacht club in Falmouth Foreside tonight. It's the season's opening celebration. It should be fun."

"Okay, but you know I don't do fancy very well."

"There are many fine people at the club. Besides, that's what you said about the Portland Andrew Wyeth exhibit last fall, and look what a meaningful experience it was for you."

"I guess."

"And I'd be wary of any art dealer who shows up out of the blue. There are a lot of shysters out there. Just because we're in Maine doesn't mean we're immune."

"Believe me, I know we're not immune—to anything."

CHAPTER TWO

AFTER FRANCIS LEFT, KATE TRIED TO COMFORT HERSELF BY HUMming one of her mother's Lakota peace songs, but it was no use. She was too agitated, with him and with herself. Back in the bungalow, she called Ginny at her gift shop. Despite feeling nervous, Kate was relieved Ginny was willing to see her. Kate said she'd be there in half an hour.

In town, as Kate approached the salt-encrusted sign hanging above *Cove Cards, Gifts & Lobsters*, she felt uneasy, in part because she wasn't sure she could tell Ginny the whole truth about what was going on in her crazy head.

A bell suspended on a spring over the door rang as Kate stepped inside. Ginny stood at the cash register counting out postcard stamps for a couple of tourists. She motioned for Kate to wait on the small deck off the back of the store. Outside, Kate leaned against a cracked wooden railing and breathed in the fine briny mist lingering over seaweed-covered rocks that formed tidal pools below her.

While at first it felt good to relax, after about ten minutes Kate became annoyed Ginny was making her wait so long. She found herself staring at a discarded whiskey bottle nestled between the rocks and suddenly had a hard urge to go get her own bottle and drink it down—every last drop. She could taste it on her tongue. "Shit—" She turned away from the bottle just as Ginny came through the screen door. Kate started when it slammed behind her.

Ginny sat in a rusted green metal chair and leaned back. "Tourists," she said. "Can't live with 'em, can't live without 'em. Seems like this season's heating up too early. Sold four stuffed lobsters already this week—the toy ones I mean—and a whole bunch of fancy new magnets. I could never keep this place open if it wasn't for all the Maine crap the Chinese keep coming up with." She looked at Kate. "You don't look so good."

Feeling uncomfortable, Kate tried to move around but there wasn't anywhere to go on the small deck.

"What ails you?" Ginny asked in a concerned voice.

Kate hesitated.

Ginny motioned with her hand. "Come on, sit down. I haven't got all day, more damn tourists'll be coming in."

Kate sat in the other chair next to Ginny. "I think I'm losing my mind."

Ginny nodded. "Know the feeling. Same thing happens to me when I don't go to enough meetings. What flavor crazy are you?"

"All kinds. Mostly I want to help String with his painting career. He has real talent, but I don't know what to do. I mean with getting him noticed, though there is some art dealer interested in him."

"That sounds promising. What does Francis think?"

"Actually, Stringer's upset with me that Francis isn't involved, but I need to do this for Stringer myself. Plus, Stringer's not really interested in selling his paintings, anyway."

Ginny looked confused but listened quietly as she picked flecks of loose paint off the arm of her chair.

Kate looked out over the gentle waves. "Sometimes I feel paralyzed by the Leland dreams I keep having. That scumbag's tried to kill me another twenty times. They're so real I can feel him on top of me. Makes me want to throw up."

Ginny waited patiently.

"And I know I should be more grateful for everything I've got now, but…"

Ginny touched her arm. "Forget that bullshit, tell me what you're really feeling."

"Mostly, I'm just *feeling*—everything—like a bear coming out of hibernation. Even the grass looks greener to me."

Ginny smiled. "I remember the first couple summers I was sober, the lawns around town seemed so bright I thought they'd been electrified. I've heard that many times from newbies at meetings."

"Good," Kate said, "I thought I was going crazy."

Ginny chuckled. "I didn't say you—or I—aren't still crazy." She scuffed an empty clam shell off the deck onto the rocks. "The first few years I was sober the hardest thing for me was hanging onto the emotional roller coaster I was on. Felt like whiplash a lot of the time."

Kate nodded.

Ginny looked Kate in the eye. "Tell me more."

Kate stood, brushed dried seagull poop off the wooden railing with her hand. "Sometimes I feel like I'm not such an awful piece of shit, that men think I'm okay." Kate felt herself blush. "You know, like I'm actually attractive to legit guys, not just scumbags."

Ginny stood up next to her. They both leaned on the railing. "Feels nice, doesn't it?"

Kate nodded. "I'm actually wide awake, looking around, you know, I'm horny."

Ginny smiled. "Of course you are. You're finally discovering how beautiful and sensual you are."

Kate looked at Ginny. "But I'm looking at other cool guys beside Francis. I can tell they notice me."

"I hear you, and I can't blame them, but it's a slippery slope for you. Don't you have something good with Francis?"

Kate rubbed the railing with her palm. "Sort of, and I know Francis is way legit, but I like that other men are checking me out. I've never had that." She shook her head. "I've felt damaged, unworthy, my whole life."

"So what's wrong with Francis?"

"Nothing, but it's like he's given his whole self to me. There's no..." Kate faltered.

"No chase to it," Ginny said. "None of that delicious playing-hard-to-get."

Kate felt embarrassed. "Yeah, it's too easy. I care about him, and I don't want to hurt him, but I want—"

"More. You want *more*, like every other drunk I know. More love, more sex, more money and security, more everything. And all it ever gets us is wanting more booze, or drugs, or anything to get us out of ourselves."

Kate nodded. "You understand."

"Of course I do. It's the way we're wired. I've struggled with everything you're talking about."

"I know I sound like an ingrate."

They fell silent as a plump seagull alighted on a large rock below them at water's edge.

"Didn't Jonathan Livingston Seagull want more than the usual gull?"

Kate asked.

"Yes, but you're not a seagull."

Kate grinned.

"So what is it you want?" Ginny asked.

Kate watched the white and gray bird lift off and fly over the water. "I want to have fun, go out, make up for a lot of lost time."

"You're free now. If you don't want Francis, move out, move on. Don't emotionally freeload."

Kate made a face. "But I don't want to lose Francis."

Ginny nodded. "Cake-and-eat-it-too—that's where you're stuck."

"Yeah." Kate pushed back from the railing. "And under all this stuff, it pisses me off that I still feel full of fear a lot of the time."

"Of what?"

"Everything, I guess, but mostly my own defects. I even worry about Leland coming back."

"From the dead?"

"I know. That's what Francis says. Besides the wicked dreams, I still jump out of my skin when a door slams, someone yells, or even a dog barks. It sucks."

Ginny nodded. "That'll take a long time to wear off, if it ever does. My old man used to take a leather belt to me and my sister. That was over fifty years ago, and I still jump if I hear a sharp crack like that belt on our backs. I swear I can feel the burning pain, and my skin welting up."

Hard emotions rose in Kate. "Sometimes I feel Leland's rough hands squeezing my breasts while he rapes me. He hurt me bad, Ginny."

Ginny moved close to Kate. "I know, but none of it is an excuse to not take care of yourself now." She looked Kate in the eye. "Why don't you go to more meetings? I haven't seen you at our home group in over a month."

"I'm embarrassed."

"About what? Being a drunk?"

"No, about the trial. I feel completely exposed, mostly about how I let Stringer get so terribly injured by Leland's crazy friends back when he was a little kid. It was unforgiveable."

"In my experience, damn little is unforgivable. Maybe Stringer's healed more than you have."

"Maybe, but my god, what do people think? That I'm a monster too?"

"I think it was clear Leland was the monster. You were a sick addict who couldn't take care of her son. And certainly not the only one. Never forget you gathered the courage to get sober and escape that bastard. That was no small feat. You saved both your lives."

Kate dug at the dry wood of the railing with her fingers. "I don't feel the least bit courageous now."

"Why don't you try and find that courage you had back then?"

"I wish I could. I feel fragmented, like an incomplete jigsaw puzzle that's had a cat jump into the middle of it."

Ginny crossed her arms. "Well, do you want to get your pieces back together again?"

Avoiding Ginny's question, Kate instead thought of what Richard's smoky voice had sounded like on the phone, and the excitement she felt about soon meeting him at the gallery. Ginny could probably tell Kate was already having fantasies about this guy, and she hadn't even laid eyes on him yet. She knew keeping secrets wasn't good for her or her sobriety, but she was going to keep Richard to her self. The good and the bad Kate were having a tug-of-war in her head.

"Kate?" Ginny said, more sharply.

"What?" She tried to refocus.

"Do you want to get yourself together?"

"Well, sure."

"That sounded convincing."

Kate looked down.

"Look, my friend, if you create more wreckage in your life, you'll then have to clean it up if you want to stay sober."

Kate looked Ginny in the eye. "I *do* want to stay sober."

"Then act sober, take estimable actions and your feelings will follow. You can't wait until you *feel* like doing what you're supposed to. And maybe it's time to turn your fears over to your Higher Power."

"I don't know what my HP is, or if I even have one."

"Then find one. Though I'm sure you've got one or you'd be dead." Ginny became impatient. "Do you actually think you have done all this on your own? Got sober, escaped Leland, made it to Maine, met Francis, and saved Stringer from the gallows? Don't you think there might be some power, some force in the universe a little stronger than Kate

Johnson at play here? You're such a typical drunk: one minute you think you're a piece of shit, the next you're the center of the universe. It's like we drive with one foot pushing on the accelerator while the other one's jamming on the brake."

Kate didn't say anything.

Ginny stepped closer. "Look, Kate, I'm sorry for all the hard stuff you've gone through, but it's not an excuse to screw your life up even more. And it's certainly not an excuse to drink. If you want a life you can truly enjoy, if you want to sleep soundly at night, get that pretty ass of yours to some meetings. Find some humility and a way to help another suffering alcoholic. Otherwise, you can die a miserable drunk, even if you're dry. It's your choice."

Ginny turned to the door.

"I really don't want to hurt Francis, but we're not on the same page. He keeps asking me how I'm doing but then doesn't hear what I'm saying. It sounds awful, but just because he helped save me doesn't mean he can have me forever."

Holding the edge of the screen door, Ginny looked back at Kate. "To me it sounds like a desperate addict has transformed into a spoiled brat."

She walked inside, letting the door slam behind her.

Shaken, Kate turned back toward the ocean where darkening clouds gathered against the islands offshore.

CHAPTER THREE

O N HIS WALK ALONG THE CLIFFS, FRANCIS TRY TO RELAX, BUT HE was upset that Kate was planning to meet with an art dealer without him. Despite Kate's believing Francis had his act together, he, too, was feeling confused and concerned about where their life was headed. He guessed that he hid it pretty well, having learned to keep things to himself while growing up under the surveillance of his critical and sometimes cruel Wall Street father. Francis wanted to understand what Kate was going through, but just as she didn't *get* parts of him, the same was true for him with her. Their extreme differences had been there since the beginning, but during the stress and crushing fear of the trial they seemed to come together almost seamlessly. Afterwards, though, as they approached something resembling normal life, a chasm opened between them, and recently it had widened. Still, he continued to feel a deep attraction to her—to her beauty and good soul—just as he had that first morning when Stringer brought her to the bungalow and Francis had wrapped his field coat around her when she was shivering out on the bluff.

After a while, Francis realized he had stopped walking and was just staring at hedge roses along the path. He turned toward the ocean and made a concerted effort to push the stress out of his mind so he could enjoy his hike. It took a few minutes, but the ever-present sea breeze and the rhythm of the waves helped clear his head.

A mile or so north of the bungalow, Francis made his way down to the smooth rocks at water's edge where he watched a trio of starfish at the bottom of a small pool. Continually washed over by waves, they deftly hung on, sometimes attached by only the tiny tip of a single foot. Francis dipped his hand in the cold water to help one of them, but then withdrew, realizing it was better if they took care of themselves. It was his nature to help, something he had learned from his grandmother and had thought was a good thing but was now learning wasn't always for the best. Thinking about his interactions with Kate, Francis realized when he didn't know what to do or felt insecure, he tended to become either apologetic or overbearing, neither of which was the way he wanted to be, especially with her.

Francis shook the salt water from his fingers then climbed up to the trail and hiked back to the bungalow. He changed his clothes to go to town then paused at the bedroom window and looked out at where Kate had sat at the edge of the cliff. He knew her aggressive attitude came from a place of pain, and he felt badly she was feeling so lost, but sometimes her words were still hurtful. Maybe the only way forward, past the chasm and the hurt, was for him to take a big risk, something not in his nature.

As his Jeep reached the bottom of the hill, Francis glimpsed what looked like a familiar car in the back of Kasa's yard. Wanting to get to Portland, he drove on, passing Wagner's Point where months of winter storms had mercilessly pounded the marooned *Maiden,* leaving only skeletal remains of the once stately sloop. Gripping the Jeep's steering wheel tightly, Francis recoiled as he recalled an image of Stringer lunging into the roiling surf to try to save Delbert. Francis realized he hadn't allowed himself to fully acknowledge how terrified he had been that Stringer would die. As he drove on, Francis marveled at all Kate and Stringer had endured. Small wonder they weren't feeling as happy and free as he wished for them to be.

Francis parked near the Portland Museum of Art, where he and Kate had visited the Wyeth exhibit the previous fall. He walked down Congress Street into Clark's, a master jeweler where he had bought Rachael's ring decades before. He took comfort in the fact that little had changed in the store, including the glass-faced oak cabinets and electrified brass oil lamps hanging from an embossed tin ceiling.

A woman dressed in a navy blue blazer approached from the back counter. "May I help you?" she asked, with a half-smile.

"Yes," Francis replied, glancing at a case of diamond rings sparkling in sunlight streaming through a window. "I'm looking for something very special."

The woman pushed her bifocals up to the bridge of her nose. "That's what we do best."

"I bought my wife's ring here almost thirty years ago."

"Are you celebrating an anniversary?"

Francis fell silent. He thought of how Rachael disappeared windsurfing that last day on the bay, how he desperately searched for her for over a year. "No, I'm looking for someone else."

"I see," the lady said, restrained judgment in her voice.

"My wife died two years ago."

The lady looked up. "Oh, you're the artist. I read about your wife at the time. I'm sorry for your loss."

"Thank you. I've met someone new, completely unexpected."

The woman forced another smile. "That *California* woman? With the son who killed the man—his father, was it—up in Winter's Cove?"

Francis felt anger rise inside. "Yes," he said flatly. Despite her judgmental inflection, he was determined to make this a pleasant experience. He focused on the diamond case, looking over several rows of sparkling rings. After a few moments he pointed to an exquisitely cut engagement ring nestled in its own black velvet box. "May I see that one?"

The lady's eyebrows rose. "Certainly. That stone would make any girl happy."

"I hope so." Francis smiled as she lifted the ring from the velvet and placed it in the palm of his hand.

CHAPTER FOUR

KATE WAS UPSET AFTER HER MEETING WITH GINNY. SHE KNEW Ginny was right, but Kate was scared of sinking back into feelings of hating herself, as in large part that was what made her drink and drug. She was not going back there, and at the moment, thinking about Richard was something that made her feel good.

Back at the bungalow, with Francis in Portland, Kate went up to their bedroom to get ready to meet Richard at the gallery. He had sounded a bit exotic on the phone, perhaps a hint of a European accent, a seductive, self-assured voice that had triggered a surge of excitement. Something breaking against the doldrums of her life in the bungalow. Though it felt a little weird, she opened the top drawer of the bureau and selected her most flattering bra, watching in the mirror as she lifted its delicate straps over her shoulders. She adjusted the soft cups against her breasts, the thin silk fabric revealing her nipples.

Embarrassed at how easily she'd become aroused, Kate quickly slid into a shirt then pulled a pair of slightly tight jeans up over her long thighs. She looked at her reflection in the mirror and shook her head. "Jesus, girl, you're crazy. You just got a talking-to from Ginny and now you're all hot and bothered to go meet a new guy."

Ginny's voice echoed in her ears. *If you create more wreckage in your life, you'll then have to clean it up if you want to stay sober.* Kate hesitated. Maybe she shouldn't go. She wanted to stay sober and part of her wanted to be a good person. But a strong part of her wanted to act out and get her due. Aware she was brewing a case of the fuck-its, she honestly didn't know which side of her would win out. She was, however, going to the gallery.

Kate turned to the bed and smoothed the quilted comforter Francis had bought her at L. L. Bean for her birthday. It was a rustic Maine print of a moose crossing a partially-frozen stream, a birch bark canoe resting on the bank in the foreground. She only wished life in Maine was that idyllic for her, though it might be, if she'd get out of her own way.

Kate sat on the bed, realized it had been a few weeks since they'd made love. She missed the passion they'd shared early on. It wasn't that Francis was a bad lover: he took his time with her, always making sure she had an orgasm. There was just something foreign to her—uncomfortable, even agitating—about his gentleness. He left her feeling like she'd barely been touched, like she was in a polite Cinderella story, not the more familiar rough-edged drama she was used to. She was aware that associating roughness with affection wasn't healthy. Her mother was an early women's libber, and the social worker who helped Kate get sober in LA had talked to her about it. She'd taught Kate it could be hard to change once that had been your experience of love.

It surprised Kate that hearing Richard's voice on the phone had released such a damned-up stream of desire, a delicious yet uncomfortable feeling of arousal colored with guilt. She momentarily thought back to what she'd been like when she was using—wearing cheap eye shadow and slinky polyester leggings, screwing guys just to get a fix. At least once she'd hooked up with Leland she'd been too scared to sleep around. He kept her in one place, which was a lot safer than where she'd been.

It gave Kate a selfish feeling in her gut that she was chafing against the good life she had miraculously found with Francis. She got up, looked in the mirror again. "You don't deserve any of this." She turned away, pushed the bureau drawer closed and walked downstairs, avoiding Francis' personal photographs lining the wall.

*   *   *   *   *   *

Kate drove to the gallery in Winter's Cove. Walking up the steps, she stopped to admire one of Stringer's paintings displayed in the front window. She'd become fascinated by his work, especially his intriguing abstract perspectives of a California-ized coast of Maine—colorful, dramatic images she found both stimulating and a bit unsettling. Kate had recently heard Francis tell Stringer that even Andrew Wyeth would have appreciated the depth of his creative exploration. Stringer had replied he thought Andy Warhol was more his speed. It seemed to have pleased Francis, showing him Stringer must have read the book on American artists he'd given him. All of this had made Kate resolute in trying to help her son build a career as an artist.

Inside, Kate noticed the faint smell of varnish used to seal wooden picture frames. It mixed with the lingering presence of Tibetan incense that emanated from Rachael's room in the back. Kate enjoyed the warm feel of the gallery with its antique rugs and dark wainscoting. She had added her own touch to the space, mounting a replica Lakota Sioux medicine wheel over the doorway, a symbol of the enlightenment and wisdom she hoped to someday attain. It also reminded her of her mother's irrepressible free spirit, some of which Kate had inherited and which often caused her to get into trouble. Kate walked around the gallery, making sure all the paintings were level and the lights were properly adjusted. Then she brewed a carafe of strong coffee, enjoying the aroma as it filled the gallery. She poured herself a cup and stood in a front window, waiting.

At nine-thirty sharp a gleaming metallic blue Ford Mustang raced down Harbor Avenue, pulled a smooth U-turn in the middle of the street and parked in front of the gallery. It reminded her of the impossibly shiny muscle cars that cruised up and down the boulevards in LA, the ones she longed to ride in but never did. Kate tucked her shirt more tightly into her jeans as she watched the driver's door swing open and a man with dark, slicked-back hair step out. He wore tight black pants and an expensive-looking white shirt—open at the top—and blue wraparound sunglasses that perfectly matched the Mustang. He closed the door, flicked a cigarette into the street then checked his image in the side window. Kate took a step back into the shadows of the gallery. He was just as she had envisioned during their brief phone call. Suddenly, nervousness replaced her excitement.

Within seconds, he was at the top of the stairs looking through the beveled glass window of the heavy wooden door. Standing on the Persian rug in the center of the gallery, Kate froze. A quick knock on the glass, the door opened and he stepped inside, polished leather shoes clicking on the hardwood floor. He slid his sunglasses up onto his head, revealing a tanned face and deeply-set blue eyes. He had a sort of severe handsomeness—square-jawed and self-assured.

He took a step onto the rug, looked Kate in the eye, and extended his hand. "Richard Corloni," he said, his arm steady in the air between them.

Kate shook his hand. It was warm and strong, perhaps held a degree of hesitation. "Kate Johnson, Stringer's mom."

"Great name," Richard said, releasing her hand. "Never heard it before."

"Yeah, it's unique, I guess. He's a cool kid."

"He's talented."

Kate watched Richard's gaze move from her shoulders down over her hips to her legs. For a spilt second he looked at her breasts then their eyes met again.

Feeling vulnerable, Kate looked at the floor, shifted on her feet. "How did you know about Stringer's work?"

"Saw a couple of pieces at a youth show in Camden."

"You don't look like you're from Maine."

Richard smiled. "You could tell?" He paused, a sexy, knowing sort of pause. "I'm opening up our family cabin north of here. I live in Manhattan but spend as much time here as I can in the summer."

"Seems like a strange place for an art dealer."

"On the contrary, this area is filled with artists, and it's a great place to discover new talent. In fact, there's a renowned art residency school outside Skowhegan that attracts artists from all over the world. If we can, we like to catch them early."

"Really," Kate said. "Maine is full of surprises."

"Yes, it is," he said, grinning.

Kate turned to several easels she had set up to display Stringer's paintings. "These are some pieces my son's done recently. He's at work or he'd show you them himself, though he's not interested in the business end of things." After she said it, Kate realized Francis wouldn't have said that. He wouldn't have shown vulnerability to a dealer.

Richard quickly looked over the paintings. "Any others?"

Disappointed he didn't seem impressed, Kate motioned toward Rachael's room. "There're a few more in the back, but they're not framed."

"I drove way over here, so let's see them all."

"Okay." He was kind of pushy, but she understood. She stepped toward the back room. Richard followed her, his shoes tapping as he stepped off the rug onto hardwood again. At the door, she glanced up at the Lakota symbol as if looking for strength. "I'll get them for you."

Richard was close enough she could smell his cologne. She wanted to tell him to wait in the gallery but couldn't form the words. Despite feeling attracted to him, her pulse quickened and a shiver of fear made its way around her ribcage. She stared at the brass doorknob, winced as she flashed to an image of Leland's cigarette-yellowed hands throwing her onto a dirty bed and ripping her shirt off.

Kate's breath caught.

Richard cleared his throat.

Kate's heart raced like a terrified rabbit bounding across a field. She opened her mouth to scream but couldn't gather the wind. Was she going to give up and just let him beat and rape her so she came out of it with less bruises, less physical pain than she was used to.

Visions of Leland's knife fight with Francis erupted in her mind. She recoiled at the sound of gunshots. Could she muster enough energy to fight this time, to knee this guy in the nuts, rupture his eyeballs with her thumbs? Could she rush past him to the front door and run up the street to get help from Charlie?

Kate heard the sole of Richard's shoe move on the floor. She hunched over, defended, prepared to take it or do battle, whichever instinct won out. She squinted, waited, but then he stepped back, away from her. "I'll wait in the gallery. Unless you need help."

Kate let out a nervous exhalation, was suddenly exhausted, as if she would collapse like a pile of dry bones onto the floor. She wanted to be home by the woodstove with Francis and Stringer. She wanted to go back to the joy and relief she'd felt after the trial, to the gratitude for all that had been done for her and for her son. Instead, she was cowering in fear. Again.

Kate's stomach knotted.

"Are you okay?" Richard asked without moving.

Kate managed to hold her hand up. "I'm fine, just a little dizziness I get sometimes."

Richard waited.

Kate reached out and turned the doorknob. "I'll get the other paintings."

"Good."

Inside, she closed the door behind her, leaned against the tapestry-covered wall and let her breathing settle. The old fear waned, like a hard-crashing wave withdrawing softly from a beach. As she had so many times, Kate hummed a Lakota melody her mother had sung to her when she was a girl traveling between Indian reservations in their station wagon. Kate breathed out the toxic mix of terror, submission, and survival. *My God, he's just an art dealer!*

Embarrassed by how much fear had flooded her, Kate knew she needed to get to more AA meetings, that she needed help. She did not want to feel crazy anymore.

Kate took two finished paintings off the sofa and returned to the gallery. Richard was in the doorway, smoking.

"You can't smoke in here." *Francis would have a fit.*

"I have the door open."

"Still…" Kate said, leaning the paintings against a chair. Richard took a long drag on his cigarette then blew the smoke outside, a pale blue wisp trailing back over the door into the gallery. Kate had the strange thought that with the light behind him, his silhouette looked like James Dean's, her mother's favorite actor. She turned away as Richard flicked his cigarette to the sidewalk and closed the door. There was something exciting about him and something obnoxious, condescending. It irritated her she found him attractive.

Richard lifted one of the paintings from the floor and held it to the light. It was an abstract piece showing a bright yellow and purple shaved ice stand on the boardwalk in Venice Beach, blurred skateboarders passing in the foreground. An off-kilter, red-and-white-striped Maine lighthouse stood just off shore, a sailboat marooned on the rocks below. Dark blue and black storm clouds loomed in the distance. The other painting showed the bow of a lobster boat breaking through the sandy cement of an ocean-side skate park, a volleyball player in the distance stretching through the air, just missing the ball.

"These are quirky but interesting," Richard said, examining the paintings from different angles. "Blending Maine and California. Great colors, though I don't know if they would interest buyers." He thought for a few moments. "Tell you what, I'll take a chance and see if either of these will sell at the Nouveau Gallery in New York. They have a few clients who take chances on new artists with unusual pieces. I'll give you a hundred bucks apiece."

Taken off guard, Kate had no idea how much the paintings might be worth. She felt stupid she hadn't asked Francis to be there, though in other ways she was glad he wasn't. This could be exciting, doing business for her son, the new artist, with a hot-looking art dealer in leather shoes driving a Shelby Mustang.

"Well, I don't know," Kate said, which was the truth.

Richard stepped closer, held her gaze. "You have no idea how hard it is for an unknown artist to break into the New York market. I could be your kid's only chance."

As Richard spoke, Kate noticed the toned muscles beneath his finely tailored shirt. She felt her nipples harden and maybe regretted wearing her thin silk bra. Richard seemed momentarily distracted.

"You are very beautiful." He slid his smooth hands over her bare forearms.

Kate was unable to break their locked gaze. She tried to step back but couldn't move. "I…I think…"

"You think *what?*" Richard asked. He pulled her toward him, leaned in and drew her lips into his. Kate slid her hands onto the front of his chest in a feeble attempt at pushing him away. She started to let his tongue slide into her mouth then turned away and took in a deep breath. It felt so good and so wrong.

Not showing any sign of rejection, Richard wiped his mouth with a monogramed handkerchief. "Perhaps you could come up to my cabin this weekend. Tell Monroe you're at the art institute for a seminar."

"There really is one?" Kate noticed his hard-on.

"Yes, it's an excellent art appreciation course. It would be good for you."

"Forget it," she said, running her hand along the top of one of Stringer's new paintings. "I don't know what happened to me."

Richard leaned in and whispered along the hair at the base of her neck. "I'd say you're horny."

Kate felt her face blush. "I can't be."

Richard reached out, gently lifted her chin with the tips of his fingers. "But you are. We can't control these things," he said with calm authority.

"You don't know what I'm feeling."

"Don't I?" Richard stared at her erect nipples. "Could have fooled me."

Who the hell was this guy? Ballsy, brash, handsome, and right on. She should get away from him fast.

Richard adjusted his pants, slicked his hair back. He pulled a business card from his pocket and handed it to Kate. The only thing on it was a phone number printed in embossed gold letters.

"I can meet you Saturday at the institute. Just say you're staying on campus like a lot of people. I'll be very discreet."

Was she *that* obvious?

Richard walked across the gallery, brought his sunglasses down over his eyes, and left. Kate stepped to the door as he slid into the Mustang. Sunlight flashed off the car as it disappeared up the street.

Kate was left with a cacophony of feelings. "Holy shit," she said, pulling on the ends of her hair.

Chapter Five

After a workout in the junior high school gym, Stringer put the weights back on the rack and hurried into the showers. Hoping Sam would be tagging along with Nelson, Stringer was anxious to get to the lobster boat. The amazing girl with a long blue streak running through the middle of her short-cropped blond hair, Sam looked tough in scuffed-up black army boots and ripped jeans belted with a length of rawhide. A painful-looking silver ring hung from her eyebrow and a thin chrome bolt pierced her lower lip. Since he had met her on the dock two weeks before, Stringer hadn't stopped thinking about her and didn't intend to. It felt like she had taken possession of his brain and pretty much everything else.

Stringer pulled off his sweaty gym shorts, taking care to keep his groin covered so other boys wouldn't see his damaged scrotum. He was used to being different, and while most of the Maine kids left him alone, some looked at him as if he was from a strange land, which he supposed he was.

That's what was so powerfully attractive about Sam. She was different, a quirky rebel with a scratched guitar case strapped on her back. And it was impossible to avoid her intense green eyes. When she'd leaned against one of the wharf pilings and looked at him that first day, he felt he might actually melt through the spaces between the wooden planks. A beautiful girl actually *looked* at him like she cared he existed. In California he'd gotten off with Leland's *Hustler* magazines, but the way Sam affected him was completely different. It felt like electric tingles traveled all through his body, directly connecting his groin and his heart. Even with his being half a man she produced a plenty powerful reaction.

Stringer's brain, on the other hand, seemed to shut down when he was around her. He couldn't remember anything intelligent coming out of his mouth during the few minutes of their first meeting. Embarrassed, he'd mostly looked at the ground, shifted around, only occasionally glancing at her face. Being with her awakened something powerful inside of him, something he'd never felt before. He would love her forever.

Stringer pulled on a loose-fitting sweatshirt and rode his skateboard into town. He raced down Harbor Avenue to the wharf where the crew of the *Look Out* was repairing lobster traps, a line of noisy seagulls watching from the rusted tin roof of the Cove Lobster Company. The air was thick with the salty stench of fish guts and herring emanating from plastic tubs lined up along the wharf, lobster bait ready and waiting.

When Stringer hit the wooden dock with his skateboard, Pike frowned from under his Portland Seadogs cap. Stringer hopped off his board and tipped it up under his arm.

Nelson, Pike's partner, looked over as he twisted a pair of wires together. "Hey, Stringer."

Stringer liked Nelson, a man in his sixties, missing the top of his right ear as well as two fingers on his right hand. They'd been torn off by a steel cable that lashed across him when he was a boy winching in a commercial fishing net that had snagged on a buoy.

"You're late," Pike snapped. His stubbly beard was a blend of gray and yellow in which black bits of chewed tobacco were caught.

"No, I'm not," Stringer said, looking around for Sam.

Pike motioned to a pile of traps on the dock. "Get them on the boat. Gotta shove off."

Stringer slid his skateboard under the workbench next to Nelson. "He's in his usual good mood?"

Nelson nodded. "Always."

"Sam around?" Stringer whispered.

Nelson nodded toward the small dockside shack Pike called his office. Stringer smiled.

Pike waved his arm. "Told you to get them pots loaded."

"I am," Stringer said, lifting a repaired trap from the pile. A seagull standing atop a streetlight stretched its neck and screamed into the air. Stringer frowned at the bird, then lifted the trap onto the boat and placed it on a stack in the stern.

After loading the other repaired traps, Stringer spoke to Pike. "You taking me out today?"

Pike spit a wad of spent chew on the dock and squinted at him.

"I'm sick of just working on the dock. I wanna get out on the water."

"You'll do what I tell you."

"Ginny said you'd let me work on the boat." Stringer glanced over at the shack. "That's why I took this job."

Pike let out a snarly laugh. "Shit, little man, this the only job a young criminal like you could get around here. I'm just doin' Ginny a favor."

Stringer hated being called *little man*. He held the gunwale as a wave rocked the boat. "It's her boat. She owns the fleet."

Pike's face screwed up tight, accentuating the stiff bristles on his chin. "Fleet my ass." He wiped his lower lip with the sleeve of his wool shirt. "Her boat alright, but she'd have nothing if it weren't for me and my boys." Pike yanked a pair of heavy rubber overalls out of a wooden box mounted to the dock.

Stringer tried to hold his breath as he loaded a tub of smelly bait onto the boat.

Pike winced as he pulled first one then the other suspender strap over his shoulders. "What do you think, Nelson? Should we bring the little bastard out with us?"

Nelson grabbed a pair of black rubber gloves off the slimy workbench. "Sure, why not? We'll find a use for him." He winked at Stringer.

Stringer heard a guitar riff coming through the corrugated metal walls of the shack. He stopped moving when he heard Sam's raspy voice singing the refrain from "Me and Bobby McGee."

Stringer sprang back onto the dock and hurried toward the shack. He opened the flimsy metal door and found Sam sitting on a stool, hunched over her old guitar, its dull brown finish scratched and gouged. She gave him a nod and kept singing. The smell of a recently smoked joint lingered in the air.

Stringer stood nervously in the doorway until she finished. "Hey."

"Hey," she said, leaning her guitar against a few cases of motor oil stacked next to Pike's tool bench. "I'd offer you a seat if there was one. It's a shithole, but at least a place to hang out of the weather."

Stringer stole a glimpse of the top of her breast showing where her bulky sweater fell off her shoulder. Her skin was smooth and white except for a Chinese tattoo on her upper arm and a few dots of red pimples on her cheek.

"You sound good."

Sam pulled a cigarette from atop her ear and lit it. "Not really. Just hacking around."

Stringer let the rattly door close behind him. "It sounds good to me."

"You're an easy audience."

"Get out here if you're going with us!" Pike yelled.

Stringer was psyched. "Guess I'm going out."

Sam looked at Stringer, spoke in a low voice. "Be careful around Pike. He's bat-shit crazy. Into sketchy stuff."

"Like what?"

"Not sure, but I think he's dealing more than lobsters. Nelson's kind of scared of him."

Stringer was much more interested in Sam than in what she was saying.

"Nelson doesn't say much, but I can tell." She stood, which in the tiny shack put her within breathing distance of Stringer. He stared at the thin chrome bolt piercing her lip. "Make sure he gives you a good life jacket and keep it on."

"Okay. I will." He was confused by a rush of feelings—mostly attraction to this wicked cool girl, but also fear because of her unexpected warning. She must care about him, which was awesome.

"Get a move on!" Pike yelled. He sounded like he was coming toward them.

"Francis told me he's got an old guitar he'll let me use, so I can practice that stuff you showed me the other day."

Sam blew cigarette smoke through her nose. "Cool."

Stringer pushed the metal door open. "See ya."

Sam held the door with her hand. "Hey! Saturday night, I'm playing the Mill Pub, seven o'clock if you can come. I'll teach you how to play a real song."

Stringer hesitated. "I'd like to but I don't know how I'd get there."

Sam leaned out the doorway. "I'll take you. I've got Nelson's old scooter. Gotta be there by six-thirty."

Pike came up and banged on the tin siding, causing the shack to shudder, startling them both. "Git moving!"

"Asshole," Sam said under her breath.

"I'll try to make it. I'll text you."

"K," Sam said. "I'd like that."

"Me, too," Stringer called back to her as he ran for the lobster boat.

Pike followed him on board, taking a pinch of tobacco from a small round tin and pushing it behind his bottom lip. "I was going to wait to take you out till next week on the fishing boat, but what the hell, we might as well show you how to lobster."

Stringer put on a yellow foul-weather jacket and pulled on a pair of rubber boots a bit too big for him. As they edged away from the dock, Sam stood outside the shack motioning to him. He realized she was imitating putting on a life jacket. He gave her a thumb's up then turned to Pike. "Where're the life jackets?"

"Don't need one," he snarled.

Stringer felt intimidated but didn't want to look weak. "I might."

Pike spit over the side of the boat, pointed to a fiberglass bin in the corner of the cockpit. "In there, you pussy."

Ignoring him, Stringer opened the bin, which held several preservers that felt stiff enough he figured they'd never been worn, which he guessed was a good thing. At least he knew where they were.

As they left the harbor, Stringer looked at the hillside where the ice slide had been during Winter Festival. On New Year's Eve, he, Francis, and his mom had had a great time sliding out onto the frozen harbor, their blazing torches held high.

As they passed the red outer marker and the mournful clanging of its bell, Stringer looked toward the open sea. The salty wind was chilly, but it made him feel alive and free. Heading east, he glanced back at the town wharf, catching a final glimpse of Sam standing next to a piling. He smiled, feeling like a sailor leaving his girl on the dock.

Chapter Six

WITH THE BOX HOLDING THE DIAMOND RING SECURELY IN HIS pocket, Francis walked down Congress then Exchange Streets past the colonial brick Longfellow House and the beautiful bronze *Our Lady of Victories* statue in Monument Square. Enjoying the familiar feel of the worn cobblestone streets of Portland's Old Port, Francis paused at Beal's Old-Fashioned Ice Cream. He looked in the window at the table where he and Kate had shared their dripping cones the September before, remembering the happy, hopeful look on her face and how much he had wanted to make love to her. He smiled, thinking how she'd rebuffed his first advances, then how they'd melted into each other's arms. It seemed so long ago.

Francis caught the reflection of his own smile in the shop's window then turned and walked past the brightly lit tourist shops down to the docks where lobster boats were unloading their haul alongside Custom House Wharf. He leaned against a heavy wooden railing and watched bearded men in orange and yellow overalls lift shiny lobsters from their holding tanks, placing them in large plastic bins to be weighed. Farther down Commercial Street on Chandler's Wharf, a small gaggle of tourists in colorful windbreakers waited to board a tour boat that would take them around Portland Head Light and Fort William Park, then out to the surrounding islands.

The heavy salt aroma of the wharf rejuvenated and comforted him as it had since his first visit to his grandmother's as a young boy. At fourteen, when he finally escaped his overbearing father and moved to her bungalow, Francis had stood next to her on the bluff watching in wonder the rhythmic rising and falling of the sea. She had held her strong arm firmly around his waist, assuring him all would be well. His grandmother had spoken words he didn't then completely understand but had never forgotten. "Remember, young Francis, the sea has many secrets: some her own, some ours she forever keeps."

Francis walked to DiMillo's marina with its unique floating restaurant built from a huge converted ferry. He admired the long, sleek yachts tied up to the maze of docks surrounding the restaurant, especially a jet-black cruiser with a Grand Cayman registry that sported gleaming gold trimmings and its name written across the stern: *Dazzler*.

After watching boats come and go in the Old Port, Francis got chilly and walked back uptown to the Jeep and drove home. Back in Winter's Cove, he stopped at Ginny's store to buy some painting supplies he and Stringer needed. Ginny was straightening up a revolving stand of souvenir magnets when she saw him come through the door. "Francis Monroe, to what do we owe this honor?"

"Stringer's been painting up a storm. We're running out of paints."

"That kid is something."

"Yes." Francis walked to the bubbling lobster tank in the middle of the shop, the dark-shelled crustaceans crawling over a layer of rocks on the bottom, their claws bound with thick rubber bands. "You ever feel bad for these guys tied up awaiting the boiling pot? Seems like an underwater death row."

Ginny kept working. "Yup, actually I do. Didn't used to bother me. Now I don't look at them much." Ginny gestured at the magnets. "Anyway, I can't make a decent living just selling the rest of this stuff. And I may have to give up the artist supplies…" She stared at him. "Unless they start buying more."

"At least there are two of us now," Francis replied, smiling.

"Thank god for Stringer."

"You can say that again." Francis looked into the tank.

Ginny glanced at the lobsters. "I guess it's their lot in life. Plus, supposedly those smart marine scientists say they have no brains. Don't feel a thing." She chuckled. "Lucky them, I say. But I think they say that just to make us all feel better."

She stepped closer to Francis and straightened a few brightly colored postcards in a rack next to the lobsters. "How you doing? Things settling down?"

Francis watched one of the bigger lobsters crawl over the others. "Sort of. Kate's feeling lost, pretty irritable, but I think I can fix that."

"How's that?" Ginny dusted off a group of lighthouse snow globes on a table beside the art supplies.

"I've fallen in love with her, Ginny."

"It would appear so."

Francis pulled the ring box from his pocket and held it up.

Ginny stopped working. "My, what have you got there?"

Francis held the box under a spotlight and slowly opened it.

Ginny's eyes lit up. "Wow, that's beautiful. You *must* be in love."

Francis closed the box. "We've got issues to work out, but my heart says she's the one. I'm not saying I believe in God or anything like that, but *some* force of nature brought us together."

Ginny looked surprised. "Sounding pretty spiritual, aren't we?"

"I think a little of your AA fellowship has rubbed off on me."

Ginny became serious. "Speaking of which—not to rain on your parade—I'm worried about Kate. I haven't seen her at a meeting in a month or more."

Francis picked up a snow globe and turned it upside down. Tiny white flakes swirled around a lighthouse decorated like a Christmas tree. "Does she really need to keep going to those meetings?"

Ginny chuckled. "Only if she wants to stay sober, not have her life turn back into a hell storm."

"Oh." He put the snow globe down. "I've told her she should call you."

"Good."

Francis wondered if Kate had called, but didn't ask

The sleigh bells over the door jingled as a mother and two young children entered the shop. The kids immediately headed for the plush toy lobsters, crabs, and dolphins. Ginny rolled her eyes, spoke to Francis in a low voice. "It takes a while to adjust to a completely new life. If you love her that much, be patient. And you can help by gently encouraging her to go to meetings, just don't push. She has to want it for herself. That's how recovery works." Ginny watched the two kids toss a black and white orca back and forth across the display.

Francis selected several tubes of paint and two canvasses and brought them to the counter. Ginny rang him up while keeping an eye on the kids. As she ran his credit card, Francis looked out the store window, reimagining the day he caught a glimpse of Kate and Stringer walking briskly up the opposite sidewalk.

"Still gawking, I see." Ginny handed him his slip. "Here you go."

33

Francis smiled at her. "Thanks. And for giving Stringer a job on your boat. You're a good friend."

"We'll see what he thinks after a few weeks with those guys. They aren't exactly Boy Scouts, but they'll teach him a lot."

"I hear Pike's a piece of work."

"Yup, but he knows lobstering. Just don't be around him when he's drinking."

The short strap of sleigh bells jingled when Francis opened the door. "Take care."

With the ring box secured under his seat, Francis drove uptown. Passing the court house, he saw Charlie on the steps of the sheriff's office waving at him. Francis waved back, but Charlie motioned for him to stop. He walked over to Francis' window.

"Hey, Mr. Monroe, you got a minute?"

Charlie seemed anxious, wouldn't look Francis in the eye.

"What's going on?"

Charlie glanced up and down the street. "It'd be better if we talked inside."

Francis felt an all-too-familiar twinge of dread as he followed Charlie into his office. He sat in the same heavy captain's chair he'd sat in the day Charlie told him about Kate's California rap sheet.

Charlie tapped his fingers on a yellow legal pad. "This may be nothing, but I'm not taking any chances."

"What is it, Charlie?" Francis asked, sternly.

"Mrs. Burns, who runs the info booth, called me this morning, said she was concerned about a strange man who stopped by yesterday afternoon. He was asking about Kate—called her by name—said she lived with some local artist but didn't mention you by name."

Francis frowned. "Who was he? What did he want?"

"Didn't say 'cept he had business with her. Had Rhode Island plates, but the numbers were banged up so she couldn't read the whole thing. AK 32—something. We train the volunteers that work in the booth to get tag numbers of anyone who looks suspicious."

Concerned, Francis leaned forward. "What would anyone want with Kate?"

"No idea, but Mrs. Burns said he looked sinister, though she's a strict Episcopalian and suspicious of most any strangers."

"Perfect for a vacation area welcome booth." Francis became more agitated. "So what am I supposed to do with this?"

"Not sure. Didn't feel right, so I wanted you to know."

Francis sat back and thought for a few moments. Charlie swallowed the last swig of coffee then threw the cup in the wastebasket.

"Far as I know, Kate doesn't have a connection with anyone from Rhode Island. You sure about the plate?"

"That's what Mrs. Burns said. The booth isn't busy this time of year, so she had plenty of time to observe it."

Francis stood. "I don't like this, but thanks for letting me know."

"Right."

As Francis walked toward the door, Charlie stood, cleared his throat. "One other thing. Mrs. Burns said that before the guy left, he reached up on the rack of free stuff and took a map of the area. She was pretty sure she saw a gun holstered under his arm."

Francis felt the muscles of his chest tighten, causing a sharp pain where Leland had stabbed him. "I've got to go find Kate."

Charlie lifted his gun belt over his hips. "We sure don't need any more trouble around here. I figured since McNeal quit and run off with his crazy cousins, they'd be the ones causing me trouble, not some stranger from down country."

Francis could think only of getting home to Kate. He pulled the door open. "Keep a close lookout for this guy."

"Sure will."

Chapter Seven

As they approached a group of lobster traps near an off-shore island, Pike jammed his beer can into a leather holder screwed to the side of the pilothouse. He leaned over the side of the boat and hooked his gaff onto a yellow and black striped buoy. Pulling the line up out of the water, he ran it over the snatch and onto the powered winch. He turned partially toward Stringer. "Always beware the winch," he said loudly. "It's an unforgiving bastard. Take a finger off quicker 'n greased lightning. Ask Nelson."

From inside the pilothouse, Nelson held up his deformed hand.

The winch motor whined. Stringer watched as the line was rapidly drawn from the ocean, at its end a wire trap with strands of green and brown seaweed dangling from it.

"Grab hold," Pike barked. "Pull it aboard!"

Stringer leaned over the gunwale and, after a couple of tries, grabbed hold and wrestled the trap up onto the plank. The trap had a strong, encrusted salt smell. Inside were several lobsters that did not look happy to be onboard. The one closest to Stringer lifted a claw and snapped at him. Stringer recoiled.

Pike grinned. "Open the hatch and pull 'em out one at a time." He reached over, grabbed his beer, and finished it with one gulp.

Stringer frowned at Pike. "They'll bite me."

"Bullshit. Grab 'em by the back and they can't get you."

Stringer opened the wire hatch, gingerly stuck his hand inside, and tried to grab the back of the smallest lobster. It quickly turned and nipped one of his fingers. He jumped back, almost knocking the trap overboard.

Pike chuckled, pulled another iced beer from the beat-up cooler at his feet. "Careful, boy, better not lose any, or we take it outta your hide."

Stringer stared at the trap.

Looking disgusted with Pike, Nelson stepped over. "Like this," he said, lifting the hatch over the part of the trap called the parlor. He quickly slid his hand onto the lobster from behind and pulled it out of the trap. He picked up a metal gauge and hooked it onto the back of the lobster's shell. "If you hold them like this they can't get you, and you can measure the carapace with this tool. It has to be between three and a quarter and five inches long or we throw it back. And we can't keep any breeding females." He pointed. "If you see eggs under here, they've got to go back."

"Hate to throw any back," Pike muttered.

Stringer pointed to another lobster in the trap that had mounds of tiny yellow eggs attached to its underside.

"Yeah, she's a breeder," Nelson said, "so we cut a "V" in a tail flipper. Other lobstermen'll know to leave her alone so she'll keep producing."

Stringer stood there looking at the lobsters crawling around in the trap. "I thought they were red."

"Only after you cook 'em." Pike waved Stringer off. "Enough, already. Don't be a damn sissy. Nothing to it." Pike spat out a wad of wet chew, which only partially made it over the gunwale, adding to the cascade of brown stains streaking down the side of the boat. He wrenched the other lobsters out of the trap and dropped them in the holding tank.

Stringer would've sworn their buggy eyes were watching him.

When all the legal lobsters were in the tank, Pike dunked his large hand into a bucket of herring and held the slimy fish up to Stringer's nose. He grimaced at the rank smell.

"Just take a handful like this to re-bait the trap. Gotta keep moving. Lotta traps to pull." He stuffed the herring into the bait bag hanging inside the trap then pushed it over the side. Stringer watched as it disappeared beneath the swirling blue-green surface.

Nelson stepped back into the pilothouse, nudged the throttle forward, and they headed for the next trap a short distance away.

Stringer held onto the gunwale to steady himself on the slippery deck. Pike leaned against the side of the boat next to him. The smells of fish, and beer on Pike's breath, were nearly overwhelming, but Stringer wanted to learn all he could so he stayed close. "How do you know where to put the traps?"

Pike looked surprised, pleased even, that Stringer was interested.

"Lobsters like places to hide, so we drop the traps down along the ledges and underwater caves, the ones that aren't too deep. Hundred foot or less."

"How do you know where those are?"

Pike pushed his cap back, scratched a scab along his hairline. "Boy, we been fishing these waters for generations. Know the bottom of this ocean better'n I know my own land. Ocean floor don't change much, at least where we fish."

Nelson brought the boat alongside another yellow and black buoy.

"All right, you haul this one," Pike said with less of a bark.

Stringer readied himself and was able to hook the buoy with the gaff on the first try. He pulled the line up, surprised at how heavy it was. With a little help from Nelson, Stinger wrapped it around the snatch and onto the winch, which whirred to life, pulling the trap from the ocean bottom. There were only two lobsters inside, and it took a bit of hand-dancing to get the first one out. Several rubber bands went flying before Stringer was able to get them over the claws, but he finally dropped a legal lobster into the tank.

"Good job," Nelson said.

Pike grumbled about how long it took. "Papers'll be out by the time we get done."

To his chagrin, Stringer dropped the second lobster, and it slid away from him. He got down on his knees on the slippery deck and tried to grab it, but by then it was riled and repeatedly snapped at him.

Pike let out a laugh.

Finally, Nelson threw an old sweatshirt over the angry lobster and Stringer was able to capture, band, and secure it in the tank.

Several hours and many traps later, Stringer had gotten the hang of it, though his hands were raw, his arms cold and aching. He'd had enough lobstering for one day. While Nelson checked the tank to make sure all the lobsters were banded, Pike sat on the rear transom of the boat and popped open another beer. "Hear your old lady's quite the piece of ass."

Pissed, Stringer tried to ignore him.

"Don't get hot California babes out here very often. Like to get a taste of that."

Stringer whirled around. "You leave my mother alone. She's not a 'piece,' you asshole."

Pike laughed. "We got ourselves a momma's boy here, Nelson."

"Give it a rest, Pike," Nelson said. He steered the boat around a large rock outcropping that jutted into the sea in a way that created a small sheltered cove. As they approached, Stringer saw a black cigarette boat that appeared to be hiding there. It had a long, low-slung bow, and he intermittently heard the growl of its motors as the outdrives bobbed up and down in the waves.

"Right on time," Pike said, squinting against the afternoon sun. He opened a locked hatch under his seat and pulled out a nylon bag.

Stringer frowned. "What're we doing?"

"Never you mind, boy." Pike stared at the other boat. "Just meetin' a friend."

Nelson stayed silent as he steered the boat smoothly into the narrow cove, like he'd done it a thousand times. Stringer kept his arms in as they passed so close to the ledges he could have easily touched them.

Stringer heard the other boat rev its engines, and it quickly came alongside. A man with a goatee in dark foul weather gear and a Miami Beach cap appeared behind the swept-back windshield. When he was close enough, Pike slung the nylon bag into the man's outstretched hand. He quickly looked into the bag then hurled a similar one to Pike. No one said a word, though the guy gave Stringer a dirty look. A few seconds later the sleek bow rose out of the water, and the black boat roared out of the cove heading south.

Pike stuffed the bag into the hatch and locked the cover. Nelson turned the boat around and they headed out around the jagged outcroppings. "Good lobster area, here," he said, which didn't seem to have any connection with what had just happened. Stringer felt uncomfortable but didn't ask any questions.

When they cleared the rocks, Pike relaxed and pulled out another six-pack. "Hey, kid—" Stringer turned as Pike threw him a can of beer. Surprised, Stringer caught it before it sailed overboard. "Have a beer. Relax."

"I'm too young to drink."

Pike grinned. "Never too young to drink."

"My mother won't let me."

"Her again." Pike raised his eyebrows. "Maybe I should talk to her."

"She doesn't talk to pigs," Stringer said, before he could stop himself.

Pike slid off his seat and glared at him. "McNeal said you'd be a pain in the ass."

"That asshole—"

"You didn't like the old sheriff, did ya?" Pike advanced toward Stringer.

Thinking Pike was going to hit him, Stringer braced himself.

"Pike!" Nelson said, sharply.

Pike backed away. "Don't be a pussy. Drink the beer."

Pussy rang in Stringer's ears. He'd hated that word ever since his father called him it in fourth grade when he'd come home and ground some of Stringer's drawings into the floor with his boot. He also was thinking of Sam's warning about Pike.

Stringer looked at Nelson for support, who shrugged his shoulders. "It's okay. What's a beer?"

As the boat rocked on the waves, Stringer stared at the beer in his hand. A lot of his friends in California drank on the weekends. So did kids here. He'd wanted to try one for a couple years, but he hadn't wanted to disappoint his mother, particularly since she'd gotten sober.

"Just drink it," Pike said, in a friendlier tone. He sat back down on the hatch where he'd stuffed the bag. "Takes the edge off out here on the big, scary ocean."

Stringer stepped under the overhang of the pilothouse, looked at Nelson. "How long before we get back?"

"Forty-five."

"K." He popped the ring on the top of the beer can. Foam bubbled over his fingers. "You won't tell my mom or Ginny?"

Nelson shook his head, raised his own beer in a toast. "Nope, won't tell a soul."

Stringer put the can to his lips and took a foamy sip. It tasted sour.

"Take a good swig, for Christ's sake," Pike said. "Like this." He turned another can bottoms-up and guzzled the entire thing. "Ahhh," he said then let out a long, resonant belch.

Stringer took several more swallows but had a hard time keeping the foam under control. He didn't particularly like the taste, but he liked the feel of the cold liquid gliding down his throat. Soon he felt lightheaded.

"What do ya think, boy?" Pike crossed his arms on top of his big belly.

Stringer took another couple of swigs then let out a belch of his own. "Not bad."

Pike and Nelson looked at each other and grinned.

On the way back to shore, Stringer drank part of another beer then found his footing a bit unsure on the slimy deck. Once inside the harbor they slowly approached the long wooden pylons supporting the main wharf. When they pulled up to the fishermen's dock, Stringer fumbled with the stern line but was able to tie it off to a heavy metal cleat. Then he sat on the gunwale. "Feel a little weird," he said to no one in particular.

Pike and Nelson unloaded the lobsters from the holding tank into blue plastic bins. Stringer suddenly retched down the side of the boat.

Pike chuckled. "That's what the sea'll do to ya."

Stringer wiped puke from his face. "It's the beer."

Pike stood over him, looked him in the eye. "Little young to be drinking, ain't 'cha." A nasty grin curled his lips. "I'm sure that alkie mother of yours won't be too happy about this."

Stringer frowned. "You told me to—"

Pike cut him off, waving his arm at the vomitus on the side of the white boat. "Clean that shit up and get out of here." He pressed a button and a cable descended from an overhead winch they used to lift the lobster bins onto the wharf.

Pike climbed out of the boat. "And don't be flirtin' with Nelson's girl. Last thing that little hussy needs is to hook up with a California killer like you."

What a prick. Stringer leaned against a piling, trying to settle his stomach.

Nelson helped Pike raise the lobsters and load them into the back of his pickup. When Pike got in and drove off, Nelson walked back down the aluminum gangway and gave Stringer a hand up out of the boat. "You're a lightweight, all right."

"Sorry," Stringer said. "I never drank before."

"I can see that. Pike's not the best influence. He can be an asshole, but he's the boss."

Stringer sat on a trap on the wharf while Nelson hosed down the deck, including the side where Stringer had thrown up. Nelson pulled off his overalls and hung them on a hook in the pilothouse. "You need a ride home?"

"Nah, Francis is coming to get me."

Nelson surveyed Stringer's face. "I guess you look okay. Rather not have Mr. Monroe know you've been drinking." He pulled a mint candy from his shirt pocket and handed it up to Stringer. "I'm going to take the boat out to the mooring. I'll see you in a couple days."

Stringer felt a little better. "Nelson—"

"Yeah?"

"You seem like a cool guy."

"Thanks."

Stringer stood and leaned against a lightpole. "What was that other boat?"

Nelson undid the stern line. "Friend of Pike's, nothing to concern yourself with."

"Looked sketchy."

Nelson leaned on the gunwale and looked straight up at Stringer. His voice was stern but not nasty. "I'll try to be good to you, but when I say something's none of your business, you'd better take note. Being out on the water can get mighty rough in these parts. We ain't in some tourist calendar. Understood?"

"Yes, Sir."

Nelson started the engine, released the bowline and, without looking back, motored toward a mooring ball to which a small skiff was attached.

Stringer watched Nelson hitch the boat to its mooring. As it turned in the light wind, the late day sun reflected off the yellow stripe on the buoy mounted atop the pilothouse. Stringer hoped he hadn't pissed Nelson off, because he wanted to spend as much time as possible with Sam. He picked up his skateboard and checked the tin shack, though he knew Sam would be long gone. Still feeling a little woozy, he started walking uptown just as Francis drove down the street toward the wharf. Stringer spat some saliva that tasted like beer on the pavement, pulled his cap down over his forehead, and walked toward the Jeep.

CHAPTER EIGHT

WHEN THEY'D DRIVEN OUT OF TOWN, FRANCIS GLANCED OVER AT Stringer. "Aren't you cold with the window down?"

Stringer kept facing out the window so Francis wouldn't smell the beer on his breath. "Nah, wind feels good."

"So they let you go out on the boat today?"

"Yeah."

"You look like you might have gotten a little seasick."

"I guess. Hard to work when it's rocking back and forth."

"Same on a sailboat, though the deck's not covered with fish slime."

"Got that right."

"What did they let you do?"

"Showed me how to haul traps, bait them, rubber band claws, all that stuff. My arms are wicked sore."

"I'll bet." Francis slowed for a pair of crows picking at roadkill in the middle of his lane. "The men all right?"

"Nelson's okay, but Pike's weird."

"How so?"

"He's a pig, says stupid stuff."

"Like what?"

Stringer wanted to tell him what Pike had said about Kate, and about the strange meeting with the other boat, but thought he'd better not. "Ah, nothing, really." Stringer sat up straighter in the seat. "But it was a good day, got to see Sam. Said she'd teach me how to play guitar."

Francis nodded. "That sounds good. I guess you're going to need that old guitar I told you about. It's upstairs in my storage room and I bet it would tune up nicely. You're welcome to use it."

"That would be cool."

By the time they turned in at Kasa's, Stringer was feeling better.

Stringer pointed. "Whose car is that? Hardly ever anyone at her

45

house."

Francis slowed. "Don't know. Hope she's alright."

Stringer brightened. "That's Buster's car. I remember it from last fall."

Francis squinted. "You're right. What do you think he's doing here?"

"Maybe they're hooking up." Stringer laughed.

Francis smiled. "You never know. Opposites attract, and she was pretty feisty with him during the trial."

"She was in my corner for sure."

As Francis drove on, Stringer strained to look. "Want to stop?"

"No. We need to get home. Your mom and I are going out for dinner at the yacht club tonight. I want her to meet some of my old friends."

"Yeah, she's nervous about that high society stuff."

"She'll be fine."

They climbed the hill to the bungalow.

"Will you be alright alone this evening? We won't be too late."

"'Course. I'm beat. Maybe I can watch something on that ancient TV of yours."

"Someday you'll thank me for limiting your exposure to all those mind-numbing video gadgets."

Stringer shook his head. "Doubt it, but luckily I have a couple friends who actually have electricity."

Francis saw Kate in the upstairs window. She moved back behind the curtain as they approached the house. He hoped she'd be in a better mood.

"Hey, Mom," Stringer called out, as he swung the front door open.

Inside, Francis enjoyed a moist floral bouquet from shower steam lingering in the hallway. Though he'd missed it this time, he loved watching Kate step from the shower.

"I'll be right down," Kate called from upstairs.

Stringer dropped his pack on the couch in the parlor and headed to the kitchen. "I'm starved."

Kate came down in a white terrycloth bathrobe. "I'll make you pasta with the cheese you like."

"Great."

She patted Stringer on the shoulder. Lately, he had not favored kisses. She turned to Francis. "I thought I'd wear that black dress you got me."

Though she still sounded hesitant, Francis was delighted she was putting effort into dressing up for dinner. "The one with the V-neck we bought in Portland?"

"Yes. I want to look nice."

"Excellent. You look beautiful in that dress. Well, in any dress, really." Francis was relieved by her good mood. "I'll shower and get ready. String says he's fine staying alone."

Kate turned to Stringer. "You sure? You could go down to Kasa's."

He gave her a sarcastic look. "I'm not a little kid anymore. Besides, she's hooking up with someone."

Kate stopped as she walked into the kitchen. "What? Who?"

"Guess."

Kate looked baffled. "No clue."

"Somebody we think is cool."

Kate thought for a moment then her eyes opened wide. "*Buster?*"

"Bingo."

"No kidding. He's down there?"

"Yup, just saw his car in back of her house, like he's trying to hide."

Kate looked at Francis, who smiled and nodded.

"Wow, you never know." Kate frowned at Stringer. "You look sore, and your wrist is bruised. You must have gone out on the boat."

"Yeah. Hard work, but it was okay."

"I know you've been anxious to get out on the water."

"Would've rather stayed on the dock today."

"Why's that?"

"Sam was there, playing her guitar in that little shack. Said she'd—" He hesitated, decided not to mention the pub gig. "Said she'd teach me to play some songs."

"How were the guys on the boat?"

Stringer looked disappointed his mom wasn't interested in Sam. "Alright, I guess."

"I worry about that Pike guy. Shelly says he can be nasty."

"He's an asshole."

At the counter, Stringer spread peanut butter on a couple of Ritz crackers and ate them. Kate filled a sauce pan with water, set it on the stove and lit the burner. Jets of blue and yellow flame enveloped the bottom of the pan.

Kate spoke without looking at Stringer. "So what's this Sam girl like?"

"She's awesome, Mom. *So* cool."

"That's it? *Cool?* What's she into?"

"Real independent, into music, even writes her own songs, plays out as much as she can. And she's got this kinda smoky voice."

Great. Another smoky voice. Putting Richard out of her mind again, Kate turned from the stove to Stringer. "Is that from all the pot she smokes?"

Stringer's expression sank. He looked stunned that Kate knew. "She mostly smokes cigarettes."

"Well, those aren't good for you, either." She looked Stringer in the eye. "You been smoking with her? Tell me the truth."

"No."

"No pot either?"

Stringer shook his head. "Hell, no."

Kate put the lid on the sauce pan. "I don't know. She's older than you, doesn't sound like anyone you should be hanging around."

Stringer got in front of her. "Why not? She's a really good person. She *gets* me."

"Uh-huh."

Stringer looked at Kate. "Mom, I've never been this in love."

"You've never been in love," Kate quipped back.

"How do *you* know?"

Sensing Stringer was getting upset, Kate leaned against the counter. "Look, String, this is the last thing we need."

"*We?* Who the hell is we? She's *my* girl."

Francis looked like he wanted to intervene but held back. Kate knew she was backing herself into a corner. "Sam may have a good heart, but she sounds like a druggie."

"Yeah," Stringer said, angrily. "Maybe she reminds you of someone."

Kate didn't seem to understand the reference.

"*You*, Mom. Weren't you a druggie with a good heart?"

Kate fell silent. Wounded again.

Chapter Nine

"I'M JUST TRYING TO PROTECT YOU," KATE SAID TO STRINGER.
He thumped down in a kitchen chair. "From the girl I love?"

"Jesus, String, you just met her."

Stringer lost the fire in his eyes.

After a few moments, Kate stepped closer. "Look, I'm sorry. This isn't the way I wanted this to go. I just don't want the same things happening to you that happened to me."

"Don't worry, they won't."

Though he tried to shrug her off, Kate rested her hands on Stringer's shoulders. He slowly pushed a cracker around the plate.

After what seemed like a long time, Kate spoke in a friendlier tone. "So, I'd like to see what this girl is like."

Stringer perked up. "Sam?"

"Who else?"

Stringer smiled. "She's cool, Mom. First girl that ever really noticed me."

Kate took a small handful of slender pasta from a tall glass jar. "Can I meet her?"

"Sure, but she's not around much—works a couple part-time jobs, plays some gigs. She sings great."

"Maybe she can come over sometime."

"You guys might intimidate her."

"Why?"

Stringer looked uncomfortable. "She's like a townie, hard-edged."

"I like hard-edged," Kate said matter-of-factly.

"Well, I mean she's had a hard life—bad stuff."

"I know what that's like."

"Exactly," Stringer said. "See, you'll like her."

Though Kate was worried about this new person in their lives, she was impressed with Stringer's empathy toward Sam. Truth was Kate worried about everything, though it was a relief for a few minutes at least, to not be worrying about Richard, whose scent she had vigorously washed off during her long shower. Even though she had pulled away, she could tell he was a good kisser.

Kate refocused, slid the pasta into the boiling water. "Well, I'd like to meet her."

"She's playing a gig at the Mill Pub this weekend. You can see her there."

"Okay, I will," Kate said, without thinking about the art seminar. She didn't let on that Shelly had told her about the pub gig.

"Cool."

Stringer walked back into the parlor, pulled his notebooks from his backpack and spread them out on the couch. After quickly looking them over, he appeared unable to focus and walked into Francis' studio, pulled a virgin canvas from beside the desk and placed it on his easel next to a floor lamp. He assembled his materials, squeezed some brightly-colored acrylics onto his pallet and started to paint. Though Kate was curious what he was painting, she knew better than to disturb a working artist. While Francis showered and the pasta cooked, Kate went back upstairs and finished dressing for dinner.

When Francis entered the bedroom, he was struck by how beautiful Kate looked. He wanted to slide her black dress up over her thighs, lay her back on the bed, and make love to her. But things had been chilly for a while and he didn't want to be rejected, plus he'd overheard her argument with Stringer, who was right downstairs.

Francis opened a small drawer on top of the Parisian bureau and took out a rosewood jewelry box. He lifted a gold necklace from the purple velvet into which it had made a permanent impression. He turned to Kate, who was brushing her hair in front of the mirror. "Would you like to wear this? It would look nice with your black dress."

Kate was surprised, looked intrigued. "Is it real gold?"

Francis smiled. "Yes. We got it in St. Thomas years ago. I think it is the right size for you."

Before she could respond, Francis slid the heavy braided gold around her bare collarbone and snapped shut the lock at the back of her neck.

Kate felt the smooth gold with her hand as she turned toward the mirror. She stared at her reflection from different angles. "I hardly rec-ognize myself, like I'm looking at a different woman." Her voice was part amazement, part puzzlement. She turned to Francis. "Thanks. It's way over the top, but beautiful." Kate looked in the mirror again. "Do you think Rachael would mind?"

Francis was surprised and moved by her question. "I think she'd be pleased."

"Okay, I'll wear it."

Francis smiled. He wanted to kiss her, but the moment wasn't quite right.

"Wonderful. I thought it might be special for you."

Holding her hand against the necklace, Kate was careful not to turn her ankles as she walked downstairs in unfamiliar high heels. Stringer was at the kitchen table chowing down the pasta while thumbing through a surfing magazine Francis had ordered for him.

Kate sat next to Stringer. "I meant to tell you an art dealer came by the gallery today."

Kate heard Francis come down the stairs to the hallway.

"Richard, the dealer, is interested in a couple of your paintings."

Francis stopped at the kitchen doorway.

Stringer showed no interest.

"String, this guy's a real art dealer, wants to sell your paintings in a New York gallery."

Francis stepped closer.

"Okay, I guess." Stringer looked up. "What does Francis think?"

"He wasn't there."

"Why not?" Stringer sounded agitated.

"Well, I need to do some things myself. He can't do everything for us."

She heard Francis step back from the doorway.

Stringer turned the page of his magazine. "I don't care what you do with them. I just like to paint."

"I'll ask Francis about it, but you have the final say. You made them."

"Whatever." He twisted pasta onto his fork, buttery bits of melting Romano and parmesan glistening in the lamplight.

Kate touched his arm. "I want to make this work for you, String. You definitely have talent. The guy even told me about an art appreciation workshop this weekend at an institute up north. I thought I could learn some things to help you out. We could do this together." She glanced toward the hallway. "With Francis' help of course."

"We'll see." Stringer finished the pasta. "That was good. Thanks." He got up and put the bowl in the sink. "Don't you guys have to get going?"

Francis stepped into the kitchen. "Yes, but I want to get that guitar out of the attic for you. Let's go up. I know right where it is."

Stringer followed him upstairs. "I didn't even know you had an attic."

"It's just an unheated storage room under the dormer."

Francis turned a dark wooden doorknob and pulled, the door squeaking as it opened. He reached in and pulled the chain on a lightbulb hanging in the middle of the room. Dry, pent-up air with a tinge of cedar escaped through the doorway.

Francis stepped inside, cracked floorboards creaking beneath him.

Stringer stayed close to Francis, looking around at plastic garment bags hanging from a pipe suspended from the rafters. There were a bunch of old boxes, including a stack under a triangular window in the dormer, on top of which were a number of faded books of "S&H Green Stamps."

"What are those?" Stringer asked, pointing.

Francis smiled. "We used to get those stamps as a bonus at the store. We'd paste them in those little books and, when they were full, redeem them for things like placemats, toasters, or even a bicycle—if you had a ton of stamps."

"Weird," Stringer said. He looked around the room and in the corner stood something with a pair of eyes that appeared to be staring at him. "What the hell is that?"

Francis looked over. "The crow? That's Charlie."

Stringer realized it was a dusty stuffed crow. *"Charlie?"*

"Yes, he was my grandmother's pet for many years. She had him stuffed when he died, kept him in the parlor next to her reading chair."

"Really weird."

"A little odd, I suppose, but if you knew her, and him, you'd understand. They were quite a pair. She even taught him to talk."

Stringer made a face. "Come on, crows can't talk."

Francis smiled. "Charlie could. When I was a kid, you'd walk into the room and he'd cock his head at you and say, 'Hello, hello, Charlie want a cracker,' and he'd keep saying it until you gave him a cracker. Like you, he preferred Ritz."

"Yeah, *right*."

"No kidding."

Stringer continued to look at the mementos hanging from the rafters, including a tarnished brass trumpet and a dusty wool pennant from an Adirondack summer camp Francis must have attended as a kid. Stringer stepped over and pushed on a couple of the sticky valves on the bugle. "It's cool that you have all this old stuff."

"Yes, memories of the past. Camp Mohawk up on Saranac Lake was one of my favorite places. It's where I learned how to sail, which was a big part of my life until, you know, Rachael died."

Stringer lifted the green and red pennant which had a tiny birch bark canoe sewn into the middle of it.

Francis looked under the eaves. "Here it is." He reached down and lifted a black guitar case from behind a couple of leather suitcases. "Got this after I moved here when I was a teenager. I mowed lawns, that sort of thing, for friends of my grandmother. Bought it with my earnings—a dollar a lawn, no matter the size, including trimming, which I hated."

"How'd you learn to play?"

"My grandmother knew many of the artists and musicians around here. She introduced me to a friend of hers up in Sebec, a great young folksinger named David Mallett. He was very kind to me, taught me chord progressions and how to fingerpick the strings. I learned how to play a few simple songs, but I had little natural ability."

Francis set the case on a wooden steamer trunk and opened it. He lifted the instrument out of the yellow velvet lining. "It's been around the block a few times, but it's made of rosewood and has a nice warm sound, or at least it did the last time I played it, which was a long time ago."

Stringer looked at the guitar admiringly. "I'll bet it's hard to play."

"If I could learn, you can. In fact, Dave is coming down to visit sometime soon. I'm donating a painting for a benefit he's doing for a local land trust. I'll bet he'd be willing to spend a few minutes showing you some licks."

"Really?" String said. "That'd be cool. Maybe Sam could be there, too."

"Sure."

Stringer felt the steel strings. "Did you play much?"

"Quite a bit when I was young and my friends and I went to folk festivals. We all had guitars—or a ukulele, banjo, or at least a Jew's harp. We camped out in leaky tents for long weekends, jammed, and hob-nobbed with the singer-songwriters."

Francis took a soft chamois cloth from the case and carefully wiped the guitar's rosewood face.

"Back then you could get close to famous people. After they performed, we'd often hang out with them and sometimes get them to sign posters or even our instruments." He held the guitar up to the light. "Wonder if you can still see their signatures."

Stringer leaned closer. He saw several bits of writing scrawled across the wood, but they were faded and he couldn't make them out.

Francis handed the guitar to him. "Why don't you see if you can tune it up? There's a tuning pipe in the case." He pointed to the strings. "You start with the bottom, the thickest one, and blow the low "E" note on the tuner as you strum the string. You tighten its corresponding tuner on the headstock until each string sounds the same as the pipe."

Stringer frowned. "Headstock? What are you talking about?"

Realizing it sounded complicated, Francis took the guitar back and cradled it on his lap. "Like this." He showed Stringer how to tune it. The strings, not surprisingly, were way too loose.

"I get it," Stringer said.

"Once it's tuned, you can play all you like. If it doesn't sound right, we'll have a new set of strings put on."

Francis handed the guitar back to Stringer. "I'll give Dave a call. He'll show you some tricks of the trade."

"Awesome." Stringer looked the guitar over admiringly. "Sam will be psyched." He leaned over and gave Francis a one-arm hug.

Stringer started strumming, but it sounded so awful they both cringed then chuckled. He put it back in the case. "I'll work on it."

"Bring the guitar down with you," Francis said. He paused at the attic doorway. "I hope your mom and I work things out so we can stay together. I mean all of us—forever."

"Me, too."

"Stringer, it's not an overstatement to say you've changed my whole life." They hugged each other for a few seconds then Stringer pulled away and picked up the guitar case. "I'll see you downstairs."

CHAPTER TEN

IN THE FOYER, KATE BRUSHED PAST FRANCIS ON THE WAY TO THE hall closet. "It's going to be chilly tonight, so I'll bring a coat."

Outside, after saying goodbye to Stringer, Francis held Kate's door as she got into the Jeep. A short way up the road, he said, "I heard you mention an art appreciation course this weekend. I assume it's at the institute in Skowhegan."

"That sounds right. Richard said it's a good place, that I could learn a lot to help Stringer."

"Yes. The institute is world-renowned." Francis thought for a moment. "It's probably not a bad idea. I'd love to go, and maybe we can get Stringer interested."

Kate's body tightened. "I was thinking of going myself. You don't need to waste your time learning basic things."

"I don't mind." Francis accelerated. "Is this Richard fellow going?"

Kate felt her pulse quicken. *She felt Richard's breath on her lips.* "He didn't say, just told me about it."

Kate noticed Francis gripping the wheel tighter.

"He probably thought it strange I hadn't taught you more."

Kate felt hot. "No, it wasn't like that. He was just being helpful."

"I'll bet," Francis said, with a little more sarcasm than he intended.

"Look, Francis, I've told you I'm trying to do this on my own. You're an expert, and it's probably hard for you to not show me everything, but you've taught Stringer how to paint and that's enough."

"Actually, he's teaching himself. I've just given him a few pointers and a little studio space."

Kate looked at Francis. "And I need you to give me enough space to learn on *my* own." She adjusted the heavy gold necklace, which was starting to feel like a choke collar around her neck.

Francis sighed. "This isn't what I had planned. I wanted us to have a nice evening out."

No response.

"Might we try again?"

"Yeah."

They rode the rest of the way to Falmouth Foreside in silence. At a fancy gold-leafed sign, Francis turned onto a narrow dirt road that led toward the ocean. As they approached the yacht club, Kate noticed rows of whitecaps rolling into the harbor. Over the gateway, a lighted American flag blew nervously in the onshore breeze. She felt chilly even before they got out of the Jeep. "So what's this dinner going to be like?"

Francis parked next to a silver Mercedes. "Well, there'll be a host of interesting people here. The club does a lot of good for the community, sponsoring benefits and offering sailing camps for disabled children. I have to admit, though, there are a few members that are too stuffy for me."

"That's what I'm worried about."

"No need to be. There are plenty of good people to mingle with during the social hour. Then there's a gourmet dinner and a brief business meeting."

A seagull screamed from atop a lamppost and flew off.

"You know I don't like being around drinking."

"It's not like everyone gets drunk. They're not that kind of crowd." He placed his hand on her thigh and looked at her. "Besides, one of the women, Mrs. Bashir, doesn't drink."

Kate recoiled. "So—what? You want me to hang out with her?"

"I thought it might be a comfort. You know, maybe she goes to meetings, too."

"Oh my god, Francis. You can't just hook me up with another *maybe* recovering drunk." Kate looked out the window. In the next row of cars sat a metallic Ford Mustang. Her heart skipped. She swore the necklace was tightening around her neck. She squinted and realized, thankfully, that the Mustang was black not blue. She didn't know what she would have done if Richard was there. Her mind flashed to earlier in the day when he stepped smoothly from the Shelby at the curb in front of the gallery. She wished she was with him. Somewhere, *anywhere* else. Still, deep down, she knew some hot new guy wasn't going to fix anything.

"Kate," Francis said. He pulled the keys from the ignition and motioned toward the club, a stately white building with a natural wood prow overhanging the entrance. Hearing no response, he raised his voice slightly. "Kate, are you ready to go in?"

"Don't yell at me," she snapped, pulling her thoughts back from Richard.

"I'm not yelling. You didn't respond."

"To what?"

Francis tried to contain his irritation. "Are you ready to go in?"

"I guess."

Raindrops sprinkled on the windshield. Francis slid Kate's coat around her shoulders and they got out. The air was heavy with a chilly salt mist. Lighted nautical flags from around the world illuminated the walkway from the parking lot, and as they approached the entrance, Kate felt like she was entering the United Nations. The glass doors had large gleaming brass pulls opened by a doorman in a navy blue blazer. She stifled an impulse to run, lowered her head, and walked inside. The threshold was slippery, and she turned her ankle in the high heels.

"Shit!" she said, starting to fall. She caught herself on the doorjamb as several people looked at her. The doorman came to her aid before Francis was able to.

Kate was angry and embarrassed, though she really didn't care what these people thought. Once she was steady on her feet, she realized the atmosphere inside was warm and convivial, the sounds of violins carrying across the room. Tables were draped with white linen and covered with crystal bowls of red cocktail sauce surrounded by circular layers of jumbo shrimp. There were gleaming silver trays of vegetables and cheeses, and other hor d'oeuvres. The air was filled with enticing aromas, laced with strong perfumes. The women wore expensive-looking dresses, and Kate couldn't help but admire their abundant but tasteful gold and silver jewelry. She paused at a white china platter stacked with skewers of beef and chicken surrounded by small bowels of dipping sauces.

Despite the urge to run, Kate was tired and hungry and couldn't resist the scrumptious-looking food. She left Francis chatting with a couple of men in summer suits, then checked to see if anyone was watching her. She grabbed several shrimp and two chicken skewers and slunk into the shadows at the side of the room.

After chewing the last tender morsel of meat off the slender wood,

Kate licked her fingers and surveyed the crowd. From the beams overhead hung rows of colorful banners and plaques commemorating sailing races and regattas which, even when she was drinking, she enjoyed watching off the beaches of LA. There also were antique nautical flags tattered by years of punishing Atlantic winds, and in one corner stood an old anchor encrusted with barnacles and deep pockmarks of rust. On one wall hung a weathered ship's life ring. Its faded blue letters read *AMORE*.

Kate shook her head. *So this is what Francis' life was like before we got here? This is crazy.*

Francis brought Kate a ginger ale, which she nursed while trying not to look at the elegant, beautifully backlit bar that called to her. It was difficult, but she tried to act interested in the insufferable small talk Francis engaged in with his friends. After almost an hour, she was startled by the sharp peal of a brass ship's bell mounted high on one of the wooden posts that supported the rafters.

From the head table, a young man in a sailor's suit spoke loudly. "Ladies and gentlemen, may I have your attention." The room quieted. "It is my pleasure to give you Commodore Charles Dewey."

A distinguished-looking man with a trim white and gray beard stepped to a lectern in the center of the table adorned with a lacquered crest of the club. He cleared his throat and spoke into a microphone, welcoming everyone to a new season, their 125th. He then introduced several dignitaries, including the governor, the mayor, the commodore of a yacht club visiting from Watch Hill, Rhode Island, and finally, two elderly World War II Navy veterans, who looked sharp in their brass-buttoned uniforms.

The Commodore paused while the guests applauded, then he turned to Francis. "And, after a two year absence, we are very pleased to have one of our long-time members back with us tonight, Maine's most famous painter and a fine sailor, Mr. Francis Monroe."

Francis smiled and waved to the crowd, which applauded. Kate stayed behind him and stared at the floor. Commodore Dewey motioned for Francis to join him at the head table. When Kate saw this, she grabbed Francis' arm and pulled him toward her. "I am *not* sitting up there in front of all these rich people."

Francis spoke deliberately out of the corner of his mouth. "Kate, these are nice people. It is an honor to be asked. I didn't know, or I would've told you. Please don't embarrass me."

Kate held firm. "Don't try to drag me up there. I will bolt out of this place. I *so* don't belong here."

Francis slid her hand off his arm. "Kate, they're not going to hurt you. You can't just wig out on me."

The muscles of Kate's jaw tightened. Squinting, she stared straight into his eyes, spoke through clenched teeth. "You have no fucking idea what I can do."

CHAPTER ELEVEN

WITH FRANCIS AND HIS MOM OUT FOR DINNER, STRINGER WAS psyched to be alone so he could work on his painting of Sam. He set his easel up in the parlor and stared at the blue-green background he had washed onto the canvas earlier. He wished he had a photograph of her, though he saw her vividly in his mind. His pulse quickened when he thought of her torn sweater partially revealing the smooth skin of her breast, though it was her eyes that most powerfully affected him. She seemed so self-assured—something he struggled with—though he could sense she really wasn't. Unable to focus, he paced about the house, pausing at the front door. He watched the orange afterglow of sunset illuminate the clouds layered over the ocean. Though he hadn't admitted it to others, he was growing fond of this other coast, which seemed more rugged than the beaches of Southern California. Though he missed hanging out along the beach in Venice, meeting Sam had dampened his interest in moving back there.

As the horizon darkened, Stringer went in and stood in front of his easel. He could hear Francis' words: "When you're struggling to create, if you stand there long enough, I guarantee you'll end up painting *something*."

Stringer picked up one of the fine French brushes Francis had given him, touched the dollop of light brown paint on his pallet and drew an outline of a neck, Sam's neck, with the small, red and black yin-yang tattoo beneath her pierced ear. He drew the curve of her cute little nose then the other side of her neck and the wave-like sweep of her collarbones. He dipped his brush in water then swiped it through jet black paint and added slightly angled eyebrows. He thought carefully about how he would bring her eyes to life. He didn't want to screw them up. They were so beautiful. Green. Intense green. He realized he'd actually never noticed anyone's eye color before.

Stringer stepped close to the canvas, steadied his right hand on his other wrist and made several delicate curved lines for eyelashes. He squinted, trying to remember every detail. Thinking of her gave him a surge of energy. He wanted to run outside and yell to the world, but he forced himself to stay focused. *How can a girl make me feel this crazy? Make me feel this good?* He thought about how his mom often talked about the gifts in her life. Stringer felt Sam was a gift. He didn't know from whom, but she was definitely a gift. He leaned in and ever-so-carefully drew an elliptical outline of an eye, then the round iris. He stepped back and studied the canvas. "Good," he said, feeling encouraged.

With wet fingers, he tightened the point on his brush, dipped it lightly in paint, drew the other eye then made a pupil in the middle of each. He pulled another brush from his box, dipped it in green paint, into which he had added a few drops of water and a sprinkling of sparkling 'stardust.' He meticulously colored the inside of one of the irises and smiled. *It looked like Sam!*

As he started on the other eye, Stringer was startled by someone pounding on the front door. He jerked his hand into the canvas, smudging green paint across Sam's cheek. "What the fu—?"

Distracted, he glanced toward the door, quickly wiping his wet fingertips on a rag. He tried to blot the smudged paint off the canvas, but it only made it worse. "Damn—"

Someone banged on the door again, so hard it rattled the glass.

"What the hell?" Angry, he dropped his brushes and rag on the paint stand, stepped quietly along the wall to the door and looked through the sidelight glass. A man in a black hat and a suitcoat a bit large for him stood on the step. It appeared the guy wasn't going away. Stringer opened the door a crack.

"Kate Johnson in there?" The man's voice was sharp, impatient.

Holding the door knob tightly, Stringer thought about the large carving knife Francis kept in the drawer to the right of the sink. "No. What do you want?"

"I'll ask the questions." The man forced the door open so hard the safety chain tore off the doorjamb. He pushed past Stringer into the hallway, quickly glancing around the house.

His arm hurting, Stringer backed away. He checked the phone sitting on the table at the foot of the stairs.

"Don't even think about it," the guy said. He took a quick look in the kitchen then faced Stringer. "You the kid who blew his old man away?" Before Stringer could respond, the man bent forward, looked him straight in the eye. "That was a *very* stupid move."

Stringer's breath caught as a bolt of fear shot through him. "Why's that?" he asked, his voice weaker than he'd expected.

Ignoring him, the man looked up the stairs. "Your old lady up there?"

"I told you, she's not home."

"I hear she's a looker."

Acid flooded Stringer's gut. Anger rising above his fear, he got around in front of the man. "Who are you?"

The man sneered. "Let's just say a friend of your dear old dad's."

Stringer was surprised, confused.

The man took a cigarette from his breast pocket, and flicked a silver lighter under it. He blew smoke in Stinger's direction. "I'll cut to the chase. Your old man owed my boss a lot of money and he can't pay up 'cause you shot him." He leaned forward again. "Dead. Five shots was it?"

Stringer's heart pounded.

"He can't deal smack for us anymore and we figure you and mommy took off with his cash." He jabbed a finger into Stringer's chest. "Didn't think we'd find you way out here, did you? We got connections all over, boy. You can't get away from us."

Stringer didn't move.

"So I'm here to collect from his estate, but I'm guessing your mother and that rich artist she's shacking up with got a lot more money than you. They're the ones I gotta see." He took a drag on his cigarette, the end glowing bright orange. He flicked gray ash onto the hardwood floor.

"I hear Monroe's paintings fetch a lotta dough." He looked over at the smudged painting on the easel, shook his head. "But I don't get why."

He turned sharply back to Stringer. "You tell them they've got two weeks to come up with two hundred thousand—cash—unmarked—no bullshit, no cops, or this little love nest won't be so cozy anymore." He scuffed the ash on the floor with his foot. "It'll be a big pile of cinders."

He took another drag on his cigarette, reached over to the easel and ground it out in the middle of Sam's face.

"Hey!" Stringer lunged forward, knocking the man's arm to the side.

In a split second, the man grabbed Stringer's hand and bent it back so hard he grimaced and fell to his knees.

"Don't ever touch me again unless you can kill me. I'm not a pussy like Leland." The man adjusted his hat with his other hand, scoffed. "Pathetic, letting a little shit like you do him."

He let go of Stringer's hand, which seared with pain. "Two weeks. Deliver the message or there'll be hell to pay." He walked to the door. "We'll be in touch."

Holding his aching hand, Stringer watched through the window as the man hurried to his car, glanced around, and got in. Stringer squinted as the guy drove off. Rhode Island plates. AK— couldn't read the numbers. Stringer swung the door closed with his elbow. "Fucking asshole."

Back at his easel, Stringer's anger and hurt grew, as painful memories of Leland wrecking his early drawings crowded in. He dampened a clean cloth and tried to wipe the cigarette stub from Sam's eye. He was surprised by a tear that formed at the corner of his eyelid. "That bastard," he said, staring at the messed-up canvas. "He still won't leave us alone."

Grinding his teeth, Stringer turned away toward a glass-front cabinet in the corner of the room. Gradually, a green and gold bottle of Jameson's Irish Whiskey came into view. He slowly walked toward it, like he was being pulled by a magnet, opened the cabinet door and firmly grasped the neck of the bottle. He squeezed his eyes shut as he saw an image of a drunk, disgusting Leland coming at him, his scraggly beard matted with beer froth. Stringer winced, then shook off the image and pulled the cork out of the Jameson's, tipped it up, and took a swig.

CHAPTER TWELVE

KATE WAS RELIEVED THAT FRANCIS HAD DECLINED THE COMMODORE'S invitation to sit at the head table and instead approached a nearby table with two empty seats. He spoke to a woman in a royal blue dress sitting next to the empty chairs. "Are these seats taken?"

The woman looked up, seemed pleased he had asked. "Oh, Mr. Monroe, no, please join us."

Francis pulled a chair out for Kate, and she hesitantly sat down.

The lady turned to Kate. "That's a lovely necklace, dear. Is it a Williston?"

Kate had no idea what the lady was talking about. She pinched Francis' forearm. He turned and smiled at the lady. "Yes, we bought it in the Caribbean years ago. The craftsmanship is extraordinary."

"Exquisite, I would say." The woman's diamond earrings sparkled in the candlelight as she spoke. She touched her husband's hand. "Maybe I, too, can have a necklace like that someday, dear."

The lady let out a fake laugh, which made Kate want to scream.

The husband smirked and took a generous swallow of his golden drink, ice cubes clinking in his glass. As he exhaled, Kate got a strong whiff of whiskey. When he set the glass back on the table, she wanted to grab it and down it.

The dinner was uncomfortable, to say the least, though Francis did try to comfort Kate with little touches under the table. The most relief she got was from eating a lot of great food and being able to stare out the floor-to-ceiling windows at the bay, her mind returning to Richard. She enjoyed the guilty pleasure of knowing she shouldn't be contemplating doing something forbidden but planning to do it anyway.

Waiting for dessert to be served, Kate felt Francis slide his hand over her palm, his fingers intertwining with hers. He leaned over and whispered. "I'm sorry this has been an awful experience for you. I got caught up in it, wanted to show you off, I guess."

Kate couldn't suppress a grin. "How's that working for you?"

"Not great. Anyway, we'll be out of here soon."

Kate relaxed a bit. "Good. Sorry I got riled. Sometimes my old fears rage up."

When they finally walked out of the club into the cool night air, Kate unclasped the necklace and put it in her coat pocket. The rain had stopped and the clouds were parting, revealing a quarter moon that reflected off crests of waves marching across the bay. "Wow, am I glad to get out of there."

"Fish out of water, huh?" Francis said, as they walked through the parking lot.

"Yeah. Sometimes I feel totally out of control. I don't like it."

"I know that's hard. I felt it most of last fall."

Kate looked at him. "Really?"

"Yes, after Stringer was arrested it felt like the whole world was wildly out of control."

"Like I said before, you hide it well."

"Probably something I inherited from my father. Not sure it's a good thing."

They drove home along Shore Road, a narrow, winding route that afforded striking glimpses of the craggy coastline. Kate rolled her window down and let the salt air blow through her hair.

Feeling like they were reconnecting, Francis slid a hand under his seat and felt for the small black box. "It's turned into a beautiful evening. Would you like to stop at a secret little overlook up ahead that has a spectacular view?"

"Sure, if you want."

He turned off the highway, drove past a field, onto a steep, barely passable road that descended through aromatic pines to a small parking area lined with knee-high boulders that protected vehicles from going off the adjacent cliff. Away from the lights of town, the clearing sky was filling with stars. He was glad no one else was there.

Francis slipped the box with the ring into his pocket and got out. Walking around the back of the car, he felt hope, mixed with some trepidation, that he and Kate could somehow create a loving, supportive family together.

Kate stepped from the Jeep and pulled Rachael's coat around her. She walked over and leaned against a boulder; beyond it the cliff fell away sharply into a deep ravine. In the distance, the ocean shimmered in the moonlight. "Wow, this is cool."

"Lovely, isn't it?" He pointed. "That beach down there is a favorite for horseback riding—and skinny-dipping."

Kate gave him a look.

"My grandmother first showed me this spot when I was a young boy. The main road up there was dirt then and there was just a hiking trail down to this spot."

"How old were you?"

"Seven or eight, I guess."

Kate sat down at the cliff's edge. She appeared to enjoy the fragrant air rising through the pines that rimmed the walls of the ravine. "At that age I was traveling around in a woody station wagon with my alcoholic mother. That jalopy was always breaking down, but no matter what, she had Janice Joplin, Jimi Hendrix, or Led Zeppelin blasting out of an eight track she'd wired to the dash." Kate shook her head. "No wonder I'm crazy. Thank god for Dylan, Neil Young, and Credence, or I would've lost the rest of my mind."

Francis sat next to her and dangled his legs over the edge of the cliff. A cool breeze ballooned his pant legs, chilling his calves. "Your mother meant so much to you, but it sounds like she was quite difficult, also."

"Yeah, she was a powerful presence—a strange woman, deeply spiritual in a quirky sort of way. Driving those long straight highways across the plains, she would regularly take a good swig off a bottle, close her eyes and chant and sing. Sometimes she'd yell louder than the music, even take her hands off the wheel for what seemed like miles. She'd dance with her arms out the window and through the leaky moon roof. I'd watch the road and grab the wheel when we headed over the shoulder. Our wheels weren't in very good alignment, and the tires were pretty bald." Kate smiled. "Life with her was crazy, but beautiful too."

"You've carried her spirit with you."

Kate pulled the coat more tightly around her. "Not very well. I started to develop a good spiritual practice, a mix of Lakota and AA, but the whole Leland thing knocked me off balance."

Francis put his hand on her forearm. "I hope you can find peace again."

"I feel pretty messed up, like withdrawing after a binge."

Francis frowned.

"Don't worry, I haven't been drinking. It's hard to explain. I just feel unstable, lost at times, like I'm back in my old life."

Francis slid his arm around her shoulders and gently pulled her closer. She let her head partially relax against his chest. "Well, you're not. You're safe, right here with me."

Francis felt for the ring box in his blazer pocket. He wanted to give it to her, to make her feel loved and at home forever.

Kate moved from under his arm. "I wish I could just settle into this new life, you know, really fit in, make everybody happy." She looked at him. "I don't know if you can ever understand where I came from, how bad it was, what it did to me."

Francis took his hand out of his pocket. "I think I got a pretty good idea when Leland arrived."

Kate nodded. "At least a glimpse."

"One helluva glimpse."

"I know, and you were such a trooper through the whole thing. You never wavered in your support of Stringer and me." Kate touched Francis' hand. "But now, I think the hardest thing for me to explain, and for you to understand, is that this kind of normal life is all new to me." She hesitated. "I know it's hard for you to fathom, but I need to figure out how to live a regular life. I've got to explore things. I mean, on my own."

Francis moved away from her a bit.

"It's really nothing to do with you. It's about me."

"Well, we *do* live together." Francis felt defensive, but tried to stifle it as he didn't want to discourage Kate from speaking her truth. He waited, the ring weighing heavily in his pocket, as he tried to read the confused emotions on her face.

Kate spoke quietly. "Francis, this life with you...it's too much, too nice, for me. I know you want us to have a perfect life in your little bungalow. No muss, no fuss, everything taken care of." She looked at him with pleading eyes. "But it's driving me crazy." She stood, turned away and stumbled, banging her knee on a boulder.

Francis grabbed for her. "Careful!"

Kate leaned against the boulder again.

"I thought you liked our life together—no more dread and fear. A stable home."

Kate threw up her hands. "I wish it were that simple. Did you think my whole past life would just magically disappear? Get flushed clean out of me? I can't go from recovering junkie to princess overnight." Tears formed in her eyes. "I don't want to be a princess. I'm not Julia Roberts, and this isn't *Pretty Woman*. This is my life, and it's *really* messy."

Silence fell between them, broken only by the distant cry of a coyote. After a while, Francis stood, stepped closer to her, and looked into her eyes. "I love you very much, Kate. And you're right, I don't completely understand you, just as you can't completely understand me. All I can tell you is I want you in my life, want to take this journey together. I can't quite imagine it without you and Stringer. Do whatever you have to do to figure it all out. Just tell me the truth, that's all I ask."

Kate nodded.

"And thank you for being honest with me."

Francis got into the Jeep. He started the engine as Kate got in.

Kate touched the sleeve of his coat. "I'm sorry, Francis. I don't mean to hurt you."

Francis nodded then backed away from the cliff and drove up the gravely path, which felt unsteady beneath their tires.

CHAPTER THIRTEEN

NEITHER KATE NOR FRANCIS SPOKE ON THE DRIVE HOME. INSIDE the bungalow, the smell of acrylic paint and a faint hint of cigarette smoke hung in the air. Alarmed, Kate quickly checked on Stringer, who was asleep, then looked around the house but found nothing out of the ordinary. She paused at Stringer's canvas. Part of the painting was smudged and his lines weren't as sharp or crisp as she was used to. Maybe he was becoming an impressionist; regardless, she knew the painting was of Sam.

Francis was tired, didn't seem to find anything unusual and went up to bed. Though Kate was glad she and Francis had been able to talk, the evening left her upset and confused. She didn't feel comfortable sleeping with him, so she walked into the laundry room and pulled a blanket and pillow from the shelf above the drier. Running her hand over the soft cotton, she remembered the first time they had made love right there on the rug amongst a pile of warm laundry. It had been wonderful, perhaps the closest she had ever felt to another human being. Surely the most powerful orgasm she'd ever had. No other guy had ever cared about getting her off.

Kate held the blankets to her chest, wondered what had happened to their passion. Had the trial irreversibly worn them down, turning the early excitement of their love into a desperate struggle to survive? Were they just too different? Parts of Francis she'd found loving and supportive early on, now sometimes felt patronizing or judgmental.

Before she lay down on the couch, Kate found the jacket she'd worn earlier to the gallery. She held it to her face, smelled the slight scent of Richard on the collar. She pulled the art institute brochure he had given her from the pocket. She lit a candle on the coffee table, pulled the blanket over her and opened the brochure. On the cover was an aerial photograph of a lake with an inset picture of a young artist hunched over a bench with an older instructor, their fingers white with clay, closely examining a sculpture in progress. She read that the institute was founded in 1947 during the creative surge that followed World War II and had been educating and supporting emerging artists ever since.

Inside, colorful photographs showed a beautiful farm-like campus with wooden buildings and a community of vibrant young people working in all sorts of creative endeavors from painting and photography to digital and fiber arts. One photo showed a young woman in waders setting up a camera at the edge of a beaver pond at daybreak. As Kate read, fatigue from the day caught up with her and her eyelids became heavy. She fell asleep with the brochure open across her chest.

Kate didn't sleep well on the couch and got up with a stiff neck around sunrise when she heard Francis come downstairs and leave for a walk. She was sort of bummed, though she wasn't sure what she would have said to him. She shed the blankets and the coat, made a cup of coffee, and took a quick shower. After packing an overnight bag, she said goodbye to Stringer, who was still sound asleep. She tucked his blankets in then left a note on the kitchen table for him and for Francis. She said she was sorry for being so irritable, and that she was going to stay in Skowhegan that night. She'd be home after the art course ended Sunday. She felt a sadness as she drove her blue Malibu down the hill past Kasa's, where she noticed a large Oldsmobile parked out back.

* * * * * *

Francis walked along the trail to Wagner's Point. A pair of snowy egrets took off from a marsh ahead of him, flying close to the ground until they disappeared in the morning mist. When he reached the point, he sat on the same sloping ledge he had the day he threw the life preserver to Stringer. He felt the same fearful recoil he had that day when Stringer jumped into the surging Atlantic to try and save Delbert Ready when his sailboat, the *Maiden*, shipwrecked on the rocks. Francis looked over the eerie remains of the once elegant sloop. Several of its wooden ribs were still trapped between the rocks, creaking back and forth with the waves like an ancient skeleton trying to speak. A seagull landed on top of one of the staves and rhythmically lifted its wings up and down to maintain its balance.

Francis still marveled at how Stringer had lunged into the sea, abandoning his own safety, battling punishing waves to try to save a drowning stranger. It was an even more astounding feat when Francis realized that one of Stringer's arms had been broken. Amazing kid.

Francis' thoughts turned to Kate, who despite her increasing irritability had not lost her good heart. He appreciated she was committed to helping Stringer develop a painting career even though she seemed to understand little about the mind of an artist. He frowned, thinking about how taken aback he was by the anger in her eyes when he had wanted to sit at the head table. He had to admit he'd sort of wanted the *Pretty Woman* story, but knew that was foolish. What he wanted more was to learn how to set his own desires aside so he could better understand Kate and be there for her.

Francis sat on the cold ledge for a short while, then, knowing Stringer would be getting up, stood and headed back to the bungalow. The house was silent when he arrived, so he walked into the parlor and looked over what Stringer had painted the night before. He was surprised to find the painting was a mess, with a strange gray smudge in the middle of the canvas. Then he noticed a bottle cork on its side in the easel tray. He lifted the cork and smelled whisky—Jameson whiskey. He stepped back, noticed what looked like ash on the hardwood floor. "What is going on here?"

Seeing that the Jameson had been moved, Francis opened the corner cabinet and checked the level he had marked on the bottle, a caution against Kate drinking. It had dropped just a tad. Concerned, he stepped to the door of Stringer's room. He was still sleeping, a pillow pulled over his head. Francis pushed the door open wide. "Stringer—"

No response.

Francis jiggled the foot of the bed with his knee. "Stringer, wake up."

Stringer partially pulled the pillow off his face. "What?"

Francis sat on the desk chair next to the bed. "What happened here last night? Did you have a party?"

Stringer pushed the pillow away. "Party?"

"Yes, did you have a party with your friends while we were out?"

"No," he replied as if the word had two syllables. He rubbed his eyes.

"The cork to the Jameson's is on your easel and some of the whisky is gone."

Stringer looked at the floor. "Oh. I must have forgotten to put it back in. It was just me. I took a sip."

"Why? You can't be drinking."

"I was pretty freaked."

"By our being out?"

"Not that. I usually like being home alone."

Francis waited, his silence implying he expected more details to be forthcoming.

Stringer sat up and stared at the floor. "Look, it was a weird night. That's all."

Francis leaned forward on the seat. "And you've taken up smoking, too?"

Stringer blushed.

"That's a different story. Kind of hard to explain."

"I'm listening." Stringer pulled a T-shirt over his head.

"I remember a kid from California I met on the bluff last fall who made me tell him the truth."

"Look, this asshole came by last night, pushed his way in and wanted money. I didn't know what to do."

Francis sat straight up. "A *robber?*"

"Kind of, I guess, except he demanded money from you and Mom that Leland owed him for selling drugs. Said he didn't pay off his dealer before he died. The guy blamed me that they didn't get their money."

Francis' mouth fell open. "*What* are you talking about?"

"Exactly. I thought we were done with this bullshit."

Francis slid his chair closer to the bed. "What did he look like? What did you do?"

Stringer held his hand up. "Give me a second." He pushed away the covers. "His license plate was from Rhode Island—couldn't read the number. He was a cocky asshole, thought my painting was one of yours." Stringer smirked. "What a joke."

"What did he say?"

"He said to tell you and Mom you had two weeks to come up with two hundred grand or there'll be hell to pay."

Francis coughed. "*Two hundred thousand?*"

"Yup. Said he knew you were rich."

"Damn." Francis sat back in his chair, remembered the guy Charlie had told him about at the info booth. "Does your mom know anything about this? Maybe that's why she's so irritable."

"Don't think so. Never said anything, and you know her, she would've gone berserk."

"That's true." Francis stood and paced. "This is crazy. I thought Leland was some two-bit street pusher, not a real dealer."

"Me, too." Stringer looked Francis in the eye. "Mom's going to freak out." He pulled on his sweatpants.

"I've got to call Charlie."

"Think he can do anything? He's just a local sheriff."

Francis looked surprised. "I think you've seen how much a local sheriff can do—good and bad. He'll help us." Francis started to walk out of the room then stopped. "By the way, drinking is dangerous for you with all the trouble your parents got into with it. And your mom would be devastated."

"Yeah."

"Have you been drinking before?"

"Once."

"When?"

"Couple days ago, on the boat. Pike made me drink a beer."

"*Made* you?"

Stringer nodded. "Pretty much."

"Another asshole."

"Big time."

"Did you like it?"

"The beer? No, tasted sour."

"So why'd you drink the whiskey?"

"Don't know. I see people drinking all the time when they're uptight. Even Buster."

"True. For most it's probably not dangerous. But with your family history…"

"Sorry."

Francis knew Stringer felt badly. "I don't want you drinking here again. Preferably nowhere until you're legal and even then you've got to be careful."

"Okay."

Francis called the sheriff's office. The deputy on the desk said Charlie wouldn't be back till early evening and that he could meet him then.

When Francis rang off, Stringer approached. "Can I ask you something?"

"Yes."

"You and Mom alright?"

Francis was taken off guard, like the first day he unexpectedly met Stringer on the lawn in front of the painting and he asked about Rachael. "I'm not sure. She seems to have changed."

"Yeah. She's gotten more like her old self, before she quit drinking."

Francis looked at Stringer. "Do you think she is—drinking?"

"Nah. I just think all this change is too much for her."

"Even for the better?"

"It's still change. She was a basket case before we came out here, a crazy woman even though we were heading for a better life. And this is *way* better."

"I hope so."

"I *know* so, and if Mom doesn't she's crazier than I thought." Stringer looked at Francis. "She loves you a lot. You going to hang in there with her?"

Relief flooded Francis. "Yes, I'm going to. And thank you for that. Sometimes I wonder with the way she acts."

"No problem. Girls can drive us nuts."

Francis smiled. "You've got that right."

"Hey, speaking of girls, Sam has a gig singing over at the Mill Pub tonight. She asked if I could go."

"Isn't that a bar?"

"I guess so. And a restaurant. She can only play till eight or something. I'd really like to watch her do her thing, and she's afraid there'll be no one there to listen. Mom said she'd come, but then she said she was going to some art thing."

"Yes, she left for Skowhegan early this morning." Francis felt bad. "There's a note on the kitchen table. I know she's trying to help your career."

Stringer made a face. "Fat chance." He got off the bed. "Whatever, I'm used to it. She used to not show up all the time."

"You really like this Sam girl, don't you?"

Stringer blushed. "Well, yeah."

"What's she like?"

"She's cool, and smart, and I think she likes me, too. Got abandoned as a little kid, doesn't even know her own parents." Stringer leaned forward. "She gets this look in her eyes that's powerful, like she knows deep things. And she doesn't look at me weird like some kids."

"Why are they like that?"

Stringer pulled on a worn sweatshirt. "I'm different. Seems everybody here's been together since kindergarten. Even the kids that are friendly act scared of me. Killing my father didn't help."

Francis nodded. "Been tough, huh?"

Stringer leaned against the door casing. "Yeah, sometimes." His voice caught. "The worst was in jail. It was so cold in that old brick cell. I was scared, especially when I started throwing up blood." He frowned deeply. "I know Sheriff McNeal wanted me dead."

Francis slid his arms around Stringer and held him. "Who locks a kid up in a dungeon like that?"

Stringer stepped back and shoved his hands in his pants pockets. "I know you and Mom and Buster worked really hard to save me. I'm so glad to be free, but I'm pissed off, too."

"What makes you angry?"

Stringer fiddled with the doorknob. "Even though it was screwed-up in California, I miss the surf and the beach, especially my seagulls."

"Your seagulls?"

"Yeah. They're all around Venice, cruisin' up and down the beach. I used to feed them all the time. They knew I'd have a pocketful of peanuts or popcorn. A whole flock of them always hovered over me. I even named some of them. One of them had only one leg. I called him Gimpy."

"That's neat."

Stringer looked up. "And I miss the sun. It's freaking cold up here."

"It can be. But summer's upon us."

"You call this *summer*?"

"Soon it will be. Tell me more about Sam."

Stringer brightened. "Sam's like the first girl I've really connected with."

"In Maine, you mean?"

"Ever, I guess."

"She good looking?"

Stringer smiled. "Yeah. Awesome."

"That always helps." Francis ran a hand through his hair. "Alright then."

"Alright, *what?*"

"You can go if you promise not to drink or get in trouble."

Stringer held up his hand. "Scout's honor."

Francis frowned. "You're not a scout."

"I could be."

Francis made a face. "What time do you need me to drive you over?"

"I just need to get to her house. I can ride with her to the gig."

"No, I'll take you to the place so I can check it out."

"Okay, whatever."

"You can get a ride back with her?"

Stringer looked dejected. "Yeah."

"What's wrong?"

"I'm bummed Mom just blew me off."

"She probably forgot."

"Yeah, she's all about her."

"Anyway, you've got me."

Stringer brightened. "Thanks for the ride. You rock."

"I'm glad someone thinks so."

CHAPTER FOURTEEN

KATE GOT LOST DRIVING, BUT AFTER ASKING FOR DIRECTIONS A couple of times, by mid-morning she made it through Skowhegan to the countryside north of town. Rolling her window down, she enjoyed the fresh sights and smells of early summer, reminding her of driving as a girl with her mother across the Blackfeet Indian Reservation in upper Montana. Kate had always enjoyed her mother's teaching about the wonders of the natural world, and had appreciated Francis doing the same since she'd arrived in Maine. Kate stuck her head out the window, felt the wind blow across her face and through her hair.

A mile up the road she slowed to admire a stretch of rich green meadow dotted with bright yellow dandelions swaying in the light breeze. Emerging through piles of winter road sand were determined clusters of purple violets and yellow tickseed. Vibrant clusters of daffodils and red, pink, and purple tulips surrounded peoples' mailboxes, many of which leaned back from the road thanks to repeated barrages from snowplows during the long New England winter. Though some guilt from leaving Stringer and Francis tugged at her, she was excited to be off on her own.

After checking the map she'd jammed in the dashboard air vent, Kate turned off the town highway and slowly made her way up a winding dirt road to the grounds of the art institute. Situated on what looked like an old dairy farm, the property was divided by a brook that flowed through a rambling campus of sun-faded wood buildings. The brook was lined with skunk cabbage, ferns, and yellow trout lilies, its water running smoothly under several wooden foot bridges.

Kate followed the arrow on a hand-painted sign directing her to a small field where there was parking for the workshop. She drove to the far corner of the field, shut the motor off and stared at a gathering of people talking outside a barn. Beyond the barn were cabins and long-porched buildings with skylights, interspersed with trees and flower gardens. Most of the people were younger than Kate, and they looked hip, dressed in loose-fitting clothing, some in bright colors, others in black. She figured they were all artists who, unlike her, knew what they were doing.

Kate held the steering wheel with both hands as she reconsidered the whole idea of coming. She felt a wave of fear. This place was not for people like her. She could learn about art promotion somewhere else without masquerading as an artist.

She started the Malibu, put it in reverse and looked over the seat to back up. She jammed on the brake when she saw Richard standing behind her car.

He walked around to her window. "Where are *you* going in such a hurry?"

Kate's heart beat hard and fast in her chest.

Richard flicked a dying cigarette into the dirt and blew smoke away from her over the roof.

"I don't think I should be here."

Richard opened her door and offered his hand. Nervous, Kate glanced around, reluctantly took his hand and stepped from the car.

"This is a special place. You'll love it."

Richard curled strands of her dark hair behind her ear. "Kind of frazzled, huh?"

"I got lost."

"How can you get lost with a GPS?"

She nodded toward the dash. "Don't have one."

He looked at the map hanging out of the dash vent and shook his head. "Somebody needs to take better care of you."

Though Kate was glad to see him, she didn't like him talking badly about Francis. "I like finding places on my own."

"I see." Richard rolled up her window and shut the car door. "Come with me. The first lecture begins in a few minutes, and they don't like people coming in late."

Richard seemed considerate, kind even, not the pompous guy in the studio. Without argument, Kate let him lead her across a trampled lawn into a beautiful old barn. Everyone else was already inside, so she and Richard sat in a couple of empty chairs in the back. Realizing she had stepped into the Performance Barn she'd admired in the brochure,

Kate's gaze lifted to the magnificent wooden structure above. The ceiling was lined with warm, yellowed wood. Sunlight filtering in through baffled skylights illuminated the hand-hewn posts and beams above and the wide-planked floor below. On the walls hung colorful murals and painted banners, most of which appeared to tell stories.

"I'm glad you came," Richard said quietly. "You seem tired, but it'll be good for you."

It struck Kate as odd that he seemed so familiar, so completely at ease with her, as if they'd known each other a long time.

"Long night. Didn't sleep much."

Richard raised his eyebrows and grinned. "Lucky guy."

Kate shook her head. "Not like that."

A woman in a black, sleeveless dress with an embroidered red hibiscus flower appeared from a doorway and walked to the front of the barn. The crowd quieted. She spoke without a microphone, her voice melodic and clear, even at the back of the room. "My name is Sidney Collins, board member of the Institute from New York. A warm welcome to all of you. We gather on hallowed ground and give thanks to the generous, inclusive vision of the founders of this unique institute set in this stunning Maine countryside." The woman motioned with a broad stroke of her arm. Then, without further introduction, she leaned forward and swept her gaze across the audience, her eyes coming to rest on a young man in the front row. "What does the existence of art mean to you?" She put her open hand to his chest. "Deep in here, where the rest of us can't see?"

The man faltered, so she moved swiftly, smoothly to the side of the audience, stopping halfway back where she motioned to an African-American woman with short-cropped hair and large dangling gold earrings. "Where do you feel art when it affects you, when it gets inside of you? In what organs of your body does the creative spirit resonate, reside, rearrange, or restore you? What does the power of art *do* to you?"

Kate shrank in her seat as Ms. Collins moved toward the back of the room to stand behind her and Richard. Kate shuddered when she felt a pair of strong hands rest on her shoulders. Ms. Collins spoke over Kate's head to the audience.

"This beautiful woman's life will be changed by how our artists, how *all* artists struggle to bring forth from within—at all costs—the magic and beauty they so generously share with us."

Ms. Collins' fingers slid from Kate's shoulders and she glided, like a dancer, down the other side of the audience and back to the front, where she raised both hands toward the cathedral ceiling. "Art does not simply fall from the sky into artists' hands like manna so that they may reveal it to us." She brought her arms down and curled her fingers into tight fists. "Works of art are pulled, gently, ferociously, desperately, from the deepest parts of their minds and their souls and, as Carl Jung would say, from our universal collective unconscious."

Ms. Collins paused for a few moments, letting the intensity of her words settle in. Then she leaned forward toward the audience and spoke as if she were telling a best friend a carefully guarded confidence. "The secret to appreciating art," she said in a loud, forceful whisper, "is already inside of each and every one of you. It resides in the place where you *feel* what a painting, a sculpture, a song, a dance, or a movement of yoga or tai chi does to you. How you're affected by a perfect moment in nature: two dragon flies mating in mid-air; a seabird gliding effortlessly above a placid ocean; brilliant bolts of lightning dancing between storm clouds over the horizon."

The woman took in a long, deep breath and brought her arms up to her chest. "You must come to know the places inside of you where these beautiful, powerful forces change you, make you a different person, a fuller, more sensual and authentic human being. Learn to listen to and appreciate how experiencing art changes your body and your mind and your heart and, yes, your soul, and you will know everything there is to know about appreciating art."

Ms. Collins fell silent. After a few moments her eyes opened widely and she looked over the audience. "And perhaps the most amazing, paradoxical thing is that as we attune ourselves to how art makes us feel, the works of art themselves will help us understand what we feel, put us in sympathetic relationship with the traditions and beliefs that brought us into this moment."

She brought her hands together and subtly bowed to the audience, which sat watching her in collective silence. "Namaste."

After a few quiet moments, applause began, then, with awakening enthusiasm, spread through the crowd. Several people came to their feet, followed by the rest of the room. As Kate rose, she realized she had a tear coursing down her cheek.

CHAPTER FIFTEEN

OBVIOUSLY EXCITED, STRINGER MADE SURE HE AND FRANCIS LEFT for Sam's gig early. As they approached the bottom of their hill, Francis saw Kasa trimming back a climbing rose that appeared to be taking over the doorway to her summer kitchen. She waved so he pulled the Jeep over next to her picket fence.

"Do we have to stop?" Stringer asked, impatiently.

"Just for a minute."

Stringer rolled his window down as Kasa walked over. She slipped a small pair of clippers into a coat pocket and pulled off one of her gardening gloves. "And where might you boys be off to?"

"I'm going to a friend's gig."

Kasa looked confused.

"You know, a concert," Stringer said.

Kasa put her hand on his forearm. "Oh, my, that sounds wonderful. Who will be singing?"

"My friend, Sam."

Kasa raised her eyebrows. "And who might Sam be?"

"A girl. She plays guitar."

"Really."

Stringer sat up in his seat. "She's cool, Kasa. I met her down on the docks. Her stepfather, or whoever he is, works on one of Ginny's lobster boats, and I've got a job on it."

"Well, aren't you the fellow about town."

Stringer shrugged. "I guess."

Francis leaned across the seat. "How are you, Kasa? I've been meaning to stop by."

"Of course you have." She pretended to whisper to Stringer. "He always says that, he does." She looked over at Francis. "I've been well, got the whole garden in, lots of tender sprouts coming up. Love this time of year, waiting for lilies to bloom, vegetables to flower. Just need it a little warmer."

Stringer cocked his head. "Anything else you been up to?"

"Not much…"

"Really?" Stringer grinned and pointed across her yard. "Whose car has been parked back there lately?"

Kasa dropped her chin, blushed. "A friend's, I suppose."

Stringer grinned. "Anything you want to tell us? Seen that big old Oldsmobile pretty late at night."

Kasa frowned, wiped a wisp of gray hair from her face. "Aren't you the little investigator?" She leaned closer. "I said, a *friend* was visiting, nothing more." She quickly turned back toward the house. "Now I'm sure you boys have somewhere to be, and I must finish pruning the dead stocks on the roses." As she walked to the house, she called back to them with a hint of a smile. "And let's all mind our own P's and Q's, shall we?"

Francis nudged Stringer and they both smiled. "I know a stonewaller when I see one."

"She's up to something," Stringer said, rolling his window back up.

"Yes. Isn't it wonderful?"

Stringer made a face. "She's pretty old to be fooling around."

Francis pulled onto the main road and headed toward town. "Never too old. You young folks don't have a corner on the love market."

"Whatever."

"She's a remarkable woman."

Stringer nodded. "Yeah, Kasa's pretty cool."

When they arrived at the Mill Pub, Sam was sitting off to the side on a rustic cedar bench playing her guitar. Her dark maroon vest was open, revealing a black and white Bob Dylan T-shirt, and she kept time with cowboy boots that looked a little big for her. Stinger was nervous as he introduced her to Francis. Sam appeared guarded, but Francis liked that they looked happy to see each other. He tried not to stare at the long, bright blue streak running through the center of her otherwise blond hair.

Francis asked Sam what sort of songs she liked to play. She hesitated, then said she was into the "old folk music" of Pete Seeger, Arlo Guthrie, Gordon Lightfoot, and Dylan. Apparently sensing that Francis was genuinely interested, she became more animated. Sam explained she also liked doing loud rock tunes on her acoustic guitar. "It surprises people," she said. "In a good way. They like it." Then she became more serious, fingering the strings of her guitar. "But there's nothing in the world like Tracy Chapman. Her songs saved me."

"She's a remarkable artist," Francis said, "one of my favorites. Have you ever heard her perform?"

Sam looked incredulous. "Like, in person?"

"Yes."

"Are you kidding?" She chuckled. "No way—I could never do that." She stared at Francis. "Have you?"

Francis felt a little embarrassed. "Yes, once in Central Park in New York the summer of '96. She was mesmerizing, a truly magnificent voice. She seems like a deeply soulful person."

Stringer was surprised.

Sam stood. She looked starstruck. "Wow, you actually saw her in person."

Francis nodded.

Sam leaned her guitar against the bench. "How close were you? Could you see her face?"

Francis thought for a moment. "We got there very early so we were way up front. Everyone stood the whole show, and being tall I could see her well. I remember her powerful eyes."

Francis was hesitant to reveal that he had actually met Chapman at a folk festival and she had autographed his guitar for him.

Sam shook her head. "What I wouldn't give…"

"I don't think she tours much anymore, but I hope you can see her one day."

Sam looked disappointed. "Pretty unlikely, a kid like me."

Stringer glanced at a couple of pickups kicking up dust as they drove into the parking lot.

Francis looked at her kindly. "I'll bet you can do anything you set your mind to."

Sam cocked her head toward him. "How? I don't have any money."

"Well, you can practice playing your guitar, write some of your own songs and work your way up, like all artists." Francis paused. "And by the way, the Chapman show was free, part of the Summer Stage program in New York."

Sam's eyes opened wide. "*Free?*"

Francis nodded. "Yes, perhaps the best concert I ever saw."

"Wow. I can't even imagine." Sam looked at Stringer, who shrugged his shoulders.

As much as he was enjoying talking to Sam, Francis was anxious to get back to town to meet with Charlie. He extended his hand. "It was nice meeting you, Sam. Good luck with your show."

"You can't stay and hear me?"

Stringer stood behind Francis and shook his head.

"Thank you. I'd like to, but I can't tonight. I have business in town. Another time, I hope."

He turned to Stringer. "Call me if you end up needing a ride home."

Stringer nodded and followed Francis back to the Jeep. "Hey, thanks for bringing me. It was cool, you talking to Sam like that."

"You're welcome."

"And you always show up when you say you will."

Francis climbed into the Jeep. "I'm sure your mom didn't mean to forget." He started the engine. "I'm glad I got to meet Sam. Enjoy yourself, and remember, no drinking."

"Promise."

Francis drove faster than usual on his way back to Winter's Cove. He didn't want to miss Charlie, who he figured would only be at his office for a short while. His cruiser was parked out front when Francis arrived. Inside, Charlie was on the phone talking in an agitated voice. Francis stayed by the door, but Charlie motioned for him to sit in a heavy wooden chair in front of his desk.

"I can't arrest someone for being loud in a bar. The whole bar's loud. You can hear that damn place way up the street. Look, Pike can be an asshole, but it sounds like whoever's with him is instigating things. Why don't you kick them out and see if things quiet down?"

Charlie listened then his expression changed, his forehead furrowing into a deep frown. "You're shitting me? *That's* who Pike's carousing with? I thought he'd stay up north."

Charlie listened for a few more moments then interrupted. "Well, I'm the sheriff now, so call me back if things get out of hand and I'll come down. You know what a peckerhead he can be. Nobody's on tonight 'cept me, but I'll bring a statie with me if need be."

Charlie hung up, took a swig of coffee from a styrofoam cup and pushed back from his desk.

"Rough day?" Francis inquired.

"Yeah. In addition to the same old bullshit—break-ins, drunks, rowdy bars—McNeal's back in town, raisin' hell at Seaman's, that dive down on South Street."

Fear rose in Francis' gut. "He and Pike friends?"

"I guess. Pike knows his cousins, grew up together near Androscoggin. Bunch of crazy loggers."

Francis shook his head. "Just what we need." He leaned forward. "And I've got more bad news."

Charlie frowned. "What?"

"Kate and I went out for dinner last night and left Stringer alone at the house. He told me this morning some jerk came by, pushed his way in, and threatened Kate and me if we didn't come up with two hundred thousand dollars. Said there'd be hell to pay. Wants it in two weeks."

Charlie stared at Francis. "What are you talking about?"

The police radio at the side of the desk crackled with static.

"Said he was collecting on Leland's California drug debts."

Charlie's face tightened. "Not that asshole again. I thought he was dead, for god's sake."

"Me, too. Stringer said he was pretty sure the guy had Rhode Island plates."

Charlie's eyes opened wider. "Must be that guy Mrs. Burns had at the info booth."

"Yes. He's a thug. He smudged a cigarette out on one of Stringer's paintings, ground ashes into our floor. Really rattled him."

Charlie thought for a few moments. "Rhode Island's full of badasses. Lotta mafia and such." He looked at Francis. "I thought Leland was some two-bit street pusher."

"That's what we thought, too, but he must have been bigger. And because Stringer killed Leland, this guy and his boss blame him for not getting their money."

Charlie shook his head, nervously fidgeted with the knobs on the radio. "Kate okay?"

"Doesn't know. She's out of town for the weekend, which is probably good."

Charlie wound the coiled microphone cord around his finger. "So what're you gonna do?"

Francis was taken aback. "What am *I* going to do? You're the sheriff. What are *you* going to do?"

Charlie sighed.

Francis stood and paced in front of the desk. "You've got to track him down before he hurts anyone."

"Look, Francis, unless this guy broke into your house, I can't really do anything."

"He pushed his way in."

"Did Stringer open the door for him?"

"I guess, but—"

"Then it isn't breaking and entering."

"That's stupid." Francis stopped and stared. "Look, I'm scared this time, Charlie. Who knows what this jerk might do. How do we protect ourselves?"

"Where's Kate?"

"Up in Skowhegan at an art workshop."

"Better let her know."

"I'll wait till she gets back. She wants some time alone."

Charlie stood and stepped around the side of his desk. "Things okay with you two?"

Francis looked at the floor. "I'm not sure. She's been terribly moody lately—restless, confrontational. Not like the Kate I fell in love with."

Charlie put his hand on Francis' shoulder. "She's been through a lot. You all have. I'm not surprised things haven't come up roses. She, and I don't mean any disrespect with this, has had some rough sledding in the past, and people can't completely change overnight."

Francis nodded. "You're not the first person to tell me that. I just want things to be simple for a change."

"Good luck with that. Even when they seem simple, they don't stay that way very long." He walked back behind his desk. "This job…it's not like being just a deputy. I know McNeal was no good, but I'm realizing all the pressures can cloud your judgment. And it's the locals that drive you the craziest." He motioned toward the harbor. "Like that damn Pike."

"Why does Ginny keep him on her boats?"

"'Cause he's one of the best lobstermen around. Brings in a good catch when others' traps are near empty. Been in his blood for generations. The hell-raisin's in his blood, too."

"Stringer's working for him part-time."

"I heard. How's it going?"

"All right, I guess. He likes it because he gets to see Nelson's daughter when they're down on the docks. He's sweet on her."

Charlie finished the last of his coffee, crumpled the cup and threw it in the trash. "Nothing sweet about that girl. And she's not his daughter, just some little orphan slut he took in. Gets money from the state to keep watch over her."

Francis frowned. "She doesn't seem bad."

"You seen her?"

"Met her today. She's a singer."

Charlie straightened the papers littered across his desk. "Pretty wild looking, wouldn't you say?"

"You mean her colored hair?"

"The whole weird get-up. Tromping around in combat boots and metal stuck in your skin." Charlie waved his hand. "I don't cotton to it."

"She's different, but that doesn't mean she's bad." Francis stood, pushed the chair back in front of the desk.

Charlie put on his hat and pulled his sheriff's jacket off the back of his dark leather chair. "I must say, you've gotten mixed up with some interesting women."

"Don't start, Charlie." Even though Francis felt defensive, he tried to grin. "I'll give you some latitude seeing as you helped save Stringer's life."

Charlie opened the door. "That kid is cool."

"You are right about that, my friend."

They walked outside and Charlie locked the heavy arched wood door behind them. "Hopefully all this doesn't amount to much. Be nice to have a quiet summer around here. Had too much chaos last year."

"Couldn't agree more."

"Anyway, we'll keep an eye out for this guy. Let me know if you see him again."

"Thanks. Goodnight, Charlie."

Charlie doffed his Stetson, climbed into his cruiser and drove off.

Francis stood alone in the parking lot, chilled by the breeze coming up from the harbor, and by his conversation with Charlie.

CHAPTER SIXTEEN

A FTER FRANCIS LEFT, SAM AND STRINGER STOOD AROUND THE bench outside the pub. "Hey," she said after a few awkward moments.

"Hey." He knew she was playing it cool but could tell she was psyched to see him. He was excited *and* nervous to see her.

Sam sat down and picked up her guitar. Stringer edged onto the other end of the bench as she tuned the taut metal strings running up the neck of the well-worn instrument. It wasn't as beat up as Willie Nelson's guitar, but it had taken its share of hard knocks.

"You ever play?" she asked, clamping a capo between frets.

Stringer shook his head.

Sam fingered a little riff leading into Tracy Chapman's "Fast Cars," which she began singing in her raspy voice.

After a couple of verses, Sam stopped playing and looked at Stringer. "You want to try it?"

Stringer leaned back.

"It won't bite you."

"I know," Stringer said, defensively.

"Here—" Sam offered him the guitar.

He reluctantly took it onto his lap and held it as she had.

Sam slid closer to him. "I'll show you how to hold the strings down to make a chord."

Stringer felt uncomfortable. "What's a chord?"

"When you hold the strings down on the neck to make them harmonize. You'll see." She placed three of his fingers on the strings and pushed them down.

He recoiled a bit.

"At first the steel strings feel sharp, hurt your fingers, but they'll get calluses and toughen up." She motioned to his other hand. "Now strum all the strings with your thumb."

Stringer ran his thumb over the strings, but they sounded dull.

"Push your fingers down harder on the strings." She held his fingers down firmly with her own.

He gave it another couple of strums and it sounded better. "Cool," he said, smiling. "Never done that before."

"It's easy once you get the hang of it."

Sam showed him a couple more chords. They spent a few minutes practicing then she took the guitar back.

Stringer looked at his fingers, which had indentations across the tips. "Thanks. I think."

"No problem." Sam sat back and looked at him quizzically.

Someone turned on the sound system inside the pub. Garth Brooks' voice came through an open window singing, "The Thunder Rolls."

Sam listened for a few moments then looked at Stringer. "You really shoot your old man?"

Surprised, Stringer looked at the ground. "Yeah."

"Wow."

"Had to."

Sam gripped the neck of her guitar tighter and plucked an E string. "I'd like to kill mine, if I knew who he was."

Stringer pushed a ripple of dirt around with the toe of his sneaker. "I didn't want to, but he was about to kill us."

Sam leaned forward. "You telling me straight? Or is that what you said to get off?"

Stringer looked up at her sharply. "It's the truth. He was stabbing Francis, had already beat up Mom and me." Stringer frowned. "My whole life with him sucked, right to the end. But that was still the worst—having to shoot him."

Sam rested the guitar on the curve of her foot. "What'd it feel like?"

Stringer was taken aback by the question but sensed her interest was earnest. "When he held the knife over Francis, I felt hot, like I was going to hurl. I don't remember the pistol going off, but I sort of felt the bullets hitting his body. Five little thuds." Stringer shook his head and looked off into the woods behind the pub.

They were both startled by a pickup with a blown muffler clamoring by out on the road. Stringer looked back at Sam. "Once I started, I couldn't stop pulling the trigger. Felt like I had to erase him."

"Weren't you wicked scared?"

Stringer thought for a moment. "I was numb. It was like I was some-one else standing behind the gun as it went off—like it had to happen. Cosmically, I mean. Like all the yelling and beatings, the busted bones and shit led right up to that gun going off. There was no stopping it."

Sam slid closer on the seat. "Sounds like you were just the worker of fate."

Stringer nodded. "Kind of like that." He glanced at her. "You get it."

Sam nodded. "Yeah, predetermined shit."

"I guess. But I still did it."

She started to reach her hand out to touch his arm then retreated. An eerie guitar riff came at the end of the song then everything was quiet save for the rumble of a lumber truck out on the road. "*What* happened to you?" Sam asked. "I mean all the stuff you must have gone through to end up there. I thought I'd been through a lot of crazy shit till I read about you. Even scared me."

Stringer sat quietly looking at Sam. She wore multiple metal rings and her wrist was wrapped in a painted leather bracelet. Her voice was softer, empathic. He knew she was trying to understand what she had read about him. Stories his mother wouldn't let him read but he knew about from overhearing peoples' comments around town and from things posted online. It had been strange, watching his own life on trial through bits and pieces from others. He figured that was why Francis hadn't allowed internet in the bungalow.

Sam leaned closer. "Your father—what'd he do to you?"

Stringer didn't know what to say. He appreciated her caring, but the load seemed too heavy to share.

Sam didn't move away from him like most kids did, and strangely, he didn't feel threatened or crowded. He felt safe.

She nodded toward his groin. "That was rad, fucked up."

Stringer slid back on the bench.

"What a prick," Sam said. "So to speak." She leaned her guitar against the end of the bench.

Stringer felt embarrassed but then managed a grin. "Yeah. I don't remember much, think I passed out. When I came to, it was bad, like I was on fire. And there was a lot of blood."

"Real bastard, huh?"

"You can't imagine."

Sam sat back. "Oh, I probably can."

Stringer looked into her bright green eyes, even more captivating surrounded by dark purple makeup. "Been rough for you?"

"Yeah, sometimes." Sam looked at Stringer's forehead. "Where'd you get your scar?"

"Somebody threw me in a dumpster."

Sam looked surprised. "Nice. Who?"

"Not sure." He motioned to a jagged scar on her arm." "What about you?"

"Barbed wire."

"How?"

"Some creep tried to fuck me and I fought him off. Scratched his eye good."

"Wow..."

"He locked me in some animal pen. I got cut on the wire trying to get out." She turned to the side, revealing a scar. "Fight in Roxbury. Got hit hard in that one, probably a baseball bat. Broke my orbit. Everyone thought I was winking." Sam winked at him. "Hope it was a Red Sox bat."

Stringer grinned. "You Sox fans are as crazy as they say."

"Yup." Sam lifted the guitar back onto her thigh. "Lotta shit I'm trying to forget. She again started picking the chords to the Chapman tune, but then fell silent.

"How *do* you forget stuff?" Stringer asked.

"I get lost in music, ride my scooter real fast, let the wind blow through me. The salt air here is awesome. Helluva lot better than the paper mill stench up in Rumford." She thrust her arms high in the air. "Sometimes down at the beach I just run along the edge of the surf and scream. Scream till I can't talk."

"Good to know," Stringer said.

"Want me to show you?"

Stringer laughed. "That's okay. I can imagine."

The sound system came back on halfway through Mary Chapin Carpenter singing, "I Take My Chances."

Sam gestured with her hand. "And if none of that works, I just say screw it all and smoke some weed or drink till I pass out."

Stringer was surprised. "Really?"

"Really." She frowned. "Haven't seen anyone get drunk before?"

"Oh, yeah. Lots of times."

Sam stood up. "I gotta get inside. Don't expect much. Shitty little stage, but better than singing alone in that tin shack."

"*I'm* here."

Sam's face softened. "I'm glad."

Stringer followed her to the front door of the pub, admiring how the leather frills on the back of her vest fell over her bottom. Inside, Sam settled onto a wooden stool on a tiny stage. She adjusted a silver mic stand littered with pieces of tape holding remnants of other singers' playlists.

"Can you cut the music?" she said into the mic. The bartender reached up and turned off the stereo.

"Test...test-one-two," Sam said into the mic.

Two roughnecks in the back whistled. "Can't hear you, sweetheart."

Stringer sat over in the shadows. He didn't like hearing men yelling at Sam.

"Please play some honky-tonk," said a polite little man in a baseball cap sitting alone at a small table in front of the stage. He had on a light green sport coat, a faded blue shirt, and a red bowtie.

"You bet," Sam said to him. "Good to see you again."

A single spotlight came on directly over Sam's head, illuminating her blue streak.

Another group of rough-looking men and women came in, unceremoniously pushed three tables together, and sat down. Stringer recognized a couple guys from the docks. One ran the big overhead winch that helped lobstermen unload their haul. A bearded man in unstrapped overalls and a stained Yankees cap whistled at the waitress and made a circular motion in the air.

She gave him a thumbs up. "Couple pitchers of PBR," she called to the bartender.

Soon, another dozen locals crowded in, and tables filled with pitchers of beer, barbequed wings, and baskets of cheese fries and onion rings. Just before Sam started, a friendly argument broke out between the guy in the Yankees hat and a couple of Red Sox fans, but soon they were toasting each other, sloshing beer over their muscular forearms.

Sam cleared her throat then put her lips close to the mic. "I'm Sam. Thanks for coming out."

Sam looked so cool under the spotlight, but Stringer and the little man in the strange suit were the only ones paying attention. Just before she started to sing, Stringer thought she glanced at him but he wasn't sure.

Sam began strumming her guitar hard, breaking into a throaty version of Bob Seger's "Hollywood Nights." By the time she got to the first refrain, practically everyone in the pub was singing along. Stringer was psyched she was singing a great California song. *Maybe it was for him.*

Sam followed with a quieter, rough-edged "Sounds of Silence," which she dedicated to the little man up front. Then she did excellent renditions of Bob Dylan's "Maggie's Farm" and "Lay Lady Lay." As the place filled up and the crowd got noisier, she pulled a harmonica out of her pocket and clamped it into a harp sling around her neck. She leaned over and turned up the small PA system. "You glad it's Friday?" she called out.

"Hell, yeah!" the Yankee fan yelled.

Sam drew a long, loud note through the harmonica and launched into a rousing rendition of Jonathan Edwards' "Shanty," which drove the rowdies in the back to their feet, clapping and shouting along with her.

As Sam came to the end of her set, she took a long drink of water from a sweaty tumbler on the floor next to her. Then she leaned back into the mic. "Thanks for *kind of* listening."

A bunch of people laughed. Stringer loved how gutsy she was. Some drunk guy in the back stood up. "We've been very attentive for us. Right, boys?"

Everyone at his table raised their beers in celebration.

Sam continued. "They'll only let me do one more song 'cause I'm just a kid and they say it's getting toward heavy drinking time." She winked. "I'd say some of you got a head start."

"Play some more!" someone yelled. "We won't let 'em run you off."

Sam fingered a few strings and spoke into the mic. "This last song is called "Fast Car," and I'm doing it for a friend of mine out there."

Thrilled and embarrassed, Stringer slumped in his seat.

The crowd settled down. Sam leaned back as she started playing then found her way back to the mic, her voice so close to Tracy Chapman's it was eerie.

When Sam finished singing, there was only sporadic clapping across the crowd. Many had lost interest, though a couple guys held up their longnecks and whistled. Stringer stood and clapped harder and longer than anyone.

With the neck of her guitar firmly in hand, and an angry look on her face, Sam hurried off the stage and strode between the tables toward the back. Stringer looked at her as she approached. "That was great," he said, smiling.

"It's all bullshit," she snapped, brushing by him.

CHAPTER SEVENTEEN

STRINGER WAS TAKEN ABACK BY SAM'S REACTION. AS HE WATCHED her push the panic bar and head outside he felt a little hurt, disappointed really, though he could relate to her being angry. And he knew it wasn't all bullshit.

Outside, Sam put her guitar in the case she had bungee-corded to the back of her scooter. Stringer hung back, not sure what to say.

Sam took a black helmet off the handlebars. "You coming?" She popped the helmet onto her head and pulled a pair of ski goggles over her eyes.

"Yeah, I guess."

"How else you going to get home?"

She unstrapped another banged-up helmet hanging from the rear fender and tossed it to Stringer.

"Thanks."

"Get on." She kicked the starter and the motor puttered to life.

Stringer hesitantly climbed onto the seat behind her. He felt the scooter sag under his weight. Sam revved the motor, and they slowly pulled out of the gravel parking lot onto the pavement. Though it sounded like she was flooring it, with his added weight it took a while to get up to speed. The road was dark and they had it to themselves. Stringer liked the wind whistling through his helmet, though without a face shield bugs were hitting his cheeks and mouth. He ducked behind Sam as much as he could.

As they headed toward Winter's Cove, Sam yelled, "Hang on," and banked sharply off the highway onto a dirt path that rapidly descended. As they picked up speed, stones kicked up under the narrow running boards. Rounding a corner, Stringer wrapped his arms tighter around Sam's waist. Shortly, they broke through an opening in the trees, revealing a bright moon reflecting off the ocean. Sam threw both arms into the air and screamed. The scooter began to wobble. She grabbed the handlebars and revved the engine again.

Stringer was scared and excited as they raced toward a beach, dark cliffs passing on either side. Sam stayed on the gas as they flew off the end of the dirt path onto the sand, where she had a hard time controlling the scooter. They lost momentum and fell over into a soft dune, Sam splayed on top of him. Stringer wiped a patch of sand from his face and was about to ask Sam if she was hurt when she pulled off his helmet, then hers. She flicked her swatch of blue hair out of her face, pushed her sandy lips onto his and gave him a kiss.

He was surprised, felt self-conscious as he didn't really know how to kiss her back, but she didn't seem to mind.

Sam rolled onto her back, spread her arms and legs out, and made a sand angel.

Recovering from the unexpected kiss, Stringer watched her arms and legs move smoothly through the golden sand. He mimicked what she did then they lay next to each other, looking up as a magnificent sky full of glittering stars came into focus.

"Look!" Sam pointed to the southwest horizon. She took hold of his hand.

"What?" Stringer said.

"A shooting star."

"Where?"

"You missed it. Wait, they'll be another."

"What do they look like?"

Sam became animated. "Like it sounds. I'll show you."

Stringer looked around the sky in wonderment. "I've never seen this many stars."

"That's cuz California's crazy bright. LA shows up on satellite photos like its own damn galaxy."

Stringer kept watching the sky but didn't see anything shooting by.

Sam pointed. "Keep your eyes over that way."

A few seconds later, what looked like a tiny bright comet streaked in front of them.

"There," Sam said.

Stringer followed the transient arc of light. "Wow."

"Cool, huh?"

"Awesome," he whispered.

Sam chuckled. "You don't have to whisper. You won't scare them."

They laughed and held hands, watching the subtle pulsations of the galaxies.

After a while, Sam sat up, held her knees in her arms. "I'd want to be a shooting star, burn wicked bright. A great show then gone into eternity."

Stringer didn't say anything.

"What about you?"

He shrugged. "Don' know. Never thought about it."

"No lingering for me as some dull dot up there. I want people to see me go."

Stringer felt a subtle sense of alarm. "I hope you won't go too soon."

"You never know."

Gentle waves washed over horizontal ripples of sand at water's edge. Sam nodded toward the flash of a lighthouse several miles off shore. "See where the light is? That's Crescent Island. Cool place. Legend says it's haunted by an old sea captain who lost his mistress in a shipwreck like a hundred years ago."

"What happened?"

"Hit a rocky shoal that stretches out from the island. Ran his ship aground in fog under a crescent moon. When the ship crashed, he raced from the helm to grab her, but she went overboard, never to be seen again. They say the captain went completely nuts.

"Anyway, that's where they built the lighthouse. Supposedly, George Washington himself commissioned it. You can see if from all over. I watch it almost every night. I think it has magic powers." She looked at Stringer. "And you know what's even cooler?"

Stringer shrugged his shoulders.

"A drunk old shipbuilder once told me there's a secret passage from an underwater cave up to the lighthouse that hardly anyone knows about. If she'd survived falling from the ship, they think his mistress might have found the passageway and made her way to safety. Maybe her spirit is what keeps the light from ever going out."

Stringer listened intently.

"I even heard that one Halloween some kids took a boat out there and tried to find the haunted spirit, but a bunch of bats and rats and eerie screeching scared the shit out of them and they rowed back twice as fast."

Sam laughed. "I think the captain's still searching for his mistress and doesn't want anyone disturbing things."

Stringer thought of Francis out in his skiff looking for Rachael. "A lot of that around here. Searching, I mean."

"Yeah." Sam tried to snuggle closer under his hesitant arm.

"No way I'd go out there," Stringer said, still thinking about the kiss. "I've been out around the island on a fishing boat. Lotta rocks, strong current."

"Yeah." Sam stared at his forehead. "Tell me more about that scar?"

Stringer felt embarrassed. "Can't."

"Sure you can." She pulled her shirt up, revealing a triangular scar beside her belly button.

Stringer looked at it, quickly taking in as much skin as he could. "What happened?"

"Hot iron. Some bitch at a half-way house got pissed 'cause I kept bugging her for cigarettes. She pushed me away with it. Burned me faster than I could jump."

"That sucks."

She let her shirt fall back. "Reminds me I'm never going back."

"Good."

Sam looked at Stringer. "You don't have to tell me what happened to you till you want to. Anyway, we're both damaged, but there's more hope for you to get a life. I will *never* trust anyone again."

"Why not?"

"I tried trusting someone once…"

"Why not try again?"

Sam shook her head. "It would kill me. An awful death—slow and torturous."

Sam adjusted herself in the sand, pulled Stringer's arm over her shoulder.

Feeling awkward again, he didn't move.

Sam cocked her head at him. "Don't you like me?"

"Yeah, a lot."

"For a kid with the balls to shoot his old man, you're pretty shy."

"Sorry. Never really hung with a girl."

Sam looked at him sympathetically then took his hand and slid it under her vest onto her breast.

Embarrassed, he started to draw back, but her smooth skin felt so good, he kept his hand where she'd put it.

"You like that?"

Before Stringer could respond, she jumped up, his fingers sliding over her firm nipple. She brushed sand off her jeans. "Let's go. Francis'll be having a fit."

"You're right." Stringer was distracted by the pleasure of touching her. "I forgot about getting home."

"The ocean will do that to you."

So will a girl.

Sam got up, took hold of his forearms, and looked into his eyes. "I think I like you."

Sam let go of his arms. Overpowered by her presence, Stringer didn't know what to say. He helped her right the scooter then they pushed and pulled it back onto the path and shook off the sand. As they headed north of town, Stringer enjoyed the subtle salty smell of the nape of Sam's neck and the feel of her warm body wrapped in his arms.

He was in love.

CHAPTER EIGHTEEN

K ATE WAS ENTHRALLED WITH THE ART SEMINAR AND RELIEVED TO feel welcomed by artists of all ages. It was a surprisingly comfortable day of learning how to appreciate not just paintings but many different kinds of art. Richard was both a distraction and a comfort as she navigated her way through the lectures, workshops, and somewhat intimidating group discussions. In the afternoon, when the last session concluded, he asked her if she'd like a tour of the area in his supercharged Mustang. She couldn't resist. He put the top down, helped her in, and loaded the Doobie Brothers' "China Grove" into the stereo. Kate felt a primal excitement as the beautiful 660-horsepower beast roared to life beneath her. She slid on her sunglasses and felt like a rock star as they pulled onto the road leading out of the institute.

Richard tore around a labyrinth of backroads, slowing down to point out places he'd been as a kid. With her hair blown back and the sun on her skin, Kate felt special, like one of those hotties she used to be jealous of who rode up and down the boulevards in LA. A man like Richard would have been an inconceivable step-up in her drinking days. Sitting on filthy street curbs, seeing the world through a haze of drugs and booze, Kate watched such men cruise around in muscle cars so shiny she had to squint against the glare. They would never have noticed her, at least not in a good way. She was one of a roving flock of pathetic addicts trying to score, attract a trick, find a cigarette butt with some life left in it, or a beer bottle with yellow spit in the bottom.

At one point, Richard pulled off the road to a turnout above a beautiful lake. He looked great behind his metallic blue shades, which reflected the golden sun as it started to set. She thought he was going to try and kiss her, but instead he only looked at her admiringly, and then headed back to the institute. Kate didn't mind when he slid his hand onto her leg and up toward the crease of her thigh. In fact she loved it.

After he parked the Shelby in a safe place away from other cars, Richard gave Kate a walking tour of the campus, leading her along a series of dirt paths connecting the buildings that housed various studios and performance spaces as well as a library.

After seeing the main campus, they walked along the edge of a stream which meandered down to an expansive lake. Richard took her hand and led her on a path which followed the shoreline, cautioning her about slippery moss-covered rocks and other unstable parts of the trail.

They crossed a small bridge then ducked under a grove of cedars that leaned out over the water. In front of them stood a small wooden cottage, dark and weathered with patches of cream-colored lichen nestled in the deeply-grained boards. Tiny tufts of plants sprouted where knots had fallen out of the boards over the years. On the southern side, beneath a window, the waning sun illuminated a row of strings running from sticks in the ground to nails driven into the casing below a window. Empty morning glory seed packets covered the ends of the sticks. Encroaching around back, a lush growth of brambles and raspberry bushes looked like they were taking over the cabin.

Richard stopped and admired the old building. "This is the first place I stayed when I came here in '73. It was more primitive then, but basically the same."

"*More* primitive?"

"Yes, no stove or anything, just kerosene lamps."

Kate was surprised. "You were a student here?"

"Sure was. Best summer I ever spent. It got me out of the sweltering city. My grandfather was the caretaker for the institute, lived in our family's cabin on the north end of the lake. Truth be told, I got accepted into the program because of him. I was no artist and a lousy student."

Richard pointed to a slightly cockeyed, screened-in porch that faced the lake. The weight of the porch and its many inhabitants over the years had pulled it away from the front wall of the cabin. Twigs and dried grass from an abandoned bird's nest protruded from the space. "Back then there were no screens on the porch, just a couple Adirondack rockers and a rickety metal bunkbed wired to the wall to keep it from tipping over. We all wanted to sleep outside, but it was first come, first serve. It was tricky knowing when you should claim your bed, because for a few hours around sunset the mosquitos would rise out of the swamps in hoards and eat you alive. So we'd mill around waiting for the skeets to disappear then rush out to claim a bunk. There were more than a few fights over it. Regardless, most of us ended up with so many welts we looked like we had chicken pox. It was fun."

"Fun?"

Richard smiled at her. "Really." He motioned toward the porch. "Come on."

She followed him through a squeaky door with a torn screen onto the porch where they encountered a dead blackbird on the floor.

Kate recoiled at the sight of the bird, which looked dehydrated.

"Must have accidentally flown through the screen."

"Hope that's not an omen."

"Just an unfortunate visitor," Richard said. "Probably late on his tuition." He picked the almost weightless bird up by a stiff leg and threw it outside.

"And you said this place used to be *more* primitive?"

"Yes." Richard pulled a skeleton key from his pocket and turned it in the lock. The dried caulking around the window was loose and the glass rattled as he opened the door. He wiped away a spray of spider webs that hung from the casing then stepped inside. Kate ducked and followed after him.

The cabin exuded a musty aroma of cedar. It was fairly dark, but she could see a round wooden table in the middle of the room, over which hung a brass kerosene lamp with a tall glass globe. Around the table were four rustic wooden chairs that looked like they were made from bent saplings.

Richard took out his lighter, lifted the globe and lit the lamp. The yellow flame hesitated then hissed to life and grew bright as it burned tiny cobwebs inside the chimney. Swaying gently over the table, the light cast slow-moving shadows on the floor and walls.

In the corner, Kate saw a log bed covered with a faded but still colorful Hudson Bay blanket. She remembered her mother took comfort in those same blankets when they were out on the road in the winter visiting reservation schools. Many a night Kate slept on them in the back of their woody station wagon, falling asleep to the sound of her mother singing and chanting.

The cabin walls were home to a collection of primitively framed drawings and paintings, some hanging askew, seemingly from the weight of long dust webs dangling off the corners.

"Wow, this place is cool."

"My grandfather and a logger friend of his built it."

"You're from up here?"

Richard shook his head. "No. Do I look like a Mainer? My grandfather was the eccentric renegade of the family. They were all Jersey longshoremen, barely knew where Maine was. When Gramps was a teenager, he raised all kinds of hell, especially during the hot summers in the city. Even with our family connections, they couldn't keep him from getting arrested."

Richard steadied the kerosene lamp. "One summer he broke into the *wrong* house, if you know what I mean. He put the rest of the family in danger, so his parents were done with him. They took everything—every dime—away from him, put him on a train and sent him up here to a logging camp. I heard they were bastards to work for, but he was tough so he survived. And who knew? He fell in love with the place, built a camp on a piece of lumber company land and spent most of his life here. After that, nobody in the family except me ever cared about him or the camp."

Kate walked over to one of the windows and gently pulled back a lace curtain. Several brittle, gray threads fell to the floor. She looked out the window. "So your camp is over there?"

"Yes, at the other end of the lake." Richard came up behind her. "It's a beautiful spot." He slid his hands around her waist. "Would you like to see it?"

"This is plenty enough cabin for me." Kate slid from his hands. "Time for me to get going, get something to eat." She walked to the door.

Richard stepped over to the kitchen area and lifted a cooler onto the table. "I just happen to have dinner right here. For the two of us."

Surprised, Kate stopped, held the screen door partially open. "Look, you've been nice to show me around and tell me about this place. I enjoyed it, but I gotta go."

Richard pulled a pack of Marlboros from his shirt pocket and tapped out a cigarette. He lit it and inhaled a long drag. He held his breath for a few moments then exhaled up into the dark rafters, blue smoke swirling in the hot column of air above the lamp. "You know you want to stay."

The screen door let out a rusty squeak as Kate stepped back inside.

"I can't."

"Says who? If you were satisfied with your life you wouldn't have kissed me the other day."

"That was a mistake." Kate felt herself getting warmer, the excitement she felt in the gallery reigniting. "You took me by surprise, and I didn't kiss you back."

Richard grinned, dropped his cigarette into an empty wine bottle on the table. Dust in the bottom burned brightly for a couple seconds then smoke curled from the neck as if from a tiny chimney.

Kate watched as Richard crossed the floor and slid his hands over her forearms, up the outside of her breasts and around her back. "We only live once, Kate."

She felt his hands slide down over her ass, which tightened. He pulled her toward him, whispered in her ear. "Might as well get the full ride."

Conflicted, Kate felt herself giving in, attracted to Richard's hint of roughness. It was as if she craved a favorite food she knew she was allergic to, knew was sure to make her sick. She wanted to taste it anyway. For most of her life she had missed out on decent men being attracted to her.

She lifted her head to kiss him but he withdrew from her and stepped back to the table. "Let's not have dessert before the main course." He lifted two plates from the cooler and peeled off tinfoil covers with a flare of fancy presentation. "For you I have magnificent crab cakes and salmon-and-cream cheese bruschetta drizzled with the best Badia a Coltibuono olive oil from Zabar's deli in New York."

"Sounds pretty highbrow."

"You're going to love it, all of it," he said in a fake Italian accent.

Chapter Nineteen

After leaving Charlie, Francis had driven home slowly, speeding up only as he passed the swamp where Leland had forced him off the road the previous fall. At the bungalow, he walked into the front hall and was struck by how quiet it was. Before Kate and Stringer entered his life he used to thrive on the silence, accompanied only by the rhythmic crashing of the waves below the bluff. Now, the house seemed *too* quiet. He felt alone.

In the hallway, Francis paused to feel the sheepskin coat Kate had worn to the yacht club, its collar still holding her scent. He climbed the stairs to their bedroom, and at the seaward window, briefly cupped his hands around the cold glass of his grandmother's whaling lamp, an heirloom left to him when he inherited the bungalow. Opening the window, he was embraced by a cleansing breath of moist salt air. He looked out at the sea, its purple and black waves churning around the rocks beyond the cliff. He wanted Stringer to come home and wondered if he should have insisted on picking him up, though he knew that letting him have some independence was important.

Francis pushed the window open wider, filling the room with the ocean breeze, which calmed him. The truth was he was more concerned about Kate than Stringer, frustrated she wouldn't let him get her a cell phone for fear she could somehow be tracked. He was coming to realize the depths of the wounds she carried from the abusive years with Leland, and before that, living alone on the streets of LA. It was hard to imagine the trauma she had endured.

He checked his watch again then walked downstairs and paced around the house. He emptied the lint filter on the drier, filled the kettle with water then rearranged the small glass containers of herbs on the shelf above the stove. He walked into his studio, picked up a couple of brushes and briefly thought about painting. He couldn't focus, so he placed them back in their wooden tray, left the house, and walked down the hill.

At Kasa's, Francis stepped around a collection of clay pots in her summer kitchen and knocked on the inner door upon which hung a string of yellow, orange, and green gourds from her garden. Through the window he watched Kasa appear from her kitchen. She turned on the outside light, opened the door wide and smiled. "Ah, my friend, you've come to see your poor old neighbor."

Inside, the warm air was scented with balsam. On a side table, a brass candelabrum with tapered candles illuminated a leather-bound copy of Anna Karenina, its pages yellowed with age. Kasa looked somehow younger—her hair brushed out, a little less weight around her waist.

"You look troubled, my friend." She motioned for him to follow her to the kitchen. "Come, sit. I'll put on some tea."

Francis didn't move. "I think I'm losing Kate."

Kasa frowned. "You *think*? What does that mean when a man thinks about something to do with a woman he loves? Crazy, you all are."

"Like Buster?"

"Perfect example, the old fool." She broke into a grin. "But a nice old fool he is. Handsome, too."

Francis sat at the kitchen table. "Has he been spending the night?"

"Occasionally—in the spare bedroom, of course."

"No midnight visitations?"

She blushed. "Do I look like a hussy to you? We don't know each other well enough. Besides, we are old."

"You two have come a long way since your first meeting in the courthouse. That wasn't the warmest encounter."

"I had to set him straight about young Stringer."

Francis nodded. "And you certainly did."

"Indeed, though alas, Mr. Hurd is a typical man with a one-track mind. At his age! The body...oh, we humans. Beastly animal instincts they are. Banal. 'Tis the heart that is essential for survival, that matters most."

"Yes," Francis said, thinking about Kate at the seminar, worried she was spending time with that city slicker art dealer.

Kasa sat close to Francis, took his hand. "So what is this trouble with Kate?"

"She's lost interest in me. She's a young spirit. I knew I was too old for her."

"What makes you think this?"

"She's in Skowhegan at the institute with an art dealer from New York. He showed up out of nowhere, says he's interested in Stringer's paintings. I think he's interested in her."

"I see." Kasa sat up straighter. "Maybe you're dreaming up things, or perhaps she's sowing some oats she never could before—and needs to."

Francis cocked his head, surprised by her take.

She leaned closer. "Maybe she's trying to survive."

Francis frowned. "What do you mean?"

Kasa sat back, let out a sigh. "Late in the War, after the Americans liberated us from the concentration camps, it was some time before we *believed* we were free, that we had actually survived the years-long nightmare. We were all changed profoundly. We hardly trusted anyone, our families mostly killed or missing, our homeland as we knew it destroyed. As grateful as I am to be sitting here safe and sound, it will take my whole life to try and recover. And even then...never fully."

Kasa wiped her hands on her apron, looked Francis in the eye. "Kate, too, has been in a war, not knowing if she would survive. I don't mean it is the same, but she also has arrived in a foreign land. As wonderful as it may seem, it is unfamiliar, disorienting."

Confused, Francis frowned.

"After the war, we made our way to England. I remember when they herded us onto the boat in Southampton to come to America. Part of me was excited but most of me, like many others, was terrified. Was this another journey to a different concentration camp? Even death? Would we sink in the frigid North Atlantic like the great *Titanic*?"

Kasa pulled her hands back into her lap. A faraway look came over her face. "Parts of the journey were most rough. Huge waves rocked the ship; we had to stay below for days, many of us very sick. We were somewhere in the middle of the ocean—I don't know where—but there was this lovely Jewish woman, a seamstress, going to New York to join her scientist brother who had escaped the Nazis at the start of the war. She knew if she could just make it into his arms, she would be safe, her life would somehow be her own again. Many times a day she prayed on the deck of the ship that we would make it. Even in the midst of storms she held onto the railing at the bow, rain soaking her malnourished body, scanning the horizon for the coastline of America. So much strength that woman had. I used to watch her from behind windows pelted by the storms. She gave me hope."

Tears formed in Kasa's eyes, something Francis had never seen before. "One morning as day was breaking, I saw the woman collapse on the deck, one thin hand barely able to hold onto the rail. She wept like a baby. I feared she'd lost her mind. Then I saw it, far in the distance, the coastline of our promised land."

Kasa leaned forward, looked Francis in the eye. "That courageous woman knew in her heart where she had to get to. She had faith enough to survive months of bombardments, unspeakable abuses by SS monsters, starvation, disease, and finally, crossing the treacherous Atlantic. All she had was her faith that God was moving her in the right direction.

"I assure you, it took me many years to recover from my hell." Kasa squinted at Francis. "My dear friend, you must know your heart, what storms you can weather to get home, to find peace you've never known. I gradually learned how to trust people and things I could believe in, depend upon. Only you will know if you love Kate enough to struggle through the battles with her, endure pain as well as joy. And I mean your pain, too."

Kasa straightened her back. "This is the reality of sharing your life with Kate, your shared humanness skinned down to essentials." Kasa touched his hand. "I know how you look at her, the depth she has lodged in your heart. You told me you missed many chances with Rachael. I pray you won't miss this one."

Francis was again struck by Kasa's wisdom, her worldly view that helped ground him, expand his own selfish perspective. "Thank you. I tend to want to make Kate into a normal Mainer, whatever that is."

"Don't think I've ever met one."

They both smiled.

Kasa got up and poured boiling water from the kettle into two cups holding silver balls filled with black tea leaves and fresh orange rind. Steam rose around her head like a halo.

She sat back down and studied Francis' face. "Might there be something else on that mind of yours?"

Francis nodded. "Yes. But I don't want to burden you with it."

"No worries. I am tougher than you."

Francis smiled. "That's the truth."

Kasa put her teacup down. "What is it?"

"It's Leland."

Kasa's eyebrows rose. "*Leland?* He's dead, for goodness sakes."

"Yes, but his miserable legacy isn't. He has come back to haunt us, or at least his drug dealer has."

A look of deep concern clouded Kasa's face. "Oh, dear..."

"Some thug from Rhode Island is in town, came to the bungalow while Kate and I were out at dinner. He threatened Stringer that we'd better settle up Leland's outstanding drug debts or something sinister would happen."

Kasa's face tightened. "Someone threatened our Stringer?"

Francis nodded. "At least threatened Kate and me through Stringer."

Kasa's open hand came down on the wooden table hard enough the teacups danced. "Cowardly bastard."

She stood, walked to the sink.

"I spoke to Charlie; he's keeping an eye out."

Kasa turned around sharply. "I believe Charlie to be a good man, but I wouldn't want him to be the only thing between me and a drug lord."

Francis stood, shook his head. "Damn Leland."

Kasa's eyes opened wider. "Francis, Leland is dead. Forget about him. Focus on the real threat." She thought for a few moments. "You should talk to Buster. He knows how to deal with these things."

Francis nodded. "I suppose you're right. He certainly worked magic during the trial."

A light flashed across the front window from the road.

Francis got up so quickly he spilled his tea. "I hope that's Stringer." He looked out her window, but the vehicle stayed on the main road heading north. "I have to go, he should be home soon. Thank you for helping me, as always."

"Anytime."

Francis opened the door. "And good luck with that new boyfriend of yours."

"Boyfriend, my stars! Don't be ridiculous."

Francis hurried toward the road.

"You take good care of Stringer!" Kasa called after him.

"I will," he yelled back.

Francis made his way around Kasa's fence and headed up the hill. As he approached the top, he slowed his pace as a pain shot through his chest where Leland had stabbed him and the chest tube had been. He'd been inside the house for only a few minutes when a light shined in the window. He moved closer and stood behind a curtain. Thankfully, it was Sam and Stringer, though he was concerned she'd driven him home on such a little scooter with a dim headlight. Francis listened through the partially open window.

Stringer got off and clipped his helmet on the rear fender. "You make me feel good," he said.

In the porch light, Francis saw Sam smile. She lifted her goggles up onto her helmet. "Me, too."

Stringer looked like he was going to kiss Sam, but she quickly shifted into gear. "But it's probably all bullshit." She snapped her goggles back down on her face, revved the engine, and took off.

"No it's not!" Stringer yelled as she vanished down the road. "I know what bullshit is."

Chapter Twenty

As Stringer walked toward the house, Francis backed away from the window and slipped into his darkened study. When the front door opened, he stepped back into the foyer.

"Hey," Stringer said, brushing sand off his jeans.

"Did you have fun?"

Stringer smiled. "It was awesome. She's a great singer, and the place was packed."

"Really?"

"Yeah. Some rowdy drunks in the back, but a lot of the crowd listened to her. And…"

Francis waited.

"She kind of sang the last song for me. Can you believe it?"

"That's pretty special."

Stringer walked into the kitchen and opened the fridge. "Yeah, till she started acting weird, like it meant nothing."

Francis stepped into the doorway. "How so?"

Stringer took the dish of leftover pasta from the fridge, slid it in the microwave, and poured himself a glass of milk. "When she left the stage I told her she did great, and she snapped at me that it was all bullshit. Did the same thing when she left me off just now."

"She's probably shy. Or, like you said earlier, women are crazy."

"Yeah."

"You look like you've been on the beach."

Stringer took the pasta out of the microwave and sat down. "Sam showed me a cool place where you can watch the lighthouse out on some island."

"Must be Black Rock Beach. Beautiful down there."

With his mouth full of pasta, Stringer nodded.

Francis frowned. "She actually took you down the old road on that little scooter?"

Stringer smiled "It was rad."

"You've even got sand on your face."

Stringer looked away and quickly brushed it off.

Francis sat at the table opposite Stringer. "You really like this girl."

Stringer wiped cheese from his lip with the back of his hand. "Yeah."

"When are you going to see her again?"

"Not sure. There's not much to do around here."

"True." Francis thought for a few moments. "Tell you what. How about I take you two down to Old Orchard tomorrow? The amusement park just opened for the season."

Stringer looked confused. "What?"

"Sorry. Old Orchard is an oceanside amusement park with rides, dime-a-dares, and a whole indoor arcade with Skee-Ball and such."

Stringer frowned. "What's a dimer-dare? And *Skee-Ball?*"

"Dime-a-dare. More like dollar-a-dare these days. They're game booths where you pay a carnie to let you throw darts at balloons, shoot moving ducks, squirt water into monkeys' mouths to win a race—that sort of thing."

Stringer grinned. "Sounds lame."

"You must have those things in California."

"Yeah, up on the Santa Monica pier, but they didn't have dumb names like that." He finished his glass of milk. "We never had enough money to play those things or go on rides. That was for rich kids."

"Well, your mother won't be back till later tomorrow, so why don't I take you and Sam. It'll be fun. I've been going there since I was your age."

Stringer looked concerned. "Is it real hokey?"

"No," Francis said, feigning being insulted. "It's great fun."

"Okay. I'll ask her, but I wouldn't count on it. She's tough."

"Let me know."

Stringer got up and took his plate to the sink. He spoke without looking at Francis. "Have you heard from Mom?"

Francis' heart sank a bit. "No."

Stringer looked agitated. "I can't believe you let her go up there with no cell."

"You know she won't let me get her one, and she wouldn't take mine. She doesn't trust them."

"That's crazy. Everybody has one."

"She's very strong-willed, particularly at the moment. Needs to do everything herself, including manage your career."

"What career?"

"You've got real talent, String. She said this dealer from New York wants to buy two of your paintings."

"He sounded sketchy."

Francis hesitated. "I don't know the man and would rather you work with one of the dealers I know to be legitimate, but it's out of my hands. She's your mother."

Stringer looked pessimistic. "I know, and she's in one of her moods." He tapped a table leg with the toe of his sneaker. "I wish you could be my dad."

Francis was touched. "I'd love that."

"It'd be cool."

"Does your mom get like this often?"

Stringer leaned on the back of his chair. "My old social worker said it's when she's down on herself, feeling worthless."

"That's awful."

"Yeah, especially 'cause this is what she was like before she'd get really drunk—like go into a blackout for a few days straight. I mean before she quit drinking."

Francis stood and pushed his chair back. "Do you think she's in danger of drinking? She's told me many times that would be a disaster."

"That's for sure."

Francis persisted. "Should I go up there and be with her?"

Stringer shook his head. "No. She probably won't drink. She really does want to stay sober, away from all that hell. And I get the thing about her wanting to do something on her own. I think you intimidate her."

"How?"

"You don't mean to, it's just you, a college grad, being famous and all. She feels like she's never really accomplished anything."

"I never want to make her feel that way."

"It's not you. It's her. Maybe this art appreciation thing will help her and her mood." Stringer picked up his glass and placed it in the sink. "I'd leave her alone. Trying to fuss over her only makes it worse."

Francis thought back to the yacht club dinner. "I believe you."

"I think she's having a hard time getting used to life out here. It's different than California."

Francis leaned against the counter. "In what ways?"

Stringer looked incredulous. "Are you kidding me? This place is so straightlaced, uptight. Nothing going on." Stringer brightened. "Well, except Sam."

"We don't like a lot of commotion. Speaking of which, I talked to Charlie about the guy who threatened you. He's looking into it, and I'm changing the locks here at the house and having a couple more yard lights put up. I'm worried what this guy might do."

Chapter Twenty-one

Kate and Richard sat across from each other at the table, which he had covered with a red tablecloth. The kerosene lamp overhead gave the cabin a warm yellow glow and the kindling burning in the stone fireplace took off the evening chill. Their secluded dinner was much more enjoyable than the pretentious affair at the yacht club. And the salmon bruschetta Richard had brought was amazing. When the last piece was gone, Kate licked the juice from her fingertips. Though she had guilty feelings being with Richard, she dismissed them, rationalizing that she deserved any attention she could get. Still, a stern image of Ginny flashed in her mind. *Screw her,* Kate thought, halfheartedly.

After dinner they relaxed on the bed. Kate was captivated by this smart, sharp-edged New Yorker, though she had a pang of fear when he opened a bottle of French burgundy and filled two long-stemmed wine glasses. She stared at the rich, red liquid. Part of her wanted to smell it, put her nose into the glass. Part of her was repulsed, frightened by her attraction to it.

"Here, darlin'," Richard said, handing her a glass. "To furthering the cause of art appreciation, in all its forms."

Kate tentatively took the elegant glass, something she had seen only in movies or on TV, but had never held before. She caught a whiff of the wine then quickly held it away from her face. Richard downed the wine in several generous swallows and poured himself another glass. She was familiar with that kind of drinking. Her hand started to tremble as if she was holding poison.

Richard looked Kate in the eye. "You are very beautiful." He slid his hand along the outside of her thigh, up over her arm then under her hair to her neck. He pulled her toward him. Inhaling the fumes of wine on his breath, she turned away.

Cupping one hand around the back of her neck and holding her ass firmly with the other, he drove his tongue into her mouth. At first repulsed, Kate swirled her own tongue against his, licking the rich, astringent taste of the wine. Even as she enjoyed the raw sensation of kissing him and the flirting with alcohol, fear danced in her stomach. *Why don't I feel more guilty? I am* so *fucked up.* She felt familiarly out of control, as if she was on a sinking ship and had no defense against going down.

Richard let go of her, drank more of his wine then pulled a metal case from his coat pocket. He carefully opened it on the table. Kate stared at a small, folded paper pouch beside which sat a tightly-rolled dollar bill and a single-edged razor blade.

"Shit," she said softly, as he unfolded the pouch and tapped a small amount of white powder onto a pocket mirror. She took a step back as he cut the powder into several lines. Without looking up, he placed the bill into a nostril and snorted a line. Kate felt the sensation in her own nose, though it had been a long time since she was with anyone who could afford coke.

Richard held a finger over his other nostril and snorted another line. Holding his breath, he held the rolled bill toward her.

Kate's hand reflexively reached for it then retracted. "I shouldn't—can't."

"But you want to," Richard leaned over the table, inhaled another line. He dropped the bill next to the mirror and sat back.

Kate looked at the coke speckled over the shiny surface.

"Go ahead," Richard said, lying against the pillows, admiring her. "We can make it big together, have a damn fine time doing it."

Kate noticed he had an erection.

He unzipped his pants, freeing his penis then reached over and deftly slid his hand inside her shorts. His fingers massaged around her clitoris then entered her pussy, giving her an intense surge of pleasure. Then he fell back against the bed, his hand sliding up over her breast. He nodded at his penis. "Why don't you see what you can do with this?"

Kate's breathing had quickened. She felt hot, drawn as to a flame.

"Go on," Richard said, folding his hands behind his head.

She stared at his hardening penis. For a second she wanted to run out of the cabin into the lake to wash Richard off of her, then to her car and back home to Stringer, who she knew she was losing touch with. Then there was Francis. *Shit.*

Richard reached over and pushed her head down onto him. She started to resist then gave in, lathered the crown of his penis with saliva and slid it into her mouth. She stroked the base of his penis with one hand, and fondled his balls with the other. His pelvis rose to meet her.

She liked the feeling of him swelling in her mouth, the feeling of power over him. She pulled on his scrotum and he moaned as he writhed on the Hudson Bay blanket. He quickly climaxed, warm cum covering her tongue.

"You're good," he mumbled, smiling. He took another long drink of wine. Satisfied, he closed his eyes and relaxed. "I'll rest a few minutes then I'm going to give you the orgasm of your life."

Kate sat there watching this passed-out naked man she hardly knew, his fingers still wet from her pussy. She felt her body involuntarily shudder; her breathing became shallow and rapid. Suddenly repulsed by the smell and taste of him, Kate grabbed a corner of the musty sheet and wiped out her mouth. Her heart racing, she was full of fear, overtaken by a wave of wanting to drink, to drown herself in the wine sitting on the table. She'd just knock the glass back then pour the rest of the bottle down her throat.

Disturbed, Kate turned away, squeezed her eyes shut, trying to force out ugly visions: pulling her baby, Stringer, from the rancid dumpster; Leland and his drunk, disgusting friends on top of her, penetrating her, one after the other as she lay in a daze of cheap booze and drugs.

Then she was jolted by an image of Francis lying naked next to her. Attacked by searing guilt, she jumped off the bed. Richard let out a snore and rolled over. Kate looked at him, noticed his muscular body. Scared and confused, she stood in the middle of the braided rug covered only by her moist panties. It felt like the dark walls of the cabin were closing in on her. She glanced to the side and saw her body trembling in a cracked mirror hanging crooked on the wall.

Kate gradually looked over at the scattered remnants of coke staring at her from the table. Terrified, her hands shaking, she grabbed Richard's pack of Marlboros and pulled out a cigarette. She tried to steady the smoke with both hands as she held it up to the kerosene lamp. After a few tries she got it to light and took a long, comforting drag.

Kate grabbed a wool army blanket off a chair and, avoiding catching herself in the mirror again, edged toward the porch. She stopped and looked at the table, then hurried over and grabbed the wine bottle. Holding it firmly by its neck, she walked outside into air heavy from an approaching storm. Far to the south, between breaks in the cedars, she watched lightning crackle between two tall banks of clouds. It reminded her of the thunderstorms she and her mother encountered out on the plains. She counted seven seconds before the low rumble of thunder arrived, and figured she was safe. If nothing else, at least she understood the weather.

Kate sat in a caned rocking chair, looked around, and noticed the jagged hole where the blackbird had crashed through the screen. A mosquito quickly found her and began circling her head. She took another drag then slowly exhaled. With the wine bottle in her lap, she dropped the cigarette on the floor and pulled the corner of the rough blanket over her head. It was hot and smoky under the wool. Kate felt terribly mixed up. Miserable. Horny. She adjusted her legs as the sensation from Richard's fingers lingered. For the first time since she got sober she desperately wanted to drink, craving alcohol more than she had in a year. Her skin felt as if it was crawling off of her.

The hand holding the slender neck of the bottle started to shake as she slid the aromatic burgundy under the blanket. She bit down on the cork with her teeth and wrenched it from the bottle. Intoxicating fumes enveloped her. *Drink it!* her alcoholic head yelled at her. *Just don't take that* first *drink,"* she heard Ginny say.

Kate started to scream, but no sound came from her mouth. Feeling like she was suffocating, she pulled the blanket down and drew in a breath of fresh air. *I can't fucking drink!*

She threw the sweaty blanket off of her and heaved the bottle clear through the brittle screen. A single black feather drifted slowly to the porch floor. Remnant of another victim.

Feeling crazy, needing relief, she glanced up and down the path that ran along in front of the cabin. There was no one around. She checked inside the screen door. Richard was still snoring. Kate ducked under the blanket, rocked back, and slid her hand down into her panties to the moist lips of her vagina.

CHAPTER TWENTY-TWO

FRANCIS AWOKE EARLY SUNDAY MORNING TO A HAZY ORANGE GLOW emerging along the eastern horizon. He stepped to the open window and watched a pair of noisy seagulls screaming at each other on the bluff. Jousting back and forth, the birds pecked at a crab, which lay on its back, legs helplessly clawing the air. "Helluva way to start your day."

Francis was excited to be taking Stringer and Sam to Old Orchard Beach. The fact that neither of them had been there before would make the day even better. On the way down the stairs he paused at a photograph of him, Kate and Stringer holding blazing torches on top of the ice chute at Winter Festival. Kate looked happy and at peace after the grueling trial.

As he stepped into the shower, the phone rang in the hallway. He was going to let the machine pick up, but then thought he had better answer it.

"Francis, we've got trouble." Charlie's voice held deep concern.

Francis felt his spirits sink. A shot of fear went through him. "What's going on?" he asked, pulling his towel tighter around him.

"We've ID'd that Rhode Island guy from a bank security camera across from the info booth. I sent the images to the feds and they came back with a match with a badass from the Providence area. Strong-arm for one of the mob families. Specializes in collecting money and is very good at it. Sounds like he's had a lot of heat on him so he's been lying low the last few months. The state police detective I talked to figures he's just been working behind the scenes. Coming up here to collect a drug debt would fit."

"Any warrants out for him, that sort of thing?"

"Nope. They'd like to pin some charges on him but haven't been able to. He's a free man unless he's caught doing something illegal."

"Can you bring him in for threatening Stringer?"

"Not really. This guy would know we don't have enough to hold him. And he didn't directly threaten Stringer, only you and Kate. We'd probably just piss him off, and he'd be all lawyered up before I got the paperwork done."

As he talked, Francis opened the front door and checked around the yard. "So what are we going to do?"

"We'll have to wait and see if he does anything else. Didn't he give you two weeks to come up with the money?"

"Yes, and that's extortion."

"If we had any way to prove it. A kid telling us, with no witnesses and no corroborating evidence isn't enough."

"I can't believe we're all in danger again."

"Anyway, I've got to go escort a wide load through town, but keep in touch if you see anything suspicious."

"All right."

Trying to push Charlie's news out of his mind, Francis took a shower then awakened Stringer. Remembering they were going to Old Orchard, he quickly got dressed and downed a glass of OJ.

They picked Sam up in front of Pike's shack on the wharf. She was dressed in black save for a neck bandana tie-dyed blue and red. She was hesitant climbing into the back seat with Stringer, but seemed to relax as soon as she hung her head out the window.

In the rearview mirror, Francis saw Stringer watching Sam, her long streak of blue hair blowing about in the wind. "Stringer says you've never been to Old Orchard before."

"Nope," Sam said, without pulling her head in.

"It's a lot of fun. An amusement park right on the ocean."

Sam didn't respond. Stringer motioned for Francis to leave her alone.

Francis didn't say anything else on the trip down Route One. The tourist season had just started, so traffic was light as they drove past a couple of campgrounds carved out of the pine forest. Several lobster shacks along the road were open for business, retired buoys, traps, and pairs of old wooden oars highlighting their signs.

Entering Old Orchard, the road wound by the stately town hall at the top of a hill that opened into a sweeping view of the *Palace Playland* amusement park, beyond which the great Atlantic shimmered in the sunlight. Francis slowed the Jeep so they could take it all in.

"Wow," Stringer said, his eyes wide.

Sam lifted her head and surveyed the scene.

Francis drove slowly down Main Street, lined on both sides with colorful tourist traps: discount camera stores, gift shops, pizza joints, ice cream and candy shops, most of which sported signs in both English and French. As they passed the *Bon Marche*, Francis smiled, thinking back to the first time his grandmother brought him there and to the jam-packed *Harold's-On-The-Beach* farther down. *Harold's* was so loaded with bathing suits, beach towels, T-shirts, multi-colored umbrellas, sand toys, and displays of Coppertone he could hardly squeeze in off the sidewalk. Thankfully there was a red and white cooler next to the cash register that was always full of cold, sweaty bottles of cola. And he still remembered the first time he saw tanned, pot-bellied men walking the streets smoking cigarettes in skimpy G-string bathing suits. "Stay away from those Frenchies," his grandmother had whispered, pulling him closer.

As they approached the center of downtown, a top-hatted juggler on a unicycle appeared at Sam's window. Dressed in red, white, and blue and balancing on his one wheel, the talented young fellow rhythmically tossed yellow balls in the air so rapidly they looked like a continuous airborne loop.

"Cool," Sam said, smiling. "Gotta learn how to do that."

"Look," Stringer said, pointing to a building filled with arcade games. "Let's go in there."

Francis smiled to himself as he turned onto West Grand Avenue and drove past the arcade, the Tilt-A-Whirl, rollercoaster, and Pirate rides. He pulled into Tom's Parking, where he was greeted by the ever-friendly George, Tom's son, who had been working the lot for over fifty years. "Park wherever you like," George said. "Got an egg-and-bacon special—$8.95 with orange juice."

Sam leaned against the front seat. "I'm hungry. Can we eat something?"

"Sure," Francis said, pulling into a parking space facing the ocean.

Sam slumped back against the seat. "I don't have any money."

Francis shut the engine off and looked at her. "Sam, today's my treat. We'll get something to eat then head over to the rides."

Rock and roll music started playing as the Adrenaline ride sprang to life across the street, the sound of hydraulics and air compressors accentuating the Rolling Stones' "Stop Me Up." Sam and Stringer's gaze followed the ride as the rotating pendulum rose high in the air. After it reached its zenith, the riders screamed as it swung back toward earth.

"Wow!" Sam said.

"Are you *sure* you're hungry?" Stringer asked.

Sam was fixated on the ride. "Not really, let's go!"

"Watch out for traffic and the train tracks!" Francis called out, as they headed toward the rides.

Francis caught up with them inside the *Palace Playland* in front of a shiny pinball machine lit up with dozens of flashing lights. Sam was pushing buttons on the side but nothing was happening. "What's the matter with this thing?"

Two teenagers came up and stood behind her, snickering. "Gotta put tokens in, stupid," one guy said. "Yeah, or get out of the way," said the other.

Sam whirled around and stepped right into one of their faces. "Who you calling stupid, asswipe?" She looked ready to fight.

Surprised, Stringer took a step back.

Francis moved to intervene, but the boys backed off. "Crazy bitch," one said, as they walked away.

A few people were staring at Sam. Francis knew she was embarrassed she didn't know how the arcade worked. "I'll get a bunch of tokens over at the booth," he said. "Be right back."

"This place sucks. I'm outta here."

"Sam, wait—" Stringer tried to grab her arm, but she quickly disappeared through the doorway. He stood there, not knowing what to do.

"She'll be back," Francis said, realizing how deprived her childhood had to have been. "Why don't you look around for something she might enjoy? I'll get the tokens."

"Okay." He looked disappointed. "I wanted this to be fun."

"Give her time. It will be."

Francis got in the line for tokens and watched as Stringer made his way through the crowd to the door. He walked outside but must not have seen Sam as he came back in and started perusing the video machines, stopping at the Mario Kart Grand Prix racing game. He watched intently as a couple of boys rocked back and forth holding onto their steering wheels as they raced down a fast-moving course dotted with exploding hazards. Stringer moved on to a glassed-in game where the player manipulated a steam shovel on a derrick over a pile of sparkling treasure trying to pick up a prize.

As Francis approached the token machine, he saw Stringer watching people playing Skee-Ball, an incline bowling game. His face lit up, Stringer turned and looked for Francis. Seeing him, Stringer smiled and motioned to the row of bowling machines. By the time Francis had purchased tokens, however, Stringer and Sam were back together over at the video games.

They got the gist of running the machines and soon were racing each other in the two-seat Mario Kart game. Francis stood behind them, ensuring no one bothered them. He took pleasure in watching them laugh and yell, leaning back and forth into each other as they skidded around curves and flew over jumps. For the first time in his life Francis felt the special joy of a dad watching his kids.

After half an hour, with Stringer and Sam still engrossed in video games, Francis wandered outside and looked at the maze of rides with the tall Galaxy Coaster in the background. To his right, the huge pendulum ride, Adrenalin, was again swinging back and forth, twirling screaming riders high in the air. From the other side, Francis heard yelling and looked up and saw clusters of riders with their legs dangling free, twisting above him on the hydraulic arm of the Power Surge. He shook his head. No way would he get on that thing.

Francis walked in the other direction and soon heard joyful shrieks from people crashing their electrified cars into each other on the Dodg'em ride. That was more like it. Francis fondly remembered riding those same bumper cars with his grandmother when he was a boy, colliding with as many other cars as possible. It also reminded him that his own father never had the time or inclination to do such fun things with him. Instead, he stayed in his mahogany-paneled study scouring the *Wall Street Journal* or was off at his club playing golf and smoking cigars with his rich and powerful friends.

Francis' attention was caught by a young boy and girl with their parents in front of a cotton candy stand. The children's arms were outstretched pointing at bags of the fluffy pink confection. Francis smiled, appreciating how much his life had changed for the better when he came to live with his grandmother. Now he wanted to pass on those same kindnesses.

Back inside, Stringer and Sam were still playing video games. He watched as they pulled their pockets inside out looking for more tokens. Satisfied they'd run out, he stepped over.

"We're out of tokens," Stringer said, looking crestfallen.

"Come outside, I want to show you something."

"But we're having so much—"

Sam crossed her arms tightly and frowned.

"This way," Francis said, leading them out of the arcade.

They reluctantly followed.

Outside, they sheltered their eyes from the bright sun then gradually took in all the rides as well as the stands selling fried dough, candied apples, and caramel corn. Sam looked around with amazement at the gleaming carousel and all the colorful game booths.

"Wow," Stringer said, pointing at the Adrenalin as it swung high over their heads, the huge pendulum covered with pulsating rows of bright lights. "Can we go on that? Can we have some cotton candy? And that caramel corn smells awesome."

"Why don't you try something a little less dangerous? And I would wait until after you ride to eat."

Sam stepped forward. "That's not dangerous. Looks like a blast."

"Yeah," Stringer said.

"Alright." Francis pulled tickets from his pocket and handed several to each of them. "Be careful. Do just what the attendant tells you to."

As she took the tickets, Sam glanced up at him. "Thanks, Mr. Monroe. This place is cool."

Francis smiled. "You're welcome. I'm having fun, too."

"You want to ride with us?"

Francis chuckled. "No thanks. I'll leave that to you daredevils."

Stringer grabbed her hand. "Come on!"

Sam looked at their hands as if she might pull away then let him lead her toward the ride.

As Stringer and Sam waited their turn in line, they looked like they would burst with anticipation. When they were finally locked into their seats and the great shiny machine started to move, they suddenly looked apprehensive, but after a couple of pendulum swings they were screaming with delight with the rest of the kids.

Francis walked over and leaned against the fence that separated the park from the beach. He looked across Saco Bay, the sun sparkling over the crests of waves crashing onto the miles of golden sand. He wished Kate were with them so she, too, could see the joy on Stringer's and Sam's faces.

"Francis!" he heard Stringer yell. He looked up and saw them twisting and turning high above the ground. Francis shook his head and waved.

When they staggered off the Adrenalin, Francis took them over to the bumper cars. Sam looked at the cars and frowned. "Looks dumb. My scooter's a lot faster."

"They're fun," Francis said, motioning to a head-on collision right in front of them. "I hope you don't do that on your scooter."

Sam made a face.

"I'm only going on those if you do it, too," Stringer said.

Francis nodded. "Okay. I used to be good at these."

"Be right back." Stringer ran toward the restrooms.

As they got in line, Francis noted that Sam seemed uncomfortable; she was having fun one minute, moody the next. "Are you having a good time?"

She stared at the ocean.

"Sam?"

She glanced at him. "Yeah, but I know you're up to something."

"What do you mean?"

"Nobody's ever nice to me unless they want something."

"I just want you to have a fun."

She became tense, scuffed her boot on the sandy cement. "Yeah, well, it won't last. Never does. I'll be right back in that nut house with Nelson and his old lady."

CHAPTER TWENTY-THREE

"I THOUGHT NELSON WAS A GOOD GUY," FRANCIS SAID TO SAM, AS they moved forward in line.

"He's alright, but his old lady's a crazy drunk. Beats on him regular." She spit on the cement. "It's better than a lotta places. I've been in way worse shitholes than that."

"It sounds like things have been very tough for you."

"Yeah, well, whatever." She looked in the direction of the restrooms. Stringer came down the ramp and ran toward them.

"I'm glad you came with us today. This has been a special place for me since I was a kid."

Sam looked at him. "You really came here? It's been here that long?"

Francis frowned. "Yes, *that* long."

Stringer ducked under the railing and joined them.

"We're next," Sam said, looking excited again.

They watched the cars cruising around, banging into each other, sparks flying off the tops of the metal poles sliding over the electrified ceiling.

As soon as the riders exited the floor, a carnie with a dying cigarette hanging out of his mouth undid a chain across the entrance and the line moved forward. Leaning against the rail, he collected tickets as everyone hurried onto the floor. "Any car you want," he called out to no one in particular.

Stringer ran ahead to a red car. Sam hesitated, not sure what to do.

Francis encouraged her. "You can ride with Stringer or pick your own car."

"Hurry up!" Stringer called. "Grab a car before they're all gone."

Sam must have noticed there were only a few cars left as she ran to a corner and climbed into a purple one. Francis quickly ducked into the last car, a green one along the side.

The carnie hooked the chain across the entrance, stopping anyone else from entering. "Everybody buckle in," he yelled, looking around the floor. His gaze stopped at Sam. "Hey you! Buckle in or you can't ride."

Sam blushed and shrank down in the seat. Stringer showed her how to lower the restraining bar in front of her.

A bell rang and the cars came to life. Francis spun his steering wheel and backed up, bumping into Stringer, who laughed, came around, and hit Francis head on.

"I'll get you!" Francis yelled, steering clear of Stringer so he could get a running start. Then he noticed Sam hadn't moved except for being bumped around by a couple hits from others. Francis drove over and pulled alongside her. "If you step on the gas and twirl the wheel around you'll move more. Now let's go get Stringer."

Sam perked up. "Okay."

They headed toward Stringer, who was stuck in the middle of a clog of cars. Francis motioned for Sam to wait, and then as soon as Stringer was free, they headed in, clobbering him in rapid succession from opposite sides.

"Yeah!" Sam pumped her fist in the air.

"You're dead meat!" Stringer yelled. He quickly came around and rammed Francis in the side then caught Sam from behind. Everyone bounced around, bumping and laughing until the bell rang and the cars were de-energized.

"No!" Sam yelled. "That's not fair—"

"Ha, ha, too bad," Stringer said, getting out of his car. "That was a blast!"

They left the Dodg'em and gathered in front of a red and white candied apple stand.

"That was fun," Sam said, smiling.

Francis nodded. "Just as much fun as I remembered." He motioned to the food carts. "Want something to eat before I take you both on at Skee-Ball?"

Sam made a face. "That looked totally lame."

Stringer pointed back at the Dodg'em. "Let's ride the bumper cars again."

"Aren't you guys hungry?" Francis asked. "You haven't eaten anything."

"Nah," Stringer said.

"Tell you what; if you try the Skee-Ball, then we'll ride the bumper cars again." He looked around. "Where's Sam?"

Stringer pointed. "Over there, having a cigarette."

Francis saw her leaning over the railing by the beach. "You can't smoke in here."

Sam took a long drag, tapped the cigarette out on the palm of her hand and slid it over her ear.

"She's not," Stringer said, with a grin.

"That's terrible for her."

Stringer shrugged his shoulders. "It's nothing."

Francis started toward her.

Stringer grabbed Francis' sleeve. "Take it easy. She's having fun. Probably for the first time in a long time."

Francis stopped and looked at him. "Really?"

"Yeah. Her life's been shit." He shook his head. "I thought I had it rough till I met her."

"What sorts of things?"

Stringer became uncomfortable. He looked over at Sam, who was still staring at the beach. "She's been abused, bounced around in some bad places." He lowered his voice. "Once a psycho locked her in a creepy basement for like a week. They'd unchain the door and throw a handful of food down to her. She broke a finger trying to dig her way out through loose cement around a boarded-up basement window. Still bothers her when she's holding a string down on her guitar."

Francis frowned. "That's criminal. I hope whoever did that to her was—"

"Nobody did shit," Stringer interjected. "I know what that's like."

"But that's not fair—"

Stringer cut him off. "Here she comes. Don't say anything."

"I won't."

Sam walked over to them. "You ready for that lame Skee-Ball?"

Francis was glad she was willing to play. He motioned toward the arcade. "After you."

Over at the row of Skee-Ball machines, they watched how others rolled balls up the sloped alleys into a series of holes worth an increasing number of points.

"That's easy," Stringer said.

Francis smiled.

Several people tore off tickets they had won and left. Sam and Stringer stepped in front of the machines. "What were those tickets?" she asked.

"If you get enough points, the games spit out tickets. If you win enough you can take them over to the prize counter and get something."

Sam and Stringer looked over at a brightly-lit counter surrounded with stuffed animals, candy, beach toys, electronics, as well as dozens of other prizes.

"Cool," Sam said. "So how do you get the balls?"

Francis pointed to a slot. "Just put a token in there and they automatically load."

Stringer looked at Francis. "We don't have any tokens left."

Francis dug into his pocket. "Well, I just happen to have some." He pulled out a handful and gave several to each of them.

Sam stared at the golden coins. "Thanks."

All three of them put in tokens, and started bowling. It took a while to get the hang of it again, but soon Francis scored on a 50-point hole. "Yes!"

Stringer frowned at him. He was struggling to get the balls to make the jump and not roll back to him.

"Look!" Sam called out as a ball went into a 20-point hole.

Frustrated, Stringer snapped a ball up the alley so hard it bounced off the ceiling of the game, jumped the side and landed on Sam's alley.

She laughed. "Thanks for the extra ball."

Francis leaned toward Stringer. "Like this," he whispered then showed him how to roll the ball smoothly at the right speed.

Stringer watched him then aimed carefully and fired. The ball flew smoothly over the jump, landing in the 30-point hole. He gave Francis a high-five then reached for another ball, but they were all gone.

"Just put in another token," Francis said.

For the next half hour they enjoyed a friendly competition that became increasingly intense as they ran out of coins. Sam had a good score by the time she took hold of her last ball. "Here goes nothing." She lined the ball up with the alley and let it rip. It flew smoothly over the jump, veered to the right and dropped perfectly into the 100-point corner slot.

She jumped in the air so hard, for a split-second her strands of blue hair stood straight up. "Did you see that?"

Stringer stared at the base of her machine, his eyes wide. "Look!" he said, pointing to a steady stream of pink tickets flowing out of a slot in the front of the game.

"Holy shit!" Sam said, as a long string of tickets flew out and landed on the floor at her feet.

Francis, too, stared at the stream of tickets spewing from the machine. "I've never seen anything like it."

"Is there something wrong with the machine?" Sam asked.

"Who cares," Stringer replied. "Let her rip!"

As layers of tickets collected at their feet, they started laughing, as excited as if they'd hit the jackpot in Las Vegas.

"Oh, my god," Sam said, picking up an armful of tickets. "This is crazy."

Francis looked around to see if any of the arcade attendants had noticed, but they were congregated around an intense Mario Kart race.

Stringer bent over and gathered up several reams of tickets as the machine just kept spewing.

Francis chuckled, and began picking up tickets himself. By the time they had collected all of them, the machine appeared to have finally run out.

"Come over here," Francis said, motioning to a red redemption kiosk. "We'll feed all these in and get a slip for a prize."

It took ten minutes to feed all their tickets into the counting machine. Then, before Francis hit the print button, he asked how many they thought they had.

"Two hundred," Sam said, hands on her hips.

"No, *three* hundred," Stringer said, with authority.

"Let's see." Francis ceremoniously pushed the button. After a few seconds a yellow slip popped out of a slot.

Stringer grabbed the slip, looked at it, and his mouth fell open.

"What's it say?" Sam tried to grab the slip but Stringer turned away, still staring at it.

Sam didn't miss the second time.

"Don't tear it," Francis said.

"Hole-lee shit—" Sam's eyes were wide. "One thousand four hundred and twenty-six."

"Wow, you guys are pros."

Stringer laughed. "It helped that the machine went crazy." He turned toward the prize counter. "Let's see what we can get."

As they waited in line, Stringer pointed at a skateboard with red neon wheels. "That's cool." Then he pointed at a slingshot. "That could come in handy."

Francis shook his head. "I don't think so."

Stringer spied a model airplane. "Hey, that would look good in my room."

Sam was standing next to them. Francis noticed she wasn't saying anything. He nudged Stringer and nodded at Sam.

Stringer shrugged his shoulders. Francis nodded toward her again and Stringer got the hint.

"See anything you like?" Stringer asked.

She took a step back. "Nah. Get whatever you want. I don't do this stuff."

Stringer thought for a few seconds. "Well, *if* you were going to get one, what would it be?"

"Eh—" she said, acting like she couldn't care. Then she pointed at a stuffed dog dressed like a pirate, a black patch over his eye, a curved plastic sword in his belt. "I'd mount him on the front of my scooter. Scare everyone." She turned and headed toward the door. "I'll catch you outside."

Stringer looked at Francis. "Why can't she just have fun?"

"Lot of tough baggage," Francis said, sympathetically.

"Huh?"

"I mean, she carries a lot of hurt with her, like you said."

"Yeah, you can feel it." Stringer watched Sam disappear through the doorway. "But there's something *really* cool about her."

Francis nodded. "I know what you mean."

"What's it going to be?" the man at the prize counter asked.

Stringer looked to Francis.

"You choose. That plane *is* pretty sharp looking."

Stringer looked up at the different prizes, pointed straight at the stuffed dog. "That one. The pirate."

Francis smiled.

The man used a hook on a pole to bring it down. "You've got another two hundred tickets. What else you want?"

Stringer picked up the pirate and looked at Francis. "You get something."

Pleased, Francis pointed at a small dreamcatcher hanging over the man's head. The black ring held a white web with a small turquoise stone woven into the middle. Three bird feathers hung from the ring by beaded strands of rawhide.

The man took it down, handed it to Francis.

"For Mom?" Stringer said.

Francis nodded.

"You got fifty points left," the man said. "Get some candy or something, but hurry it up. People waiting."

Stringer selected a bag of rock candy containing a small metal hammer. The man motioned behind them. "Next."

Stringer tucked the stuffed pirate under his arm. "Let's go find Sam."

They walked outside onto the downtown plaza. The sun was still warm as it descended over the west end of town, casting long, moving shadows from the rides onto the white sand beach. Sam was up the street by the railroad tracks, leaning against a light pole, smoking. Stringer headed toward her. Francis followed, proud of Stringer for getting the pirate.

As Francis made his way up the sidewalk, he noticed a car with Rhode Island plates passing slowly by them. His heart jumped. He squinted and stared into the car. It was just an older couple with a pair of little kids in the back. He shook his anxiety off and continued walking but slowed when he saw Stringer had caught up with Sam. Francis watched from a distance as Stringer brought the dog around from behind his back and gave it to her. She paused for a few seconds then smiled and took it from him. She leaned forward and gave Stringer a kiss on the lips.

The two of them waited as a Boston and Maine railroad engine clanged by then they crossed the tracks and headed up Old Orchard Street toward the many brightly-lit stores hawking their kitschy wares. Stringer and Sam sat on a bench in front of a pizza place and started talking.

Francis waited a few minutes then walked over to them. When she saw him, Sam looked down and sort of hid the stuffed dog, seemingly embarrassed.

"You guys must be hungry by now."

They both nodded.

"I'm going to take you to a great place for dinner. It's on a salt marsh just north of here. Anything you don't eat you can feed to the seagulls."

"Sounds good," Stringer said.

Back in the Jeep, they drove up East Grand Avenue past the old Snows Chowder Estate into Scarborough, where they soon pulled into the Clambake Restaurant. In the parking lot dozens of seagulls circled overhead and inside the smell of fresh seafood and melted butter filled the air. After ordering, they walked around and looked at the nautical memorabilia as well as a room filled with taxidermied animals, including several life-sized deer and bear. "Weird," Sam said, looking up at the head of an elk mounted over the door.

When their number was called, they picked up their tray of food and took it to a table overlooking the salt marsh, where they watched egrets and blue herons hunting in the tall grasses. Francis was surprised and touched that Sam brought her stuffed dog inside with her and sat him in the fourth chair at their table.

Francis put on a white plastic bib and bit into a heavily-laden lobster roll, melted butter and mayonnaise oozing out both ends. He chewed the delicate meat slowly then licked his lips, savoring the taste. Stringer and Sam leaned over the table and devoured an order of heavily-battered onion rings, followed by a couple of cheeseburgers, a pile of coleslaw, and two large plates of golden French fries. As they ate they kept glancing outside at the parking lot where kids were feeding fries to a congregation of screaming seagulls. The impatient birds hovered anxiously overhead, repeatedly swooping down and snatching pieces of food from peoples' outstretched hands.

Stringer and Sam left a good pile of fries on their plates, and after downing their lemonades, headed outside to add to the feeding frenzy.

"Don't let them peck you," Francis called after them.

He stepped to the window by the door, watching as they timidly held out fries for the birds to grab, quickly withdrawing their hands as soon as the food was swiped. They warmed up to the birds and seemed to have a great time, laughing and throwing food onto the pavement, which brought a sudden noisy rush of gulls to retrieve it. As much as Francis enjoyed being with them, he again felt a wave of sadness that

Kate wasn't there.

After a short time, Francis noticed that Sam had left the rest of her plate of food on the ground, which was immediately devoured by the birds. She appeared to be withdrawing again, walking away from everyone to a far corner of the parking lot where she sat on an old picnic table and lit a cigarette. Through the dancing flock of birds, Francis saw Stringer walk over and sit next to her.

Sitting at the picnic table, the constant screaming of the gulls became unnerving. Sam seemed fidgety and uncomfortable. Stringer didn't look at her when he spoke. "I feel bad it's so hard for you to have fun."

Sam moved away from him, blowing smoke through flared nostrils like a horse getting ready to bolt.

CHAPTER TWENTY-FOUR

STRINGER WAITED PATIENTLY, WATCHING A WHITE EGRET STEALTH-ily step among the tall reeds.

"I'm broken," Sam said, getting up so abruptly she startled a gaggle of gulls that had assembled around her. She flicked the stub of her cigarette to the water's edge, where it fizzled and died. "Damaged beyond repair, as they say." She glanced at Stringer then looked away. "You don't know me."

Stringer slid toward her end of the bench. "Then tell me."

"My life's a mess. I told you the only things that hold me together are music and weed." Sam scuffed an empty clam shell into the swampy water. "Being with you, you guys being nice to me, makes me sadder."

"Why?"

Sam became agitated. "Jesus, Stringer, 'cause it gives me glimpses of what my life might have been like."

"You're not more broken than me, or lots of people. We're all kind of messed up. You've got your whole life ahead of you. Don't talk like it's over."

Sam picked up a stone, threw it far into the marsh. "A lot of the time it feels like it. Sometimes I'd like to shed my own skin."

"But you're cool, way cooler than me."

"Well, that's true..."

They both grinned.

"See, it's not that bad."

She gave him a quizzical look. "What planet are you from, Mr. Optimistic? With the shit you've been through..."

"It's from my mom."

"What?"

"Optimism. No matter what happens to us, she always says, 'It'll be okay.'"

Sam shook her head. "It won't. It's never okay."

"You have to *let* it be okay."

Sam stared at the orange sun reflecting off the headwaters of the marsh as it descended into a pine forest to the west. "Easy for you to say."

"No it isn't. I just don't give up."

Sam looked at him. "Well, maybe I..."

He waited.

"Never mind," She walked back through the middle of the seagulls toward Francis, who was waiting by the restaurant door.

Francis led them to the attached gift shop, where he bought a box of salt water taffy. On the drive home, Sam lightened up again, and she and Stringer fooled around in the back seat, getting taffy stuck in their teeth and talking like Hannibal Lector. After a while, the two of them fell asleep leaning against each other.

When they arrived back in Winter's Cove, Francis pulled up in front of the shack by the harbor, where Sam's scooter was chained to a metal lamppost. He gently woke them.

"Can't I give you a ride home?" Francis asked. "It's almost dark."

"I'm fine." Sam turned to Stringer, who was slowly awakening. "See ya."

"Yeah."

Sam walked to her scooter, set the stuffed dog on the seat then walked back over to Francis' window. "This was way cool. Never had a day like this."

Francis smiled. "It was great being with you, Sam."

She squinted and nodded. "But just so you know, I don't think I can do this."

Before Francis could say anything else, she hurried around the front of the Jeep back to her scooter.

Stringer climbed into the front seat. "Let's get out of here before she gets weird again."

Francis watched Sam unlocking her scooter. "You think she's all right?"

"Yeah. I told you, she thinks people want something when they're nice." He looked at Francis. "I felt the same way when you bought me my easel. Trust me, there aren't many like you."

"Feeling's mutual."

Sam stared at Stringer and motioned with her finger for him to come back over to her.

"Hang on—" Stringer got out and walked over to Sam, who seemed uncomfortable. They turned away from Francis. Sam pulled a partially smoked cigarette from behind her ear and tapped it on the back of her hand. "Listen," she said, looking at the ground, "you're a good kid. I know you guys are trying to do something nice for the poor orphan. But you have no idea how screwed up I am."

Stringer leaned on a parking meter post with his hand. "Look, we both are. It's not like I've had some kind of perfect life."

Sam started getting agitated. "Okay, so we're both messed up, but there's a lot more hope for you. I don't care how many trips to Old Orchard I take, I will *never* trust anyone again."

"Why not?"

"Can't."

Stringer looked her in the eye. "Why?"

Sam fidgeted. "I told you trusting someone again would be like an awful, slow death. Don't you get it?"

"Come on, Sam, you don't mean that."

Sam nervously licked the bolt that pierced her bottom lip. "Get away from me, Stringer. I can't do this." She took hold of her scooter handlebars.

"You can if you want to." Stringer was upset and angry. He turned away and hurried back to the Jeep.

Glancing in his side mirror, Francis saw Sam affixing the dog to the front of her scooter with a bungee cord. As soon as her headlight came on, he sped up, passed the sheriff's office, and headed home. When they climbed the hill past Kasa's, he was aware he and Stringer were both anxiously looking for Kate's car. As they pulled up to the bungalow, Francis' jaw tightened, a combination of fear and anger. No car in sight.

CHAPTER TWENTY–FIVE

KATE'S FITFUL SLEEP ENDED WHEN SHE HEARD THE SOUND OF young voices passing in front of her. Confused, she lifted her heavy head from a sweaty blanket and pulled matted hair away from her face. She shifted her body, her back and hips stiff from sleeping in the wooden chair. Through rusted screens she watched two young couples holding hands walk past the cabin.

"What have I done?" she whispered, realizing she was naked save for her panties. As she rubbed the night out of her eyes she smelled the aroma of fresh coffee. *There is a god.*

The screen door squeaked as Richard stepped onto the porch carrying two mugs of hot java. "Figured you might need one of these."

Kate tucked hair behind an ear and took a mug with both hands. She blew across the steaming surface then took a sip. "Thanks."

Richard sat in the other rocker, his waist wrapped in a towel. His body was moist, like he'd just taken a shower. "There's an excellent lecture at nine on reflective observation."

Her brain clogged with confusion and remorse, the last thing on Kate's mind was the art seminar. "What?"

Richard spoke matter-of-factly, like nothing unusual had happened the night before. "You'll appreciate the first lecture—if we hurry we can make it. Sidney Collins, the woman who did the welcome address, is giving it. She seemed to hold your interest."

"Yeah," Kate said, hoarsely. She cleared her throat and took another swallow. "Look, I'm a wreck, in no shape to show up at a lecture."

Richard motioned toward the shore, barely twenty feet in front of the cabin. "Take a quick swim in the lake. I just did. It's cold, but it feels great." He pointed. "There's a big flat rock down there with a bar of soap on it." He got up and opened the screen door. "When you're ready, we'll go up and have breakfast."

Kate frowned. "Why are you being so nice to me?"

He spoke from the other side of the screen. "You have chutzpah. I like that." He grinned. "And a terrific body."

After Richard disappeared inside, Kate shed the sweaty blanket, picked up a thick white towel he'd left by her chair and wrapped it around her. Barefoot, she stepped carefully down to the edge of the water, which lapped gently against the smooth rocks. The water was so clear she could see every pebble on the bottom as well as a small school of tiny fish darting about under the surface. She hung the towel on a branch of a cedar then slid her naked body into the water. At first it felt uncomfortably cold, but soon a wonderful cleansing relief came over her.

Kate scrubbed her whole body with the bar of soap then dove toward deeper water. As she swam under the surface, she felt the night before rinse off of her. She went as far as she could before she had to take a breath. When she surfaced, she must have come up under a catch of gadflies as she had one of the little black devils on her nose. She shook her head and it flew off. Feeling refreshed, she slowly treaded water, breathing in the soft scent of cedar.

Kate let her arms relax. Feeling nearly weightless, she looked back at the rocky shore and the primitive cabin just visible through the trees. *This place is so beautiful.* She dipped under the blue-black surface and swam back, coming up just in front of the large rock, where she was surprised to see Richard holding her towel in one hand and a lit cigarette in the other.

"Time for the mermaid to get out or we'll be late."

Kate tried unsuccessfully to hide her breasts with her arms as she climbed onto the slippery rock. She took the towel and wrapped it around her.

Richard snuffed out the cigarette with his fingers. "This lecture will help you help your son. That's why I want you to hear it."

She stared at this man with slicked-back hair and a fresh gray shirt unbuttoned to mid-chest. Strangely, he already seemed familiar, had an edgy comfortableness about him. "Okay. Then let's go." Kate reached out, let him guide her off the rock.

Richard looked her over, raised his eyebrows. "Like that? Every man in the place will be after you."

She gave him a push then followed him up the short trail to the cabin.

Kate put on her clothes from the day before. Not wanting to be seen coming in with Richard, she left him and hurried through the woods and across the field to her car. She pulled clean clothes from her bag in the trunk and, with no one nearby, quickly changed. As she walked toward the Performance Barn, several artists said good morning, making her feel more comfortable. Kate stopped at a table set up with coffee, tea, and baskets of warm muffins, bagels, and blueberry scones. She leaned over, breathing in the delicious aroma of the fresh baked goods, which felt surprisingly like home, though not a home she'd ever known.

Kate and Richard attended a provocative lecture by Ms. Collins, who explored how painters reflected in their art "the undersides of the fascinating, frustrating, painful, joyful, and sometimes boring world around them." She emphasized that the shape, thickness and firmness of every brush stroke, every color variation, blend, shade and hue revealed each artist's interpretation of the world, *their* world at a particular moment in time. "Part of the magic of art is that it is limitless; it has no defined boundaries," she said. "It invites, seduces us to get lost outside of ourselves. And what a relief that is."

During the day, Richard and Kate did a sort of dance, acknowledging each other from afar: glances across a classroom or a studio, watching each other draw, touching elbows while moving along the lunch table.

"I can smell your scent across the room," Richard whispered in her ear as she placed spinach and baby carrots on her plate. "You are incredibly sensual. That should not be wasted."

Kate felt heat in her cheeks. She moved along, quickly scooping a spoonful of pasta and broccoli salad onto her plate. She picked up a glass of lemonade, walked over and sat in the sun on a bench near an apple tree. Richard followed and sat next to her. After eating his couscous and bean salad, he looked at her. "Why don't you drink?"

Kate finished chewing a piece of pita bread followed by a swallow of the tart lemonade. "I've got a pretty checkered past."

He scoffed. "Don't we all."

"Yeah, well, I could've died many times. California was not the Land of Milk and Honey for me."

"I figured you weren't a Mainer." He looked at her face. "You have some Indian blood in you?"

Kate was surprised. "How can you tell?"

"The angle of your jaw, your eyes." He smiled. "You have that beauty."

Kate looked at him.

"Italian," he said, with an exaggerated accent. "Sicily. We've got our own bad actors in our olive tree. And a little misplaced Cherokee got in there somehow."

"Really?"

"Yes. My grandmother supposedly had an affair with an Indian while working on a reservation."

"That's an interesting mixture."

He nodded. "I'm proud of it."

"I see it gives you your way with the ladies."

He grinned. "Many."

Though he was obnoxious, Kate was attracted to his frankness. She finished her lemonade. "You're probably a softie at heart. All but the worst assholes are."

Richard tipped his head and looked at her. "Have you known any?"

A vision of Leland's scraggly, bearded face snapped across her mind. Kate stared at a lush green field beyond the barn. "Yeah. One too many bad men."

Then she imagined Francis sitting next to her at the trial, his artist's hands holding hers. "And I've known a good one, too." She suddenly felt a hard pang of guilt tighten her diaphragm.

Kate collected her plate and cup. "I'm heading to the afternoon workshop then I'm out of here."

"I'm sorry to hear that."

"Richard, we can't do this again."

"Do what?"

"You know what."

"Kate, there's so much more we can share together."

She turned and walked to the studio building where she spent the afternoon learning the basic concepts of media, mixing paints and applying a base layer to a virgin canvas. It was difficult and fun, intimidating and freeing, all at the same time. She felt inklings of creativity coming to life, stimulating her in ways she hadn't felt in years. She marveled at how both Francis and Stringer had such natural talent. They saw things in ways that allowed them to internalize unusually deep meanings and translate them through their brushes into powerful paintings. At one point she paused, thinking of Wyeth's painting "Barracoon," the beauty of that cruelly confined, naked slave and how that print had been a talisman for Stringer and for her. She wished she had it with her now.

When the sessions were finished for the day, Kate walked to her car. Though seeing Richard made her feel guilty, she was pleased to find him leaning against the trunk. She put her things on the back seat and rolled the windows down.

Richard came around and stood next to her as pent-up heat escaped from the Malibu. "I've never been good with this sort of thing," he said, in an unusually quiet voice. "But if you have any interest, there is a follow-up workshop next weekend, and I'd be glad to see you again."

Kate was disarmed by his seeming humility, his sincerity. She glanced at his face then looked away. "I've got a good life, Richard, one I don't appreciate enough." She squinted against the golden late-day light. It surprised her that she wanted to be honest with him. "Still, it's like I'm coming to for the first time in twenty years. I want to run around crazy like a teenager, experiencing everything I missed in a chaotic haze of drugs and booze." Kate shook her head. "I was dying. I missed so much."

She leaned against the car, ran her hands through her hair. "I can't believe I'm talking to you like this. I feel out of control, and I'm not being true to anyone right now, even my son, which is *so* not me. I'm back to messing up the world around me."

"Come on, you came here to learn how to appreciate art, to better understand that part of Stringer's life."

She turned and looked at him. "Did I?"

She stared into his eyes for a few seconds then climbed into the car and pulled the door shut. Holding the steering wheel, she looked at the young artists packing up their things and saying goodbye.

Richard reached in and gently ran his fingers behind her ear into the soft hair at the back of her neck.

Kate's pulse quickened. She felt tingling in her breasts. Gripping the wheel tightly, she glanced up and forced a smile, then started the engine and drove off. Needing to clear Richard from her head, she decided to take the backroads out of Skowhegan. She stopped and walked around a beaver pond ringed with last year's fuzzy cattails and hundreds of newly budding lily pads. She chuckled when bug-eyed young frogs saw her and dipped below the surface, leaving tiny waves spreading outward in concentric circles. She stood silently and watched as a blue heron took flight from the opposite shore, its prehistoric wings gradually lifting it above the trees and out of sight.

After a while, Kate became anxious to get home. She drove back onto the main highway and soon found herself stuck behind a tractor-trailer. The first chance she got, Kate floored it and pulled out to pass the long truck. When she did, she heard a loud bang under the front end and the Malibu lurched to the right. Speeding down the highway with the steering wheel shaking, Kate jammed on the brake and tried to wrestle the car toward the shoulder of the road.

Chapter Twenty-six

S TILL RECOVERING FROM WHAT COULD HAVE BEEN A DISASTROUS accident, Kate crouched at the side of the road as a young mechanic strained to loosen the rusted lug nuts from her wheel. By the time he was finished changing the tire, it was getting late. She was exhausted, dirty and discouraged. She felt stupid for taking backroads instead of the highway out of Skowhegan, but despite the two-hour flat tire fiasco, she had enjoyed the beautiful countryside and it had given her time to try and forget Richard. That, however, was not going particularly well. There was something undeniably delicious about the confident way he'd touched her. She'd wanted him to seduce her right there on that Hudson Bay blanket. After she had satisfied him, she had felt pissed and frustrated when he fell asleep. She was hungry for something more than Francis' gentle touch. She wanted a rougher-edged man to rock her body, force her out of her head, and, at the moment, she didn't feel guilty about it. Well, maybe a little. And a little slutty, but that was an old familiar feeling. And despite her feelings of guilt and wanting to see Stringer and Francis, Kate was already scheming how she could meet up with Richard the next weekend for the follow-up seminar. She was smart enough to know she'd better wait a couple days before bringing *that* up.

Kate followed the mechanic's red pickup onto Route One, where she was glad to be back on solid pavement. He reached a blond-haired arm out his window and pointed her south. Kate waved, tooted her horn and drove off. Figuring Francis and Stringer might be worried about her, she stopped in the next small town and found one of the few remaining phone booths outside an abandoned gas station. Tufts of witchgrass grew between cracked cement slabs surrounding the decaying pumps, their nameplates having been pried off long ago. Above the front of the garage a rusted Firestone Tires sign hung from a twisted metal arm. Broken glass littered the cement in front of the two service bays, and Kate had to park carefully to avoid it. The darkened garage had elaborate spider webs in the corners of the windows, and inside, pieces of old equipment looked like suspicious people standing in the shadows.

Kate checked around her car before she got out and stepped to the phone booth. Mounted to a slab of broken cement, the booth was no longer level, causing its accordion doors to not fully open. She squeezed inside and looked at the phone. Much of the black paint was scratched off and dried chewing gum was stuck in two of the coin slots. The receiver was sticky, the dial tone scratchy. She felt eerily alone, like she was standing in an empty stadium after everyone else had left the game.

Kate pulled Francis' credit card out of her pocket and swiped it several times. Nothing happened. She banged on the side of the phone, swiped the card again and a woman's computer voice welcomed her to *Northeast Telecom*. Feeling anxious, she dialed the bungalow and let it ring a long time. She was bummed no one answered and that the machine didn't pick up. As the distant ring echoed in the heavy plastic receiver, she again glanced around the grounds of the garage. She felt disconnected from her life and knew it was her own fault. She hung up, the flexible metal cord causing the receiver to spring off its cradle. Dangling, it twisted in the flashing neon light from a motel sign across the street.

Kate was startled by the sharp, mournful cry of an orange and white cat standing outside the door of the booth. One of its ears was missing and only one eye seemed clear and able to see. Kate stepped out of the booth, and the cat rubbed against her leg.

"Nice kitty," she said, reaching down to pat its head. Its fur was matted and stiff, but it appreciated the attention. Over the years, she'd befriended many an alley cat on the streets of LA. In the depths of her using, they'd often seemed to be her only friends.

"Hang on," Kate said. She retrieved a paper bag from the Malibu, emptied what was left of a scone onto the ground, and the cat immediately began to eat, its tail rising into the air in approval.

It was starting to get chilly, so Kate pulled on her fleece, got in and rolled her window down. The cat looked at her expectantly. "Go on, now, stay away from the road."

She pulled out and headed south, watching the cat disappear in her side mirror. Half an hour later she approached the turn for Falmouth Foreside. She thought back to the other night, felt badly she had acted out at the yacht club. She couldn't stand being around what she presumed to be pretentious, highbrow people but had to acknowledge, at least to herself, she had been hard on Francis and that the people weren't that bad.

As Kate approached the road leading down to the overlook, she slowed the car. The sun was setting, the sky streaked with bright peach and pink. She bet the view of the clouds over the ocean would be spectacular. The boys weren't home anyway, so she turned off and parked at the edge of the field where the old washed-out road began. Figuring her car wouldn't handle the road like Francis' Jeep, she got out and walked down the rocky descent to the small parking area. Portions of ledge showing through the ground were worn smooth, revealing that this was a popular spot, not the secret outlook Francis had made it out to be.

Carefully approaching the cliff, Kate leaned against a large rock and gazed over the thick forest that swept far down to the ocean. She found herself in awe of the changing pastels of pink, orange, and purple lining the undersides of cumulous clouds offshore. Just to the south, a subtle fog hung in the pointed tops of a stand of tall pines. "Beautiful," she said softly, feeling another pang of guilt. Francis would love this.

Sitting on the rock next to where they had talked, Kate pulled her legs up into her arms. Resting her chin on her knees, she stared out toward the ocean. On the far side of the ravine, a hawk took flight from a branch of an especially tall pine, spreading its wingtips as it glided down toward a strip of beach in the distance. As a strong breeze drifted up to her, Kate closed her eyes and breathed in the sweet scents of the forest. Sitting above the cliff, she felt like she was hovering over the landscape in a hot air balloon.

Kate must have started to nod off, as she was suddenly roused by a strange noise coming down the trail above her. She looked behind her just as someone came crashing through the underbrush on a motor scooter. Hitting the small parking area, the driver yelled, dragging sandaled feet through the gravel, trying to slow down.

"Holy shit!" Kate sprang off the rock, catching a glimpse of a wide-eyed girl just before she and her scooter glanced off one of the large boulders.

The girl screamed as she careened off the cliff, out of sight. A moment later Kate heard metal crashing onto rock.

"Fuck—" For a few seconds, Kate was unable to get in a full breath. Then she gingerly peered over the edge of the cliff, saw a torn piece of fabric caught on a broken branch of a cedar. On a narrow ledge below, the mangled scooter lay jammed into a rock outcropping.

Chapter Twenty-seven

AFTER THEY RETURNED FROM OLD ORCHARD EARLY SUNDAY EVEning, Stringer stayed in the parlor working with a pair of tweezers to get the last of the cigarette off his damaged painting. Francis mostly kept to his studio, which had the best view of the driveway. Every few minutes, he peered out the window, looking for Kate's car. As darkness descended, he watched for the shine of headlights on the trees, his anger melding into anxiety and then fear. After a while, he threw the latch on the iron-cased window and nudged it open. Cool air from the ocean comforted him.

Shortly, Francis was jostled out of his reverie by Stringer stepping into the doorway behind him. "I'm worried about Sam."

"Why?"

"I haven't heard from her, that she made it home."

"Would you expect to?"

"Yeah, well, for the last week or so."

Francis glanced out the window again. "You'll hear from her, then."

"I don't know." Stringer picked up a fine paint brush and twirled it in his fingers. "You watching for Mom?"

Francis nodded, looked at the antique Regulator clock on the wall. "She should have been back a while ago."

Stringer placed the brush back in its tray. "So what if I don't hear from Sam?"

Worried about Kate, Francis was getting annoyed. They'd seen Sam just a couple hours before.

Stringer looked at him for an answer.

"Have you tried texting her?"

Stringer nodded. "About twenty times. Can we go look for her?"

Francis shook his head. "Look, String, she's probably busy at home. It's Kate I'm worried about. We haven't heard from her all weekend."

Francis tapped his fingers on the window casing. "And that mob guy from Rhode Island is lurking around somewhere." He looked out the window again.

Stringer patted Francis on the back. "I'm sure she's fine. Damn girls, always causing trouble."

Francis sort of grinned. "Always."

Stringer's eyes opened wide; he pointed outside. "Lights! Mom must be home."

"Thank god," Francis said, "I was really getting worried."

They both held a hand up to shield their eyes from the bright headlights.

Francis frowned. Kate never parked in front of the studio window. He recoiled as the car door opened and a gold sheriff's badge reflected in the house lights. Charlie got out of his cruiser.

"What is *he* doing here?" Francis hurried to the front door. Stringer followed close behind.

Francis opened the door before Charlie could knock. "What's happened to Kate?"

Charlie looked confused. "Kate? I don't know anything about Kate."

Francis motioned for him to come in. "What then?"

Charlie nodded at Stringer. "Got a call from Nelson, said he hadn't seen Sam since you took off with her this morning. He and his old lady are drinking as usual so he wanted me to check into it. I was out this way so I thought I'd stop by."

Stringer's face narrowed into a frown. "Something's happened to her—"

Francis closed the door. "We left her off at Pike's shack when we got back from Old Orchard. She wouldn't let me give her a ride home."

"She seem okay?"

"Yeah, I guess," Stringer said. "We mostly had a great time."

"We did have a good time," Francis said, "though Sam gets pretty moody, struggles with relaxing and having fun. Stringer says she's been through a lot."

Charlie nodded. "That's for sure. She's pretty rough around the edges, if you know what I mean." He looked at Stringer. "No offense."

"She hasn't texted me since we left her off." Stringer's countenance hardened. He hit himself in the thigh. "I *knew* something was wrong."

Charlie pushed his Stetson back. "Any idea where she might be? Nelson said she's probably off playing her guitar somewhere."

Stringer looked a little hopeful. "Maybe she stopped at a club."

"There aren't many places around here that'll let a teenager play at this hour on a Sunday." He looked at Stringer. "Why don't you call any place you think might have live music?" He turned to Francis. "If she doesn't turn up in the next hour, we'll have to start searching for her." Charlie shook his head. "That's a helluva windy road to Nelson's place."

"And she likes to go down to Black Rock Beach," Stringer said.

Charlie looked at the sky. A few high clouds far out over the ocean still had a hint of purple on them. "Going to be dark soon. I'll take a ride down to the beach then check Thatcher Road out to Nelson's. Let the office know if you hear anything."

"Alright," Francis said. "We'll make some calls."

Charlie opened the door to leave.

Francis stepped toward him. "Have you heard about any accidents between here and Skowhegan?"

Charlie shook his head. "Nothing. Is that why you're worried about Kate? An accident?"

"One of the reasons."

Charlie started to leave again.

"Any more word on that Rhode Island guy?"

Charlie shook his head. "Nobody's seen him. I assume you haven't."

"No. Maybe he was just bluffing and has already left town."

Charlie glanced at Francis. "Possibly, but he doesn't sound like the type to make idle threats. Makes his money intimidating people, making them pay."

As Charlie walked into the darkening world outside the bungalow, fear and anger rose in Francis' chest. One second he was worried Kate had gone off the road or had been attacked, the next he could see her lying on her back, enjoying wild sex with Richard.

Stringer looked at Francis. "How am I supposed to know what clubs to call?"

"Look in the phone book."

"The *phone book*?"

"Yes. The Yellow Pages."

"This sucks! You've got to get internet in this place. We're living like the stone age." Francis tossed him the phone book and Stringer started looking for local clubs or bars and quickly called several that advertised music. Though a couple knew of Sam, no one had seen her.

Stringer slammed the phone back onto its caddy. "Something's happened to Sam." His chin started to quiver. "I know it."

"Come on," Francis said, grabbing his keys off a hook. "We can't stay here and do nothing, and we can't drive all the way to Skowhegan looking for Kate. But we can check the roads around here for Sam."

Stringer yanked a hoodie over his head and pulled on his sneakers. "I'll grab your big flashlight."

Descending the hill in the Jeep, they saw Kasa standing beside her small car. Francis pulled in.

Stringer tugged on Francis' sleeve. "Come on, let's go—"

Kasa hobbled over to Stringer's door, her arthritic hip clearly paining her. "Did you have some of that splendid fresh caramel corn down on the Old Orchard Pier?"

Stringer nodded, though Francis saw he was too worried for chitchat.

Kasa frowned. "Good heavens, what's happened?"

"We don't know," Francis replied. "Kate hasn't returned from the art institute and Sam never made it home after we got back to town."

Kasa's screen door banged, and Buster walked slowly toward the car, a pair of suspenders hanging at his sides. His protuberant belly was mostly covered with a white T-shirt, and he looked a bit winded.

"Buster, okay?" Francis asked, quietly.

Kasa waved her hand. "It's nothing. He's been a little short of breath is all. He was trying to exercise and it was too much for him. Of course he won't let me call the doctor." She shook her head. "Stubborn, that man."

Kasa looked at Buster disapprovingly. "You should not be in public looking like a bum. What kind of heathen are you?"

Francis was also growing impatient.

"Lovely, we have visitors," Buster said, acknowledging both Francis and Stringer.

Kasa shooed him away. "They have to go find Kate and Sam."

Buster looked confused.

"They're missing."

Buster immediately became serious. *"Missing?"* He stepped around Kasa and spoke to Francis. "Where do you think they are?"

"We don't know, but we're going to check the roads. Sam was alone on her small scooter."

Buster put first one, then his other arm through his suspenders and stretched them over his shoulders. "We will go at once. I will get my coat and keys. Just tell me where we should search." His forehead contracted into a deep frown. "Poor dear. We *must* find her."

All three of them knew Buster had to be thinking of his son, who many years before was driven off the road on his bicycle by a drunk driver and died alone in a roadside ravine.

Kasa put her hands on his chest to stop him. "You know you aren't feeling well. You must rest. Francis and the sheriff will search."

He turned away from her. "Nonsense. There is no time to spare."

"They don't need to also worry about an old man stumbling around in the dark!" Kasa called after him as he hurried into the house. She shook her head. "Don't worry, I'll keep him here."

Stringer shook Francis' arm. "Let's go."

"Thanks," Francis said to Kasa. "We've got to get going. I'll let you know."

"You do that."

He backed the Jeep out of her yard and sped away. Crossing the salt flats on the way to town, Francis glanced over at Stringer, who was staring hard at the sides of the road. He reached over and touched Stringer's shoulder. "We'll find her."

Stringer shrugged him off then rolled his window down and hung his head out.

In town, Francis turned down Harbor Avenue toward the main wharf.

"Where are you going?" Stringer asked, annoyed.

"Back to where we left her."

"But we saw her drive off."

"Just checking." Francis pulled up to Pike's shack. They got out and looked around. Francis walked over and checked where Sam's scooter had been locked to a post. Nothing looked out of the ordinary.

Stringer got up on his toes and peered through the window into the shack. He pushed back. "*Shit—*"

"What?" Francis said. "Is she in there?"

Stringer pointed to the window.

Francis hesitantly looked through the dirty glass. There on the work bench were the remains of the dog, its stuffing gutted and littering a collection of engine parts. The dog's head was jammed on top of a tool rack, its unpatched eye staring at the window. "What in the world?"

Chapter Twenty-eight

DESPITE FEELING DIZZY AFTER WATCHING THE GIRL FLY OFF THE cliff, Kate got down on all fours at the edge and searched for her, for any sign of life. It was hard to see in the waning light, but Kate thought she saw something—an arm perhaps—move on the ledge beyond the bike. "Are you all right?" she yelled.

Kate listened but there was no response.

Perhaps another subtle movement. She had to get help, but had no cellphone and was way outside of town, beyond any houses.

Kate cupped her hands and yelled down toward the wreck. "Hang on! I'm going to get you out of there!" She had no idea if that was true or not, but she wasn't going to let the girl die alone with no hope that someone was coming for her.

Kate ran back up the trail, screaming for help as loudly as she possibly could, turning so that her voice projected in every direction. Hearing nothing, she decided she had to somehow get down to the injured girl herself. Kate remembered there was a long pair of jumper cables in the trunk of the Malibu, so she retrieved the cables and a small flashlight. On the way back down the trail, she yelled several more times but still heard no reply.

Kate tied the cables to a piece of rusted angle iron driven into the rock then lowered them down over the edge. They reached far enough she figured she could shimmy down to the ledge and make her way over to the scooter and the girl.

"Help me..." she heard the victim moan.

"I'm coming. You're alive, thank god."

Kate lay down next to the cables and took hold of them with both hands so she could control her slide over the cliff. She looked up toward the darkening sky and said a sort of prayer. "I know I haven't been very responsible lately, but I'd appreciate some help here."

Despite her considerable fear of heights, and tendency to sea-sickness, Kate nudged herself over the edge and, without looking, slid down the cables, her hands burning as she descended to the narrow ledge. She was relieved when her feet touched rock, though the broken shale was unstable beneath her. Holding tight to the cables with one hand, she reached out with the other and took hold of a thin cedar tree miraculously growing from a crevice in the cliff.

"Help…" Kate heard again, weaker than before.

The gathering fog and enclosing darkness made it difficult to see the injured girl so Kate focused on the direction of her voice. "I'm coming for you."

Kate pushed the fingers of one hand into a crack in the rock face then gradually let go of the cables with the other hand. Steadying herself, she took a couple of small steps and rested next to the cedar. Jammed between the rock face and an outcropping she couldn't possibly get around, the wrecked scooter blocked her way. Below, the cliff dropped off into the deep ravine. She reached out with her foot and nudged the rear fender, which seemed solidly jammed between the rocks. Kate crouched, let go of the cedar and lunged forward, grabbing hold of the fender, then the flattened tire. The smell of hot oil made her fear the scooter might catch fire.

She heard the girl stir. "I…can't breathe."

Kate's heart beat so furiously she thought it might knock her off the ledge. Scared she might be about to die, Kate tried to calm herself by quickly humming one of her mother's Lakota lullabies. She slid the flashlight from her pocket, and with the light in her mouth began carefully climbing over the wreckage, testing each piece for stability. She stepped up onto the torn vinyl seat, maintaining her balance as the bike settled. Despite feeling dizzy, she squeezed past the outcropping, lowering herself onto an even narrower section of ledge. She tried to avoid a trickle of water coming from a crack, but one foot skidded on a section of wet, unstable rock, sending pebbles and pieces of shale over the edge. She freaked when she heard how long it took for them to hit the bottom. "Shiiitt."

This *really* could be the end, leaving the girl and Stringer and Francis—even Richard—alone.

The girl cried weakly. "My back hurts so bad…can't breathe."

"Almost there," Kate said, refocusing on the girl. Staring straight ahead, she started crawling again, catching a glimpse of the moon coming up over the ocean. It was beautiful, hopeful, some sort of spiritual guide. She glanced skyward again. "Thank you."

Kate lifted her head so the flashlight illuminated the girl. She saw short, tousled blond hair mixed with blood, and strangely streaked with a blue tinge. Anxious to reach her, Kate edged closer, moving her hands from one crevice to another. As she got close to the girl, Kate realized one of her legs was twisted oddly behind her, a bare foot jammed into her spine. Her denim shorts were partly torn off and there was a deep gash running down her flank revealing dark red muscle. The girl's chest was wedged between another, smaller outcropping and the rock face, upon which were streaks of bloody prints from the one hand she could move.

The sight of the blood startled Kate. She looked away, tried to focus on the ocean. With the help of the moon's brightening reflection on the water, she thought there might be something moving on the beach far below. Something sizeable, a horse perhaps. She vaguely remembered Francis had mentioned it was a place where people liked to ride.

"Gotta—help me—" the girl whispered, "—get out of here." It was painful to hear how hard it was for her to get air into her lungs.

"I think there's someone down on that beach. I'm going to scream really loud."

"Good."

Kate got up on her knees and braced herself against the girl, which was the only way she could cup her hands around her mouth without falling. The girl murmured in pain. Kate took in a huge breath and yelled. Her voice echoed sharply down the walls of the ravine. As soon as the echoes stopped, she yelled again, as hard as she possible could. Taking the flashlight from under her arm, she aimed it at the beach and rapidly waved it back and forth.

With a hand cupped behind one ear, she listened.

Nothing.

The girl started to whimper.

"You gotta hang in there."

Kate repeated yelling and flashing the light several times, waiting in between for any sign from the beach.

After a brief silence, the girl spoke again. "We're fucked…"

I know.

"Not yet," Kate said, with as much confidence as she could muster. She again flashed the light up and down the beach. Suddenly, she got dizzy again, felt like she was going to fall. She had the sensation someone was pushing her over the edge. She took hold of the girl's good ankle to steady herself. Her skin was cold and clammy, and even though she cried out, Kate held on till she felt more stable.

"Sorry. I thought I was going over. There's nothing else I could hold onto."

"No problem," the girl whispered in a gurgling voice, containing a hint of welcome sarcasm. "You're only—on a cliff—trying to save me."

Kate liked this kid. A few seconds later, Kate thought she saw a flicker of light on the beach.

Yes, there was a weak light! Kate turned her flashlight on again and vigorously waved it back and forth. Then she thought of the SOS Morse Code signals her railroad father had taught her when he used to let her ride with him up in the locomotive. *SOS: dot-dot-dot / dash-dash-dash / dot-dot-dot.* She was pretty sure that was it.

Kate braced herself again, directed the flashlight where she'd seen the light, and with her thumb on the switch, clicked out the signal.

She waited.

She aimed the light and clicked out the signal again, this time more slowly.

Several faint flashes of light returned from the beach. "They know Morse Code! Three dashes, then something else." She waited, hoping they would repeat it. It came again: - - - / -·-

"'O-K," she said to the girl. "They sent back, 'O-K.' They got the SOS signal."

"Cool," the girl said, weakly. "They got a helicopter?"

"I'm sure they'll get help." Kate rested against the rock face.

The girl whispered something Kate couldn't hear. She squeezed her head in closer to the girl's. "What did you say?"

"So much pain…I know I'm dying."

Kate made sure the girl's back was covered, taking care not to touch the gash in her flank. She smelled beer on the girl's breath, pot in her hair.

"We'll get you out of here." Kate touched the girl's cold arm. "I'm Kate."

The girl coughed up some blood. "Too hard to talk…"

Kate wanted to ask her name, tell her she, too, used to drink and do drugs and drive. But she could do that later. Maybe.

"Just rest. I wish I had water for you, but I don't dare try to get back up to my car."

The girl's body jerked. "Don't leave me."

Kate laid her head on a small mound of shale close to the girl's. "I'll stay right here. Don't talk; save your strength."

Kate held the palm of her hand lightly on the girl's back and again softly hummed the Lakota lullaby.

"Nice," the girl said, in a barely audible whisper.

Realizing the girl was shivering, Kate unzipped her fleece and did her best to curl around her as much as she could. The girl's back and buttocks were cold against Kate's warm belly. She gingerly covered the girl's exposed leg with her own.

One of the girl's arms was twisted partially beneath her, her swollen fingers sticking out at unnatural angles. It was as if it they were asking for help. Kate reached over and intertwined her fingers with the girl's.

Lying there cradling another suffering human being, Kate thought of the many times she'd gotten hurt drinking. Never on a cliff, but almost as bad. Feeling the girl struggling to breathe, Kate felt intense compassion for her, wanted badly to save her. Strangely, as Kate tried to warm the girl she wondered if she'd ever felt this close to another human being.

Kate put her mouth close to the girl's ear. "I won't leave you, no matter what."

Before long, Kate also started to shiver. The whole world seemed to have become stone cold. Her left leg started to cramp up so she straightened it, inadvertently disturbing an unstable piece of ledge, which shifted under them. Startled, Kate held the girl tighter. Several pieces of loose rock went over and fell into the ravine. Scared to move, Kate barely dared to breathe, lest the whole side of the cliff collapse. Feeling desperate but needing to keep herself together, she closed her eyes and tried to think of comforting slogans she'd heard at AA meetings.

Another piece of ledge broke off and fell from the cliff. Scared herself, Kate tried to think of how terrified the girl must be. Kate settled her breathing then leaned forward. "Remember, you are not alone," she whispered softly in the girl's bloodied ear.

The girl's lips parted. "Are you afraid of dying?" she asked in a raspy whisper.

"A little."

"Me, too."

Kate felt a wave of gratitude for the gift of her sobriety, of being delivered from the hellish life she and Stringer had lived in California. "There was a time I didn't care, but now I do."

The girl ever so gently squeezed Kate's fingers then fell silent again.

CHAPTER TWENTY-NINE

STRINGER HAD RECOILED AT THE SIGHT OF THE SHREDDED DOG, A mixture of fear and desperation overtaking his face.

Francis, too, was shocked at what he saw. "Why would she do that?"

Stringer frowned. "How do you know it was her?"

"Who else?"

"Maybe that mean-ass Pike. He might have threatened her." Stringer shook his head. "Or she's just given up again."

Francis faced Stringer. "What do you mean, 'again'? This sounds like trouble."

Stringer became agitated. "What's that supposed to mean?"

"I mean I'm scared what might be going on."

"I told you she's been abused and shit. And *so what* if she's trouble? She's not as much trouble as Mom and me. You didn't throw us out like trash. At least not yet."

"Stringer, that's not fair."

"Look, she's weird. It's like she gives up on life *and* is a survivalist at the same time." He headed back to the Jeep. "Come on, we've got to get to the Mill Pub. There's a place near there she goes to be alone. Maybe that's where she went."

Francis got in and they headed up Harbor Avenue. As they passed the jail, Charlie saw them, pulled his cruiser alongside and rolled down his window. "Any luck?"

"No sign of her," Francis said. "But we found a cut-up stuffed animal in Pike's shack."

Charlie looked confused.

"Stringer won it for Sam in Old Orchard. She, or somebody, ripped the stuffing out of it and left it on his workbench."

"What the hell's that supposed to mean?"

"She's upset, Charlie. I'm worried she might try to hurt herself."

Stringer leaned across the seat. "She's done it before."

Charlie shook his head. "I can't believe all the trouble you two get into."

"Neither can I," Francis said. "We need to find her."

Charlie put his cruiser back in gear. "Let's keep looking. I've let the state police know what's going on. Call me with anything. Otherwise, let's meet at the info booth in half an hour." He leaned toward Francis. "Any word from Kate?"

"No."

"You all are having quite a night. Hang in there, we'll find them."

Charlie drove around the perimeter of the town looking for evidence of a crash—a broken guardrail, fresh skid marks, or where someone had flattened weeds along the road. After several miles, he hadn't seen anything and remembered Stringer had said Sam liked to go to Black Rock Beach, so he turned around and headed in that direction. The muscles of his neck were tense as he raced down the road. He did not want to find another disaster; the town had had enough.

Trying to focus on looking for Sam, Charlie was distracted by the speaker from his police radio crackling on the dash. Same old bullshit: trespassing, another B&E at a summer camp up on Shadow Pond. The experienced thieves liked to get in and out before most of the summer people arrived. But no matter how many times he told homeowners not to leave valuables in their camps, they always left some sentimental family heirlooms behind, and then were in his office crying about losing them. The robbery sprees hadn't been nearly as bad before drugs invaded the area. He'd barely heard of heroin five years ago, and now it seemed to be everywhere, as easy to get as beer at a package store. It alone was fueling crime at a rate many people could only deal with by ignoring it. "This is Maine," people would often say, like that was some kind of immunization against the bad things going on in the rest of the country. They should spend a week working with him.

Charlie turned off the main road and descended a steep hill to the beach, a beautiful sweep of sand in a cove carved out of a rugged hill by the receding glacier. It was almost dark when he drove into the unlit gravel parking area bordered by large logs laid end-to-end. He parked close to the beach. It was the first time he'd had a few minutes to himself all day so he got out, leaned against the warm hood of his cruiser and admired the last glow of sunset as it disappeared like an apparition from the tops of the offshore clouds. He watched a series of waves break over the sand then fizzle back into the blue-black sea.

Growing up in Port Clyde, Charlie could never get enough of the ocean, especially at night when he'd listen to the waves rhythmically churning around the rock outcroppings below his family's modest home. He was fascinated by the foam spray rising above the rocks in the moonlight. He felt like he had his own Old Faithful right there in Maine.

Charlie thought back to his father taking him fishing for striped bass off the beach after work. Walking into the surf in their high rubber waders, they'd cast out as far as they could then return to the beach and set their poles deep into the wet sand. They'd collect dried seaweed and driftwood and build small campfires just beyond the tide's reach around which they sat on bait pails and talked. If the Red Sox were playing, his dad hung a transistor radio off their lantern pole, a metal coat hanger jammed into it for an antenna. Charlie could still hear Curt Gowdy's voice calling the game, especially his rising excitement when Yastrzemski flew through the air to catch a ball in front of the *Green Monster*, or when he would belt one of his soaring homers clear out of Fenway Park.

On Saturday nights, his father let Charlie have a sip of his cold Narragansett, describing his forays into France on D Day as a paratrooper with the 82nd Airborne as if they'd been a great adventure. In his father's face, though, Charlie saw the true horror of the War. It wasn't until his dad's funeral that Charlie learned from another veteran, only a handful of his father's comrades survived that first harrowing night.

Charlie pushed himself off the hood of his cruiser and adjusted his gun belt. He knew Stringer was a good kid and felt bad he was mixed up with that Sam girl. Charlie was sure she was no good. And that asshole from Rhode Island? He'd like to shoot the bastard, sink him in a bog somewhere.

Then he caught himself. "Probably better not."

He thought about Francis and how much he'd helped his struggling son, Nathan, by teaching him to paint. Nobody knew the term autism back then, or at least Charlie'd never heard of it. He smiled, thinking back to when he rather dramatically broke from McNeal during Stringer's trial and told the truth about that bastard. He had been scared to do it, but it had felt good and led to McNeal being run out of town and Charlie becoming sheriff. Truth was, Francis and Stringer meant a lot to Charlie. Kate, he still wasn't so sure about, but he accepted her because those two loved her.

Charlie realized the reception on his radio was poor because of the surrounding cliffs. As much as he was enjoying a little respite from everything, he figured he'd better get back up to the main road in case anything was happening.

When Charlie crested the hill his radio came alive again.

"Sheriff One, come in." It was Nancy McGreevy, the dispatcher. Her voice held an unusual urgency. "Charlie, come in."

She never called him Charlie on the radio. He snapped the mic off the dash. "Charl—ah Sheriff One here."

"Need you up off Route One, near the old lookout. Report of someone yelling for help. A guy horseback riding on the beach called it in. Sounds urgent."

Charlie thought for a moment. "You're talking about the overlook, right?"

"10-4."

"Long way up from that beach. You sure that's right?"

"That was the report. Whoever called said the voice sounded desperate."

"All right, I'll head over."

"Where've you been?"

"Searching down by Black Rock. Poor reception. You heard from Monroe?"

"He called a little while ago, said they were waiting for you at the info booth."

"Roger, I'll pick them up on my way through."

"Do you want me to send fire and rescue or the staties?"

"Send rescue with their tactical team, but they don't need to bring every damn fire truck in the county. That old road's narrow and steep. They'll need their four-wheel-drive brush rig with the litter and ropes and all."

"10-4."

Charlie felt bad he had been out of radio range. He flicked on his blue lights and floored it, tearing through loose gravel onto the main road back to town. He reached to turn on his siren but decided not to get everyone riled up. He didn't need a line of yahoos racing to the scene.

Chapter Thirty

At the info booth, Charlie saw Francis' Jeep parked in front. He pulled to an abrupt stop. "Get in," he called out.

Francis was alarmed by Charlie's urgency. "What's going on?"

"Get in. I'll tell you on the way."

With Francis and Stringer aboard, Charlie headed north.

Stringer was uncomfortably jammed between Francis and Charlie. "Where're we going?"

Charlie turned onto Route One, his cruiser's engine roaring as he passed several cars.

"Got a call somebody's yelling for help from the overlook. Dispatch said a horseback rider on the beach heard a woman up on the cliff."

Francis frowned. "The beach? That's way below the overlook."

"I know, but that was the report."

Stringer looked at Charlie. "You think it's Sam?"

Charlie cleared his throat. "No idea, but somebody's in trouble." He hit the siren, racing past two cars and a lobster truck.

"Falmouth Ambulance on the air responding," came over the radio. "Engine One, Heavy Rescue responding."

Charlie grabbed the mic off the dash. "Orton, bring your four-wheel-drive brush truck. They must be near the old overlook. Road's probably washed out."

"10-4, Charlie."

Charlie continued driving at a high rate of speed with one hand on the wheel while talking on the radio with the other. He glanced at Francis, pointed to the glove compartment. "There's a flashlight in there with a red wand on it. When we get there I want you to flag down the rescue folks and keep others out. Back-up's coming, but at this hour on a Sunday it'll be a while before they get out here."

Charlie took a hard right onto a secondary road, its pavement cracked and broken from many winters' worth of salt. "Mostly keep the gawkers away from the entrance to that old road. Don't need a bunch of rubber-neckers clogging it up."

Charlie pulled to a stop in a sandy spot just off the road, a cloud of fine brown dust passing through his headlight beams. He clicked the mic. "Dispatch, I'm on the scene."

Charlie aimed his cruiser's spotlight at the opening in the trees that led to the old road. They all got out, and Charlie pulled a long black flashlight from under his seat and turned it on. That's when he and Francis both saw Kate's blue Malibu parked at the edge of the woods.

"What the...?" Francis said, running to Kate's car.

Stringer started down the old road then suddenly stopped. "Oh my god—" He reached for something inside the underbrush. "No!" he yelled, slowly picking up a piece of broken plastic.

Francis wheeled around. "What is it?"

Stringer didn't respond.

Francis hurried over and shown his light on what Stringer was holding—a piece of plastic from the scooter with a scraped yellow "Music Heals" bumper sticker.

"It's Sam's," Stringer said, his jaw trembling.

Francis put his hand on Stringer's shoulder, turned and yelled. "Charlie, over here. It's a piece of Sam's scooter."

Stringer looked up at Francis. "What's happened?"

"Not sure, but we're going to find her."

Charlie and the firemen began searching the road and the edge of the woods, where they figured Sam might have gone through the under-brush.

"Sam!" Stringer yelled.

Sirens approached from the highway, flashing red, blue, and white lights lighting up the night. A pumper truck pulled in next to Charlie's cruiser, followed by a state police cruiser and an ambulance. Suddenly the scene was lit up like a Christmas pageant.

The door of the pumper opened and a large fireman in bunker gear climbed down. He put on a white hat, stretched suspenders over his T-shirt, and hurried to where they were standing. "What you got, Charlie?"

"Hey, Chief, looks like someone on a scooter crashed through here.

We just started searching."

Chief Simon surveyed the scene. "Know who it is?"

Charlie lowered his voice. "That Sam girl, with the guitar."

Stringer wheeled around, his eyes wide. "She's my girlfriend."

"Okay," the chief said, in a comforting way. "Let's find her." He turned to the other personel. "Set up the floodlights, bring the ropes and litter. We'll search along the road down to the overlook. Got to be in the woods here somewhere. And remember, the county closed this area because the cliff is unstable. Stay away from it."

Stringer grabbed his arm. "You gotta find her."

Chief Simon looked at Stringer. "We'll do our best."

A group with bright headlights methodically worked their way through the woods, descending toward the overlook. The terrain was thick and rocky, and they encountered pockets of fog as they made their way down.

"Hey, Chief," a fireman called out. "There's fresh scrapes on the ledge in the middle of the old road, here. Maybe they went straight down."

Several men joined him and they followed the scrape marks to a set of foot-drags at the bottom. The fog reflected off their light beams but they were able to see that the marks led straight to the cliff.

A state trooper knelt at the edge. "Damn. Went right over." He turned and yelled up the road. "Get some floodlights down here!"

Several men shone their flashlights over the edge, where the earth seemed to just disappear into thickening fog, its particles illuminating like a million tiny sparklers. Stringer saw only vague outcroppings of ledge and tree tops. He yelled for Sam.

The trooper touched Stringer's arm. "Be careful." He gently coaxed Stringer back from the edge. "While they're bringing the equipment down, let's just listen and see if we hear anything."

Stringer got down on all fours. The only thing he heard was the muted, long-off hoot of an owl and the creaking back and forth of tall trees lining the ravine.

Stringer stayed close to the trooper. "You think she's okay?"

"I hope so," he replied. "Just got to find her as fast as we can. Gets real cold out here at night."

Stringer stared over the cliff into the foggy darkness.

Behind them, the fire department's brush truck made its way down the old road, parking so that the winch on the front of the rig was close to the edge.

Francis and an out-of-breath Charlie came up behind Stringer. "See anything?"

Stringer shook his head.

"Why is Kate's car here?" Francis said.

"She ever been here before?" Stringer asked.

Francis hesitated, blushed. "Once. The other night."

"But why would she come back—at night?"

"Be quiet," the trooper said. "I thought I heard something."

Everyone listened. After a few seconds, Stringer raised a hand. "I heard something, too."

"Probably the wind," Charlie said.

"No," the trooper said, "it was someone."

"Help us…" came a distinct cry.

Stringer's eyes opened wide. "Mom!"

"That's Kate!" Francis said, leaning over the cliff as far as he could without falling. "Where are you?"

"On a ledge, with a girl trapped under the rocks."

"Mom!" Stringer yelled, "Is she okay? Are you okay?"

"Don't move!" the sergeant yelled, cutting Stringer off. He spoke sternly to the others. "Let me do the talking."

Frustrated, Stringer obeyed.

"This is Sargent Leblanc, Maine State Police. Can you hear me?"

"Yes—" Kate's voice was weak.

"Can you tell us your condition? The girl's? And exactly where you are? The fog is making it hard to see with our lights."

"On a narrow ledge, just beyond the scooter. The girl's wedged under a rock. She's…"

Kate's voice trailed off. A chilling breeze blew up from the cold surf in the distance.

"What did you say about the girl?"

"Unconscious."

Kate's voice faded again.

Francis nudged the trooper. "You've got to get them out of there."

The trooper looked straight at Francis. "You see all these people rigging up rescue equipment? I need to keep her engaged and get as much info as possible while they're getting ready. And I need you to stay out of the way."

Francis nodded and stepped back.

The trooper yelled again. "Is she breathing?"

After a few moments, Kate responded. "Sort of. I've been lying next to her, but now I'm so cold I can't warm her up."

"Are you injured?"

"Just scraped up."

Francis put his arm around Stringer's shoulders, which were quivering.

Sergeant Leblanc looked over at Chief Simon. "Sounds about twelve or fifteen feet down and over a ways, but I haven't gotten a good look yet."

The chief frowned. "The boys are about ready to repel, but if it's too dangerous, we'll have to back off. If we need it, do you think a Coast Guard chopper can fly in this fog?"

The sergeant straightened his back. "Possibly. Depends how thick it gets. This ravine is a helluva place, rock walls on both sides, but those guys are the best."

"Yeah."

Maggie Sheltra, a firefighter with red hair escaping from under her helmet tapped Sergeant Leblanc on the shoulder. She held up a rope with a large loop on the end. "Sir, we'd like to tie you off to the rig just in case."

"Good idea." He put his arms through the loop, which she tightened around his waist.

A couple of the firefighters had set up searchlights secured to the front of the brush truck. They leaned them out over the cliff and turned them on. Powerful beams of light shown through the fog. Everyone moved closer to the edge to try and get a better look.

Maggie pointed. "There, I see the scooter, wedged between the rocks."

Thick white fog again obscured the view.

"Quiet!" Stringer said. "Mom said something."

"What's her name?" asked the sergeant.

"Kate," Francis replied.

"Kate!" Sergeant Leblanc yelled down to her. "What did you say?"

"I feel like I'm slipping—going to fall. My arm's numb. I can't tell for sure."

Francis' heart pounded in his throat.

"What's the rock ledge like between here and there?" Leblanc yelled back.

"Shale. Keeps breaking off. It's a long way down."

"Kate," Francis said, "there's a great crew here to get you off of there."

"You'd better hurry."

Stringer stood. "Mom!"

Francis grabbed his arm and pulled him back down.

"String—" came Kate's slightly more energetic reply.

Stringer shot up again. "Hold on, Mom. We're coming to get you!"

"Love you, String."

He leaned dangerously close to the edge. "I love you too. And Sam…"

Sergeant Leblanc abruptly turned to another trooper and told him to move Stringer away from the cliff. The trooper took hold of Stringer's arm.

"You gotta get down there!" Stringer yelled as he shook the trooper off. As Stringer moved out of the way, he caught a glimpse of the jumper cables tied around the angle-iron protruding from the rock.

Firefighters tied two members of the tactical rescue team to the heavy front bumper of the brush rig. As they prepared to rappel, the rock beneath them broke loose. The lip of the cliff collapsed, dropping them until their ropes caught, slamming them face-first into the remaining wall of the cliff.

"Shit!" one of them said, pushing himself back from the jagged rocks.

"Pull 'em up!" Chief Simon yelled.

Everyone grabbed hold of the ropes. Straining, they pulled them back up over the collapsed rock. Maggie immediately attended to one of the men who was bleeding from gouges in his forehead and cheek.

The chief gestured to the brush rig. "Move all this back—now! The whole cliff could let go. Must be two—three hundred feet to the bottom of that ravine."

"I'll back it up," a fireman said, jumping into the rig.

Sergeant Leblanc moved off to the side. He keyed the mic on his lapel. "Dispatch, find out if the Coast Guard chopper can fly. This cliff is falling apart on us. Got to get these people out of there."

Static came over the mic. "You're breaking up…did you say, call for the bird?"

"Roger that."

"10-4."

In the confusion, no one untied the tactical team members from the front bumper, so when the brush rig backed up, it yanked them backwards, almost knocking them over again.

"Sorry," the fireman called from the cab.

One of the team members waved him off. "No problem."

Stringer stood by himself in the darkness outside of the floodlights. He stared at the jumper cables, figured they must be what Kate used to shimmy down. He didn't understand what exactly was going on except he knew the two women he loved were injured, scared, and trapped on a collapsing cliff. A wave of nausea swept through him. For a few seconds he thought he would throw up. He squeezed his eyes tightly, trying to focus on Sam's face, the one he had tried to paint. She was beautiful. And she was damaged, like she'd told him. *I know why Sam went over.* Thoughts raced through Stringer's mind as he flashed back to Old Orchard and how hard it was for her to believe people just wanted to be nice to her. All she'd ever known was manipulation, people trying to get something out of her. That's why she kept saying, "It's all bullshit." But it wasn't. It was real.

Stringer looked over at the rescuers. They didn't seem to be making any progress. He'd have to do something himself. He thought back to Walker's Point when Delbert was drowning off the shipwrecked *Maiden.* He felt his feet trying to stay steady as the bow rocked back and forth in the pounding waves. Stringer felt the strength of his body in the moments before he dove into the stormy Atlantic.

"Stringer, you okay?" Francis called to him.

Stringer nodded. "Yeah, just staying out of the way."

"Okay."

Sergeant Leblanc was talking on his radio. Sounded like it would take at least forty-five minutes to get the helicopter out there, if it was able to fly.

Stringer's face tightened. His head was hot as he felt a surge of adrenaline. The skin on his forearms tingled. He glanced over at Francis and Charlie, and the others. They were still trying to figure out what to do. Stringer knew they'd stop him if they saw him make a run for it. He stared at the jumper cables, which were just at the edge of the area illuminated by the floodlights. He had to do this.

CHAPTER THIRTY-ONE

COMMANDER SAMSON OF STATION SOUTH PORTLAND STARED AT the large, multicolored weather radar screen in the command center. He spoke in a seasoned though urgent voice, the recent crash of a chopper in rough seas heavy on his mind. "On the topo, it looks like there's a fairly narrow ravine—maybe 200 feet across—that runs from where they're trapped, east down to a strip of beach. In this fog it'll be treacherous trying to get a Jayhawk up in there." He squinted, leaned toward the display, and pointed at several breaks in the cloud cover. "At least it's not a solid fogbank."

Lt. Jeremy Cooke, the station's most experienced pilot, nodded. "I agree, Sir, and offshore there are even more clear spots."

"Though there's a fairly fast-moving storm coming up from the south." The Commander looked at Lt. Cooke. "I know you want to get those people off of there. You're a hell of a pilot, but you know what I think about cliff rescues, especially with the winds they're predicting." He looked at the screen again. "This is a tricky one, not out over open ocean where we belong."

Lt. Cooke studied another screen. "Potential wind shears are worrisome, but we've done these successfully before."

"Damn fools, out on that cliff—" The commander shook his head. "In the dark, no less." He turned to Lt. Cooke. "So, what's your plan?"

"We'll attempt to come up through the ravine from the shore, see how badly the winds are kicking up. We'll use our searchlight, of course, but if the fog-glare prohibits it, we'll depend on the fire department to light up the scene. Hopefully, we'll be able to see so we can hover low enough to drop the basket and not hit the rock face on either side."

"Or disturb that cliff, which is already unstable." He looked the lieutenant in the eye. "If you go down in that ravine, it may be all over."

Lt. Cooke stayed steady. "If we don't try, Sir, it'll surely be over for those two women. If we can't get into an acceptable position, or they tell us the rotors are causing more of the cliff to break up, we'll pull out."

The Commander stroked his chin. "All right. I'll send a second Jayhawk as backup. We don't have a boat in the area, but that wouldn't help anyway. It'll be you and the local squads. Luckily, those guys up there are good." He glanced at Lt. Cooke. "But they aren't Coast Guard."

"Yes Sir." Lt. Cooke saluted then walked to the staging room and looked out the window at the flight line where two helicopters were being readied. Pulling on his flight suit, he watched Chris Duvall, his flight mechanic, inspect their sleek red-and-white bird. Even after eight years as a search and rescue pilot, Jeremy always felt a rush as he got ready to fly. He couldn't imagine doing anything else with his life, even if missions like this were some of the most dangerous. He adjusted his helmet strap then pushed through the door into a gusty wind. He carefully checked the outside of the helicopter then climbed aboard.

Inside the tight cockpit, Lt. Cooke and his co-pilot strapped themselves into their seats. As the ground crew prepared them for departure, Lt. Cooke methodically went through his pre-flight checklist. He verified that all his green, yellow, and blue displays were up then entered the coordinates of the mission into his GPS. As soon as they were cleared for liftoff, he pushed the throttles forward with his right hand, holding the stick with the other.

As they rose above the tarmac, co-pilot McAndrew activated his mic. "Pretty gusty from the southeast."

Lt. Cooke nodded, pulled back on the stick and they banked up into the wind coming off the ocean. It was bumpy getting up out of the unpredictable surface currents but they were soon over Peaks, then the Chebeague Islands, flying north toward Winter's Cove. Though it was choppy, the winds didn't start getting really bad until they entered Maquoit Bay on their way to the target area.

As they began descending toward the shoreline, strong gusts buffeted the Jayhawk. "Tighten up those belts," Lt. Cooke said into his mouthpiece. "Going to be a rough ride."

CHAPTER THIRTY-TWO

STRINGER TIGHTENED HIS BELT, TOOK A DEEP BREATH AND BOLTED for the cliff. Several people shouted his name as he did a baseball-slide across rough gravel and broken shale, desperately grabbing for the cables as he careened over the edge. As if in slow motion, he felt his legs enter free air, his hands desperately searching for the jumper cables. Fog and shale dust clouded his eyes. As gravity hauled him downward, his left hand felt the cables and he grabbed them as hard as he could. His descent slowing, he twisted in midair, slinging his other hand onto the cable. As he jerked to a stop, his palms felt like they were on fire. The outstretched cable swung back toward the cliff, slamming him into crumbling rock. The air was momentarily knocked out of him as shards of stone punctured his forehead and tore his shirt.

After a few seconds, he got his breath back and felt the cables start to lift. He knew they were pulling him back up over the cliff. He relaxed his grip and slid down till his feet hit the clamps. From the reflection of the rescue lights, he saw a ledge just a few feet below him. He felt another strong tug on the cables, raising him up another foot. He let go and dropped, landing on the narrow shelf of rock. The rescuers must have lost their grip as the cables came down next to him.

He heard men cussing and yelling up above him. "Crazy kid!" A foggy searchlight swept over his face. Then he heard Charlie's familiar voice; he sounded frightened. "Stringer, now you listen to me. You stay right where you're at. It's a long way to the bottom of that ravine, covered with sharp pine trees that'll skewer you like a chicken. You got to let the professionals get you and the others out of there."

Sitting, Stringer tried to shimmy back against the rock face, but the shelf was so narrow he couldn't get a good purchase with the heels of his sneakers. The leg he'd landed on cramped and burned, but he was able to push himself up into a standing position. He hung onto a small tree branch to steady himself. Standing on his injured leg, the painful charley-horse subsided. He picked up the cables and slung them around his neck. He might need them.

"Stringer!" Charlie's voice was more urgent. "Can you hear me, boy?"

"Stringer, don't move!" This time it was Francis, stark fear in his voice.

"I'm going to help them," Stringer yelled up. "All you guys do is talk."

"Stringer, this is Sergeant Leblanc. You are breaking the law being down there!"

Stringer let out a nervous laugh. "Like I give a shit—"

"Now stay put while rescue figures out what to do."

"While you're at it, I'll get to my mom and Sam."

Ignoring their ongoing pleadings and ultimatums, Stringer crouched down and started crawling along the rock shelf toward the mangled scooter. He caught glimpses of its rear reflector as searchlights intermittently cut through the fog. After making it about six feet, he was feeling optimistic when his right knee landed on a patch of crumbling shale that gave way. He lurched forward so hard his chin smacked into the rocks, banging his teeth together. Holding perfectly still, he heard the shale hitting the side of the ravine as it fell far below him. Stringer tasted warm, salty liquid on his tongue, grasped for anything and caught hold of another small tree. He spit blood over the cliff then adjusted the jumper cables so they didn't choke him.

"Who's there?" A weak voice a short distance ahead of him.

"I'm coming for you." He didn't know if his mother realized it was him.

"Thank god."

Stringer felt stable rock in front of him, took hold of it and edged past the portion that had collapsed.

"Do you have—ropes for us?" The voice was so weak it barely sounded like his mother.

"Hang on." Stringer kept crawling, the lip of the cliff starting to dislodge under his weight. He felt a rumble as a section collapsed behind him. Knowing he was about to go over, he lunged forward, grabbing what was left of the rear frame of the scooter. His arm muscles strained as he held onto the flimsy metal, digging into the crumbling wall with his sneakers and knees. He kept struggling till he found solid rock cradling the scooter. As he wrapped his arm around the crumpled machine, he realized most of the shelf behind him was gone. There was no going back.

Stringer collapsed onto the scooter, panting to fill his lungs. When he tried to right himself his hand slid off the slippery gas tank. He realized it was covered with gas and blood. *Her* blood. And so was the rock shelf in front of him.

He heard sirens as well as vague voices above the cliff. Concentrating, he lifted his head, unwound the cables and hooked them on the crooked handlebars so they wouldn't fall. He saw a dim flashlight lying next to what he thought was his mother's leg. In the fog, he couldn't see Sam but assumed she was just beyond his mother. He quickly examined the scooter and realized it was jammed into what appeared to be a solid outcropping of rock, an obelisk of sorts.

Feeling the scooter was fairly secure, he cautiously pulled himself over it, crouching down just a couple feet from Kate. "Mom, it's me," he said softly, wanting to comfort, not shock her.

"What?" she said.

He moved closer. "It's me, Stringer."

Kate's head came up off the rock an inch or so. *"Stringer? What?"*

"Somebody called from the beach. The fire department is figuring out how to get down here." He searched for Sam. "'Cause the cliff, you know, it's falling apart."

"You can't be down here," Kate said, weakly.

"Well, I am." Stringer gently took hold of Kate's leg, partly to reassure her, partly for something to hold onto. The fog cleared for a few seconds and he got a better look at her. His mom's fleece was torn, her hair disheveled and wrapped around her neck. She looked cold and miserable.

Kate pointed. "The girl—I tried to keep her warm, but we're both freezing. She's barely breathing."

Stringer picked up the dying flashlight and shone it beyond his mom. His spirit sank when he saw Sam's blue shock of hair in the middle of her blood-stained head. "Sam…"

He started to crawl over his mom's feet to get closer to Sam, but there was not enough room on the narrow ledge. "Sam…it's Stringer."

Kate's eyes opened wider. "My, god, String…this is *Sam?*"

Stringer recoiled back from Sam's unmoving body. "Is she…alive?"

Kate touched Stringer's arm. "I think so."

Stringer's breathing became rapid. His chin quivered.

Kate tried to slide toward him, dislodging more loose shale. "I can't really move, String."

Stringer was frozen, dizzy.

"Can you crawl over to her?"

Stringer was terrified this girl he loved was gone, that he was looking at her dead body. "She *can't* be dead," he whispered.

Kate lifted her head a bit more. "Can you check her?"

"How?"

"Put your ear to her chest. Listen for a heartbeat, some breathing."

Stringer tightened his jaw. He wiped his eyes, put the flashlight in his mouth and gingerly crawled over Kate's legs, staying against the rock face.

Kate backed up a smidge to give him a little more room.

Stringer slid his body in next to Sam's, his heart pounding in his ears. He very gently touched her shoulder.

She was so cold.

He shimmied in a little closer, smelled the faint odor of weed on her hair. "Sam…" he whispered over her ear. "Can you hear me?"

No response. He couldn't even tell if she was breathing.

He lifted himself up on his bad elbow, and with the flashlight in his mouth, leaned over Sam. Her thick wool sweater was torn and matted with blood. He gently pulled the sweater away from her neck, revealing a disturbing, unnatural blue hue to her skin. He lowered his ear to her upper chest, which was so cold it didn't feel real. Scared of what he might not hear, he held his own breath and listened.

All he heard was the whistling and whooshing of rising winds in the pine trees.

Suppressing panic, Stringer plugged his other ear with his finger, held his breath again and laid his left ear against her firm flesh.

There was a distant, rapid thumping. Intermittently, a slight wheezing sound. He listened for a few seconds to make sure, then covered her up and looked at his mom. "She's still alive. I can hear her heart and some wheezing."

Stringer suddenly felt a surge of energy spiked with anger. He carefully rolled away from Sam and steadied himself against the rock face.

He looked up at the cliff. "She's alive!" he yelled with a voice that echoed through the ravine. "She's alive!"

"That's great!" someone yelled back down to him. "Which one?"

"Sam. Sam's alive!"

"So'm I!" Kate added.

"Can you keep her warm?"

"I'll try," Stringer said.

"The Coast Guard is sending two helicopters from Portland."

"They better hurry the hell up!" Stringer moved back toward Sam.

Kate tried to stay back out of Stringer's way. "Be careful, String. You're so close to the edge."

"I will. You alright?"

"Yeah." Her voice was emotional. "I had no idea it was her."

"It'll be okay, Mom," he said with conviction beyond his years.

Kate managed a faint smile. "Heard that before."

Stringer slid in next to Sam. He unbuttoned his shirt, nestled against her back, and wrapped his jacket around her as best he could.

Kate reached over and held onto his shoulder.

"I love her, Mom."

CHAPTER THIRTY–THREE

A S MUCH AS HE WANTED TO GET SAM OFF THE CLIFF, STRINGER knew there was nothing he could do but wait for the rescuers, and try to comfort her and keep her safe. He lay wrapped around her as closely as he could, occasionally stroking her long blue hair. Though exhausted, his mind raced. What in hell was his mother doing on a cliff with his girlfriend? Did they have a fight? How could they both even be there? He feared Sam drove off the cliff intentionally, but there were those foot drags in the gravel. Maybe she changed her mind at the last moment. His mother hadn't seemed to like his being with Sam, but Stringer knew she had to have slid down the jumper cables to try and save her. As he lay there, he realized it was a comfort having his mother behind him, holding tight to his shoulder.

Increasingly gusty winds swirled up through the ravine. A storm was blowing in, the air getting even colder. He felt his mom tuck the back of his shirt into his pants then he thought he felt the slightest movement of Sam's arm next to his. "Sam," he said, hoping it was true. He leaned closer and said her name again.

Her arm *definitely* moved—not a lot, but it moved. Her parched lips parted and her dry tongue tried unsuccessfully to moisten them. She attempted to speak but couldn't get words to form.

"Wait," Stringer said. He wet her lips with his then placed his ear close to her mouth. He listened intensely.

"String-er…" came a whisper, dry as desert air.

Stringer's heart sped.

Kate nudged him. "Did she say something?"

Stringer stayed focused on Sam. "I'm here. You had an accident."

Sam's right eye partially opened. "Shit—I'm alive."

"Yeah. I'm damn glad."

"Fuck—" Her eye closed again. "Where am I?"

"Partway down a cliff."

"Shitting me?"

"No. They're going to get us out of here."

Sam's arm moved a little. It looked like she tried to move her left leg, but it was broken and twisted under her. "I'm going over."

"The hell you are." Even though she couldn't really move, Stringer put his arm over her just in case.

"Push me—finish it."

Stringer was torn apart by her words, her giving up. He would help keep her alive until she could see some light in her life. "Just rest."

Kate lifted herself up on her elbows. "Do you hear that?"

"What, Mom?"

"A beating in the air, like a helicopter."

Stringer heard it, too. "'Bout time."

A flood of white light lit up the face of the cliff.

"The choppers are here," someone yelled over a megaphone from above. "They're going to make a pass over the ravine to figure out the best approach and how to deal with these winds. Just stay where you are."

"We're not going anywhere," Stringer murmured.

Within seconds, the rhythmic roar of the chopper approached from the direction of the ocean. As it slowed overhead, Stringer hunkered down against the nearly deafening whop-whop-whop of its rotors. The powerful wash from the blades blew his hair back as he tried to protect Sam. Kate covered both of them with her fleece jacket. Through squinted eyes he looked up and at first could see only the vague flashing of red strobe lights, but as the helicopter hovered, the fog partly cleared and he saw the letters USCG on the bottom of the aircraft. He felt a fleeting sense of relief.

As the chopper gradually descended, it started rocking side-to-side. The engines roared more loudly then it disappeared up into another cloud bank.

"Where're you going?" he yelled.

"Ha—" Sam said, weakly.

"They better come back." Stringer stretched his bruised leg, which was cramping again.

"Give them a chance," Kate said, holding his arm.

Within a couple of minutes, the thudding of the rotor blades returned as the helicopter made another approach. This time it stayed higher.

A voice came from a loudspeaker on the aircraft. "This is the United States Coast Guard. I'm Petty Officer Chuck LaVoie. I'll be coming down with a metal basket on a cable to get you out of there. Please stay—"

A savage gust of wind hit. The loudspeaker cut out as the chopper wobbled.

"Winds are too strong. We'll be back."

Again, the chopper pulled up out of the ravine and headed out to sea.

"Shit," Kate and Stringer said, together.

By then the fire department had illuminated the ravine and the cliff like daylight. With the fog thinning, Stringer could better see what was going on. He hadn't realized there was such a large rock overhang above them making it difficult for the chopper to get in close. Then he glanced down over the edge and about shit himself at how far it was to the bottom.

Someone above them spoke through a megaphone. "The pilot's having a hard time hovering in these winds, but if anyone can get you off of there, they can." There was a pause. "We'd try to rappel again, but the cliff keeps collapsing."

Kate tightened her grip on Stringer's arm.

The megaphone again. "They're coming in one more time with the rescue basket already down. They can't get in as close as they want because of the overhang, but the pilot will swing the basket with the rescue swimmer toward you so he can lasso that rock outcropping next to Sam. It looks pretty solid."

This sounded like a pretty crazy plan, but Stringer couldn't think of a better one. He looked up at the cliff and yelled. "Tell them Sam is caught in the rocks. They'll have to pull her out."

"Okay." Charlie. Hearing his voice was comforting.

Moments later, the chopper approached again. This time Stringer caught a good view of the sleek red-and-white machine, its whirring rotors suspended in the lights. The winds were still gusting, but hanging below the aircraft was a cable attached to a metal basket holding a guy in an orange suit and a helmet. He was hanging onto the sides of the basket with both hands, steadying himself like he was in a circus act.

When Officer LaVoie was about twenty feet away, he yelled over to

Stringer, who cupped his hand behind his ear trying to hear through the noise of the helicopter. "The pilot's going to try to swing me over so I can lasso that obelisk with a rope. That should steady me enough that I can pull the basket over."

"Okay," Stringer yelled back.

Stringer could see that LaVoie couldn't hear him, so he gave him a thumb's up.

"Be careful, String," Kate said, holding onto him while cowering against the vertical rock face behind her.

Stringer heard the subtle change in the helicopter's noise as the pilot gradually rolled back and forth, swinging the basket. LaVoie held a coil of rope in his hand, bracing himself with his knees against the front of the wire cage. As the pilot swung him a little harder, he straightened up, and like a cowboy trying to rope a steer, lifted the lasso above his head. As the basket swung toward the cliff, he let the lasso fly. It landed short of the rock and slid over the cliff.

After a couple more tries, LaVoie was able to securely loop around the outcropping. Just then, a hard gust of wind whipped the basket into the edge of the cliff, breaking off another section of rock. LaVoie was thrown about, losing his grip on the rope, which fell out of the swinging basket before he could grab it.

Kate screamed, drew her hands up to her face.

Regaining his balance, LaVoie quickly righted himself, got back into position and yelled into the microphone on the front of his suit. "Rope's on the rock but I lost the end. Going to try to grab it this time," he yelled.

Due to the erratic wind, the movement of the basket seemed even less controlled. Another gust hit, and it swung hard toward Stringer.

"Pull back!" LaVoie yelled into his mic as the basket suddenly dropped then jerked upwards under the rock outcropping. The rim of the metal cage caught on the sharp under-edge of the rocks, trapping the basket. The overly taught steel cable twanged, jolting LaVoie onto his back. "Go down. You're caught on the cliff!"

"Negative," came the urgent reply. "Rotors don't have enough clearance."

"Shit—" Stringer heard the helicopter's engine strain as he watched disaster unfolding in front of him. There was no way the guy was going to grab the rope now dangling over the cliff. Then Stringer thought of the jumper cables, which seemed pretty heavy duty. He leaned over and grabbed them off the handlebars. "Hey!" he yelled. "Maybe I can hook these onto your rope and throw you the other end. If they can just lower you a little bit, I think your basket will swing free then I can pull you over to get Sam."

"I can't endanger you!" The metal frame of the basket squeaked as it scraped against the hard rock.

Stringer looked at him like he was crazy. *"Endanger me?* What the hell do you think we've been doing?!"

"Hurry up!" the pilot yelled over LaVoie's radio. "I can't hold this position much longer."

LaVoie looked at Stringer. "Okay, hook the cables onto my rope and throw me the other end." Officer LaVoie readied himself as Stringer crawled back and hooked the cable clamps around the rope.

"When you're ready, throw me the other end of the jumpers!"

Stringer took careful aim and, without hesitating, let the cables fly through the air right into the rescuer's gloved hand.

"Good job!" LaVoie yelled. He asked his hoist operator to let him down, but the basket was still caught under the rock. He tried to maneuver so he could push off, but his movement changed the angle of the basket and broke off another piece of rock.

Without hesitating, Stringer lay down, held onto the rock with his arms, stretched his good leg over the edge and kicked the steel frame of the basket as hard as he could.

"Be careful!"

Stringer coiled his leg and kicked the metal solidly again. The basket swung free, the jumper cables tentatively holding it.

"Great!" LaVoie spoke into his mic. "Raise me up a few feet." The cable started to rise, bringing the basket even with Stringer. "Hold there!"

Stringer was face-to-face with the basket only six feet away. Officer LaVoie pulled hard on the jumper cables and when he was within a couple feet of the ledge, he tied them off to the frame of the basket. Stringer watched the chopper's rescue cable whipping in the wind, tugging on the basket. He hoped the jumper cables were strong enough to hold.

LaVoie quickly assessed the situation. He pointed to Sam. "She's the most serious?"

"Yeah. And she might jump if she could." It pained him to have to tell the guy, but he had to know.

"Okay, I get it. Looks like she's trapped behind that big rock. Can you pull her out of there?"

"Her leg is broken bad."

Officer LaVoie seemed to try to figure out how he could get onto the ledge, but there was no way. He looked at Stringer. "You're obviously a brave kid. I need you to pull her straight out by the legs, trying to straighten the broken one. And keep her spine in alignment. If you can get her close to the edge, I'll get her into the basket."

"You can do it, String," Kate said.

Stringer's jaw tightened. His mind again flashed back to that moment he jumped into the surging Atlantic. Somehow, the cold, pounding surf seemed more hospitable than dragging a badly injured Sam off a cliff.

He got down on his knees at her feet. "Sam, this is going to hurt, but we're going to save your life, whether you like it or not."

He first took hold of her normal foot then braced himself and gripped the twisted leg at the ankle.

"Leave me alone," Sam cried, in a stronger voice.

"Can't." Stringer started to pull. He was concerned how tightly she was jammed between the rocks.

"Pull her!" LaVoie yelled more urgently. "We've got to hurry!"

The pounding of the rotors made Stringer's head hurt. It was hard to see well with all the dust and fog. He tightened his biceps and pulled as hard as he could. Sam's twisted leg started to straighten; he felt things snap and grind. As he dislodged her from the rocks, she cried out in pain. He grit his teeth and kept pulling. Sam clawed her fingernails across the rock shelf with her one good hand, resisting as much as her weak body could, but it didn't stop him. She screamed like he was killing her, but he kept pulling, dragging her across the narrow shelf.

Bracing himself in the basket, which kept straining against the jumper cables, LaVoie leaned dangerously far forward and took hold of Sam's ankles. As he dragged her past Stringer, she tried to spit on him, but he just kept helping move her over the gap toward LaVoie, who was sitting low in the basket. When he finally had hold of Sam, she was so weak, she just slumped against him.

"I'll release the jumper cables and take her up. The other helicopter crew will come in for you and your mom."

Stringer watched Officer LaVoie cradling Sam's nearly lifeless body.

LaVoie undid the cables. Within seconds he was hoisted up into the fog. Feeling completely drained, Stringer knelt dangerously close to the edge. Dizzy, he started to lose his balance then felt his mother grab his belt. He caught a glimpse of the abyss below him, felt a wave of nausea and retched over the cliff. Kate pulled him back and he fell into her arms.

CHAPTER THIRTY-FOUR

A S THE CHOPPER ROSE ABOVE THEM WITH THE BASKET CARRYING Sam, the thumping of the rotor blades intensified and another section of shale broke loose. Holding Stringer tight to her chest, Kate leaned back against the rock face. They seemed to shiver in unison. Though it was a relief not to be under the oppressive roar of the helicopter, Kate felt a growing fear they wouldn't get off the cliff alive. Deep down, however, there was no way she was giving up.

Soon, someone spoke over a megaphone above them. "They took Sam straight to Maine Med. Their second chopper had engine trouble so the Coast Guard has a backup enroute from Portland." The voice was more muffled than before, as if they had moved farther back from the collapsing edge.

Kate looked up. "Hurry up! Stringer's freezing."

"Hang in there, it's going to take a while longer. We can't get anything down to you. The whole cliff is giving way."

"No shit—" Stringer grumbled as cold, gusty winds buffeted their sore bodies. Stringer curled into a tighter ball. "Do you think she'll make it?"

Kate was struck that he was thinking only of Sam. "I hope so. She's tough."

"I don't mean just physically. You heard her, she wanted to jump."

"I've wanted to jump a few times."

"What?" Alarmed, Stringer looked at her.

"Not today. Over the years when I was using. But something always saved me."

"Like what?"

"Like you—loving you so much I couldn't do it."

Kate noticed the fog had thinned and the clouds were breaking up. She looked out toward the ocean, saw the moon for the first time. "I think the brunt of the storm has passed."

"Good. Enough for one night." Stringer nestled his head under Kate's chin. She felt a cold rigor travel through his body. "Where's the other chopper?" he asked.

"They'll get here."

Stringer lay quietly.

"We've been in some pretty tight spots, but this takes the cake."

"Nope," Stringer said. "Nothing compares to Leland trying to kill Francis. I could've lost you both."

Kate held him tighter. "But you didn't."

"That was *so* bad, Mom. Seeing you beat up again, having to shoot…" Stringer fell silent then spoke again, in an angrier, more fearful voice. "That's why you can't mess everything up." He turned and looked at her. "This is our chance. You understand me?"

Kate was taken aback, though she had no question what Stringer was talking about. It reaffirmed how much Francis meant to him. "Yeah, I know." She felt a warm flush of guilt. "And I'm sorry I wasn't at Sam's performance. I completely forgot."

"Like you forgot lots of things when you were drunk."

"I wasn't drinking."

"I know. You were all tied up with that art dealer."

"For you. I'm learning how to help your career."

"What career?"

"You *can* have one, if you want."

"I want you and Francis, a family. A normal one."

Feeling chastened, Kate fell silent, reflexively stroking Stringer's hair. Soon, he fell asleep. As her hearing recovered, Kate was comforted by the wind moving through the pines. Exhausted, she too must have nodded off as the next thing she heard was another chopper approaching. As a blazing spotlight hit them, Kate put up her hand to shield her eyes. When the light moved off them, she saw another rescue basket descending on a cable. A loudspeaker crackled above her. "This is the United States Coast Guard. I'm Rescue Swimmer Adam Turner. Do you think you can throw me that same rope or the jumper cables so I can pull the basket over?"

Kate's body was so stiff it felt like a shell of ice cracked and broke off of her when she moved. She looked for the jumper cables, but they were gone. They must have fallen into the ravine after they loaded Sam.

Kate forced herself to crawl over to the rope still lassoed around the rock obelisk. Fatigue had worn her defenses down so she was not as afraid to reach over the edge and grab hold of the rope, though she was surprised how heavy it was. She felt Stringer holding onto her jeans.

Kate looked at the new rescuer. "I can throw it to you."

"Be careful! I'll have the pilot swing me in as close as he can. Throw me the rope when I yell."

Kate gave him a thumb's up then pulled up several loops of rope. When she threw it to him, he tied it off to the basket and pulled it toward them. "I will help one of you in at a time so that you can go up to the helicopter. The basket won't hold all of us."

"Get in, Mom," Stringer said.

"No way," Kate said, pointing. "You're going right now."

"But you're a girl."

Kate frowned. "Get in—now."

Kate watched as they hoisted Stringer up to the chopper, which then flew up over the cliff. The chopper returned quickly and she was finally, blessedly, taken off the cliff.

Kate was lowered toward a meadow next to a staging area littered with ambulances, cruisers, fire trucks, and a line of pickups that stretched far up the road. Several EMTs waited beyond the reach of the rotors. As the basket carrying Kate landed, Francis ducked under a yellow police tape and ran to her. He helped her get out of the basket and limp to a waiting stretcher. She was surprised by how weak her legs were.

"My god, Kate, are you alright?" Francis wrapped his coat around her.

"Is String okay?" she asked, sitting on the stretcher.

"Yes, the EMTs are attending to him. That kid is amazing. He just wants to get to Portland to see Sam."

Though Kate was glad to see Francis, her exhaustion held a complex mix of relief, guilt, and fear. "I would've tried to save her, but she came careening down that old road and straight off the cliff. Like in two seconds." Kate shook her head. "Crazy."

"What were you doing?" Francis cut himself off. "Never mind, we'll talk about everything later. Right now, I'm just relieved you're all safe."

Kate saw Stringer sitting on the back of an open ambulance. She threw off Francis' coat and ran to him. "You okay?"

"Yeah," Stringer said, as an EMT bandaged his arm. Another applied ointment to the cuts on his face. Charlie was holding court with a group of firemen and others standing nearby. Stringer looked over at them. "Jerks."

Kate frowned. "Why'd you say that?"

"They're talking shit about Sam, that she caused all this."

"Well...she did."

"Wasn't her fault," Stringer snapped.

Kate turned and listened to the men. She, and apparently, Stringer, heard one of them—a big scruffy guy, not one of the firemen—refer to "that little slut." Kate was about to confront them when Stringer tore away from the EMT and charged into the group of men. He tried to tackle the big guy, who grabbed hold of Stringer's arm and threw him to the ground.

"Hey!" Charlie yelled. He and a couple troopers quickly moved in. The troopers immediately man-handled the roughneck away from Stringer, who was slow to get up off the ground. He took a couple of steps forward and looked the man right in the face. "That's my girl-friend, you asshole. You don't know shit."

"Why you little, fucker—" The man tried to break free of the troopers.

Charlie pulled his metal flashlight from its belt ring and rapped it hard on the guy's collarbone. "Shut up or I'll split that stupid head of yours in two."

The man finally retreated, so the officers let go of him.

Charlie stood at his full height, pointed with his long black light. "You get the hell out of my county, or I'll throw your ass in jail."

The man shook his torn shirt back into position and took a few steps away from everyone. He forced a laugh. "Just wonderin' if I could help." He kept glancing back at the lawmen as he walked to his truck.

"Goddamn loggers," Charlie said. "Nothing but trouble." He turned back to the others who were obviously upset.

"Asshole," Kate said.

Francis seemed to agree.

Charlie slid his flashlight back into its ring. "He'll take off, the shit-for-brains." He stepped over to Stringer, patted him on the back. "You're something else, young man. Crazy to have gone over that cliff after them, but I don't think they would've made it off alive without you."

Stringer took hold of Charlie's arm. "How's Sam? Have they got her to Portland yet?"

"Let me check." He keyed his radio mic and asked dispatch for an update.

Soon the dispatcher was back on the speaker. "Getting her ready for surgery now. Unconscious. Leg's real bad. She's lost a lot of blood. Said they're doing everything they can."

Stringer's body appeared to weaken. He dropped to his knees, his head hanging almost to the ground.

An EMT leaned over him. "Let's get you to the hospital so they can check things out. Your arm is pretty banged up."

"I'm fine," Stringer said, weakly shaking her off.

Kate knelt next to him. "Do what they say. We don't want to miss an injury."

Stringer perked up a little. "I'll get checked out if you take me to that Portland hospital, not the local one."

The EMT looked at Kate, who nodded.

"We'll have to check with our hospital to get permission to bypass them."

Charlie leaned toward the EMT. "Just tell them the patient is refusing to go here. They'll okay it."

The EMTs strapped Stringer to a gurney and Kate climbed into the ambulance with him.

With red-and-white strobes lighting up the night, they took off.

Charlie gave Francis a ride back to his Jeep at the info booth and he headed to Portland. He had a nasty headache, and it disturbed him that Sam might have done this on purpose. He knew how worried Stringer was about her, and how complicated their lives had suddenly become.

CHAPTER THIRTY-FIVE

STRINGER TRIED TO JUMP BACK AS HE FELT HIMSELF GOING OVER the edge of the cliff. As shale collapsed under him, he grabbed for something to hang onto. He thought he had hold of something solid, but then it was pulling him over. He fought hard to stay on the rock ledge, but he was being yanked harder and harder.

"Stringer...Stringer!"

In a panic, his eyes opened and he saw a fuzzy view of his mom leaning over him, holding his hands. Though the lights were low, her image reflected in a large glass window, outside of which shown the lights of a city.

Stringer blinked hard and looked around. "What the...?"

He was on some couch, with a thin blanket over him.

"String, it's okay, we're at Maine Med in Portland."

Realizing where he was, Stringer sat up. "How's Sam?" He rubbed his eyes. "Shit, I fell asleep."

Kate sat next to him. "She's out of surgery. They've taken her to intensive care."

"Why did you let me fall asleep?"

"We all did. We were exhausted. There was nothing else we could do."

"Where's Francis?"

"Gone down to the cafeteria to get coffee and something for us to eat."

"Can I see her?"

"Not yet. She has to recover for a few hours. It took two orthopedic surgeons to fix her leg. They hope she can keep it."

Stringer frowned. *"Keep it?"* He visualized her legs wrapped around him on the beach that night. "She could lose her leg?"

Kate nodded. "All I know is what the nurse said."

Stringer lay back against the vinyl couch. He puffed his cheeks and let out a long breath. "This is so crazy, Mom."

"I know."

Stringer looked around. "Where are we?"

"They let us stay overnight in this lounge. The people are nice here."

Francis backed through the door with a cardboard carrier of coffee cups and plastic-wrapped pastries. "Stringer, you're awake." He sat next to Kate and handed her a steaming cup, then another to Stringer. "I got you hot chocolate with whipped cream, the way you like it."

Stringer took the cup. The warmth felt good in his hands. "Thanks."

Kate took a sip. "That helps."

They all sat looking out over the city, streaks of red dawn appearing beneath linear clouds outlining the horizon.

Stringer stood. "I gotta pee bad."

Francis pointed. "Down the hallway to the right."

When the door closed behind Stringer, Francis slid his hand over Kate's. "I was really worried about you this weekend, that you might have been hurt—I mean *before* the whole cliff thing."

"I thought it'd be fun to take some backroads home from Skowhegan but got a flat and had to wait for some kid to come along to change the tire. Afterwards I stopped in a little town, and called the house, but no one answered."

"How'd you call with no cellphone?"

"I think I found the last phone booth in Maine, in front of an abandoned gas station off Route One. Pretty creepy, though I met a nice cat."

Francis looked confused.

"Anyway, the answering machine didn't pick up so I figured you guys weren't home. I decided to stop at the overlook. I was thinking about our talk the other night."

"Me, too. I don't want to lose you."

Kate settled into the couch. "I've been pretty mixed up."

"I'm sorry."

Kate became agitated. "Stop...*please* stop saying you're sorry. It drives me nuts. My life is *not* your fault."

"It's a habit."

Kate shook her head. "*I* guess—" She got up and stepped to the window. "I feel like I've barely taken a whole breath since we left California. Like I'm trying to get myself oriented, to stop spinning after being on some wild ride."

She turned and looked out over the Portland skyline, what there was of it, focusing on a large red neon sign flashing 6:02 AM from atop the tallest building. "It may sound weird or ungrateful to you, but it's been hard going from the mess I was in California to being a famous guy's girlfriend in Maine."

She turned back to Francis, who was obviously listening carefully. "I haven't felt free for so long. I don't mean I want to be totally free, I just need to plant my feet somewhere under my own power."

"I do understand," Francis said, quietly.

Kate shook her head. "I can't believe we just got my kid, and me and his girlfriend, off a collapsing cliff." Then an image of a naked Richard unexpectedly crossed her mind. Searing guilt attacked her from within. Before Francis could say anything, she left the room.

In the hallway, Kate felt sick. She leaned against a metal windowsill and closed her eyes. She saw Richard standing on the rock at the edge of the lake, waiting for her. "Screw you," Kate said then headed around the corner, where she found Stringer outside the large glass doors to the intensive care unit.

"What'd you say?" he asked.

"Nothing. I didn't know you were here."

"Are you having another fight with Francis?"

"No. I was talking to myself."

Stringer slid down the wall to the linoleum floor and stared up at the ICU sign over the doors. "I want to see her. Just for a few minutes, to make sure she's okay."

Kate ran her hand over his head. She couldn't help but notice the scar, that painful remembrance she wished would disappear. "I'll see if someone can tell us how she's doing."

Stringer nodded.

Kate found an information phone on the wall and talked to someone inside who said it would be at least another hour before anyone could see Sam and then only next of kin. Kate explained the situation but was told that, due to privacy rules, she would have to get hold of Sam's legal guardian, Nelson. Kate tried to argue with her, but it was no use, though she was told the hospital was trying to contact him. She sat on the floor next to Stringer. "So, we'll wait."

After a few minutes, Kate spoke. "The art appreciation thing was cool. I learned a lot."

"About what?" Stringer asked, without raising his head.

"How to really look at art, how it makes you feel, and how it helps you understand what you feel."

Stringer shook his head. "No idea what you're saying. Did you talk to Francis?"

She looked at Stringer, annoyed. "Can I have an opinion about something without running it by Francis? I do have my own brain, you know."

"It's just..."

"Just *what*?" Kate said abruptly.

"He's an artist. He cares about us—and you."

Kate tried to be patient.

Stringer lifted his head. "You've been really hard on him lately. I don't get it, Mom, don't you like this new life we have?" Before Kate could answer, Stringer continued. "And I don't think you're going to any of your meetings, and you know that makes you crazy."

Kate wanted to defend herself, but really couldn't. "You're right."

Stringer looked at her. "This is the first time I ever felt safe. I've been pissed about a lot of things, but this is home now. And knowing Sam is so cool. I don't want us to blow it." Stringer put his hands up to his head. "I'm so tired I feel dizzy. I'm going to lie down in the lounge till we can see her."

After Stringer walked away, Kate looked out over the bay that partially encircled the city. Even though it was early, there were several boats plying the water, including a car ferry leaving a large dock in the distance. Dozens of sailboat masts waved back and forth in marinas along the harbor. Even having been chastised by Stringer, she was thinking of Richard, the thrill of being with him, of having a new man want to touch her, to do new things with her. And *to* her. The wine and cocaine had scared her but it also added excitement to what was for her such a conventional life. Then she heard Ginny's voice at the last AA meeting she'd gone to a few weeks back: *Kate, you're a chaos junkie. Learn how to enjoy an ordinary day.* "Who the hell wants an ordinary day?" Kate said out loud. Had she ever had one?

There was a clicking noise and one of the metal doors opened. A heavy-set woman motioned to Kate. "I'm Clara, the supervisor. We got ahold of that Nelson fellow. He's not coming in but said it was okay for you folks to visit."

"Great. I'll get Stringer."

Kate found Stringer asleep again. Back at the ICU, she kept her arm around him as Clara spoke. "Dr. Jacobs, one of the surgeons, wanted to give you an update himself, but he was called to another emergency. It's been quite a night." She held the door open and they walked inside, where the cool air was strong with the smell of antiseptic. "Have you ever been in Intensive Care?"

"No," Kate said.

"It's a different world. It can be intimidating with all the machines beeping, seriously sick and injured people, and lots of staff running around. This girl, Sam, has what we call an external fixator on her badly injured leg. It looks weird if you've never seen one."

Stringer perked up. "What's a fixator?"

Clara demonstrated on her arm. "A metal rod structure that runs along the leg attached to pins that are drilled into the broken bone fragments to hold them in place."

Interested, Stringer opened his eyes wider. "Oh, one of those," he said, like he had any idea what she was talking about.

Clara bent toward him. "You're going to be okay in there? We don't want you getting sick or passing out."

"I'm fine." He motioned to Kate. "But she doesn't look so good."

"Stringer—" Kate nudged his shoulder. "I'm okay."

Clara looked at Kate. "You sure?"

"Yeah."

"Then follow me."

Before they could step through another doorway, they were made to lather their hands with white foam which had the strong smell of alcohol. It made Kate feel a little light-headed, so she turned her head away as it evaporated.

Clara swiped a security badge and the inner door opened. Inside, staff members bustled around in various colored scrubs, some with face masks, in what looked like a carefully orchestrated dance. They carried bags of IV fluids, clipboards, medications, bandages, and armfuls of clean laundry. One man was rolling a strange-looking machine with tubes sticking out of it down the hallway, a couple others stood clicking away on mobile computer stands.

Kate and Stringer stayed close together as they followed Clara around a long, semi-circular nurse's station. In the first room, Kate caught a glimpse of a bloated patient with a green tube in his nose and a bigger, clear tube coming out of his mouth connected to a machine making puffing noises. An elderly woman stood holding the bedrail, patting the man's thin black hair through a mess of technical spaghetti that surrounded him. Kate looked away.

Clara paused outside the next room, where a young woman held an injured boy's hand. Clara spoke in a low voice. "Poor woman. Her son crashed his car into a cement abutment over by the South Portland docks two days ago." She shook her head. "She's been here ever since."

"Where's Sam?" Stringer asked, moving toward the next room.

Clara kept walking. "Bed five, down here."

As they approached the room with a red 5 on the door, Kate hesitated. Stringer headed straight for the door and was met by a young nurse in blue scrubs with blond hair pulled back in a tight braid. She was beautiful despite a noticeable scar that ran through her slightly indented upper lip.

"I'm Cindy," the nurse said, extending her hand first to Stringer then to Kate.

Stringer tried to peek around her, but she blocked the view.

"How do you know, Sam?" she asked in a friendly, professional voice.

Stringer and Kate briefly explained.

"Well, you can come in for just a few minutes as I'm about to do her wound care. The ventilator is breathing for her, but we hope to get her off it in the next day or two. She also has a warming blanket covering her, as her body temperature was quite low when she got here."

"I tried to keep her warm." Stringer said, disappointment heavy in his voice.

"I'm sure you did," Cindy said. "I heard you both kept her alive."

"Can she hear me if I talk to her?" Stringer asked.

"I'm not sure. She has a head injury with a small fracture of her skull. She was down a long time."

Stringer's jaw tightened. "It took them forever to get her out of there."

Cindy nodded. "I'm sure it seemed like it, but cliff rescues are some of the most challenging and dangerous. My fiancé is a paramedic."

"Oh," Stringer said. He tried not to look at Cindy's scar, though it made him feel like he had some sort of connection with her.

"We also don't know if she has any anoxic injury."

"What's that?"

"A brain injury from not getting enough oxygen, perhaps from all the bleeding.

Cindy stepped aside, allowing Stringer an unobstructed view of the complicated hospital bed. He first noticed the bottom of a strange looking, orange foot, Sam's foot. He followed her swollen leg up to where the long metal rods began. He could see where several pins attached to the rods pierced her skin like she was in some kind of trap. Then there was a long incision down the front of her thigh which was covered with clear plastic. Most of her leg was bruised like she had taken a terrible beating. Except for her injured leg, most of the rest of her was covered with some kind of inflatable blanket.

Stringer glanced back at Kate, who stood in the doorway, her hand to her mouth. He stepped to the bedside and took hold of the railing. He gradually looked up over the blanket. Sam's face came into view. She was pulled slightly to the side by a large tube coming out of her mouth and taped tightly across her cheeks. Her swollen eyelids were closed, her lips dry and cracked. Her pale skin was marred by scrapes and red blotches. Sam's hair looked like a dull lawnmower had sheared it off and he couldn't see her signature blue mane, which must have been tucked under her.

Stringer had to look away, his gaze crossing over the bright displays and blinking lights of monitors suspended over the head of the bed. He recognized the bouncing green EKG tracing, thought it was going too fast, the red number next to it varying between 120 and 124.

He looked down, saw another clear plastic tube emerging from under the blankets. Clear yellow liquid tinged with pink trickled down the tube toward a collection bag hanging on the bedrail. After a few moments, he made himself look at her face again. That wicked cool face that had so attracted him. Her beautiful, slightly sarcastic mouth that spoke the truth to him. The once moist lips that kissed him on the beach.

Stringer desperately wanted Sam to open her swollen lids so he could see her amazing green eyes. For a second he felt a hot flicker of rage, thinking of that asshole from Rhode Island who had ruined his painting, which would have captured her eyes forever. Now they might never open again.

Stringer turned to Cindy, whose presence seemed to ease some of his fear. "Can I touch her?"

She smiled and lifted the sheet, revealing Sam's hand. It, too, was swollen. Two fingers were splinted together and she had a large pink IV needle stuck in the back of her hand. It was connected to a skinny tube that snaked along the side of the bed to another machine.

"I'm sure she'd appreciate that."

Stringer looked at Cindy, a lump forming in his throat. "You think she'll know me?"

Cindy put her hand on Stringer's shoulder. "I bet she will."

He stared at Sam's hand for a few seconds then reached out and gingerly touched her with the tips of his fingers. Feeling her cool, puffy skin, he withdrew then slowly, gently curled his hand around her wrist. "She feels cold."

"That's why she's under this warming blanket. She's getting warm IV fluids also."

Cindy stepped back, pulled on a pair of gloves and attended to something on the bedside stand. Kate stayed in the doorway.

Stringer stared at Sam's face, moisture racing in and out of the breathing tube in synch with the puffs from the ventilator. He was scared, hoped she'd want to live when she woke up. He didn't think he could bear it if she really wanted to die. That was so crazy. He had never wanted to die: not when Leland savagely beat on his mother or his drunken, douchebag friend had shot Stringer; not when Stringer was arrested and locked up in McNeal's ancient jail where he threw up blood in that dark, cold cell. *Never.*

He stared at Sam's face. "How could you want to do that?" He wiped a stray tear from his cheek. "You *have* to want to live and get better. Nobody else can do that for you." He leaned close to Sam's ear. "I love you. Don't you leave me here alone."

Stringer turned to Cindy. "Sam has one long bunch of bright blue hair that's her favorite. Do you think you could get it out from under her? It doesn't look like her without it. I know she'd want you to be able to see it."

Cindy nodded. "I understand. As soon as I finish with her wounds, I will try."

"Thanks. I'm glad you're taking care of her."

"I'll be here until three then one of the other girls will come on."

"Other girls?"

"Yes, we have two or three shifts of nurses a day." She smiled. "You didn't think I lived here, did you?"

Stringer was disappointed.

"They're all great." She smiled. "And I'll be on again tomorrow."

"Good."

As Stringer stepped to the doorway, he realized Francis was standing behind Kate, his hands resting on her shoulders.

"Are you okay?" Francis asked.

Stringer nodded. He walked past them and through the sets of heavy doors. He made his way down the hallway to the lounge where he found an open window. He hung his head outside and took in a couple deep breaths of cool morning air. *Sam had to make it.*

CHAPTER THIRTY-SIX

THE DAYS AFTER THE RESCUE WERE AN EXHAUSTING BLUR. After one night's fitful sleep at home Stringer essentially camped outside the ICU where he heard the doctors talking about how close Sam came to dying. Her blood alcohol level wasn't quite over the legal limit but they figured it had been higher, and worn off during the hours she was trapped on the cliff. He heard them say that, assuming she survived, they'd try to get her to go to rehab.

Thankfully, the school year was just ending and Stringer's teachers were very understanding of the situation, so he was able to sit with Sam for hours. He talked to her quietly, told her she made him feel good about himself, whispered that he thought he was falling in love with her. "You can't stay in a coma, Sam. You've *got* to wake up." He tried to will her awake, but her eyes didn't open; only her chest rose and fell with the rhythm of the respirator that was keeping her alive.

Stringer had brought Francis' guitar and a couple of songbooks to the hospital and occupied himself practicing when he couldn't see Sam or wasn't catching a nap. Despite the tips of his fingers being sore, he kept at it, determined to learn a special song for her.

Cindy was truly an angel, letting Stringer be with Sam way more than official visiting hours allowed. She kept him informed about what was going on medically, and though it was scary to hear, her calm explanations relieved some of his fears. On Tuesday, she asked Stringer if he wanted to help shampoo Sam's hair. He felt a little awkward, but appreciated being able to do at least something for her. And he was psyched when he realized Cindy had brought in a bottle of hair coloring so that they could freshen up Sam's blue streak. He felt close to her, gently running his blued fingers through her long hair. He so wanted to hear her smoky voice again.

By Wednesday morning Sam was able to breathe well enough on her own that her breathing tube was removed. She still didn't respond to verbal stimuli, but she did withdraw her good leg when they pinched her, something that upset Stringer but Cindy said was a good sign. The place buzzed with activity as a parade of doctors, therapists, and techs came and went many times a day. Sam had several x-rays of her fractured leg and a CT scan of her head but still no one could tell Stringer whether or not she was going to wake up or when. He was scared, confused, and frustrated, despite support from Kate and Francis. Playing the guitar seemed to be the one thing that kept him chill enough to function.

Stringer was scheduled to work the lobster boat that afternoon, which was a needed break from the hospital vigil. Regardless, he was angry Kate made him go. Pike wasn't as much of an ass as usual, seeming to act a little skittish around Stringer, who was relieved there wasn't another rendezvous with the cigarette boat. On the way home, Pike drank his beer sitting alone on the stern. Stringer welcomed the change in Pike's behavior, but it was also a little concerning.

After work, Stringer talked Kate into driving him back down to the hospital, where she stayed with him overnight in the now-familiar visitors' lounge. He knew Cindy was working the late shift, so after Kate fell asleep, Cindy let him back in with his guitar to sit with Sam. She looked better without the breathing tube taped across her cheeks, and the swelling in her face had gone down. Still, it was weird having her lie there not saying anything.

Cindy situated Stringer in a recliner with a blanket, and he continued to quietly practice until well after midnight, when he finally fell asleep. Every little while he would wake up and look over at Sam and was happy her hair was blue again. It looked cool draped over her white pillow. Thursday morning, as the first light of dawn appeared at the window, he couldn't sleep anymore, so he decided to practice the special Tracy Chapman song he'd been working on. It was difficult because his fingers were painful from the guitar strings and his arms hurt from working on the boat. As he played a particularly sour chord, he winced and placed his palm on the strings to silence them. He leaned his guitar against the recliner, closed his eyes, and tried to relax.

"That was bad…"

"I know," he said, thinking it was Cindy. Then his eyes snapped open. He looked at Sam. "Was that you?" He threw off the blanket and took hold of the bedrails. "Did you say something?"

"Who else?" Sam said, struggling to clear her throat.

Stringer thought he might be hallucinating.

"Need water."

"Oh, my god, Sam!" Stringer started to reach out for her then whirled around looking for a water glass. He banged his knee on the recliner, knocking over the guitar, which made a hollow echo when it hit the floor.

"You trying to play again?" Sam whispered, sarcastically. "Where am I?"

"Maine Med, in Portland."

"Shit, I'm alive."

"Damn straight."

"That sucks."

Stringer held the glass so she could grab the straw with her teeth. He looked into her eyes. "I was so scared."

"Why?" she said in a raspy whisper.

He started to answer, but stopped when he saw her lips curl into a weak smile.

He pulled himself over the bed rail and kissed her cheek.

She turned toward him. "That all you got?"

Stringer smiled and blushed, felt an intense rush of love for her. He dropped the side rail and leaned in, spilling water on her johnny. He gently kissed her dry lips, joyfully sliding his tongue into her mouth. His heart soared when she let out a little whimper of pleasure, a sound that assured him she was glad to be alive.

Within a few minutes Sam fell back asleep. Stringer hurried out and told Cindy the great news. Delighted Sam had regained consciousness, Cindy briefly woke Sam up again and did a cursory neurological exam, which, except for the leg in the fixator, seemed to be fairly normal. With her arm around Stringer's shoulders, Cindy watched Sam fall off to sleep again. "Seen a lot of miracles in here," she said, with a reflective smile.

"Is that why you keep doing this?" Stringer asked. "It must be hard."

Cindy nodded. "Yes, a lot of the time, but not with moments like this. Though it was a whole different story this morning for another patient."

"What happened?"

"Can't talk about it. Just sad stuff." She adjusted the sheet so that it lightly covered Sam's injured foot. "Reminds me every day how fragile we all are. As they say…'seize the day.' This is all we've got."

Cindy pulled on a pair of gloves, and turned her attention to Sam. "I've got to do my morning wound care so this would be a good time for you to get some rest."

"I've got to tell Mom and Francis," Stringer said, excitedly. "And hey, you're great."

"So are you, Stringer."

He gave her a quick hug then grabbed his guitar by the neck and headed out the door.

Stringer left the unit and hurried down the hallway to the lounge. His mom wasn't there, but he saw a subtle indentation in the vinyl couch surrounded by a cocooned blanket from the bungalow revealing where she must have slept. He figured she'd gone downstairs for coffee. Through the large windows he saw the sun had lifted over Portland Harbor, illuminating the city in clear yellow light.

Stringer had to tell someone the good news. He looked around. The only person in the lounge was a big, pot-bellied man in the corner who filled one chair and had his feet up in another. The visor of a faded Hamilton Marine ball cap hung low over his eyes and he was snoring so hard his white moustache fluttered with every exhalation.

Stringer walked over to the open window and cranked it all the way out. He cupped his hands around his mouth and yelled to no one in particular, "She's awake! Sam's awake!" He listened to his voice echo off an adjacent building then turned into the first warm rays of the morning sun.

"That's great!" someone yelled up to him. Stringer shielded his eyes, looked down, and saw Francis waving to him on his way in from the parking lot.

"She's going to be okay!" Stringer yelled back.

Francis gave a thumbs-up then broke into a trot and disappeared inside the hospital entrance. Stringer pulled his head back inside. The big man in the corner had awakened, his cap repositioned higher on his head. "Good for you," he said, in a sleepy voice. With some effort, he pulled his legs off the chair and straightened his back. "I seen you in there with that girl." The man sounded gruff but caring, not the voice Stringer would have expected to come out of him.

"Yeah, it's great." Stringer took a couple steps toward the man. "I'm Stringer."

The man sized Stringer up for a couple seconds. "Cap'n Tom," he said, extending his large hand.

"Why are you here?"

The man coughed up some phlegm and spit it into a spent coffee cup. "Daughter's in there."

"What's her name?"

"Kendra. My baby."

Stringer sat on the arm of a once green couch, much of its vinyl worn down to an ashen grey. "What happened to her?"

Captain Tom hesitated, cleared his throat and took in a short breath. "Overdose. Again. Goddamn heroin." He wiped his mouth with his hand. "Drug-dealing bastards from down country. New York—wherever—up here all over the place, killing our kids." He grit his teeth so hard his cheek muscles bulged.

"I'm sor—"

"No good peckerheads." He cut the air with his arm. "If I could find them I'd teach 'em a lesson they wouldn't forget—line 'em all up, mow down every last one of them."

Stringer retreated a bit.

As Captain Tom growled with anger, his neck swelled a purple-red. When he ran out of breath, he fell silent, his bristled jowls seemingly weighted down with sadness. His tirade made Stringer uncomfortable, but he could empathize. His mom and dad had amply demonstrated how bad the ravages of drugs could be.

Stringer got up and took a half-step toward him. "I hope she gets better."

Captain Tom lifted his cap, scratched the top of his head, a shiny bald eggshell save for a few irregular dark patches. He nestled the cap back onto his head, its frayed edge resting in the groove ringing his receded hairline. "No gettin' better this time. She was down too long. Doc says her brain's dead." His face tightened. "Missus and I give up yesterday. They convinced us."

Emotion choked him, his already bloodshot eyes tearing up. He raised his hand to his chin as if to steady it. "We're waitin' on transplant teams from Boston and Pittsburg to take her org—" He gasped for a breath then started crying, tears trickling down through thick whiskers that covered his cheeks.

Out of respect and fear, Stringer didn't move. He felt terrible for the man and his daughter. Stringer knew it could be him, mourning for Sam.

After a few minutes, Captain Tom settled enough to speak again. "Coordinator said they can help five or six other folks, but my little girl's organs won't be where they're supposed to be." He continued in a painful whisper. "I said no way to takin' my baby's eyes." He continued to speak through tears. "I hope that wan't selfish, but I couldn't bear..."

Stringer became emotional, thinking of Sam's amazing eyes. He stepped over to Captain Tom. "That's awful. Of *course* they can't take her eyes. Gross. Crazy."

Captain Tom looked up. "Yeah?"

"Hell, yeah." Stringer reached out and touched the captain's shoulder which was moist with sweat.

He hung his head. "Worst day of my life."

"I bet. I'm really sorry."

Stringer stood silently in front of this broken man, his large, tough shell melted by incomprehensible grief. In those long, poignant moments, Stringer felt himself change in some uncomfortable, but essential way. Like he was suddenly older.

"Why are you called captain?"

"Run a fishin' boat up the coast a ways. Used to lobster, but the body couldn't take it no more. Pulled my last trap three years ago."

Stringer sat on the arm of a chair. "I work on a lobster boat part-time. I'm just learning."

Captain Tom looked up. "Run from it while you're young and can." He half-smiled. "If the sun and the salt don't ruin you, your achin' arms and back will."

"But you're still running a boat. Why don't you quit?"

"Ahh," Captain Tom said, as if it had three syllables. "The sea—once she gets her tentacles around ya, there's no letting go. Yer hooked, as they say."

"I love the ocean," Stringer said.

"Whose boat you on?"

"The *Look Out*, up in Winter's Cove."

Captain Tom perked up, frowned. "You don't say. That bastard, Pike, who runs Ginny's boat?"

"Yeah. You know it?"

"Yup, I go out from the other wharf on the south end of the cove, far away from Pike as I can get. *Sunset Baby*'s my boat." Captain Tom choked up again. "Named for…"

Stringer waited a few seconds. "I've seen your boat over there."

The captain got control of his emotions again, shook a finger at Stringer. "You watch yourself with Pike. He's crooked as a water snake."

"He's a weird old asshole."

Captain Tom nodded in agreement.

"I gotta go find my mom." Stringer looked at the floor. "I don't really know how to pray, but I'll be thinking of you."

"Thanks." Captain Tom pushed up off the chair and stood. "I'm glad you came around; I needed someone to talk to." He slowly arched his back then walked out of the lounge toward the ICU.

Stringer tried to squeeze the image of Captain Tom's poor daughter out of his mind. He'd seen that girl in the bed two down from Sam. "Damn…" he said then turned away and went looking for Kate and Francis, whom he found rushing off the elevator to see him. They were ecstatic that Sam had woken up, perhaps equally so that Stringer felt she was okay with being alive. It was a huge comfort to him that both Francis and his mom understood what he was feeling.

Friday afternoon Sam was moved out of intensive care to the step-down unit. Kate had wanted to talk to her privately but hadn't had the chance. With school out and Stringer back working on the boat, Kate decided to drive to Portland to see Sam alone. Though not outright fighting, she and Francis were in what seemed like a cold war, especially since she told him she was going back to Skowhegan for the follow-up workshop the next morning. Kate didn't suggest he go with her and he didn't offer.

When Kate found her way to Sam's new unit, the nurse said her leg was paining her a lot, and that she needed to rest. Kate walked back upstairs to the familiar ICU lounge and sat looking out over the Fore River, which flowed around the city into the south end of Casco Bay. Kate enjoyed watching planes taking off and landing in the distance at the jetport, their wings flashing brightly in the sun. The interstate arteries were jammed with Friday afternoon traffic, though they didn't compare to the massive rush hour *parking lots* that encircled LA. To the southeast Kate saw a couple of cranes loading an enormous pile of rusty scrap metal onto huge barges that a man near her in the lounge said were bound for China to be melted down to make more junk for us to buy.

As Kate rested, an image of Richard standing on that rock at the edge of the lake returned to her. She felt the cool water flowing over her naked body, as well as the lingering effects from what his fingers had done to her the night before. Part of her was glad they hadn't had sex, but part of her wanted to, and she knew that was a primary reason she was going back to the institute. Yes, she wanted to learn more about art, but Richard was drawing her north again. He was hot, and so was his Shelby Mustang. Kate fantasized riding with him in the California sunshine, top down, cruising up the Pacific Coast Highway past the Santa Monica Pier.

"Miss—Miss, you can visit now."

Kate pulled out of her reverie to focus on a woman in a volunteer vest. Aware her erect nipples were pushing against her bra, Kate pulled her fleece around her. "Thanks."

She followed the young woman down a set of stairs to the unit where Sam had been moved. Inside, it didn't smell as overwhelmingly antiseptic as Intensive Care, and the fluorescent lights weren't as bright. A nurse met Kate at Sam's door. "I told her you were coming. She seemed a little nervous but said it was okay."

Kate felt nervous, too, but tried not to show it.

Sam's eyes were closed when Kate entered the room. Stringer's guitar stood in the corner. She was impressed by how hard he'd been practicing, though he seemed to be a natural, as with his painting. He just amazed her, though she felt bad disappointing him, knowing he was worried about her not going to enough meetings. It would crush him—and her—if she drank again. Despite knowing the 'don't-give-a-shit' warning signs of her disease, Kate wasn't doing much to combat it. That expensive wine in the cabin smelled deliciously tempting and had almost made it to her lips. Ginny had reminded her many times that they shared a cunning, treacherous disease, but Kate lost sight of that quickly when she wasn't around other recovering people.

Kate realized she was staring at the fluid flowing through Sam's IV. She turned her gaze to Sam's face, which looked less swollen and bruised.

She smiled at her bright blue hair, knowing Stringer had helped Cindy dye it.

Sam lifted her head, moaned and reached for one of the fixator pins piercing her skin. She rubbed the muscle around it for a few seconds then her head fell back against the pillow.

"Are you in pain?" Kate asked, quietly.

Sam's eyes opened slowly. She looked up. "A little."

Kate slid a chair over and sat next to the bed. "We haven't had a chance to talk since, you know, the cliff."

"Yeah. Pretty rad—you and Stringer rappelling down like that. You guys are crazy."

Kate smirked. "Look who's talking. You scared the hell out of me when you flew off that cliff."

"Sorry," Sam said, sounding sincere.

Kate leaned forward. "I couldn't just let you die there. Alone."

Sam closed her eyes. "That was the plan."

Kate stayed cool. She had some understanding of how Sam felt. "How come?"

Sam didn't respond.

"You must have felt desperate. Scared."

The corner of Sam's mouth curled into a subtle grin. "Can't be scared if you jump off a cliff."

"Yeah, you can."

Sam crossed her arms, tucked her hands into her armpits. "Maybe." She glanced at Kate. "Got any beer or dope—anything—with you?"

"You crazy?" Kate said, surprised at Sam's forwardness.

"Obviously." She adjusted her leg. "They aren't giving me shit for pain meds."

"You can ask for more."

"I already did but they shut me down." She motioned to a small gizmo attached to a pole. "I got my own med pump here but they won't turn it up."

"They're worried about you after what happened." Kate leaned back in her chair. "I was scared shitless when I tried to kill myself. Tried to overdose out in the dessert near Joshua Tree. Thought I'd be cool and do it like Gram Parsons."

Sam's eyes opened wider. "Of the Byrds?"

"Yeah. You know him?"

"*Sweethearts of the Rodeo*'s one of my favorite albums. I love that old seventies country-rock. I'm always playing those songs."

Sam strained to reach down and rub her lower leg. "How'd you do it?"

"Cheap tequila, Quaaludes, a bunch of other shit I got out of Leland's stash. Not sure what. I was *really* crazy back then."

Sam tried to move her injured leg and winced. "Cramp."

Kate looked at the complex fixator. "Can I rub it for you?"

Sam arched her back with another spasm. "I guess…"

Kate lowered the side rail. "Tell me where."

"The muscle in the back. And they don't let me touch the pins, you know, for infection."

"Okay. Tell me if I'm not doing it right."

" 'K. Be gentle."

"I will." Kate reached through the fixator and slid her fingers over the back of Sam's calf. She stayed away from the pins, which looked cruel and painful. Very gently, she massaged the still-swollen muscle, suspending her arm with her other hand so she didn't lean on the device.

After a few minutes, Sam adjusted her shoulders and seemed more comfortable. "That feels good."

"I'm glad." Kate continued massaging for quite a while.

"Thanks, but you can stop before your arm falls off." Sam smiled. "Stringer only lasted two minutes."

"Wimp."

"And he nearly knocked this contraption off the bed."

Kate's arm was starting to ache so she pulled it back through the fixator and lifted the side rail. "So how'd you get *your* courage up?"

Sam tightened her lips, took in a breath through her nose then let it out, "I'm a Jack Daniels girl when I can get it. And good reefer. But anything'll do." She looked out the window. "I felt nuts after Old Orchard, got really pissed back at Pike's shack. Drank my little stash and some of his, too. I don't remember much driving out there, but I was real high when I came down that old road. I didn't know it was that steep, and I think I tried to stop at the last second, but I still had the throttle cranked." She shook her head. "Dumb shit…"

"Yeah, you were moving, but you did drag your feet before you went over, like you were trying to stop."

"I got scared too late."

"Almost," Kate said. "Do you drink a lot?"

"When I get the chance. That's one reason I like playing out. I can usually get a few for free under the bar." Sam looked at Kate. "Were you drunk that night, too?"

Kate shook her head. "No. I used to drink all the time. Couldn't stop, but I had to quit, like a year ago."

Sam looked interested. "How come?"

"I was losing it. I mean, going *crazy*."

"Oh that. I can relate." Sam looked away. "I don't think I could stop."

"Me neither. Not till I got real desperate, getting beat up and almost drowning off Venice Beach, shit like that."

Sam looked surprised, nodded. "Me, too."

"Who beat you up?"

Sam shrugged. "Other foster kids, bullies. And a couple of older assholes in the houses they put me in. Almost got gang-raped on a pool table once, but I fought my way out."

"Getting beat on sucks."

Sam nodded. "Yeah."

Sam and Kate both looked out the window. The sun was setting behind the tower at the jetport, and to the east, the bright lights of the harbor were coming on.

Sam looked back at Kate. "How'd you quit?"

Kate thought for a moment. "I got really messed up out in LA. My husband beat me so badly I ended up in the hospital. I was broken—literally—so done. The only reason I cared about staying alive was Stringer. Fortunately, a cool social worker came and talked to me, helped me figure out how to get sober *and* get away from my old man. He didn't let me out of his sight much, but she told me about a woman's underground AA meeting, and luckily it was on a night he was normally out carousing, selling drugs, so I met her there.

"I know it sounds corny, but almost from the minute I walked into that room, I felt at home for the first time in years. We call it the fellowship, a bunch of desperate drunks trying to keep each other sober. They saved my ass."

Sam listened carefully. "How'd you guys end up in Maine?"

"After I'd been sober a while, I got a plan together to escape Leland with the help of an old railroad friend of my father's. Rode across Canada as stowaways on a freight train. Then all the shit with Leland happened."

Sam pushed a button on the side rail and raised the head of her bed. "That was nuts, saw it in the news. I was rooting for you guys." Sam frowned. "I'm glad he shot that bastard."

Kate slowly nodded her head. "String didn't want to, but he had no choice. Leland would've killed us all. He was a ruthless prick."

"Glad he's gone. For all of us."

Kate looked at Sam. "Me, too, though String went through hell because of it."

A nurse stepped into the room. "Sorry to interrupt, but physical therapy is here."

Kate nodded. "I'll be gone in a minute."

"Do you have to go?" Sam lifted herself up on her elbows.

"Got to get home. String'll be wondering what happened to me."

"Can you guys come back tomorrow?"

Kate stood and zipped up her fleece. "String probably can, but I'll be away at an art workshop."

Sam nodded. "I know he doesn't act like it, but I think he's glad you're doing that."

Kate was surprised. "Really?"

"Yeah." Sam adjusted the sheet over her fixator. "He knows you want to help him but he's not interested in any business stuff."

"Thanks for telling me."

"Sure. Thanks for coming. This was a lot better than on the cliff."

"Got that right," Kate said, lingering on Sam's previous comment. Kate put her hand on the bed rail. "I'm really glad you're safe, Sam." Kate touched her forearm. "If you ever want to go to one of my meetings, I'd be happy to take you."

Sam considered it for a few moments. "Sometimes maybe I drink too much."

"Only you know," Kate said sympathetically.

Sam looked up. "How often do you go?"

Kate felt herself blush. "Not often enough."

Sam grinned.

CHAPTER THIRTY-SEVEN

STRINGER CAME THROUGH THE DOOR AS SOON AS KATE DROVE UP TO the bungalow. "How's she doing?" he called out.

Kate got out and gave him a hug. "She's good, I think. I'm glad I went to see her."

Francis appeared in the doorway, backlit by the foyer lights.

"Did they move her out of ICU?" Stringer asked, excitedly.

"Yes, now she's in a regular room." Kate put her arm around Stringer. "Her leg is bothering her a lot, but otherwise she's doing pretty well."

"I can't believe you got to see her and I didn't."

"You'll see her soon." Kate stepped inside and gave Francis a half-hug.

"I was getting worried about you," he said.

Kate tried not to get defensive. "I had to wait quite a while to get in, but then we talked till they kicked me out."

"What'd you talk about?" Stringer asked.

"Girl stuff."

"Like what?"

"Well, things we have in common."

"Tell me!"

Kate unzipped her fleece and Francis hung it on the coat tree. "Why don't you let your mom catch her breath for a few minutes?"

"Thanks," Kate said, heading for the kitchen. "String, she's improved a lot."

Stringer followed after Kate, who filled a glass with water, leaned against the sink and looked at him. "Sam's cool. I get it now."

He smiled broadly, came in for a hug, and she kissed his head.

"Mom, I knew you'd come around. You just needed that bonding time on the cliff."

Kate rolled her eyes.

Stringer motioned to Francis. "Come on, get in here."

Francis hesitantly stepped in, sliding his arms around them both. "I'm glad everyone's safe. It's been quite a week."

"*I guess,*" Stringer said.

They held the hug for a few moments then Kate withdrew and drank the rest of her water. "Did you guys get something to eat?"

"I made a pizza," Francis said.

"It was good," Stringer added. "Someone finally put enough pepperoni on it. And Francis called that musician friend of his, the Mallett guy. He stopped by on his way to a gig in Portland and said he would try and go by the hospital to see Sam. He played me a couple of his songs. He's pretty good…for an old guy."

"That sounds cool." Kate yawned, ran her hand through her hair. "I'm too beat to eat, think I'll get ready for bed. I've got to be at the conference by ten."

"What are they presenting this time?" Francis inquired.

"I've barely looked at the brochure, but the main talk is about getting other people interested in art. Tomorrow morning there's a breakfast session with an agent from New York—I think his name is Wentworth."

Francis raised his eyebrows. "James Wentworth?"

"That sounds like it."

Francis nodded. "He's top notch, has handled several famous artists."

Tired and not wanting to get into an argument, Kate took a chance. "Do you want to come with me?"

Francis looked at her. "Would you like me to?"

Kate's pulse quickened. A shot of fear went through her. She forced herself to sound normal. "If you'd like to."

Francis looked at Stringer. "We had planned to go visit Sam. I don't want to disappoint you."

Kate kept an honest face on. "Whatever you think."

"I think it's best that you go, and besides, you've really wanted to do this yourself, which I understand."

Kate felt relief. "Okay. I'm sure they'll be other workshops." She didn't look at Francis but felt him watching her. "I'm going up to bed."

"All right. I'll climb in quietly in a little bit."

Kate forced a smile and stepped back into the kitchen to say goodnight to Stringer, who seemed upset.

"Mom, I'm scared about Sam and her drinking. She almost killed herself." He looked at Kate. "Can you help her?"

Kate pushed his hair back with her hand. "I'm going to try, but she has to want it for herself. We had a good chat, but you can't force someone to get sober. It just doesn't work."

"But you can show her there's a way. Like you do in your meetings."

Kate nodded. "You're absolutely right, and I really want to help her. I asked her to go to a meeting and shared some of my experience with her so I hope she'll feel comfortable talking with me. I also know it takes a while to trust someone."

"Especially with her. What'd she say?"

"Not much, but she heard me. My sense is she knows she has a problem."

"Okay." Stringer brightened. "And thanks for going over that cliff for her. If you hadn't been there and got help, she would have died for sure."

"As they say, God—whoever He or She is—works in mysterious ways."

"I never heard that."

"Oh, you'll probably hear it again."

Kate kissed Stringer on the forehead and went upstairs. In the bedroom, she stood in front of the hurricane lamp, the bottom layered with different colors of smooth melted wax. She looked at the cloudy moon reflecting vaguely off the dark ocean, thought about Francis out in his skiff searching for Rachael. Every day. For a year. Though really tired, Kate had a hard time settling her mind: Richard, Sam, AA, Stringer, Francis, deceit, lust, and love all tugging at her. She knew Ginny was right, that she needed to get honest in all aspects of her life. But her wild side was calling to her again, and her behavior with Richard made her want to stay away from Ginny and the other AA people so she didn't have to tell on herself.

Kate closed her eyes and tried to hum a Lakota lullaby, but it wouldn't come. Anxious and irritated, for the first time in a while she got down on her knees, and leaned her elbows on the windowsill in front of the whaler's lamp. She felt a refreshing lick of sea air sneak in through the window, which was open a crack. "Help," was all she could whisper. She knelt there with her head bowed for a few minutes then got up, pulled on one of Francis' T-shirts and slid into bed.

Sometime during the night, Kate felt a warm hand on her back, gently rubbing the tight muscles around her shoulder blades. She almost said Richard's name then realized it was Francis. "Thanks," she said, softly.

Francis curled around her; she felt the weight of his once-comforting arm lying across her hips. Her pulse quickened, not from desire, but from guilt. She hoped he wouldn't try and seduce her. She lay perfectly still as if she had fallen asleep. Soon she drifted into pleasant thoughts about the next morning, knowing she had to rise early to get to the institute and to Richard.

Chapter Thirty-eight

Late Saturday night, after a delicious dinner with Richard, Kate sat at the cabin table, picked up the tightly-rolled fifty dollar bill and stared at the thin lines of blow on the white-speckled mirror. Appearing to shimmer in the lamp light, the cocaine drew her toward it. Nervously holding the rolled bill to her nose, Kate leaned forward then jerked back as if scorched by a flame. Fighting hard against a near-overwhelming temptation to use, she dropped the bill on the table and turned to Richard, who was behind her unbuttoning his shirt, revealing his tight abs.

Richard lifted a dark chocolate-covered strawberry from the cooler and presented it to Kate. She let it melt in her mouth while he kissed her neck, smoothly running his hands over her shoulders and down her arms. She didn't run, didn't even think of running.

Kate watched Richard lick drips of chocolate from her breasts, intermittently sucking on her erect nipples. She felt desirable, sexy, delicious. As she lay back on the Hudson Bay blanket, with confident hands he slid off her jeans, her shirt, and then her panties. She watched him take off his leather pants. Standing there naked, he opened a bottle of expensive-looking olive oil which he had warmed by the fireplace. Straddling her, he poured the golden liquid into his palm and let it seep between his fingers, drizzling it over her swollen breasts, and down onto her abdomen, where it trickled into her belly button.

He spread the warm oil over her tense skin with his tongue, intermittently leaning up to kiss her. She licked chocolatey oil from his lips, sliding her wet tongue into his mouth. Her muscles tightened as she felt him massaging her pelvis with his. Kate let her thighs fall apart. Richard put on a condom then reached down, covered his hard penis with oil and slid it deep inside of her. Kate's breathing was rapid and shallow and she moaned as he smoothly penetrated her over and over again. Furiously horny, but distracted by guilty thoughts, Kate came to a disappointing climax.

After a short rest, Richard was aroused again. Lying on his back, he positioned her on top of him. Her heart beating uncomfortably fast, she straddled him, her sweaty palms sliding over his abdomen as she bounced up and down with him inside of her. She winced when he spanked her wet ass. Shortly, he moaned and tightened and she felt him cum. When his thrusting ceased, Kate was broadsided by a powerful wave of guilt. Not able to look at him, she slid off and rolled away. Standing by the bed, feeling disoriented, she reached down, picked up a slimy condom packet and pushed it into Richard's pants' pocket. Then it hit her. She'd brought *two* condoms. They'd had sex again. She lifted the trapper blanket and saw one of the spent condoms stuck to the sheet, but she didn't see the other one. She checked her pants and shirt. Nothing in the pockets; nothing stuck on them.

Panicked, Kate frantically searched the cabin, grabbing hold of something cold and metal. Pulling on it, it gave way and suddenly fresh air surrounded her. Kate withdrew into a ball, shielding herself from harm. As she came to, she realized she was in her car and had hold of the door handle. She checked herself. Though disheveled, she was fully dressed. Sitting up, Kate was frightened by the face—her face—in the rearview mirror. As her head cleared, she was greatly relieved to realize she'd been dreaming. Her back was knotted up, and her butt was sore. She pulled her jeans down, revealing a red handprint.

"Shit—" She remembered Richard *had* spanked her, that it wasn't all a dream. "Did I fuck him?" She was confused, had a hard time getting her bearings. She had sometimes liked it rough in her drunken days, made her feel desired, *hot* even. But she didn't like it this time, or the imprint left on her soft skin.

Kate stretched her arms against the steering wheel, tried to remember exactly what had happened the night before. After the seminar, when they got to the cabin, Richard had pulled her shirt over her head and ripped off her black bra. He'd leaned her back against the table, forcefully kissing her. Things were a bit fuzzy, but she remembered him drinking from a bottle of Smirnoff which he left on the table next to her torn bra. While she had stared at the bottle, Richard snorted lines of coke off his small travel mirror.

Kate felt the clasp of her bra. It was torn loose. *"Fuck..."* she whispered, wondering if she had used the night before. Had she guzzled the Smirnoff? To enhance the passion, drown the guilt? She put her finger to her nose, sniffed one side then the other. She didn't taste any particles of coke in the back of her throat. *But a little blow right now would be nice.*

"You are so messed up!" she yelled inside the car.

She remembered Richard drizzling olive oil over her chest, putting on a rubber, but... Kate squinted, couldn't remember him penetrating her. "No—" she said, shaking her head. Just as he was going to enter her, she felt sick, pushed him away and jumped off the bed. She'd grabbed a wool blanket from the floor and wrapped it around her. The musty wool was rough against her skin, but she had clung to it tightly.

With Richard trying to coax her back onto the bed, Kate had put on her damaged bra, moved away from him and pulled on her fleece. She had been relieved she didn't have any major bruises, no black eyes. But that wasn't fair. Richard wasn't abusive; he was passionate and strong, caught up in their sexy games. She'd wanted it—all of it—but the tremendous wave of guilt that hit her had forced her out of there. In those moments, she'd known it was one of those choices Ginny had talked about: whether to make more of a mess of her life, or not. To knowingly hurt a good person, someone she cared about, or not. As much as she had wanted Richard to screw her brains out, she had left and made her way across campus in the hazy moonlight. Sleeping in her car, and despite feeling like shit, she'd done the right thing. It almost felt good.

Now that it was morning, Kate had an impulse to drive straight home, but she needed to be at the seminar to help Stringer. And she sure as hell should hear the lecture by James Wentworth, as Francis would ask her about it.

Needing to clean herself up, Kate grabbed her old sweatshirt from the backseat and hurried across campus to the flat rock at the edge of the lake where she'd swum the week before. She undressed, slid into the cool water and washed her body as best she could. As she turned under water and swam back toward the rock, part of her hoped Richard would be standing there with a towel and fresh coffee as he had before. When she surfaced, though, only her sweatshirt was there, which was actually a relief. She dried off, loosely clasped her bra, and dressed. She was sure she looked like hell, but at least she hadn't really cheated on Francis.

That was something.

Kate slipped into the Performance Barn and sat in the back corner, where sunlight streaming through skylights couldn't find her. She kept her head down, didn't acknowledge anyone, though she intermittently scanned the doors to see if Richard showed up. Mercifully, he didn't. She tried to focus on James Wentworth. Speaking from the podium, he had on a finely-knit cream sweater, khaki pants, and dark penny loafers. A small gold ring hung from his left earlobe beneath graying hair. His tortoiseshell glasses stood out prominently on his light skin, making him look like the professor he was.

Kate's head was a jumble of fears, disgust, dread, and doom. Her stomach churned with acid, and despite how good the coffee smelled she knew she wouldn't be able to keep it down. The night before re-emerged in her head. Her right hand started to shake, like the old days, though thankfully this was an emotional hangover, not a chemical one. She uncrossed and recrossed her legs. Despite the swim, her pelvis felt moist and sticky. She felt dirty and desperately wanted a hot shower.

Kate sweated it out for two hours until Wentworth finished at the first break. Grabbing a croissant and a banana from the breakfast table, she went out the side door and made sure Richard wasn't in sight. She hurried across the lawn to the Malibu, and drove down the winding driveway beneath the canopy of trees and onto the road. The next thing she remembered was turning onto Route One, heavy with traffic. She followed a lumber truck for several miles, watching an imposing load of logs swaying side-to-side just in front of her. She wondered if they would let go and crush her right there on the highway. A good Maine death. Nothing to explain.

CHAPTER THIRTY-NINE

KATE FOLLOWED THE LOGGING TRUCK INTO A TRUCK STOP WHERE she saw a sign for "Diesel-Food-Showers." She parked between two jacked-up pickups and checked the back seat for something to use as a towel. She grabbed a hand towel and her overnight bag, which had a change of clothes. Inside, the air was heavy with the smell of bacon and fresh coffee. The lunch counter was full of men in vests and flannel shirts. Several of them had large leather wallets bulging from their back pockets, attached to their jeans by small chrome chains. A man on the end with long sideburns blending into a pointed goatee looked over and caught Kate's eye. He lifted his eyebrows and grinned.

Kate turned away, glanced around and saw a sign hanging from the ceiling in the back: "Restrooms-Showers." She ducked behind a display of electronic items: CB radios, antennas, cellphone chargers, coffee cup holders, and metallic license plate frames. A rack of souvenirs looked uncomfortably familiar as she'd seen several of them in Ginny's store when they were talking about their AA program. Kate bee-lined past a table of fresh donuts and pastries, and slipped into the restroom area in the back where a young guy in a black hoodie was talking on his phone in a hushed voice. Kate pushed open the *Darlin's* door and locked herself in one of the two shower stalls. She felt a vague, disturbing deja-vu. She'd shot up in shitty bathrooms around Venice Beach many times.

Kate stripped off her clothes and, holding her arms against her chest to stay warm, stepped onto the cold, grimy tile of the shower and pulled the plastic curtain closed. She reached to turn on the water but was greeted by a coin-op box attached to the hot water valve. '50¢ for 5 minutes.' Her shoulders sunk. *You got to be kidding me.*

She had no money in her pockets and didn't have the energy to get dressed and go back out to the car. She felt filthy—had to take a shower, even if it was a cold one. "What the hell," she said, stepping to the corner and turning on the cold, which was thankfully only cool. She lathered up with liquid soap from a wall dispenser and stepped under the water. A shiver spread over her back as goosebumps formed on her forearms. She pumped more of the strong-fragranced soap into her hands, washing her armpits, breasts and belly then her pelvis and the inside of her thighs.

Though the water was uncomfortable, Kate kept scrubbing her body, turning around in the stream several times while rinsing everything off. It was like she couldn't get clean enough. Finally she turned off the water and stood there watching swirling soapsuds gurgle down the tarnished metal drain. As she shook water off her head, she heard footsteps outside the shower stall. She was startled by two quarters flying over the shower curtain, spinning as they landed on the tiles. She stared at the silver coins for a few seconds then picked them up and jammed them into the coin slot. "Thank you," she called, turning the chrome handle. She heard the coins drop inside the box and suddenly hot water burst from the shower head. She lifted her face into the stream. It felt wonderful after the cold, especially that a stranger would do something nice for her. Then she wondered if it was that creepy guy at the lunch counter. She turned and pulled the edge of the curtain back, but no one was there.

Standing in the hot water, Kate realized how worn out she was, having once again thrown her life into chaos. Deep down, she didn't want to be a shithead, to hurt people she cared about. To sabotage herself. *Why am I like this?* She leaned back, slid down the cold tile wall, and huddled in the corner. As warm water continued to rain down on her, she dropped her head on her knees, and cried.

Soon the timer dinged and the hot water ran out. Kate wiped herself off with her sweatshirt and pulled on a pair of jeans that felt a little too tight.

As she drove south from the truck stop, Kate was tense behind the wheel, increasingly anxious about getting home. This whole Richard thing was wrong; it had to stop. She desperately needed to get to an AA meeting and knew there was one in Winter's Cove that afternoon. Though she dreaded to see Ginny, it would be a good thing. Her sponsor would set her straight.

An hour later Kate slowed as she climbed the driveway toward the bungalow. She glanced in the rearview mirror. *You look like shit.* She parked away from the house, left her wet sweatshirt on the floor in the backseat. Zipping up her fleece, she walked to the door, peered through the side window, and saw no one. Inside, she heard a baseball game on the radio in Francis' studio and figured he was listening to the Red Sox and painting. She stepped farther into the hallway, and then into the kitchen.

"Hi, Mom," Stringer said, pulling his finger out of a peanut butter jar.

"Hey," Kate replied, feeling like a cat burglar breaking into her own home.

She heard the chair in the studio move. Francis appeared at the door, his painting shirt open in front. "Oh, hi. I didn't hear you drive up. I had the game on." He seemed friendlier, in a good mood.

"Just got in." Kate started to look at him then turned toward Stringer.

"You're home early," Francis offered.

"Yeah, I was tired. I left after Mr. Wentworth spoke."

Stringer spun the lid onto the peanut butter jar and came toward her. Both he and Francis were staring at her head. She tried to pat down the frizziness left by the harsh soap at the truck stop, but it was no use.

Stringer cocked his head. "What'd you do to your hair?"

"Yes—" Francis chimed in.

Kate tried to smile. "I forgot my regular shampoo and conditioner. Had to use some soap."

"Great look," Stringer said, apparently accepting her explanation.

"How was it?" Francis asked. "Did Wentworth give a good talk?"

Kate felt dizzy, like she might fall over. Hoping he wouldn't notice, she reached out for an arm of a chair and sat down as if to take her shoes off. "Yeah, it was good, but I think I've had enough art training for a while. I'm beat."

Francis stood over her. "Well, I'm glad you're home early. Stringer wants to go see Sam later."

"That's fine, but I think I'll take a rest. Then I really should get to that late afternoon meeting in town."

Francis looked surprised. "Absolutely." He stepped toward her. "That would be good for you, Kate."

She nodded. "I know."

"Can I take your jacket and get you into something more comfortable?"

"Sure," she said, without looking up. "I just need a nap."

"Did you not sleep well?"

Kate stood and unzipped her jacket, her heart racing with guilt. "Not really. Those old cabins are pretty rough."

"I told you I'd have been happy to get you a nice hotel room."

"I know, but I wanted the whole art institute experience."

Francis took Kate's fleece as she pulled it off. She felt a moment of unidentifiable dread as he held it by the neck, gently shook it out and laid it across his arm. As he turned toward the coatstand, a torn foil packet slipped from the pocket. She lunged forward to catch it but it hit the tile floor with a subtle noise.

Francis stopped, bent forward and haltingly picked it up. "What's *this?*"

CHAPTER FORTY

FRANCIS STARED IN DISBELIEF AT THE TORN CONDOM WRAPPER. After several long moments, his face morphed from blank shock to sadness then anger. He dropped the shiny black and gold wrapper on the phone stand and slowly turned to Kate.

Kate reached out to touch his arm. "Nothing happen—"

He withdrew his arm. "That's not what it looks like."

The anger—hatred almost—in Francis' eyes was something she'd seen before, but never in him.

"Don't even try—" He glanced at Stringer, who had stepped into the kitchen doorway.

"Meet me by the skiff," Francis said coldly to Kate then moved toward the door.

Kate followed him outside. Stringer looked frightened as they left the bungalow.

A strange coldness coursed through her body as they crossed the lawn. On the way down the cliff stairs, Kate's hands shook so badly she could barely hold the iron railing. She was scared but knew she had no choice but to follow him down to the water's edge for what she hoped was just a talk. She thought a beating might almost be easier.

When they reached the cement landing, a cold wave crashed over the rocks, soaking Kate's legs. Beginning to shiver, she stood at the bottom of the stone steps, watched Francis pace back and forth alongside the white skiff which rhythmically tugged against its lines. When he stopped pacing, he leaned against the dark rock wall with an outstretched hand. Kate couldn't tell if he was crying or seething. She retreated when he lashed out, repeatedly kicking the rock wall with his boat shoe.

Kate didn't dare move. She knew what enraged men were capable of—probably even civilized men like Francis. She glanced up the cliff stairs to see if Stringer had followed them, but there was no sign of him.

At least Francis was trying to shield Stringer from the effects of what she'd done.

Francis turned to her, his sandy hair blown back by the tidal breeze. His eyes squinted against her. "How *could* you?"

Kate braced herself for a barrage of yelling. But he didn't yell. Instead, he continued in a stark voice of barely controlled emotions.

"I don't understand you, Kate. What do you want your life to be? Nothing stable, just shitty chaos?" He shook his head. "You're breaking what little faith I have left in people, and you were the one that gave me new hope." He gestured with his hand. "You're like the one who steals a man's wallet, empties it then helps him look for it."

Kate wanted to say, No! That's not true, but it was. And it hurt.

"Rotten—" Francis continued, sounding emotional. "It feels rotten." He stared at her. "Drugs, booze, deceit? Why'd you bother to get sober? Anybody can have a life based on that crap. It's horribly hurtful to those who care about you, who probably care more about you than you do."

Kate cowered under his words. It felt like he was battering her. Crushing feelings of being a no good piece of shit overtook her. It was as if after all this time her life had gone nowhere. "I feel terrible. I never deserved you."

Francis glared at her. "That's bullshit, just making excuses."

Francis put his foot down hard on the gunwale of the skiff and stared into the bottom of the boat. "If only you knew what a beautiful human being you are, underneath it all. If you only believed in yourself enough…"

Kate was surprised, relieved by his more sympathetic words. Tears filled her eyes. She reached toward him. "Francis, I'm *so* sorry, but it's not as bad as—"

His hand cut through the air, silencing her. "I don't want to hear it." He turned away sharply. "You've got one week to decide what you're going to do. Choose your old, wayward life and I want you out of here by next Sunday. There'll be nothing to discuss. Ever."

The emphasis on *ever* rang in Kate's ears.

The muscles around Francis' mouth were tense, his eyes squinting hard. "Make no mistake, Kate, this will either be your last week in this house or the first of a new life. I'm done with your deceit and lies. I'd rather be alone. At least it's peaceful."

As Francis' rage and pain hit her, Kate felt like she was falling backwards. She knelt on the rough cement to catch herself. A cold wave hit her backside, stinging where Richard had spanked her.

Francis did not flinch or come to her rescue. He took hold of the iron railing. "I will say nothing of this to Stringer—*yet.*" He started up the rock steps. "We'll leave to visit Sam in two hours. You can come, but I'm not talking about this any further." He walked straight up the steps and disappeared over the top of the cliff.

Crouching on the cold concrete, Kate stared at the skiff as it pulled on its mooring lines trying to break free. She thought of Francis rowing out onto the bay searching for Rachael. Kate knew in her heart what a good man he was, that he was way too good for her. She also knew that was no excuse for what she'd done. She closed her eyes, watched in slow motion as that torn condom package fell from the pocket of her jacket. She winced, remembering the incredulous look on Francis' face. One of *his* old condoms she had taken from his sock drawer.

The fire of her deceit rose like lava in Kate's chest. She retched violently, hot vomit erupting over the side of the cement into the water. Acid burned in her throat. If there had been a chance of drowning, she might have jumped headlong into the ocean, but she was surrounded by ancient rocks and shallow tidal pools.

When the retching stopped, Kate cupped seawater into her hand and washed out her mouth. She sat back and watched waves break and foam over the exposed ledge, which came in and out of view with the rise and fall of the surf. She watched a small, flesh-colored starfish swaying back and forth, hanging onto tiny barnacles that lined the bottom of a pool. She felt uncomfortably heavy, knew there was no escaping this time. She was too whipped to run.

* * * * * *

Francis was so agitated he didn't go inside but walked out back and wrested his hatchet from its chopping block. He split a pile of kindling, shooting thin pieces of maple onto the lawn. By the time he was done, he had split a pile two feet deep and had worked off at least the veneer of his anger.

His arms tired, Francis drove the steel blade deep into the chopping block and straightened his back. He wiped a layer of sweat from his forehead then started to walk around to the front door. Despite not wanting to see Kate, he was concerned about her, so he walked over to the bluff. He was surprised to see she was still down there, head bowed, sitting cross-legged in the bottom of the skiff. He had an impulse to tell her it was getting too cold to be there without a jacket, but at the moment he just couldn't be near her.

When Francis entered the house, Stringer was upstairs practicing his guitar. Francis quietly closed the front door and stood in the hallway, listening. He was impressed by the many hours Stringer had spent teaching himself to play. It was nice having some live music in the house, and it was a good outlet for Stringer with all that was going on. And for what might soon be coming down.

As he listened to Stringer singing "Hey Jude," Francis' anger and hurt subsided. He did not want to lose Stringer from his life and reminded himself Stringer and Kate were forever entwined. He'd better be careful. Though he was deeply hurt by Kate's behavior, Francis knew he was still in love with her. She'd crossed a dark line, and it frightened him that he didn't know if she, or they, could cross back over it.

Francis glanced at the clock then yelled upstairs. "Hey, Stringer, how about we head to Portland in an hour?"

The guitar playing stopped. "What?"

"Portland. You want to go in an hour?"

"Soon as you're ready. Mom going?"

Francis hesitated. "You'll have to ask her." He pulled on his field coat. "I'll be back in a little while."

The air was brisk as he walked down the hill from the bungalow. At the edge of the road, a squirrel stood on his hind legs, examining a dark brown butternut with his tiny paws. He quickly took off when he saw Francis.

There was probably another hour of daylight before darkness fell, which would be a relief after the tumultuous day. He walked to Kasa's garden, admired the rows and hills of tender green spouts. There were a few weeds poking through which was unusual for her, but her meticulous gardening had been apparently distracted by a gentleman-in-waiting named Buster Hurd.

Francis rapped on the door with the lion's head knocker. He waited patiently, wondered if she might be taking a nap. When Kasa opened the door, however, her hair was nicely done up and she was wearing a bright, flowery dress. She looked great, younger somehow. "Come in," she said, welcoming him as always.

Francis hesitated on the step. "I don't want to interrupt anything."

"No, never." She motioned him inside. "Come in. Buster won't be along for a bit." She made eyes at Francis. "We're going to a show."

Francis managed a smile and sat in his usual chair at the yellowed oak table.

"I'll quickly reheat the water," Kasa said, putting the tea kettle on. She took two white porcelain cups and saucers from the hutch and sat next to him. She looked him over. "Oh dear..." she said, "what has happened, now?"

Francis' smoldering anger turned to sadness.

Kasa reached over and touched his forearm. "Tell me."

He stared at the salt and pepper shakers standing in the middle of the table; a miniature pair of Scotsmen in full bagpipe regalia with little holes in their heads. "I don't want to ruin your evening."

Francis started to withdraw his arm, but Kasa held it. He looked into her large, knowing eyes, felt ashamed, embarrassed. "Kate...she's having an affair, with that art dealer." He shook his head. "I knew he was trouble from the moment I heard about him."

Kasa listened patiently. As usual, she appeared to understand way more than he had said. She shrugged her shoulders, as if discarding all the emotional drama involved. "What can you do?"

Francis straightened, pulling his arm from beneath her hand. "I let her have it down by the skiff, told her she's got a week to decide what she's going to do. Not just about him, but about her life."

He stood, stepped to the cookstove, reached out and touched a couple of ladles hanging overhead. "I love her, Kasa. I know this is not who she really is."

Kasa stirred a white sugar cube into her tea cup and took a couple of sips. "I understand hurt. Had a young soldier disrespect me once when I was sixteen. Loved that man, even after he broke my heart. I promised my mother I wouldn't, but I would have taken him back in a second."

"Why didn't you?"

Kasa paused. "He was shot and killed outside of Berlin at the end of the war, just before the Germans surrendered to the Allies."

"I'm sorry."

"I was, too, but I got along." Kasa sounded not dismissive, but realistic, seasoned. She motioned for him to draw closer to her.

Kasa took his hands. "So, my dear friend, I see Kate as a trampled flower learning to grow again, and despite how much I know she loves you, women have irrepressible desires and hers have been repressed for too long. Your relationship is real, not a dream romance from a movie." She squeezed his hands. "As I see it, a beautiful, spirited Lakota horse has ridden into your life and you can hang on for the wild ride, or you can give up, let her go. Only your heart knows." She leaned toward him. "But if you banish her, there'll be no second chances when she's gone."

Chapter Forty-one

SURPRISED BY KASA'S SEEMINGLY HARSH WORDS, FRANCIS' FACE tightened. "Isn't Kate the one that will need a second chance?"

Kasa frowned. "You don't think worse things have happened to people? That they have had to recover from more devastating tragedies? Moved larger mountains to go on with their lives?"

Chastened, Francis sat back. "You get right to the point, don't you?"

"When you're in turmoil. Isn't that why you visit?"

There was an awkward silence then Kasa sat up straighter, finished her tea, and set her cup in its saucer. "The great writer, C. S. Lewis, said it best. You know him?"

"Of course. *Narnia*."

Kasa nodded. "He once said, 'Not forgiving is like swallowing rat poison and waiting for the rats to die.'"

Her words took a few moments to settle in, and though not particularly ready to hear them, Francis found himself somewhat comforted by them. "Food for thought," he said.

Kasa picked up their cups and set them in the sink.

Francis pushed his chair back and stood. "I'm sorry to have held you up. I appreciate your wise counsel."

Kasa spoke while rinsing the cups under the tap. "Wise, I don't know. But I have seen enough to know truth when I see it." She turned with a dish towel in her hand. "Despite the considerable challenges you and Kate have had, I have seen deep love between you. Something on a soul level. Now you will have to find out if your love is strong enough to overcome it all." She set the clean cups on the drain board and faced him. "None of us are angels, Francis."

He nodded then stepped to the door.

Kasa followed after him. "When you were married to Rachael, I loved her as my friend for many years, but Kate…" Kasa shook her head. "She is from another place, has worked magic in your life. And in mine. She is a beautiful, powerful woman. A rare treasure."

Though he felt confused, Kasa's words rang true. He opened the door. "Thank you. Have fun tonight."

Her countenance lightened. "I believe we will. Are you all right?"

"Yes." As he left, he saw Buster walking over from his Oldsmobile, a dozen roses in one hand, a box of chocolates in the other. He held up both of his gifts. "These ought to do the trick," he said, with a mischievous look.

"Certainly should." Francis smiled, held the door for Buster then walked along the garden fence toward the road, hearing the joy in Buster and Kasa's voices as they greeted each other. He walked slowly back up the hill. Inside the bungalow, he found neither Stringer nor Kate, so he walked to the bluff. They were down below in the skiff, a blanket covering Kate's shoulders and back. Stringer looked angry. He was pointing his finger at her. Through the crashing of the waves, Francis could hear only part of what Stringer was saying.

"...the best thing that's ever happened..." he yelled. "How could you screw it up?"

Wincing at Stringer's words, Francis pulled back out of sight. He had never seen Stringer so furious. Crouching down, he heard Stringer yelling again. Francis inched forward, peered down at them from behind the hedge roses. Stringer was waving his arms, shouting something Francis couldn't hear. Then the word "slut" rose sharply through the air. Kate fell forward in the boat, like Kennedy when he was shot. Stringer didn't move for a few moments. Then he leaned toward his mom and gradually slid his arms around her.

Francis heard Kate sobbing. He felt bad she was so upset. He hated to see Stringer treat her like that. It was not okay. Part of him wanted to go down the steps and admonish Stringer then bring them in to warm up by the parlor stove, tell them everything was going to be all right. But he couldn't fix this; they each had to work it out on their own. And damn it, it was her own fault—at least most of it. Stepping back from the edge of the cliff, Francis thought of Kasa's words. *Rat poison might be better than this.* He made himself walk toward the bungalow.

Francis lit a fire in the woodstove then went into his studio and tried to paint, but couldn't. Back in the parlor he pulled a leather-bound

Collected Dickens from the bookcase and sat in his grandmother's maple rocker. He turned to one of his favorite passages of *Oliver Twist*, when, after Oliver has robbed him, Mr. Brownlow takes in the sickly boy and nurses him back to health. Francis always loved that in the end Mr. Brownlow adopts Oliver and they live happily as a family ever after.

Francis rested the gold-edged volume in his lap and watched yellow flames lick around the edges of the split kindling. He thought about how attached he had become to Stringer and to Kate, how empty his life would be without them.

Soon Francis felt the warmth from the stove on his face and closed his eyes. He must have nodded off as it was after dark when he heard Kate and Stringer come inside. Feeling anxious, Francis wasn't sure what to say, felt out of place in his own home, a home that no longer belonged to just him. Still, he was glad to hear their voices in the foyer.

He swung the afghan off and looked at Stringer's easel holding the repaired portrait of Sam. Francis' mind was filled with conflicting emotions, including the odd thought he wished he belonged to some kind of religion, at least for a few minutes, so he would know how to pray, ask for help, do *something* to get beyond his pain. He hated being confused or incompetent, not knowing how to fix things when they were awry.

Francis listened as Kate and Stringer shed their damp clothes. Someone slowly climbed the stairs—probably Kate—as he soon heard the metal lid come off a jar around the corner. Francis walked into the kitchen where Stringer was scooping peanut butter with a spoon. He didn't look at Francis, just shifted back and forth from one untied sneaker to the other. Francis was struck by how quickly he was growing into a young man.

Stringer nudged a table leg with the toe of his sneaker. "You probably don't care, but she feels like shit. I know what she did was fucked-up." He slid his hands into the pockets of his baggy pants. Sounding more like a parent then a kid, he continued. "I'm disappointed in her, too, but she's still my mom, and she's hung in there with me through everything."

Francis listened quietly.

Stringer looked over at him. "Do I...do I have to stay away if you kick her out?" The rims of his eyes were red. "I'd miss you a ton."

Francis' heart sank. He hadn't expected this, hadn't thought it out this far.

"I could never say goodbye to you, Stringer."

"Well, Mom and I are sort of a package deal, no matter what she's done."

"Your mom has hurt me deeply. I'm angry and confused."

"I know. I'm wicked pissed, too, but I know it's not the same."

Francis was again impressed with Stringer's maturity, his ability to understand other people's feelings. "I want to always be here for you. I just don't know about Kate's and my future right now. I hope there is one."

There was a long silence then Francis spoke again. "Do you still want to go see Sam?"

Stringer shook his head. "It's too late; we're all beat. Plus I talked to her earlier. She's doing all right."

Francis smiled. "I'm glad." He gave Stringer a hug. They lingered for a few extra moments. As had always been the case, being in Stringer's presence warmed Francis' heart, especially when it felt like it could freeze over.

"Your mom is going to need your support."

Stringer looked surprised. "I don't feel very supportive right now."

"And you need to treat her with respect."

"Then she needs to treat us with respect."

Francis wasn't going to argue with that. "I don't want her to do something stupid—like drink."

"Me neither. I'm pissed, but I'm here for her."

"Good."

"By the way," Stringer said, "your friend Mr. Mallett came by the hospital, showed Sam and me how to play a couple of his songs."

"That was nice of him."

"He's a great guitar player. Kind of a crusty old guy, but cool."

Francis turned when he heard Kate coming down the stairs. She was carrying a couple of pillows and a comforter. She kept her head down as she crossed the foyer. "Is it okay if I sleep on the couch?"

"No," Francis said, quickly.

Kate stopped, stood there sadly, not knowing what to do.

Francis took a half-step toward her. "I mean, no, I want you to stay upstairs near Stringer. I have the cot in the studio."

Kate looked beyond exhausted; she looked broken, how he imagined she looked before escaping from California.

"Please, let me sleep on the couch. That's all I want." She glanced at Francis. "Would you mind taking that liquor bottle out of there?"

Francis didn't have to ask how she was feeling. "Sure."

He nodded to Stringer, who led Kate to the couch. Francis took the Jameson out of the cabinet while Stringer tucked her in and sat next to her in the rocker. As Francis slowly walked up the stairs he heard Stringer take out his guitar and start singing.

At last, a few moments of peace.

CHAPTER FORTY-TWO

THE NEXT MORNING, FRANCIS WAS AWAKENED BY THE VAGUE SOUND of a car in the driveway then a single, sharp rap on the door. As he hurried downstairs, he found Kate standing in the archway to the parlor looking frightened, a disheveled blanket partially wrapped around her. "Somebody banged on the door and took off."

"Did you see them?"

"I was asleep. Just saw the tail end of a big car. They were moving."

Francis looked out the sidelight as he pulled on his field coat. Seeing no one, he opened the door and stepped out onto the stone landing.

Kate screamed, causing Francis to whirl around and come face-to-face with a hunting knife stabbed into the door, pinning a bloody brochure to the wood. Startled, he reflexively pulled the knife from the door, ducked back inside and threw the deadbolt. "Call Charlie!"

Stringer appeared at the top of the stairs. "What's going on?"

"Get back in your room!" Kate yelled.

"Why, what's—"

"Now!" Kate grabbed the phone from its charger and hit the red emergency button.

Stringer's door slammed.

"We need the police," Kate said then gave their address. "Somebody just stabbed a bloody knife into our door."

Francis grabbed the Louisville Slugger he kept inside the hall closet and led Kate into the kitchen where they crouched by the stove. He pulled the blue paper off the knife; it was a tourist brochure for the Winter's Cove area that had been smeared with what looked like blood but was actually ketchup.

"Yes," Kate said urgently into the phone. "Hurry!" She turned to Francis. "Charlie and a trooper are coming."

"Tell them about the car. They may meet it on the way."

Kate told the 911 operator about the large sedan she saw.

Stringer, in a hoodie, hurried into the kitchen. "What's going on?" He got down with them and saw the knife. "Where'd *that* come from?"

"In the door," Kate said.

"Shit—" He glanced around.

Kate held him close to her. "Cops are on the way."

"You think it's that drug dealer again?"

Francis wiped the ketchup off the brochure with a dish towel. "Must be."

"I figured he'd taken off."

Francis opened the brochure. Someone had printed across it with a black marker. "Monroe, you have 48 hours to collect 200K—unmarked, no bullshit, no cops or your friends' Maine vacation will have a tragic end. Wed 6 AM—be alone— park outside solid waste depot—walk in and wait behind metals roll-off. We'll call your cellphone to give you directions. I've been easy on you. Don't test me, we're watching."

Kate shook her head. "That sonofabitch."

Francis heard a siren coming up the hill.

Stringer started to get up, but Francis held his arm. "Wait till they get to the house."

Soon they heard Charlie's voice at the door.

"Coming!" Francis got up and unlocked the door.

Charlie rushed inside. "Rhode Island Jimmy's back?"

"Yes." Francis handed him the note.

Charlie took a whiff, frowned. "Ketchup? Nice touch."

He studied the note and the knife then showed them to Sergeant Leblanc who'd arrived just after him. After Leblanc checked out the bungalow and found nothing else of concern, he recognized Stringer. "How's your girl doing?"

Stringer perked up. "Good. Learning how to use crutches."

"Excellent. Tell her the troops say hi."

"I will."

He stepped closer to Stringer. "You were something else, going over that cliff to help them."

Stringer looked at the floor. "Thanks."

Leblanc took photos of the door, the knife, and the brochure then placed them in a large plastic bag marked EVIDENCE.

Stringer looked at the bag, the inside of which was smeared red. "Maybe this guy's just a jack-off, trying to scare us. I mean…*ketchup?*"

Sergeant Leblanc held up the bag. "Looks like a dangerous knife. He just didn't have any real blood handy." He looked at Stringer. "We take this kind of thing seriously." He sealed the top of the bag. "Besides, our colleagues down in Rhode Island say this guy's bad news. Violent history. They'd love to get their hands on him."

Stringer looked dejected. He backed away, sat on the bottom of the stairs. "Shit never ends."

Charlie spoke to Francis, who was watching Stringer. "You find anything else?"

"No, but I haven't looked around outside."

"Why don't you folks get out of here? We'll finish investigating, dusting for prints, all that. Go somewhere safe for a while. I'll call you when we find out anything."

Francis looked at Kate, who nodded.

"All right. We'll go to Portland to visit Sam. The hospital ought to be safe."

Charlie nodded. "Sounds good."

They quickly got ready and headed down the hill in the Jeep. Buster's car was still at Kasa's. Francis thought of stopping to warn her about what was going on but decided to just head straight to the hospital. The guy had no beef with her.

In Portland, Francis felt relieved to be inside the large medical center. They found Sam up walking in the hallway with a physical therapist. She smiled when she saw the three of them come out of the elevator. Stringer ran ahead and gave her an awkward hug as she balanced on her crutches. Francis and Kate stayed back, letting them have a few moments together.

"You've probably had enough for one outing," the therapist said, motioning down the hall. "Why don't we go back?"

Stringer walked next to them. "How'd she do?"

"Very well," the therapist said, unhooking a canvas belt from around Sam's waist. "You'll be walking on your own tomorrow."

Sam sat on her bed and smiled. "Then I can get out of here?"

"Well, that's up to the doctors, but it won't be long. You've made remarkable progress."

"Cool. You've all done a great job piecing me back together, but I'm getting pretty claustrophobic."

The therapist smiled. "I understand." She slid a pencil over her ear and picked up her note pad. "I'll see you tomorrow."

Stringer helped Sam lift her injured leg up onto the bed then sat next to her.

Francis and Kate came in and said hi to Sam. Kate leaned against the wall by the window. Francis stayed near the door.

Everyone was quiet.

Sam closed her eyes and rested. Soon, she shifted her leg a bit and looked at them. "You're a lively bunch."

Stringer tried to look more upbeat but was unconvincing.

Sam frowned. "Something happen?"

Stringer glanced at Francis, who said, "Nothing to do with you, Sam."

"That Rhode Island guy back?"

"Yeah," Stringer said. "He left a calling card."

"What do you mean?"

Stringer adjusted himself on the bed. "You don't want to know."

Sam sat up straighter. "Tell me. I'm bored to death in here." She looked over at Kate. "Though they made me talk to a drug and alcohol counselor this morning."

"How was that?"

"I'd rather talk to you."

Kate smiled. "Good. We'll have plenty of time."

Sam looked back at Stringer. "So…?"

Francis leaned forward. "Maybe it's better if we don't—"

"Come on, I'm not some pussy."

Stringer looked at Sam. "Some asshole stabbed a note into our front door with a bloody knife—actually a knife with ketchup all over it. Demanded money in 48 hours."

Sam didn't flinch. "Sounds like a real douchebag. *Fake* blood? Lame."

"That's what I said, but the trooper and Charlie are taking it real serious. Oh yeah, Sergeant Leblanc said to say hi to you. His men are psyched you're getting better. He was pretty cool that night."

"I don't remember."

Stringer snickered. "I do."

"Me, too," Francis said.

"Me, three," Kate added.

They all fell quiet again. Francis felt the palpable awkwardness between Kate and him. He was trying to think of something to say when a young woman knocked on the open door and walked into the room. She had on a red polo shirt that said, Volunteer.

"I'm sorry to interrupt, but is there a Mr. Monroe in here?"

Francis was surprised. "Yes, I'm Francis Monroe."

"They asked me to tell you a friend of yours is in the hospital and she'd like to see you." The woman looked at a piece of paper. "Her name is Kasa Makano-something."

Francis stepped forward. "Makanovitch?"

"That's it."

"Where is she?"

"Upstairs, Room 410, the cardiac unit."

CHAPTER FORTY-THREE

ALARMED, FRANCIS STEPPED TOWARD THE VOLUNTEER. "WHAT happened to her?"

"Sorry," she said, "that's all I know. But I can show you how to get there."

"Thanks, I'll find her."

Francis spoke to no one in particular. "I just saw her yesterday. She was all gussied up for Buster, who was arriving with flowers and chocolates."

"Maybe too many chocolates?" Stringer said.

"Who's Kasa?" Sam asked.

"Our neighbor," Stringer said. "Cool old lady."

Francis moved toward the door. "I'll go see what's happened."

"Do you want me to come with you?" Kate asked quietly.

"No, thank you, I'll go." Francis walked out without looking at her.

He ran up two flights to the cardiac ward and found Kasa's room. When he walked in he was surprised to find Buster in the first bed and Kasa in the far one. Buster smiled but Kasa turned and looked out the window. They were hooked up to several monitors and had green oxygen tubing in their noses. Thankfully, they didn't look like they were in any distress.

"What happened?"

Kasa didn't look at Francis. Buster broke into a big grin and started chuckling.

Francis was confused. "What's going on with you two?"

Buster rolled his eyes toward Kasa. "You want to tell him, dear?"

Kasa shooed him off with her hand. "Keep still!" she said, sharply. "Have you not an ounce of couth?"

The door swung open. Kate came in followed by Stringer pushing Sam in a wheelchair.

Kate went to Kasa's side. "What happened? Are you all right?"

"Good heavens, will you all leave us alone?" Kasa pulled her blanket up higher, partially covering her face. "Can't you see we are very ill?"

Buster let out a laugh then started coughing. "Ill?" he said, between coughs. "We are simply recovering from a most eventful evening."

Kasa turned and glared at him. "Hush now. You are the furthest thing from a gentleman!"

Everyone else in the room stood confused.

"Would someone tell me what's going on?" Francis felt agitated. His mind on the Rhode Island guy, he wasn't in the mood for fooling around.

"I'm not feeling well enough for visitors," Kasa said, turning back to the window.

Buster pushed himself higher up on his pillows. "Well, I am." He put on his black glasses, and straightened his hospital gown. He spoke in a formal tone. "Ms. Makanovitch and I have each suffered minor heart attacks." He sounded pleased, proud, almost. "And we certainly had a good time having them."

Francis frowned. "*Heart attacks?*"

Stringer cocked his head at Buster.

Buster appeared to be trying to keep his composure, but his face cracked into a smile. "Why, yes. When Kasa gave me my pleasure, I knew I was either having the biggest orgasm of my life, a heart attack, or both!"

There was a collective dropping of jaws.

Kasa's face turned redder than a rimmer on a stove. "Against my will! The big oaf fed me cheap wine that went straight to my head."

"I certainly did not!" Buster replied indignantly, but with a grin.

Kasa crossed her arms tightly. "I temporarily lost my mind, but I assure you it won't happen again."

Stringer started to laugh. "You blew it, Buster."

Kasa put her hands to her face. "I am so terribly ashamed."

Buster waved his hand at her. "Don't be such an old prude. Besides..." he said to Stringer on the side, "she was enjoying herself right up until she infarcted."

Suddenly Kate cracked up. Then Sam and Stringer started giggling.

Preoccupied with the sight of the 'bloody' knife in the door, Francis was the last to catch on, but when he did, he laughed so hard tears formed in his eyes. Buster, laughing and coughing, knocked the oxygen out of his nose causing an alarm to go off.

Within a minute, an older nurse with a white cap brusquely entered the room. "What's going on in here? This is a cardiac ward, for heaven's sake."

Seeing the serious look on her face, Francis and the others tried to contain themselves but started cracking up again, finally driving Stringer and Francis into the hallway to try to compose themselves. Kate walked out after them, and when she and Francis looked at each other, they continued to laugh, reflexively leaning against each other, which made Stringer smile. "I told you they were hooking up."

Francis shook his head. "You were right, but they *both* had heart attacks?"

After a couple minutes they walked back into the room, where Sam had rolled her wheelchair over to Kasa. Sam was showing her the fixator.

"I'm glad you two had a chance to meet," Francis said.

"I'll go to my grave regretting this," Kasa sputtered at Buster. "I shall never forgive you."

Francis looked at Kasa. "Really? Beware the rat poison, my friend."

The others gave Francis a strange look.

"Private joke," Francis said, as his cellphone began ringing in his pocket. He quickly stepped back out to the hallway. It was Charlie. "We talked to Rhode Island, sounds like your guy's been down there raising hell with some of the family's gambling operations. That may be why he's back up here. Who knows what he'll do. I'll keep a deputy up at your place till this is over. Nobody wants to put you in danger, but if you're up for doing this, we'll have that recycling place completely covered, and with Stringer out on the lobster boat, he should be safe." Charlie paused. "This has to end—one way or another. I've had enough of this Leland bullshit."

"Me, too," Francis said. "I'm in. And I'm counting on you."

"The state police and I want to come out to your house in the morning to go over the plan we're working on."

Though the prospect of meeting this guy by a dumpster frightened him, Francis was ready to do whatever it took.

"They'll be a deputy waiting for you in your driveway."

"Okay. We'll head home soon."

"Not alone. There's a trooper waiting to escort you home." Charlie's voice became even more serious, sympathetic. "You're a good man, Francis."

"We'll see."

CHAPTER FORTY-FOUR

OUTSIDE THE HOSPITAL, BEFORE THEY HAD GOTTEN IN THE JEEP, Francis took Kate aside and told her it felt good to have a laugh but he had to stick to his ultimatum about whether or not she would continue to live at the bungalow. She looked disappointed but said she understood. Besides a few lingering chuckles about Kasa and Buster's romantic misfortune, the ride home was quiet. Feeling anxious about what this guy might do, Francis appreciated the unmarked state trooper following behind them.

As they turned the corner at Kasa's, Francis was pleased to see a sheriff's cruiser parked at the side of the road. He slowed and waved to the deputy then continued up to the bungalow. Before going inside, Kate and Francis stood next to each other looking at a striking collection of stratus clouds layered over the outer bay, the last purple hues of sunset softly illuminating them. The sea was unusually calm.

"Beautiful," Kate said.

"I'm going in," said Stringer.

When Stringer was inside, Kate touched Francis' arm. "I'd like to explain what happened in Skowhegan."

Francis stared at the ocean. "I don't think there is much to explain, Kate. There was a used condom wrapper in your pocket."

"But, we didn't…"

Francis put his hand up. "I can't hear it. Not now."

"Okay." Kate walked to the house, paused at the threshold as if she was going to say something else, then walked inside. Watching her, Francis was again struck by her beauty, and he respected her for breaking her anonymity to try and help Sam with her addiction issues. Despite feeling wounded, he hoped she would choose to embrace their life together and stay.

Inside, as Kate stepped through the archway into the parlor, she sud-

denly stopped and let out a shrill scream. A stab of fright pierced Francis'
chest. Coming up behind Kate, he saw a pair of black leather shoes resting on the coffee table. Leaning back against the quilted pillows on their
couch was Rhode Island Jimmy. Hands behind his head, he appeared
disturbingly comfortable.

"Welcome home, folks. Sit down."

Francis backed up half a step to the closet and felt for the Louisville
Slugger then realized he'd left it in the kitchen beside the stove. Kate
stood trembling in the hallway. "What do you want?" she said, weakly.

Jimmy pulled his feet off the table, knocking over a crystal dish holding a candle. Kate and Francis started at the sound of glass breaking on
the floor.

Francis stepped in front of Kate. "How'd you get in here?"

"Your stupid rent-a-cop let me in."

Francis frowned. He didn't know what to believe. "Listen, we've got
nothing to do with Leland and your drug business."

Jimmy slid an ominous-appearing black handgun from under his
coat, motioned toward the two chairs opposite the couch. "No, *you* listen,
Monroe. I said, sit down."

They sat in the chairs. Francis hoped Stringer would take off out the
back door and get help.

"Why don't you leave us alone? Kate doesn't know anything."

With the gun resting across his lap, Jimmy leaned forward. "Oh, yes,
she does." He looked at Kate. "Don't you, honey? You were right there
dealing with that scumbag, keeping everybody happy." He smirked and
thrust his pelvis.

Kate's face tightened. "You pig—"

Jimmy sniffed then wiped his nose. "A pig you owe money to. We
know a lot of Leland's money went right up your nose."

Kate looked uncomfortable. "Not for a long time."

Jimmy gestured with the gun. "Bullshit. You were doing blow last year,
you lying bitch."

Francis sat forward. "Don't talk to her like that."

Jimmy lifted the gun and turned to him. "What are you going to do
about it? Call the cops? Wake the guy up at the bottom of the hill?"

Francis felt his chest muscles tighten.

"So I got a message for you from the boss. Now it's 400 grand. Taken too long to get his money—makes him nervous—so he added a surcharge."

"What if we can't get the money fast enough?" Francis said.

Jimmy abruptly stood, glared. "Don't fuck with us or you're all history. Killing someone's no big deal. And there's nothing your little copper friends can do about it." He took a quick step toward Francis, stuck the cold muzzle of the gun in his forehead. "Ever seen what a nine millimeter'll do to a brain? It ain't pretty."

Francis' breath caught. He looked up at Jimmy, saw his dilated pupils.

Jimmy pulled the gun off Francis' head, jammed it inside his belt. "Tomorrow morning. Six o'clock. Don't be late."

He walked out of the parlor, glanced into the kitchen at Stringer. "And you better not fuck things up this time, you little puke."

He quickly left through the front door, which partially closed behind him.

Francis and Kate hurried into the kitchen, where Stringer stood on the far side of the refrigerator, gripping the baseball bat. Kate took him in her arms. Watching them, Francis realized they were losing their ability to fight. They'd spent too much survival energy on the trial, never dreaming they'd have to do it again. He felt like their batteries might not take another charge. But he was resolute in doing whatever it took to get rid of this guy, and Leland, forever.

Through the partially open front door, Francis thought he heard a power boat take off below the cliff.

"Why don't you run down to the deputy?" Stringer said.

"That Jimmy guy will be long gone, and I've got to figure out the right thing to do. He's brazen, ruthless. But it doesn't make sense to me. He's a city gangster. What's he doing up here for a few hundred thousand?"

Kate turned to Francis. "Didn't you say when Charlie first talked to the cops in Rhode Island they thought he was up here getting away from the heat down there?"

Francis nodded. "That's right."

"Well, maybe that's it."

"Seems like there's got to be something else. Some local connection, maybe?"

"So what are we going to do?" Kate looked at Stringer. "I'm so sick of running."

"Charlie and the state police are coming up with a plan."

"You going to tell them he was here? He threatened to kill us for god's sake."

Francis thought about it. "I don't know, I'm trying to trust my gut, but this is way out of my league." He tried to grin. "At least until I met you two."

"Lucky you," Stringer said.

"I don't like it but I think we should just do what they say. Seems like they hold the cards."

The phone rang in the hallway. It was Charlie, who said he and the state police didn't have time to come out to the bungalow, so he went over the basic plan on the phone. They'd put Francis in a bulletproof vest and have him go to the drop site with a bag of marked bills where they would take down these bastards. Assuming they would try to pull something unexpected, the police would have the recycling depot and the surrounding roads heavily covered. Francis didn't tell Charlie that Jimmy had paid them a visit, but he did ask to have the deputy drive up and park in front of the house. Truth was, Francis wasn't convinced the local police, despite their best intentions, were adequately prepared to deal with this. He'd go along with their plan, but he was going to try and keep his options open and above all, keep Kate and Stringer safe.

Francis watched Stringer sitting in the kitchen, aimlessly rolling the baseball bat back and forth on the kitchen table. Kate walked around the house, pulling all the window shades down. Afterward, she sat on the couch by the woodstove, fidgeting with her hair and looking at the cabinet where the whisky bottle had been.

After a couple minutes, Francis walked in and sat near her. He spoke in as calm and friendly a voice as he could muster. "Would you like me to take you to a meeting? It's been a while."

Kate seemed surprised. "Wow," she said, quietly, "that would be good. What day is it, anyway?"

"Monday, I think. It's been a whirlwind."

"I know Ginny used to go to a Monday night meeting in town."

"Would you like to call her?"

Kate nodded. "She will *not* be happy with me, but it's the right thing to do. I need to face some music." She looked at Francis. "You don't mind taking me?"

Francis felt himself soften. "I'd be happy to."

"You'd better tell Charlie, so he knows where you are."

"Yes."

Kate looked up. "Thank you."

"You're welcome."

She looked at him with sad, exhausted eyes. "I'm sorry, Francis."

He nodded, touched her hands, and went back to the kitchen to check on Stringer.

On the phone, Ginny said she'd catch up with Kate at the meeting then give her a ride home. Charlie sent a cruiser out, which followed them into town. Francis left Kate off at the Congregational Church then idled at the far end of the parking lot, watching to make sure she got safely inside the basement door, from which a warm yellow light shone onto the pavement.

On the way back out of town, Francis slowed as he drove by the information booth, remembering the day the Rhode Island asshole first showed up. Francis pulled onto the shoulder of the road. He tried to push Richard and Kate—together—out of his mind, *whatever* had happened. And he acknowledged for the first time, to himself at least, that he felt inadequate, too old for Kate, so he'd stopped trying very hard. It was as if he knew she would eventually run off with some younger guy and helped her do just that.

After the back door to the church closed behind Kate, she stood alone in the dim light. There was a subtle mustiness in the air, and downstairs she heard members of the fellowship talking and laughing with each other. The irreverent and often self-deprecating humor of the groups was an important part of what had attracted her to AA. Though now, after having not attended meetings for a couple of months, it sounded almost foreign to her. *How could I have screwed things up so bad?* She put her forehead against a cold concrete wall. *Cause that's all you've ever done.*

Chapter Forty-five

After Francis left, Kate felt a strong wave of the old panic, the feeling she had to have a drink at any cost. She knew her bad behavior had caught up to her and if she didn't take some sober action, it would drown her. As she'd often heard in meetings, it was sure to be a slow, agonizing death.

Starting to sweat, as if in withdrawal, Kate peered through the corner of the window. It looked like Francis was out of sight. She had an intense urge to run cross-lots to a nearby bar and drink till she passed out. Blotto. Dead drunk. She didn't want to die; she just wanted to not feel anymore.

She stepped into the shadows of a small utility closet and stood with the brooms and mops and wash pails. She stared at a spray bottle of "Green Clean," an "all-purpose environmentally safe cleaner" that hung from a nail pounded into a two-by-four. *Would that help?*

Kate heard a bell ring downstairs. The meeting was about to start. Ginny would ream her a new one if she didn't get down there. But how she hated to admit all the deceitful stuff she'd been doing and how stupid she'd been to stop going to meetings.

Kate descended the stairs and quietly took a seat in the back. Ginny must have sensed she was there as she turned in her seat, looked directly at Kate, and pointed to an empty chair next to her.

While the chairperson opened the meeting, Ginny kept staring, her expression increasingly severe. She raised her hand even higher and continued to point at the seat she'd obviously saved for Kate. Several members glanced back to see who Ginny was looking at.

Kate stood, slunk down the side aisle to the appointed chair next to Ginny.

"I wondered when you would've had enough," Ginny said, without looking at Kate.

"I feel like shit."

"Of course you do. You've not been sober."

"I didn't drink," Kate whispered.

"There's a lot more to being sober than not drinking."

"I know. I'm sorry."

Ginny looked at her. "Don't be sorry for my sake. It's your life. You chose not to heed my warnings."

A woman stepped to the lectern and read the Twelve Steps. Kate took some relief in hearing them. The word *powerless* rang sharply in her mind.

After a couple minutes, Ginny patted Kate's thigh. "You're in the right place. Now stay here."

Kate tried hard to listen as they went around the room taking turns reading about Step Two from one of the fellowship's books. "Came to believe that a power greater than ourselves could restore us to sanity." Kate remembered when she first heard that and was offended by the implication she could be insane. But after the last nine months of chaos and her own recent behavior, she had no doubt she was certifiably nuts and had no problem admitting it.

Though at times it was hard to keep her focus, Kate got a lot out of the group discussion about the step. She really *had* come to believe in some kind of Higher Power, even though she didn't know what it looked or sounded like. She knew for her it wasn't religious. It was more a spiritual force like the one her mother had communed with. It was something Kate felt most strongly when she was out in nature or when she was surrounded by other recovering alcoholics. It baffled her why she had stopped going to meetings as they always made her feel better.

After the meeting, several people came up to Kate and said they had missed seeing her. She, Ginny, and a couple other women had a cup of coffee together then they helped clean up the hall and headed home. Ginny drove slowly so they had plenty of time to talk. Fearing they might be attacked, Kate kept an eye out for suspicious-looking vehicles, but saw none.

"I know what it feels like to be out of control," Ginny said, after they'd pulled onto the main road. "My life was a tangled mess before I got sober."

"You seem so together now," Kate said.

Ginny pointed to her head. "Ha! If you only knew what goes on in here."

"Oh, I have a pretty good idea." Kate pointed to her own head. "I've got one, too."

Ginny grinned. "Looking back, I don't know how I survived, but somebody up there must not have been done with me. I was drinking almost two fifths a day. One summer, shitfaced drunk, I nearly sank a boat in the middle of the harbor. If it wasn't for Delbert Ready I would've drowned, surer than hell. Or killed somebody else. And back then I was kind of married *and* screwing two other guys at the same time."

Kate grinned.

Ginny laughed when she realized what she'd said. "Well I don't mean simultaneously!"

The night was ink black, not a star in the sky. A subtle, wispy fog snaked along the side of the road in the tall reeds. With a lot of the white line worn off from winter road salt, it was hard to see where the edge of the pavement was. Ginny squinted as she drove. "Kate, I hurt so many people, mostly my poor family. After I came into AA, I decided I would avoid any more romantic relationships. I'm not equipped for them. I'm happier alone in my shop and keeping my little lobster fleet running."

Kate smiled. "I love your shop. Francis said he was in there the first time he saw me and Stringer walking up the sidewalk, said he almost broke your door down trying to catch up with us."

"Oh, I remember. First time he'd shown any life since Rachael died. He was smitten with you alright, and with Stringer."

They rode along in silence for a couple of miles.

Ginny glanced over at Kate. "How you two doing?"

"Not good."

"Anything you want to talk about?"

Kate looked out the window into the darkness. "I don't know. We grew apart fast after the trial, which was strange because things had seemed so good with us. After he and Stringer had the successful art show, I started working in the gallery. I was getting the hang of it, even sold a couple pieces, but Francis seemed jealous of every guy I talked to, especially if they were younger. It's like he lost his mojo just when I was finally coming to life."

Ginny waited a few moments then spoke. "So did you have an affair?"

"Jeez, you get right to the point."

"Well?"

"Sort of—"

Ginny chuckled. "Like *sort of* being pregnant?"

"A one-nighter, well, maybe two—an art agent that's interested in Stringer's paintings."

"And you."

"I guess. He's slick, from New York, a decent guy with a hot blue Mustang."

"Sounds dangerous."

"He is."

"What's Francis know?"

"We haven't talked about it, but he knows something happened. We were together up at an art appreciation course in Skowhegan a couple of weekends."

Kate thought about the night in the cabin. "It could have been real bad, Ginny. He had good wine, not that I ever cared, and a lot of blow. He got pretty drunk and passed out, didn't really push me, but staring at those white lines on his little mirror scared me."

"It should, for Christ's sake. You're a drunk, a drug addict. You nearly died in California, almost killed your newborn son." Kate slid closer to the window as Ginny's voice rose. "How many chances do you think your Higher Power is going to give you? Have you no gratitude for this amazing gift you've been given?"

Kate knew she had it coming, almost welcomed it.

Ginny slowed the car and pulled over at the side of a swamp.

Kate grimaced. "Do we have to stop?"

Ginny jammed it into park. "Yes, we do. Right here where Francis could have been killed trying to protect you. The man who's turned his life upside down to give you and Stringer a good home."

Kate remained silent.

"You, like me, are a self-centered drunk, and if you're not practicing the program, living the Twelve Steps, then that's *all* you are—a damn drunk." Ginny looked Kate in the eye. "Nobody's going to babysit you, Kate. You're a big girl. Make your own choices, but I'm here to help if you want to live an emotionally sober life, not just *not drink*. I've got no tolerance for your behavior, though, if you keep on like you've been."

Without waiting for a response, Ginny pulled the shift back into drive and drove Kate straight home, passing the sheriff's cruiser parked on the corner at Kasa's.

"Strange he's running radar way out here. Must be a slow night."

"Yeah," Kate said, flatly.

When they pulled up to the bungalow, Kate wanted to tell Ginny about the Rhode Island guy and the extortion, but she couldn't muster the energy. She got out and shut the door. "Thanks for the ride. And for the lecture. I needed it."

"You know," Ginny said through the open window, "when Bill Wilson and Dr. Bob started this whole AA thing, it only worked because one alcoholic was willing, or desperate enough, to help another get sober so they could stay sober themselves."

"Yeah, I know."

"So why don't you commit to helping that girl, the singer who went over the cliff. You've got a lot to offer. You can help each other."

"I actually talked to her at the hospital, told her a little about my story."

"You offer to take her to a meeting?"

"Yeah. I think she might go sometime."

"Well, you need to take her and yourself to a lot of meetings." Ginny put the car in gear. "Let me know if I can help."

"You already have."

As Ginny drove off, Kate realized she had no idea what the next couple of days would bring, but she was determined to stay sober and do her best to help Stringer. And to be truer to Francis.

CHAPTER FORTY-SIX

THE NEXT MORNING IT WAS STILL DARK OUT AS FRANCIS WATCHED Kate pace back and forth in the foyer.

"I don't get it, Francis. This is too dangerous. Why can't they just arrest this asshole?"

Francis checked that the marked money was secure in his valise. "Kate, we've been over this. He hasn't done anything illegal they can pin on him. They want to nail him for extortion, but they've got to catch him in the act."

Kate gestured. "We find a knife stabbed in our front door and that's not enough?"

"You heard Charlie. There were no prints, no witnesses. They've got nothing solid on this guy."

Kate shook her head, put her hands on her hips. "This is *such* bullshit."

"Look, it's going to be okay. They've got an army of cops waiting for the guy after I give him the money. And Stringer's headed out on Ginny's boat, so he's out of danger."

"What if they trick you or something?"

"I'm aware that anything can happen." Francis looked at her face, which was replete with concern. "You're really scared, aren't you?"

Kate looked him in the eye. "You may not believe it, but I care a helluva lot about you, and I don't want anybody else getting hurt. I want this over."

Francis closed his valise and secured the leather strap. "That's why I'm doing this."

Kate felt both sides of his chest. "You have the vest on, right?"

"Yes, Sergeant Leblanc adjusted it for me before he left."

"And your cellphone's charged?"

"Yes."

"Can't I go with you?"

"No. We don't need anyone else at risk. A deputy is going to be here with you till it's over. Why don't you go down to Kasa's like we talked about? Water her plants, do whatever you can to stay calm."

Kate stepped between Francis and the front door and, for a few moments, held him close. Outside, before climbing into the Jeep, Francis noticed the first pink glow of dawn appearing over the Atlantic. He drove down the hill feeling uncomfortably confined in the Kevlar vest but was glad he had it on. The police had said there would be absolutely no contact with him until after they—hopefully—arrested Jimmy and whoever was with him. This whole thing was beyond weird, but thankfully his fear had largely been replaced with sheer determination.

Approaching the entrance to the recycling depot, Francis couldn't see evidence of police anywhere. He had to assume they were nearby looking out for him. A beat-up van with a flat tire sat in the grass off the side of the road. He wondered if someone was in it. He drove past the locked gate and parked in the weeds. As instructed, he ducked under the chain and walked down a short road into the still-dark recycling yard. He disturbed a small animal which glanced at him then slunk off into the underbrush. Francis' heart accelerated.

In the yard, the uneven ground was crisscrossed with deep tire tracks, and as Francis headed toward the large roll-offs, he tripped on a piece of half-buried scrap metal. He guessed, hoped really, there were swat cops hiding in some of the many dumpsters scattered about the yard. He checked his watch—5:53. Seven more minutes. He looked at his cellphone. No missed calls.

Francis found the large container with METALS painted on the side. He leaned back against it, the cold from the steel quickly penetrating his windbreaker. He kept his valise tight against his leg. Consciously keeping his breathing slow and steady, he waited, though he could hear his heart pounding hard in his chest. It finally hit him that this might be a really bad idea. He should have listened to Kate.

His phone lit up and started ringing. Startled, he dropped his valise in order to hold onto the phone. He fumbled turning it on, realizing he was shaking when he lifted it to his ear. "Hello—"

"Move to the other side of the roll-off." The voice sounded computer-altered but came through clearly.

Francis hesitated for a second, not sure where to go.

"Now!" the voice said, sharply.

Francis grabbed his valise and hurried around to the back side of the container. He struggled to keep the phone on his ear.

"Go straight to the chain-link fence in front of you. The bottom section has been cut so you can crawl through it. Then lock the fence back together with the padlock. Wait by the railroad track."

Francis looked over at the fence.

"Do it now!"

Hurrying up a short embankment of uneven gravel, Francis fell hard on his knees.

"Get moving!" the voice yelled.

Francis pushed himself up off the ground, protecting the phone so he didn't accidentally shut it off. His hand was bleeding from the fall, but that didn't matter. He scrambled to the fence and pulled on the cut section but couldn't open it enough to get through. He dropped to the ground and kicked the fence out the other way.

"You have one minute to get to the train tracks."

Francis pushed the valise through the opening then crawled through the cut section, the ends of the sharp wires ripping through the nylon shell of his windbreaker.

He looked up and saw the railroad tracks just beyond him.

"Lock the fence!"

Francis pulled the fence together and secured it with the padlock they had left hanging on the wire.

"Now go down the track till you get to the first signal pole and hide in the bushes."

"To the right?"

"Yes!"

"Okay."

"Run. There's very little time!"

Francis ran along the track, stumbling over piles of crushed stone and discarded railroad ties. He was winded by the time he made it to the pole. Up ahead of him, a train whistle blew two-long, one-short, then another long blast.

"Stay in the bushes until the third car after the last engine comes into sight. Then get as close to the tracks as you can and throw the bag in the open door. You get one chance. Or you won't see this kid again."

Francis felt a lead weight drop in his stomach. "*What* kid?" he asked, barely able to get the words out.

"Do it, Francis!" The computer voice had disappeared. Stringer. They had him.

Panicking, Francis' eyes opened wide. He had to tell the police. *But then they might kill Stringer.*

He gripped the phone with his bloody hand. "Don't you hurt him!"

A man's voice came on. "Just throw the fucking thing into the train like I told you."

Francis felt the ground rumble as the train's bright yellow headlight came into view. As the massive engine picked up speed, its horn let out another deafening blast. Francis tried to cover his ears and dropped the phone. He had no time to pick it up. The first engine passed, then the other, their hydraulics hissing loudly. The third freight car came into view. Stepping up as close as he could he felt a cold draft pulling him along the track.

He squinted. There was no open door!

He kept watching the third car and just before it reached him, the metal door slid partially open. He slung the valise as hard as he could. It hit the edge of the door and started to fall back but an arm appeared out of the darkness and snatched it into the car.

As the rest of the train passed, Francis looked around and found the phone amongst the crushed stone. It was still lit up. Shaking, he held it to his ear, heard the computer voice again. "That 400 K was just a deposit on the kid's life." There was a pause. "Are you listening?"

Francis winced as he heard Stringer cry in the background. "Yes. Yes."

"Listen carefully if you ever want to see him again."

CHAPTER FORTY-SEVEN

FRANCIS WAS DESPERATELY AFRAID FOR STRINGER. "DON'T YOU DARE hurt him," Francis said into his cellphone.

"Shut up! Now go to your bank and get ready to wire another half-mill to an overseas account. We know you've got it. We'll text you the account number at eight-thirty when the bank opens."

Francis bit his lip, tried to get control of himself.

"You got that, Monroe?"

"I'll be there when they open."

"Remember, no cops."

"Do what they say!" Stringer yelled into the phone.

Francis had never heard him sound so terrified. "I will!"

The phone went dead. Francis stood there, reeling. "My god—" He momentarily put his hands to his face. Then he made himself snap out of it. He glanced around. Daylight illuminated the recycling yard. The train was already out of sight when he saw several swat officers heading toward the METALS container.

"Oh shit—" he said, motioning for them to stay away. Instead they must have thought he was asking for help as they started running toward him, converging on the padlocked fence. He knew he was being watched, so all he could do was act like everything had gone as planned.

Sergeant Leblanc made it to the fence first. "What happened? What'd you do with the money?"

Francis thought lying would better protect Stringer, as the cops seemed to be a step behind the bad guys. Francis stalled, bent over, and acted like he was too out of breath to talk.

Leblanc shook the fence. "Monroe, where's the money bag?"

Francis had to tell him. "They told me to throw it..." He hesitated, took an extra breath he didn't really need.

"Where?" Leblanc demanded. "Where'd you throw it?"

"Into the train."

"The *train*? Where on the train?"

"Into one of the cars."

"Which car?"

"I'm not sure."

Leblanc shook the fence with both hands. "Are you shitting me?" He turned to two other officers. "The money's on the train and every cop in Maine is surrounding this place. Sonofabitch." He pointed. "You guys stop that train. I don't care if you park a cement truck on the tracks."

The men ran back through the yard and up the access road.

Leblanc radioed headquarters and told them what was going on. Francis couldn't believe he was doing his best to help the bad guys escape, but maybe it would save Stringer. He looked at Leblanc. "I'm going to walk around the fence back to my Jeep."

"You'll have to. I haven't got any bolt cutters." Leblanc looked straight at Francis through the fence. "Anything else? Anything that would help us?"

Francis wiped his forehead with his sleeve. "Sorry. It all happened so fast: they kept yelling directions into the phone then when I heard..." Francis almost mentioned Stringer.

"Heard *what*?" Leblanc stepped close to the fence.

"That I had to crawl under the fence."

Leblanc cocked his head, looked at Francis suspiciously.

He held his bleeding hand up. "I fell and cut my hand, barely made it to the train to throw the bag up. I didn't know what else to do, had no idea where you all were."

Leblanc stared for a couple seconds then shook his head. "We didn't think of the train, with this fence and all. Tricky bastards."

"I'll say."

"We should have thought of it. There's a bunch of dirt bike trails near here. We figured they'd use those."

"It's only money," Francis said, thinking of the half-million he now had to get together.

Leblanc gave him a strange look. "It's actually extortion and robbery."

"I know." He didn't want to piss off Leblanc. "I'm going to get moving, got to get this hand bandaged." He didn't let on it was just a minor cut.

Since he had to fight his way through several thickets of long-thorn blackberries, it took Francis a while to make it all the way around the fence. By the time he reached the Jeep he was tired, sweaty, and badly scratched-up. As he climbed in, he realized all of the police had taken off after the train. That was a relief. No one should bother him when he went to the bank. His head raced. He felt terrible. Stringer was caught up in another life-threatening situation. He wanted to tell Kate but decided telling her would not be for the best. He realized again how much he cared about them both.

Francis looked in the rearview mirror and saw what a mess he was. Even his cheek was scratched and beaded with tiny drops of dried blood. Knowing he was not presentable enough to go into the bank, he decided to go to the gallery and get cleaned up in the small shower Rachael had installed years before. He figured he had a change of clothes there somewhere. He kept his baseball cap low across his forehead as he drove into town and parked behind the gallery. No one was on the street so he hurried up the steps, noticing an abstract painting of Stringer's displayed in the window.

Stepping into the back room, the smell of Rachael's favorite jasmine incense lingered. He ignited the small propane stove and shed his torn, wet clothes. As the odor of burning dust rose from the stove, he held his hands over it to warm them.

The hidden door to the little bathroom was cut out of the carved, mahogany planking that covered the back wall. Rachael had found an artisan in Bali who carved traditional scenes into beautiful boards and had had a local carpenter assemble them into a wall. Many a day work-ing in the studio, Francis slipped out back, relaxed on the couch and marveled at the intricately carved scenes.

The door creaked as he opened it. Cobwebs dangled from a wicker-framed mirror over a small porcelain sink. Hanging on the back of the door was a green and black-checked flannel shirt and a pair of semi-retired jeans. He turned on the hot water and after a minute or so, the pipes began to squeak. He stepped in, pulled the curtain closed and lathered himself with shower gel. As the stall filled with fragrant steam, he breathed in deeply. Bowing his head, he tried to relax, the hot water soothing his sore muscles as it flowed over his back.

Francis lifted his head and thought of Kate: her deep blue eyes, her long dark hair, the smooth curve of her hips. He realized he needed her to help him look into his own soul more clearly. She completed him in ways he'd never before experienced and figured he never would again. Despite the recent turmoil, he more fully realized what a beautiful gift she was and that he had to accept and embrace—unconditionally—exactly who she was.

Francis turned off the shower and dried himself. He had no clean underwear, so he pulled on the pair of old jeans and the slightly musty flannel shirt. He wiped his hand across the foggy mirror. Not great, but he looked better. He had to keep moving. When he left the gallery, the clock read 8:15.

Francis drove to the back parking lot of the bank which was in the middle of Harbor Avenue, just down from the sheriff's office. He only had to wait a few minutes before the lights came on and someone unlocked the door, though unfortunately it was Ms. Wheeler, the oldest and most suspicious teller.

Francis' cellphone rang. He flipped it open and realized the screen was partially obscured with blood. He grabbed a pen and an old envelope from the cup holder.

The computerized voice again. "Bank of Cayman accounts: Z2165970062, and AF8966721347. Routing number—"

"Wait—" Francis interrupted. "I can't write that fast."

"You'd better," the voice said.

"Okay."

"You get the account numbers?"

Francis read them back. They were correct.

"Routing number 00167328745."

Francis wrote quickly. "Got it."

"We're not fucking around, Monroe. We *will* kill this kid if you don't get the money transferred."

"How will we get Stringer back?"

"Wire the money then I'll tell you."

Francis became acutely anxious again. "I can't control the cops, but I won't say anything."

"We know. They're off chasing an empty train." The voice snickered and the phone went dead.

Again, Francis wanted to call Kate and Charlie and tell them what the hell was going on, but his gut said he should do what they said. He ran a comb through his hair, took in a deep breath, and got out. He straightened his flannel shirt and walked to the back door of the bank, where, like a stern schoolteacher, Ms. Wheeler stood waiting for him.

Chapter Forty–eight

CHARLIE PULLED HIS CRUISER TO A STOP IN A CLOUD OF DUST NEXT to a railroad crossing a few miles south of town. He got out and yelled to one of his deputies following him in another cruiser. "Park right on the track, leave all your lights on and get the hell out of there." He heard the train coming in the distance and figured it had cleared the slow, tight curves coming out of town.

"You sure?" the deputy asked.

"Do it!" Charlie keyed the mic on his lapel. "Dispatch, did you hear back from the railroad? They going to stop this thing?"

"10-4, Sheriff. They radioed the engineer. He's not happy, has no idea what we're talking about."

"No matter. You just get this train stopped."

"Yes, sir."

Three blue Maine State Police cruisers, as well as a black tactical unit came racing up the road and pulled in behind Charlie.

Sergeant Leblanc climbed out of the truck and walked straight to Charlie. "How'd you get here so fast?"

"My county," he said, with a grin. "I can't tell you all the shortcuts."

"Wiseass." Leblanc turned to the tracks and listened for a few seconds. "Haven't they stopped that locomotive yet? Judas priest! We're not going to lose these guys."

At Leblanc's command, the tactical team set up behind Charlie's cruiser and one of the swat officers rested his sniper rifle across the hood. As it came into sight, the train sounded like it was powering down. It slowed until it was fifty yards from the blocked crossing, its steel wheels squeaking to a stop. The swat team immediately made their way to the engine, rifles trained on the cab in case someone had taken control of the engineer. Charlie followed them down the short section of track as fast as he could.

"Hands in the air!" one of the officers yelled up to the engineer, who was leaning out his window.

"What's going on?" the confused engineer yelled back.

"Anybody in there with you?"

"Just my brakeman."

"We're looking for a robber, maybe more than one. Come down out of there and keep your hands in the air."

"Cain't climb down without my hands," the engineer grumbled.

"Just come down."

Both trainmen were soon on the ground. Two officers immediately entered the cab, one from each side of the tracks. The engineer shook his head, lit a cigar, and stuck it in the corner of his mouth.

"Nothing in here," an officer yelled down.

"All right. Fan out," Leblanc said. "Take both sides and check every car. There's another team coming up from the caboose, so watch out for them."

"T'aint no caboose these days," the engineer said with a tinge of sarcasm.

Leblanc waved him off. "You know what I mean."

The officers made their way down the tracks, but found that none of the boxcars had an open door. Charlie took his time, walking behind them, inspecting each car for himself.

Leblanc became increasingly agitated. He looked at Charlie. "What the hell was Monroe talking about? Now we've got to search the whole damn train."

"I don't think so." Charlie nodded at the boxcar next to him, the third behind the engine. "I bet they used this one."

Leblanc frowned. "How do you know that?"

"A hunch."

"A *hunch*?" Leblanc shook his head. "Just what I need, a hunch."

"It's the only one I've seen that isn't latched tight."

"Good point." Leblanc turned to his men. "Search it."

Two officers pushed the sliding door open, looked around inside then climbed in. One of the men quickly stepped back into the doorway holding a leather briefcase.

Charlie pointed. "That's it. Francis' bag."

Leblanc stepped closer. "And I'll bet it's empty."

"Correct," the officer said.

The sergeant turned to a couple of men with 'Crime Scene' printed on their jackets. "Do your thing. Let me know if you find anything, but I bet you won't."

The men were given a hand up into the boxcar by the swat guys, who then jumped down.

Charlie held his chin. "I'll bet they jumped out on Beckman's Curve, 'bout a mile back. The train has to slow way down there; be easy for someone to jump off. All kinds of 4-wheeler trails around there."

Leblanc was angry. "So we've got basically nothing and the perps have the money." He looked at Charlie. "Where's Monroe? He's got to know more. Come to think of it, he was acting strange after we found him by the fence."

"Probably traumatized," Charlie said, matter-of-factly.

Leblanc frowned. "We'll see. Find him, will you?"

Charlie nodded. "Sure. I'll call you when we find him. Then why don't we all meet at my office. I'll put out an APB for the Rhode Island guy's car. We've got a good description. Maybe they'll be stupid enough to head south through the toll plaza."

"That'd be convenient." Leblanc looked around. "In the meantime, let's get these men a quick coffee."

"Cartwright's Diner's just a couple miles from here on the way back to town."

"Okay." Leblanc motioned. "Saddle up—all but the Crime Scene guys. Meet you at the diner."

* * * * * *

As Francis entered the bank he tried to be especially friendly to Ms. Wheeler, who gave him her usual suspicious scowl. Luckily, there was another teller on duty behind the granite counter where iron bars separated the tellers and their money from the rest of the people. Francis always felt safe inside The First Casco Bank and Trust. It had been robbed only once during its long history, and that attempt was thwarted, rather definitively, by Sedge Rainville, a farmer who was perched atop a crow's nest built up in the corner of the stately, high-ceilinged building. On payroll day when the railroads, lumber yards, and fishing fleets paid out their wages, Sedge volunteered to sit in the nest to protect the bank from attack. Early on a Friday in 1928 two armed Quebecquois brothers came through the front door and fired shots through the large chandelier. Having everyone's attention, they held up both tellers at gunpoint.

Before the last piece of fractured crystal tinkled to the marble floor, old Sedge had those bad boys in the sights of his lever-action Winchester 30-30 and, without hesitation, fired two shots in smooth succession. The first bullet pierced the younger brother's heart from behind, dropping him right where he stood. Before the older brother could turn with his Colt 45, Sedge squeezed off another round, killing him. Francis remembered his grandmother's postman relating the incident when Francis was a young boy. "By God, the rob'bry was over b'fore it begun," the man had declared. The oft-repeated, graphic account at first frightened Francis, but by the time he was a teenager, he was proudly and dramatically repeating it to his friends in New York.

"Can I help you, Mr. Monroe?"

Francis realized he was staring up at the nest, though there was no local marksman in it these days.

Francis stepped to the window. The teller was young Alicia Tabor, now Mrs. Alicia Miller. She had been a student back when Francis used to teach painting classes at the local high school.

"So nice to see you, Mr. Monroe. What brings you in this morning?"

Francis realized he hadn't thought through what he was going to say. He paused and made up what sounded to him to be a plausible, but bold-faced, lie.

"I'm starting several art schools for underprivileged children in Guatemala and Nicaragua, and I was supposed to send my grant money by yesterday. I'm a little late but figured I'd get it out as soon as I could today. I have the overseas account the funds need to be wired to."

He glanced sideways to see if Ms. Wheeler was watching. She was raising the blinds in the large plate-glass windows that faced the street.

Alicia was staring at his face. "That looks sore. Did you have an accident?"

He touched his scratched cheek and shrugged. "Oh, I got into some blackberry bushes cleaning around the yard." He surprised himself at how easy it was to lie, something he prided himself on not doing.

Francis tried to keep his hand steady as he took the folded envelope on which he had written the account numbers from his pocket. He slid it partway through the opening beneath the bars.

Alicia took the paper. "How much do you want to wire to these accounts?"

Francis leaned over the counter, spoke in a lower voice. "Two hundred and fifty thousand to each."

Alicia's eyebrows rose slightly. "Really?"

"Yes. I'm passionate about these schools, and, well, I've been very fortunate in my career over the years."

Ms. Wheeler retrieved her pocketbook from beneath her desk. "Alicia, I'm going for tea," she said in her schoolmarm voice. "May I bring you anything?"

"No, thank you," Alicia replied, appearing a bit nervous.

Ms. Wheeler left the bank.

"So, Mr. Monroe, I see you have plenty of money in your account. I mean, I wasn't questioning, I just meant it shouldn't be a problem."

"Thank you."

Alicia did some typing then printed out a multipart form. She stared at it for a moment. "I haven't done many of these. I suppose I should have Ms. Wheeler check it over, co-sign it perhaps."

Feeling increasingly anxious, Francis leaned toward the bars so as to get a better view of the form. "Does it require that? I am already late for a meeting with an important collector from Rhode Island."

Alicia scanned the form again. "Well, I guess not."

"Then let me sign it and you can transfer the money. It's such a good cause."

Alicia nodded. "I guess it's okay." She slid the form through the window. Francis acted like he was carefully reading it then signed on the two lines beside which she had placed an asterisk.

Alicia checked the form again but seemed like she didn't know what to do next.

"Aren't you going to enter the transfer—into the computer, I mean?"

"It's a lot of money."

"I know," Francis said, unable to avoid a hint of annoyance.

Alicia entered a collection of numbers, scanned the barcode on the form, hesitated, and then hit Enter. She stared at the screen for about ten seconds then smiled. "Accepted. Wow, I've never handled that much money before."

Francis smiled. "The children will be grateful."

"Wait a moment," she said, putting her finger to the screen. "Now it says 'pending approval.' I think that means they need to confirm the funds are in your account, which should be pretty automatic."

Francis wrote his cell phone number on the back of a deposit slip and slid it through the window. "Please call me right away if there is any delay. I want the funds to be received today."

Alicia smiled. "No problem, Mr. Monroe. Now you have a great day, and thanks for banking at First Casco."

Francis nodded and left the bank. On the way to the Jeep he felt creepy, like he was pulling a heist or something. But it was his money, and he would do anything to bring Stringer home safely. And why would they want to hurt him if they got their money?

Gripping the steering wheel with his sweaty palms, Francis realized he had to go home and tell Kate, who had no idea what had happened. She was going to go crazy.

CHAPTER FORTY-NINE

As Francis headed north out of town, a sheriff's cruiser raced up behind him with its blue lights flashing. He immediately pulled over and realized it was Charlie. Francis rolled his window down as Charlie approached. He looked dead serious.

"I need you to come on into the office. Leblanc wants to talk to you, see if you can give us any more information."

Francis glanced up at Charlie. "I told him what happened this morning."

Charlie seemed unusually on edge. "Well, you need to talk to him again. I'll meet you back at the office." He scratched his right temple. "And, Francis, if you know anything else, you'd better spill the beans. Whole lotta shit's goin' down."

As Charlie walked back to his cruiser, Francis' heart raced, like the anxiety attacks he had as a kid when his father arrived home from Wall Street and made fun of his paintings. Francis knew he was in trouble. He felt nauseous but held it down. His mind raced through a cacophony of ways he was screwed. Obstructing justice? False statements? Aiding and abetting? There'd be no one who could get him out of this one.

Francis could no longer hold the hot bile down. He grabbed for the door handle just as a hard spasm knotted his gut. He threw the door open and vomited. Stifling an impulse to race north, he better understood what Kate had felt that night after Stringer shot Leland and she took Stringer in Kasa's car and made a desperate run for the Canadian border.

Francis had to get to the sheriff's office or things would get worse. Bottom line, he had to do whatever it took to save Stringer. He pulled a linen handkerchief from his glove compartment and wiped his mouth then threw it on the floor in the back. He pulled a U-turn and drove the short distance to Charlie's office where several state police cruisers were parked prominently in front. A group of troopers talked by the front steps.

As Francis approached the officers, the muscles around his jaw were so tight his face hurt. The heavy oak door squeaked as he pushed it open and stepped into the sheriff's office. Over the last year, he had been in there way too many times.

Charlie stood behind his desk, pointing at an aerial map laid out between him and Sergeant Leblanc. Leblanc was stone-faced as Francis approached.

Charlie motioned to one of the captain's chairs—the same chair Francis sat in the fall before when Charlie had told him about Kate's rap sheet. "I'll stand."

Leblanc looked at Francis, and spoke in an accusatory tone. "Who told you to put your briefcase in the train?"

"Some guy on the phone—called at six like they said they would."

"You recognize him?"

"No. It was a garbled computer voice."

"No idea?"

"No."

Charlie spoke in a more sympathetic tone. "Do you think it was the Rhode Island guy?"

Francis shook his head. "I'd tell you if I knew. I couldn't tell." He relaxed a bit. The line of questioning wasn't as bad as he'd expected.

Leblanc took a step toward him. "Where'd you go after I talked to you at the fence?"

"Back to my Jeep."

Leblanc became agitated. "I know *that*. Then where?"

"To my gallery."

"Why?"

"I was a mess from crawling under the fence and getting cut. I wanted to get cleaned up before I went home."

"Kate sensitive to a little dirt?"

Charlie cleared his throat. "Let's get back to what happened. Did the guy say anything that would help us out? Anybody else get on the phone?"

Francis forced himself to keep his cool, even spaced out a bit, just wanting to get through the inquisition, go home, and somehow face Kate.

"Francis—" Charlie said again, more sharply. "Anybody else get on the phone?"

"Just Stri—" Francis stopped the word as it emerged from his mouth. Charlie's eyebrows slanted.

Leblanc stared in disbelief.

Charlie spoke deliberately. "Did you say *Stringer* was on the phone?"

Francis couldn't get in a full breath.

"Francis!" Charlie snapped.

Francis' jaw started quivering. His face felt like it was fracturing into pieces.

Leblanc's face reddened. "I don't look kindly on people who lie to me, Mr. Monroe. Tell us what happened."

Charlie walked around the desk. He got Francis into the captain's chair then sat on the edge of his desk, partially blocking Leblanc's view. "Listen, my friend, you have to tell us everything—right now. Stringer may be in grave danger and we're not doing anything to help him."

"And you're obstructing justice!" Leblanc barked.

Francis looked at the worn hardwood floor. He felt like his whole world had imploded into that moment. "I tried to help him." Francis struggled to control his emotions.

Charlie put a hand on Francis' shoulder, bent down so he could see his face. "How, Francis? How did you help him?"

"I paid the ransom."

Leblanc could no longer contain himself. "*What* ransom?" He gestured sharply with his hand. "Are you kidding me? They've kidnapped Stringer, demanded ransom and you didn't think you should tell us?" Leblanc paced around a few steps. "Then you paid it? This is un-fucking-believable. Are you trying to get this kid killed?"

Francis' jaw tightened into a knot. He squinted up at the sergeant. "I would do anything for Stringer." He stood, looked Leblanc in the eye. "Don't you ever ask me that again."

Leblanc backed up a half-step, spoke deliberately. "You need to tell Charlie and me everything right now. I mean *everything*. Do you understand?"

Francis nodded and lowered himself back into the chair. He told them the whole story, leaving nothing out. Both Charlie and Leblanc seemed to try to hide their incredulousness with only partial success.

Leblanc called the FBI to have them start working on the bank connections. When they were done, Francis stood in front of them. "I realize what I did was crazy, if not downright stupid. I thought I could save him myself. I'm sorry."

Charlie nodded.

Leblanc checked the notes he had taken. "When Stringer was on the phone do you think they were on Pike's boat like we expected? Could you hear anything that sounded like a boat engine, or water, you know, waves in the background?"

Francis shook his head. "I don't think so. I might have heard the train whistle in the background, though I could also hear it down the track from me, so I'm not sure. I think they were on land, maybe even with whomever was watching me." He looked at Leblanc and Charlie. "They don't have any reason to hurt Stringer now that they've got the money, do they?"

"Hopefully not," Charlie said, "but who the hell knows what they'll do."

In his pocket, Francis' cellphone started ringing. It was Alicia at the bank. He felt himself tighten as he listened to her. After he hung up, both Charlie and Leblanc were staring at him.

"The bank says the transfer hasn't been approved. I've got to go back and sign more paperwork, get something notarized." In frustration, Francis made a fist. "What will those guys do when they find out there's a delay?"

Leblanc appeared relieved. "We'll use it to our advantage."

The phone on Charlie's desk rang. He reflexively hit the speaker button. A computer-altered voice entered the room.

"We're not playing games. Make the transfer by two this afternoon or we start taking your little shithead here apart. We'll mail you his fingers first."

Charlie and Leblanc appeared speechless.

A voice sounding like Stringer yelled something in the background, but with the computer modulation it was hard to tell for sure.

Charlie abruptly yelled into the phone. "There'll be hell to pay if you hurt that kid!"

The voice laughed. "You bunch of hicks have no idea who you're dealing with. Now the three of you get busy. No more second chances." The line went dead.

Charlie frowned, looked around the room.

"What are you looking for?" Sergeant Leblanc asked.

"How could they know there're three of us in here?" Charlie whirled around and looked at the black plastic clock over the door leading to the holding cells. "McNeal put that up last year. "Gotta be a camera in there. Francis, get it down."

Francis stretched and took the clock off the wall.

Charlie pulled the back off, and sure enough, there was a tiny digital camera mounted through the face. Leblanc looked at it carefully then pointed and mouthed *microphone*. He used a paperclip to flip the little battery out of the camera. "Obviously, they've heard everything."

Charlie looked angry, crestfallen. "That bastard McNeal's involved. He's probably been watching everything for months. I had no idea."

"How could you?" Francis shook his head. "All our ghosts are back to haunt us."

CHAPTER FIFTY

SERGEANT LEBLANC CALLED THE FBI AND GAVE THEM AN UPDATE. They immediately set up a trace on the wire transfers to Grand Cayman and figured a judge in Portland would okay it when he got back from striper fishing that afternoon. Kate kept calling the sheriff's department and leaving messages trying to find out what was going on. Since Francis had to go back to the bank, Charlie said he would go and talk with her. Francis felt bad he wouldn't be the one to tell Kate, but there was no other choice. While Charlie headed north to the bungalow, a couple of detectives briefed Francis on exactly what they wanted him to do.

At the bungalow, Charlie's boots hadn't touched the ground when Kate came running out the front door. She looked frantic. "Charlie, what's going on? Where's Francis? Did he make the drop? Is he okay?"

Charlie left the door of his cruiser open and leaned on it. He felt anxious as hell. "Look, Kate…"

Kate lunged at him, grabbed both his arms. "What happened? Where's Francis?"

"Settle down. I'll tell you."

"Is he alright?" she demanded, shaking him.

Charlie had a hard time looking at Kate, her eyes wild with fear. "Something's happened—"

Kate searched his face. "Charlie! What?"

He scratched his temple. "Francis made the drop in a train car."

"Train?"

"Yeah. Long story, but now the bastards have demanded another half-million in ransom."

Kate's breath caught.

Charlie realized what he'd said.

Her eyes dilated. "No—" she said, her voice shuddering. She screamed at Charlie. "Not my baby!"

She screamed so loudly it scared Charlie. He wished Francis were there.

Kate fell to the ground, crying. She pounded the thin sandy grass with her fists.

Charlie struggled with his bad knee to kneel beside her. He gently put an arm around her shoulders. "We think they're still nearby. We've got everyone working on it. But..."

Kate slowly lifted her tear-streaked face. "But *what?*"

"He was trying to help out, trying to help Stringer, so Francis paid the ransom, but..."

Kate clasped her hands over her ears and started rocking back and forth. "This is too crazy."

Charlie waited until she settled down. "Kate, I've got to bring you down to the office where we've set up a command center. We may need you to help get Stringer back."

Kate's expression glazed over. She had stopped crying. "You *may* need me?" Her lips tightened. "I'm his mother, Charlie."

"Sorry, I just—"

"We're leaving," Kate said, cutting him off.

Charlie motioned to the hall closet. "Bring a coat. Cold front coming in."

Kate looked at Charlie with desperate eyes. "Is he going to be okay?"

"We're doing everything we can. The staties and the FBI have taken the lead. They'll have every cop in New England and beyond looking for him." Charlie paused, looked at her sympathetically. "He's one tough, resourceful kid."

"Yeah." Kate pulled on Francis' field coat, and Charlie led her to his cruiser. He told dispatch he was enroute then paused, looking out the windshield. "I gather things have been pretty rough this spring, and now, with this, the stress, must be...well, unbearable." He looked at her. "Kate, you need to know Francis loves you and Stringer very much. He'd do anything for either of you. That's what he did this morning."

Kate softened, became emotional again. "Ah, Charlie. I just feel crazy, but I appreciate all you've done for us. Now you've got to find Stringer."

Charlie drove down the driveway and raced toward town. Back at his office, the state police incident command unit—basically a high-tech

RV—had set up in the parking lot. Inside the office, things were buzzing as a group of detectives as well as the search and rescue unit had taken over.

When Charlie and Kate arrived, she was relieved to see Sergeant Leblanc. "Have you heard anything?"

Leblanc held up a finger, finished a phone call then offered her a chair. "I have just a minute to update you. We figure this guy may be heading down to familiar territory somewhere south of Boston or back to Rhode Island. Not taking any chances, we've set up roadblocks in every direction and a plane from our Air Wing Division is searching for this guy's sedan. Two Border Patrol helicopters are also joining the search."

"Charlie said they were still nearby."

"We think they were in the neighborhood when Francis was at the recycling depot, but after the drop on the train they disappeared. Nobody's seen them so we just don't know. Perps tend to either hunker down and not move or they run like hell."

Hearing all this made Kate even more anxious. It was real. Her son had been kidnapped. Questions intruded into her mind, but all she could really think about was Stringer getting hurt or killed, or her never knowing what happened to him, like countless tragic stories on the covers of checkout magazines.

She looked at Charlie. "Stringer was supposed to be on Pike's boat."

"I know. Francis left him there early this morning as planned. He said Pike was bringing the boat into the dock when he left."

Kate frowned. "You mean he didn't see him get *on* the boat?"

"Not sure. Anyway, there's a chopper looking for Pike's boat, and a Coast Guard boat searching for them, too. But we don't think Stringer is with him. That would mean those guys are in on it somehow. Seems farfetched. I've known Pike for forty years. I don't much like him but can't imagine him kidnapping a kid. The Rhode Island guy must have grabbed Stringer before he got on the boat."

Kate winced at the awful image conjured up in her mind.

"They're searching Pike's usual lobster grounds but haven't found him yet."

"Where else would he be?"

Charlie made a face indicating he didn't know. "Hard to tell. Lobster boats have to cover a lot of territory."

Kate nodded. Part of her wanted to scream, tear her hair out, run out there and find her son, wherever he was. Another part of her felt like the fabric of her body was so spent she might simply disintegrate at any moment. She spoke to Charlie without looking up. "I need your restroom."

"Sure." He pointed. "You know, toward the cells, first door on the left."

Kate pushed herself up on the arms of the chair and walked through the door. The cool, brick-lined hallway caused a chilling déjà vu—the same hallway they'd walked down to visit Stringer when he was in jail. Remembering how terrified and sick he had been, Kate had to steady herself against the chalky red bricks. Once she regained her balance, she walked to a door with a large, frosted glass window where "Bathroom" had been lettered across the top. The 'th' was partially worn off so it looked like "Baroom." Not a place she should be.

Inside, there was an old porcelain toilet with a wooden seat. The sink was rust-stained from a dripping faucet. As she pushed her jeans down to her knees and sat on the cold seat, she felt desperate, like she'd been badly beaten-up. She leaned forward, covering her face with her hands so that everything went completely dark. The subtle drip-drip-drip in the sink next to her was somehow comforting.

"God, if you're out there, please help String. Keep him safe, let these cops rescue him. I will do anything you want me to for the rest of my life. Anything if you'll save him."

Kate felt warm tears trickle down her cheeks. She wiped her eyes with her sleeve. Then she listened, half expecting God to respond to her right then in that cold jailhouse bathroom.

After a few minutes, she reached for paper to wipe herself but the roll was down to one thin sheet stuck to the cardboard. She leaned forward, opened a stained white cabinet and took out a new roll. As she closed the door, the light glinted off something behind the loosely stacked toilet paper and plastic bottles of bathroom cleaner. Kate squinted, and despite sensing danger, slid her hand between the white rolls and edged them to the side. Standing in the back of the cabinet was a half-full bottle of George Dickel Tennessee Sour Mash Whisky.

Kate reached in as if retrieving lost treasure, grasped the fifth by the neck and pulled it into the light. She cradled the bottle in her hands like a newborn, staring at the fancy embossed black label, the clear golden liquid moving smoothly behind it. As if in a trance, she methodically unscrewed the cap and lifted it to her nose. Her nostrils flared and she took in a long, deep breath, letting the intoxicating aroma rise up into her head as if racing up a chimney. She leaned forward and stared into the neck of the bottle. Her body shivered with anticipation, relief, and paralyzing fear.

* * * * * *

Francis pulled his dark blue Red Sox cap tight over his eyes and walked out of the sheriff's office. As he passed the Incident Command Unit, he was startled by his cellphone ringing in his pocket. He turned away from a couple of troopers standing beside a cruiser, hurried to the far side of the parking lot and answered his phone.

"I said *no cops.*" The computerized voice sounded angry, though with a faint hint of desperation.

Francis ducked around the back of a large oak tree. "I didn't go to them. They pulled me over. There was nothing I could do."

"You get the money transferred today or this kid's had it." The line went dead.

Though he was tempted to make another deal with the devil, Francis knew he could not go it alone. He had to stick to the plan with the police. He'd taken but a few steps before his phone rang again. Anxious, he answered it.

"Francis?" It took him a couple of seconds to recognize Sam's voice.

"Yes." He forced himself to sound normal. "How are you?"

"Where's Stringer?" Her voice sounded urgent, frightened.

"Why?"

"I haven't heard from him. He texts me every morning. Is his phone broken?"

"I don't know. He went out on the boat early this morning. Maybe it doesn't work offshore."

"But he always texts before he leaves the harbor. Is he alright?"

"Far as I know." He hated lying to her. "You'll probably hear from him when he gets back."

"I wanted to tell him I'm getting out of here today. Can you guys come get me? Nelson's working."

"Well, we have a lot going on, but we'll try to figure it out."

"I really want to get out of here. They said I can go this afternoon."

Francis hated putting her off. "We probably can't get down there till later."

Sam went silent.

"Sam?"

"Remember Kate said I could come stay at your house for a week or two."

Shit. He couldn't think of anything to say.

Sam's voice changed abruptly "I knew you didn't want me. Just like everybody else." She sounded angry and hurt. "Forget it."

The phone clicked.

Francis felt like his head and his heart would explode. He jammed the phone into his pocket and kept his head down as he walked toward the bank.

"Well, good morning, Mr. Monroe."

He looked up. "Good morning, Ginny."

Ginny stopped in the middle of the sidewalk. "What happened to your face?'

Francis nervously touched where the blackberry bushes had scraped him. "It's nothing."

"No offense, but you look like hell."

"Thanks."

"At least you said 'hi' this time. Saw you drop Stringer off on the wharf before daybreak, but you never waved."

"I didn't see you."

"I was walking Fitz. He can't seem to make it till dawn these days. Old dogs are like old men."

Francis gradually moved around her. "I suppose. Have a good day."

Ginny gave him a strange look. "Hope Stringer doesn't mind the big waves out there," she said as he started walking away.

Francis quickly turned around. "What was that?"

"They're on the deep-sea fishing boat today. It goes out a lot farther than the lobster boat."

Francis walked back to Ginny. "Where do they fish?"

"They're after cod and haddock, so they're probably eight or ten miles out. Supposed to get a good storm around suppertime, so they should be back early."

"I didn't realize they were fishing. I thought they were on the lobster boat."

Ginny shook her head. "It overheated yesterday, can't get parts till Monday. Might as well fish."

Francis tried to act normally. "What direction did they head?"

Ginny shrugged. "Depends on where the fish are. Usually down east from here, way out beyond the islands."

Francis needed to get back and tell Charlie. But he had to get to the bank. He started fidgeting.

"You look like you gotta take a leak," Ginny said.

"Yes, well, I've got to go."

She laughed. "I'll say."

Francis started walking past Ginny, back toward the sheriff's office.

Ginny frowned. "Weren't you going the other way?"

Francis hit his forehead with his palm. "Yes. Thanks."

Ginny shook her head. "Nutty artists."

Panicking again, Francis moved slowly down the sidewalk, glancing back to watch Ginny, who disappeared inside The Claw. As soon as she was out of sight, he hurried down an alleyway and ran up through several back lots, emerging behind the sheriff's office.

Inside, Charlie and Sgt. Leblanc looked surprised to see him. "Back so soon?" Charlie asked.

Kate was nowhere to be seen.

Francis explained what had happened. Charlie stepped over to a chart of the coast mounted on the wall behind his desk. He pointed to an area off-shore. "Those sons-of-bitches. I doubt they're fishing. They're probably using the boat to get away."

Leblanc cleared his throat. "You didn't think these local guys were involved."

Charlie shook his head, turned away from the chart. "I should have known."

He looked at Leblanc. "They're smart, keeps them off the roads. There're a million places to hide out on the islands."

Leblanc looked at the chart. "Or they could rendezvous with another boat. We'll keep all the roadblocks up for now, but we need a lot more coverage on the water. If these bastards make it to the Caribbean or Mexico, we may never find them, or Stringer." He paced to a window, and turned back. "I'm starting to get the picture. Remember, the Rhode Island authorities said this guy was hot, that they'd been after him and he was up here to cool off. I'll bet he and his cronies were about to make a permanent break for the Caribbean—likely where they launder their money—when the issue with Leland's dealer came up. They were greedy enough not to leave any cash behind."

"You may be right," Charlie said. "They found out Francis is a rich artist and couldn't resist ripping him off before they left. All they had to do was read the papers from last fall to pretty much know everything."

Leblanc looked disgusted. "Damn—we should have connected the dots, figured this out."

Francis looked around. "Where's Kate?"

Charlie looked puzzled. "Don't know. She went to the bathroom a while back, haven't seen her since."

Francis walked into the brick hallway. The bathroom door was closed. "Kate—" He tried the glass doorknob several times but it was locked. "Kate, are you in there?"

"Go away," came the monotone reply.

Francis called to Charlie to open the door, which he did with a brass skeleton key from his ring. As the door swung open, the strong smell of whiskey was nearly overpowering. Francis entered the room, waving his hands as if clearing smoke. Kate sat in the corner, head down, arms wrapped around her knees, rocking back and forth.

Chapter Fifty-one

STRINGER HAD NEVER GOTTEN SEASICK BEFORE, BUT THIS WAS DIF-ferent, spending hours rolling back and forth banging into the wooden bunks of Pike's fishing boat. He had a pounding headache and his stomach had churned into an angry tempest. Still, he forced himself not to hurl. The tight duct tape across his mouth might cause him to suffocate on the puke. At least they hadn't blindfolded him, though he had no idea where they were. Seemed like they had gone out a long ways then doubled back or gone in circles, something like that.

As he lay there, Stringer heard fragments of conversation between what sounded like three men up on the bridge. Pike, as usual, sounded like he'd been drinking. Nelson said very little. The other guy had gotten onboard after Stringer was bound and shoved below. Stringer didn't recognize the voice, but it sounded vaguely familiar. He thought they said something about meeting another boat, but between the noise of the engine, the wind, and the waves pounding against the hull, it was hard to hear. With his hands duct-taped behind him, and his feet bound together, it was next to impossible to try and help himself. The odd thought came to him that he should be scared shitless, but really he was just exhausted and angry as hell.

After a while the boat slowed and stayed on a straight course. Stringer thought if he could sit up it would help his headache, so after considerable maneuvering, he righted himself. He quickly scanned the cabin and saw an old bottle and can opener in the shape of a lobster hanging on a hook next to the sink. He nudged the opener several times with the side of his head. It swung back and forth then fell onto the floor. He shimmied around so that his hands were close to the opener. He bent back and felt it, and after several tries, lifted it between two fingers. He figured out which was the pointed end and struggled to puncture the several layers of duct tape binding his wrists.

Just as Stringer started popping through the tape, he heard Pike say something, and then footsteps tromping down a ladder to the fishing deck just above Stringer. He twisted so his hands were out of sight but lost hold of the opener. He quickly covered it with his body.

Pike stuck his head into the gangway. "You comfy?" He spit a wad of wet chew into the metal sink next to Stringer.

Stringer stared at him, hoping desperately he wouldn't notice the opener was missing.

"Your artist friend better wire that money in the next hour, or we're going to start cutting your fingers off." Pike let out a beer belch, reached in and picked up a tarnished fish knife from the sink. He stared at Stringer. "Don't you think I don't know how to use one of these, boy."

A wave hit the port side of the hull and the boat lurched to starboard. Pike steadied himself, dropping the fillet knife back into the sink. He grabbed hold of the side rail and clomped back up to the bridge.

Pike was drunk enough he'd left the knife behind. Stringer felt a shot of optimism. It might come in handy.

It was getting hot and harder to breathe under the tape, which partially covered Stringer's nostrils as well as his mouth. He slowed his breathing and focused on what he had to do. Adjusting himself on the floor, he trapped the can opener between his fingers and went back to work punching through the duct tape. As he started to make progress, he again heard someone move up top then footsteps on the stairs again. They were different than Pike's—heavier, more sure-footed.

Stringer lay back on the floor, glanced sideways as a large man came into view. He kept his back to Stringer as he checked something on the rear fishing deck. Stringer didn't move. The man turned and stepped back toward the bridge. For a moment, he lifted his head, revealing a glimpse of his face beneath a black baseball cap.

Stringer's heart hesitated then pounded hard against the inside of his chest. For a split-second, he'd seen the unforgettable face of Larry McNeal. *Shit!* There was no one who'd rather see Stringer dead than McNeal. But what the hell did he have to do with all this? Stringer felt even more out of breath.

As soon as McNeal was out of sight, Stringer worked like mad to cut the rest of the way through the tape.

A cellphone rang up above. The boat slowed to a crawl. Everything was briefly quiet then McNeal's angry, chillingly familiar voice boomed from the bridge. "You son-of-a-bitch! You can't leave us out here! I can't help it was delayed. Monroe'll wire the money soon. He won't abandon the kid. Don't you get it? He's our ticket to the money!"

Silence again.

"What do you mean, it's too dangerous?" McNeal growled. "You aren't the one riding around out here with a kidnapped kid. We're partners, you peckerhead!"

"What the hell's going on?" Pike demanded.

"Shut up!" McNeal snapped.

"Listen, you take off on us, and I will hunt your sorry ass down. I don't give a shit if you're in the Carifuckingbean or not."

Then whoever was on the other end must have hung up. Stringer realized the boat had drifted broadside to the surf because suddenly they were pushed hard by a series of strong waves breaking against the hull. He frantically worked to finish cutting through the tape. As it started to loosen, he twisted his hands back and forth, trying to force it to tear.

Stringer heard Pike again. "Those bastards took off on us?"

"Yup."

"You mean we can't get to the seaplane?"

"No, we can't, goddamn it!" McNeal barked.

"What're we goinna' do?"

Someone stomped on the floor over Stringer's head.

"We gotta get rid of this kid," Pike said. "They can't catch us with him onboard."

"Look, Pike, he's all we've got left for leverage to get the money. We'll try and get the ransom ourselves."

"How?"

"I'm thinking. It's all screwed up 'cause we can't get away to the Caymans like we planned. The only chance we've got is to make a run for Sliver Cove, where we usually make the drops. Roger is supposed to be waiting in his cigarette boat to take us to the seaplane. He doesn't know they're taking off without us. At any rate, he should be able to take us somewhere in that fast boat of his. If we stay out here on this old clunker, they'll catch us surer 'n hell."

"Haven't seen any choppers for a while," Pike said.

"'Cause of the storm. They'll come after us in boats. Monroe's got a lotta clout. To hell with the weather—he'll have a whole goddamn armada out here searching for that punk."

"Fog'll be rolling in by Crescent soon. We can try making it around the east side where it gets really thick. They'll have a harder time seeing us there."

"Okay."

Stringer heard the engine rev, and they picked up speed, crashing through what felt like increasingly rough surf. He frantically twisted his wrists back and forth, the tape burning his skin until it finally tore apart. He pulled the tape off his lips then stretched his stiff arms out in front of him. On his knees, he reached up into the sink, grabbed the filet knife and cut his ankles free. There'd be no more pretending he was still bound.

Stringer heard the men moving about again. He crouched down on the musty carpeting holding the knife behind him. Hopefully the men would stay up on the bridge. Even though Stringer'd had enough violence for a lifetime, he'd use the knife if he had to.

CHAPTER FIFTY-TWO

BROKEN GLASS CRUNCHED UNDER FRANCIS' FEET AS HE HURRIED over to Kate. "Are you alright? What happened?"

Kate lifted her head. "I found a bottle of whiskey...and dropped it."

"I can tell."

She didn't sound drunk, at least not yet. The smell in the room was so strong Francis couldn't tell if there was whiskey on her breath.

Kate lifted her hand, pinched her index finger and thumb together. "I was this close to throwing in the towel, saying to hell with everything." She looked up at Francis. "If we don't find Stringer, I will drink till I'm dead."

Francis' feet were sticky from the spilled whiskey. He slid his arm under Kate and helped her stand.

Kate looked at Charlie, who was standing in the doorway. "Sorry about the Dickel. I was staring down the neck and started shaking so bad I dropped it."

Charlie looked a little embarrassed. "I'd forgotten it was there. McNeal had it around for emergencies, like every Friday afternoon. The guys would play poker and tip a few back."

Francis helped Kate to the sink, where he washed the whiskey off her hands. "I wanted to tell you myself about what happened, but I had to go back to the bank."

Kate stared at him. "Did you really pay them ransom?"

Francis nodded. "I thought I was doing the right thing."

Kate looked incredulous. "You were going to handle this on your own? The guy who always tells me to let the authorities take care of things."

"Look, I'm sorry. That's all I can say. This isn't exactly my area of expertise." Francis wanted to get back to the matter at hand. "I ran into Ginny on the way to the bank. She said Stringer went out on her fishing boat this morning because the lobster boat had engine trouble. She didn't act like anything was amiss. She can't know Pike and Nelson are involved, but they have to be. They must be holding Stringer somewhere offshore."

"You don't think they're on the road to Rhode Island?"

"We don't know for sure," Charlie said.

Kate frowned at him. "You don't seem to know much—any of you. Every five minutes you change your plan." She threw a moist paper towel at a wastebasket and missed.

Charlie's voice stayed steady. "If the weather doesn't get too bad they're redeploying the choppers over the coast and the islands, and we're going to head out on the harbormaster's boat."

"I'm going to come with you," Francis said.

"Me, too," Kate chimed in.

Francis was concerned.

"No, I'd throw up," she said, dejectedly.

"She gets seasick easily."

Francis felt how scared Kate must be. He started to give her a hug, but she ignored him. "Maybe it's best if you stayed here, anyway, in case anyone calls. You might be able to persuade them to let Stringer go."

"Yeah," Kate said, without a hint of hope in her voice.

✳　✳　✳　✳　✳　✳

Winter's Cove is a small, fairly close-knit town where it's hard to keep anything secret for very long. By the time Charlie, Francis, Leblanc, and two heavily-armed state troopers boarded the harbormaster's patrol boat, word had spread that something unusually dangerous was happening. Francis felt uncomfortable with all the firepower on the boat but understood they needed to be ready for anything. Leblanc had him wear the same Kevlar vest he'd worn that morning, zipping his foul weather jacket over it. With a storm approaching from the south, as they headed out of the harbor, other boats were on their way in. The only other boat preparing to leave was a large white and green fishing vessel, *Sunset Baby*, which was tied up at the harbor's south wharf.

Charlie stood next to Francis as Reg, the harbormaster, checked his radios and radar up in the cockpit, readying to depart. Charlie pointed at the other boat. "That's Captain Tom, one of my auxiliary deputies. Not sure what he's up to. Poor fellow just lost his daughter. Drug overdose, they said."

"Sad," Francis replied. "She was in ICU near Sam. Stringer said they were harvesting her organs for transplant."

Reg grimaced. "Shove off," he said, turning back to the helm. Charlie and a trooper freed the lines from the heavy steel cleats.

Francis grabbed hold of a chrome rail as the boat powered away from the dock. He observed the old harbormaster's shack as they made their way past several returning lobster boats. He thought back to the night he and Kate talked on the shack's weathered deck, supported high above the water on tall creosoted pilings. He'd known then he was falling in love. Less than a year later, he was struggling with how to handle those same feelings.

Up at the console, two-way radios crackled with activity, but then the twin 300 horsepower outboards roared to life and Francis couldn't hear much of anything else. As they approached the granite breakwater protecting the harbor, the men up front huddled around the radios.

Charlie said something into a microphone then motioned for Francis to join them. "The choppers had to back off because of the winds picking up, but one of border patrol guys might have seen Pike's boat about a mile out from Crescent Island."

"Did he see Stringer?"

"What?" Charlie said, cupping his hand behind his ear.

Francis yelled his question at Charlie.

"No, but they didn't get a good look."

"What is Pike up to?"

Charlie shook his head. "Don't know, but we're going to find out."

Everyone hung on as the boat cleared the breakwater and Reg put full power to the engines. The surf was increasingly rough, but the patrol boat was plenty capable of cutting through the waves. Francis stayed inside the cockpit out of the cold spray as they crossed the wide bay and headed for open ocean.

The radio crackled again. A Coast Guard boat was on its way from Portland but could maintain only about 12 knots because of the building surf.

"Damn, they won't be here for an hour," Charlie said.

Sergeant Leblanc looked at him. "Then we'll take these guys down ourselves."

Charlie nodded but looked less than confident. Francis knew he was no stranger to boats, but this wasn't his usual sheriff activity.

The farther out they got, the larger the seas became. With binoculars pressed tightly to their eyes, Leblanc and the other troopers scanned the horizon. There wasn't a lot of daylight left, and already a thin fog was forming around the islands. It was going to be a very dark night.

A scratchy transmission came over the radio from what sounded like a lobster boat. "Reg, what're you looking for?"

Reg kept one hand on the helm and picked up the mic with the other. "You seen Pike?"

"I think his boat's docked for repairs."

"Yeah, but he's out on Ginny's fishing boat."

"Saw a boat like hers couple miles down east from Crescent an hour ago. Didn't look like they were fishing."

"Any idea where they're headed."

"Storm brewing. I s'pose they're coming in like everybody else." The radio crackled with static. "That old bastard in trouble again?"

Reg hesitated then keyed the mic. "Maybe."

"I wouldn't chase him too far. Bad squalls off Cape Elizabeth coming this way."

"Thanks."

Reg kept a steady hand on the helm as he piloted them into larger swells that slowed their progress.

Looking over the rising, tumultuous sea, Francis felt increasingly anxious. There were no other boats in sight. He worried on one hand they might capsize and on the other Reg would turn back. "We've got to find them."

Reg looked at Francis. "Yup." He again stared over the bow, and turned on the windshield wipers, which flapped back and forth clearing the heavy salt spray. For another half-hour everyone continued to scan the horizon. Reg worked the throttles trying to keep the boat on as even a course as possible.

A large wave crashed over the bow just as Sergeant Leblanc pointed to the east side of Crescent Island, mostly surrounded by fog a half-mile south of them. "Looks like a boat close to the island."

Reg turned to Francis. "Take the helm and head for the island."

Francis did as he was told, the vessel rolling back and forth as they rose and fell over the crests of waves.

Reg steadied his elbows on the dash, training his long binoculars in the direction of the island. "Could be them. Fishing boat all right. No one else crazy enough to be out here."

"Speed it up," Reg commanded. Francis nudged the throttles forward, and the boat sped up, rocking harder in the waves. "Don't let her yaw. Keep her on course."

Reg opened a plastic trunk on the floor of the cockpit and checked his equipment, which included rescue ropes, floats, a flare gun, and a hunting rifle with a scope. Francis felt his chest tighten as the reality of what might happen settled in.

Leblanc lowered his binoculars. "What's the name of Pike's boat?"

"*Chaser II*," Reg said.

"That's it. Caught the name on the stern."

The radio came to life. "Coast Guard Station Portland to Winter's Cove harbormaster. Come in."

Reg took the helm back from Francis and clicked the mic. "You got him."

"We're making pretty good headway. Where do you want to rendez-vous?"

"We're heading for the east side of Crescent from the north. I think Pike's boat is there, though the fog is sockin' in so it's hard to keep him in sight."

"Roger that. We're about three miles south. Be careful. There are strong, unpredictable currents around that island."

"No shit," Reg said, off the air.

"Why don't you wait for us to get there?" the Coast Guard officer asked.

Reg didn't respond.

The Coast Guard came back on. "Any other boats in the area?"

Reg took a quick gander around. "One boat way back near the cove. Not sure where he's headed."

"Roger. Keep in touch."

Reg double-clicked the mic and clipped it back on the dash.

The wind let up a little as they approached the lee of the island. Soft patches of fog passed by them as Reg held a steady course, narrowing the distance between them and *Chaser II*. Francis figured Pike had yet to see them as their boat didn't appear to be underway. A minute later, they were close enough to get a good look with their binoculars. Nobody saw Stringer, but it looked like Pike was at the helm. Suddenly, his bow came up, and a roostertail of water rose behind him as he headed south. Large sprays shot off their bow as they crashed through the waves.

Reg pushed the throttles all the way forward. Francis held onto the rail for balance. Weapons drawn, Leblanc and his two troopers braced themselves against the cockpit. Taking advantage of the island sheltering them from the strongest winds, they gained speed. Pike's engine was no match for the 600 horsepower Reg had behind him. Soon they were bearing down on *Chaser II*. Pike took a sharp turn toward the island, trying to trick Reg into running aground on a reef that extended underwater off the southeast corner. Reg knew exactly where the reef ended. He curled toward the island in pursuit.

Probably fearing he would get trapped, Pike abruptly turned southwest and circled around the back side of the island into a larger fog bank.

Francis held on with both hands.

Reg checked the radar screen trying to keep sight of Pike's position, which was difficult with the signal bouncing off multiple rock outcroppings. Catching glimpses of the boat's radar target, Reg intermittently pushed and pulled on the throttles. Coming around the other side of the island, they lost Pike again. Reg abruptly slowed the boat, a wave of water washing over the stern and the crouching troopers.

Though they couldn't see Pike's boat, after a few moments they heard his engine come to life. *Chaser II* appeared from the fog and tore past within thirty feet of them. Francis got a glimpse into the boat. He didn't see Stringer, but clearly saw that Pike and another man had guns.

"Who's with him?" Reg snapped, as he brought his boat around.

"Don't know," Francis said. "Didn't look like the Rhode Island guy."

"They're both armed!" Leblanc yelled. "Be ready for a fight.

Francis felt a sharp fear go through him. "Stringer's probably on board. Be careful!"

"Just stay down," Leblanc yelled.

Out of the lee of the island, stronger winds hit them as they headed south again, trying to follow in the wake of Pike's boat.

Reg squinted as hard spray strafed across the windshield. "He's heading for Sliver Cove. Don't know what he's up to, but if the damn Coast

Guard would get here, we could trap him."

They unexpectedly emerged from the fog bank into a clear area and saw *Chaser II* approaching the narrow cove, where, legend had it, pirates used to lie in wait for British merchant ships heading toward Portland in the 1800s.

Reg followed after Pike's boat, which slipped between the jagged rock outcroppings.

"Be careful," Leblanc said, "may be a trap." He and the other troopers were tense as they braced themselves, ready to shoot.

Reg pulled back on the throttles and they slowed. He leaned forward, peering into the darkening cove. A shard of sunlight escaped through the clouds and momentarily blinded them. A sharp clap of thunder reverberated along the coastal cliffs to the south.

As Reg edged their boat into the mouth of the cove, Francis crouched low behind the cockpit. He peered out the window, though intermittent beams of sunlight were so bright he couldn't see much.

Francis winced as something pinged off the metal hull next to him. Several rapid gunshots followed. The men ducked. Two boats came surging out of the cove, each hugging the sheer rock sidewalls. One was a dark cigarette boat, which had a gun mounted on its bow. Francis realized they were coming at them from both sides, leaving them terribly exposed. With nowhere to go, Reg jammed the throttles to full power and drove straight into the center of the cove. Francis hit the deck as Leblanc and the other troopers opened fire. Bullets ricocheted off the metal cockpit as the attacking boats tore by.

One of the troopers yelled and grabbed his arm. Blood oozed from a hole in his tactical jacket. "Got me," he said, but continued to fire with his other arm.

"You all right?" Leblanc yelled.

"Yeah."

Francis grabbed a towel from a tool cubby and wrapped it tightly around the injured trooper's arm, seeming to stem the bleeding.

Reg had little room to maneuver inside the narrow cove, so he pulled up abruptly, threw the boat in reverse then they came around, just missing the rock sidewall. "Sons of bitches!"

As they emerged from the cove, Francis saw that another boat, *Sunset Baby*, had arrived and appeared to be trying to cut off the cigarette boat.

"Captain Tom's here!" Reg yelled, with unusual exuberance. "He'll stop that bastard!"

"*That's* why he was coming out of the harbor," Charlie said. "He's a tough old fella."

Francis hung on as they raced out of the cove in pursuit of Pike's boat, which now had three people on deck. Leblanc, pissed off that one of his men had been hit, steadied himself against the gunwale and took several shots at *Chaser II.* Its green starboard light exploded, but it didn't look like he'd hit anyone.

Francis yelled, "They'll probably use Stringer as a shield."

Heavy clouds closed in overhead choking out the last of the sun. A stiff wind arrived with a sheet of cold rain. Nearing Crescent Island again, both Pike and the cigarette boat had to turn to avoid the under-water shoals, allowing Reg to get closer. Though all the boats were pitching up and down in the rough surf, the two troopers raised their guns. Leblanc held up a hand. "Careful, that's the kid in front of them. If you get a clear shot, take it, otherwise hold your fire."

"You can't get a clear shot like this!" Francis yelled.

"Stand down, Monroe!"

Francis squinted against the driving rain, training his eyes on Stringer, who suddenly elbowed Pike in the gut and wrenched himself free. Pike bent forward, firing his pistol, though apparently missing Stringer as he lunged forward and grabbed something mounted under the gunwale. The guy at the helm threw the throttle and they headed past the island toward open water. As Reg gave chase again, the black cigarette boat passed Captain Tom's *Sunset Baby* and raced ahead, trying to get along-side Pike's boat. Captain Tom, whose boat was slower and more lumber-ing than the others, kept after them.

It looked like Pike was trying to get off his boat into the cigarette boat, but it was too choppy and he fell back onto the deck. Stringer came up with something in his hands. Pike lifted his pistol and fired at Stringer, who ducked. Leblanc and his troopers unloaded a barrage of bullets at Pike just as the surf tossed his boat behind a large wave.

Francis was frantic they might have hit Stringer. "Don't hit him!"

"Stay out of this!" Reg yelled.

Leblanc said something to his men and they lowered their weapons. When *Chaser II* surged into view, Pike was pointing his gun at

Stringer again. A puff of smoke rose from in front of Stringer, and a harpoon shot into Pike's leg. He fired his gun in the air, staggered to the side and fell to the deck.

"Holy shit!" Francis called out.

The guy in the cigarette boat fired a couple of shots at Stringer then steered away from Pike's boat, firing instead at Captain Tom as he tried to escape.

Francis noticed a Coast Guard boat approaching from the south. He could just barely hear their megaphone over the surf. "Stand back! Retreat!"

"Screw that!" Reg yelled, and again headed straight for Pike's boat.

As they approached, the man at the helm turned and fired a shot, punching a hole through the windshield next to Reg.

Gun drawn, Charlie ducked then looked over the dash. "That's McNeal!" he exclaimed. "Why that bast—"

Francis couldn't believe it. "*Sheriff* McNeal?"

"*Ex*-sheriff," Charlie said. "I should'a known that asshole was involved in this."

Another gunshot spidered a corner of the windshield. Charlie ducked again then broke out the remaining glass with his gun barrel and fired several shots at McNeal. With all the boats pitching and rolling in the surf, it was impossible to get off a good shot or to know if they'd hit anyone.

The cigarette boat's propeller came roaring out of the water as the vessel pitched over a wave. Slamming down in a trough, it turned sharply back toward Pike's boat, where Stringer clung to the side as Pike slid back and forth on the deck holding his injured leg.

Captain Tom, whose larger boat wasn't tossed around as much as the others, came up alongside Reg's boat.

Reg keyed his mic. "Cap'n, that guy's a drug dealer—heavily armed."

"That so?" Captain Tom replied as he passed them. His ruddy, bristled face tightened into an angry reddish purple. He continued toward the other boats as the guy in the cigarette boat took hold of the machine gun on the bow and aimed at Stringer.

"Shoot him!" Francis yelled. Fighting to steady themselves, none of the cops on board had a good shot.

Closing in on Pike's boat, Captain Tom pulled a shotgun down from his cockpit ceiling, poked it through his open windshield and, without hesitation, fired. Loud, flaming blasts erupted from both barrels. The torso of the guy in the cigarette boat exploded in a red, fleshy mess. With no one at the wheel, the boat turned broadside to a wave which drove it into the side of Pike's boat. Glancing off, the cigarette boat's bow submarined into another large wave which swallowed it whole.

"Take that, you drug-running bastard!" Captain Tom bellowed, ebullient and enraged.

Stringer looked terrified as he held onto the side of Pike's boat with both arms. As Reg closed in on him, McNeal let go of the helm and skidded his way across the deck. He got Stringer in a headlock with one arm and held his pistol to Stringer's head with the other.

"Back off or I'll blow him away!" he yelled.

Reg yanked the throttles back. The boat abruptly slowed.

The Coast Guard approached. "Drop your weapon!" came over a loudspeaker.

Keeping Stringer in front of him, McNeal nervously turned back and forth between Reg and the Coast Guard. Then another man in dark clothes came up out of the companionway carrying a short-barreled machine gun. Stringer elbowed McNeal in the groin, causing him to lose his grip on the pistol. A wave hit the boat, which spun it partially around as Stringer lunged across the deck. The other man lost his balance and fell back against the gunwale. The boat pitched violently, water arcing over the roof of the cabin. With the yawing of the boats, and in the confusion, no one had a good shot at McNeal or the other guy, who Francis realized was Nelson.

As the deck of *Chaser II* momentarily came back into view, Francis saw McNeal raise his gun, hesitate for a split-second then fire at Stringer, who careened over the side into the dark surf.

"Noooo!" Francis cried out, lunging forward.

Nelson fired off a burst from his machine gun and was instantly blown away by a hail of gunfire from the Coast Guard boat.

"Get over there!" Francis yelled at Reg.

"I don't know where he went," Reg said, his gaze trained on the water.

McNeal dropped his gun and put his hands in the air. His boat pitched sharply then slammed into a trough, spraying a cold sheet of water over Francis and the troopers. Francis held onto the rail with both hands, searching the water for Stringer. He was panicked one of the boats had landed on top of him. "Do you see him?" Francis yelled.

No one responded.

A Coast Guard Zodiac came alongside *Chaser II*. Officers with guns drawn boarded the boat and quickly handcuffed McNeal. They searched for Stringer, but between the unpredictable currents and the surging storm, the sea had churned into an ominous, inky-black whirlpool.

Grabbing a rescue line, Francis continued to scan the water, but saw no sign of Stringer. It was too dark to see below the surface. "Oh, my god," he said, trying to steady himself against the side of the boat. "Oh, my god."

CHAPTER FIFTY-THREE

STRINGER WAS DISORIENTED, FELT HIMSELF FALLING, HIS EARS screaming from gunfire. Then all was watery and quiet. His legs were pulled by a swift current, and above him he saw the vague image of the hulls of boats jostling in the dim light, gradually moving away from him. He started waving his arms aimlessly until one caught on a rope, which he realized was a lobster trap line. Thoughts punched in and out of his mind. He was underwater, not a fish, needed air. He didn't know who was still after him or exactly where they were. If he surfaced too quickly they might finish him off. He looked down and noticed a wisp of blood coming from his right thigh where a bullet had grazed him. He was glad there were no sharks in these waters—at least that he knew of.

Despite the strong current, Stringer managed to hold onto the trap line with both hands. His lungs burned, his head felt like it was swelling. As his mind cleared, he realized he had to get air or he would drown.

He let out what little air was left in his lungs and, fighting the current, pulled himself up along the line toward the surface. It frightened him how fast his arms weakened in the frigid water, but hand-over-hand, he made it up to the marker buoy, which he hoped was big enough to hide behind. He tipped his head back and, bouncing with the waves, sucked in a huge gulp of salty air. He ducked back down, blew the air out and repeated this several times until the burning in his chest started to ease.

Not really knowing where he was, Stringer decided to take a quick look above the surface to see where the boats were. He pulled himself up, his face rising behind the buoy. It took a few seconds for him to blink the salt water from his eyes then he peered around the buoy and caught a glimpse of the stern of Pike's boat maybe fifty yards away. Just then a wave broke over him. The buoy slammed hard against his cheek. He tried to get in another gulp of air but instead sucked in a mouthful of sea water, which shot down his windpipe. He instantly gagged, but worried someone would hear him, ducked underwater, where he continued to cough. He felt like he would drown.

Stringer forced himself to settle down, pushed the water out of his mouth then pulled himself back up to the surface. As he and the buoy rode up onto the crest of a wave, he looked around and saw he was probably a quarter mile away from Crescent Island, which was by far the closest landmass. He thought of yelling, waving an arm, but didn't trust he wouldn't be killed. That bastard McNeal still had a loaded gun, and was shooting it, when Stringer went overboard. Though injured, there was Pike also. Stringer felt Pike was the most dangerous, as he was pretty sure McNeal could've killed him if he'd wanted to.

Stringer figured Pike's men would search the island for him, but then he remembered on the beach that night Sam talking about a secret passage from an underwater cave up to the lighthouse that hardly anyone knew about. Stringer hoped it was true.

Luckily, there was a field of lobster traps between Stringer and the island. It was an area with countless underwater crevices and caves that Pike had taught him were rich with crabs, clams and mussels. If his energy held up, Stringer figured he could swim toward the island from one buoy to the next, resting on them as needed. With it getting late and the storm overhead, the sky was quickly darkening, but he could still see the mostly white buoys riding on top of the waves.

Stringer rested briefly, thinking of Sam, how much he missed her quirky smile, and sparkly green eyes. How much he'd like to have her kiss him again, the wonderful feel of her tongue on his. He'd had no idea girls tasted so good. But he'd never see her again if he didn't get moving. With heavy arms he swam from buoy to buoy, the changing currents first helping to propel him forward then pulling him back so forcefully he could hardly hang on. He knew at any moment he could get swept out to sea.

He was about halfway to the island when more thunderheads moved in, sharp white lightning crackling between dark gray clouds. South of the island he heard several loud rumbles of thunder. He remembered his mom saying that meant the gods were bowling. Sheets of rain swept over the island and over him. He kept looking at the light from the lighthouse, which guided him in a fairly straight line and kept him from wasting energy. The cold water made his legs ache, especially the one that had been shot. His arms were so tired they felt like petrified wood, and again he thought he might not make it as relentless waves crashed over him. Up ahead, he heard the surf pounding against the rock outcroppings. Buoy by buoy, he kept swimming, closing in on the place where he thought Sam had said the cave was.

When he was but a couple of lobster buoys away from the rocks, he realized his legs were so cold he could no longer kick. He wrapped his arms around a red and white buoy and rested, knowing he had only his arms left to get him to land. In the distance, he heard a boat approaching. It displayed no running lights, so he figured it was McNeal coming back for him. It looked like they were headed in the direction of the island, so he had little time to find the secret hiding place, if in fact there was one. Sam said legend had it that the captain's lover climbed from the cave to the base of the light tower, so Stringer lined up with the lighthouse and made one last push. He pulled himself through the water with his arms, passing the last buoy without stopping. Mercifully, he was finally pushed onto a rock outcropping by a wave. Despite scraping his ribs, he was able to drag himself out of the water, up along the spine of the ledge and into a small tidal pool protected from the surf. He collapsed on his back in shallow water, the rocks beneath covered with barnacles, snails and starfish. He let his head rest back on a mat of slippery black seaweed.

Within a few minutes, the boat got closer. A searchlight shown through the fog. It swept right over his head, shining on the rocks around him. He pushed himself up enough to look and saw no official markings or blue lights on the boat. Fearing his kidnappers would find and kill him, he had to get back in the water and try and find the secret cave. As the boat approached the island, he crawled on all fours into a crevice in the rocks and slid back into the sea. The water seemed colder than ever.

Stringer felt like his body was seizing, his muscles so tight it was hard to move. Gusts of wind whipped the waves into a frenzy. Regardless, he made himself dive into the water and search for an opening. Several times the waves slammed him into the rocks before he finally felt a hollow area under a ledge. Deafening thunder cracked overhead as he saw a huge wave was about to crash over him. Fearing he would be crushed against the rocks, he took in a deep breath and dove toward what he hoped was the hidden cave.

As he swam into an opening, the wave roared onto the rocks above him. He pulled and swam his way under the ledge for about ten feet before he surfaced in a dark cave which had only the faintest sliver of light coming through a crevice overhead. There was only about a foot of water in the cave, warmer and more peaceful than the stormy ocean outside. For a few minutes he felt relief but that was soon replaced with a rushing fear of being trapped in this underwater den where, surely, no one would ever find him. With high tide approaching, he knew he would have to get himself out of this one. He backed into what felt like a corner, wrapped his arms around his chest to try and get warm, and took a short rest. He would find Sam's secret passage. Or die trying.

Chapter Fifty-four

Since she'd hung up on Francis that morning, Sam had been immersed in old, familiar feelings of abandonment. By late afternoon, feeling restless and not knowing how she'd get a ride home from the hospital, she walked on her crutches to the lounge that looked over the city of Portland. She took hold of the fixator, lifted her leg up onto the windowsill, and looked out toward the ocean. Soon, the door opened behind her, and she felt a hand touch her shoulder. She knew it was Cindy, her favorite nurse when she was in intensive care.

"How are you doing?"

"My social worker called you, huh?"

"Yes. Thought you were having a rough day."

"I guess."

"Even though it's exciting to go home, it can be scary."

Sam crossed her arms against her chest. "Not that. It's the same old bullshit. I knew they wouldn't be any different."

"Who?"

"Francis, Stringer—all of them. Nobody gives a shit."

"Oh, I think they do." Cindy stepped around in front of her. "So I hear you need a ride home."

"Yeah. I want out of here."

"Do you feel like you're going to be okay? You could have died, Sam, and we all think it would be best for you to go directly to rehab. I guess they aren't going to make you, but I wish you'd reconsider. It can be really tough trying to get and stay clean on your own."

"Kate said she'd help me, take me to some AA meetings. That's if she hasn't given up on me, too."

"I'm sure she hasn't. None of them have."

Cindy glanced around the lounge, saw that no one else was there. "I need to talk to you about something that will be hard to hear."

Sam felt a sense of alarm. "What about?"

"My fiancé called me and said he had to cancel our dinner plans because all the area rescues are at a major incident up near Winter's Cove."

"That's where I live."

"I know."

Sam swung her leg off the windowsill. "What's going on?"

Cindy motioned to a couch. "You want to sit?"

"No."

"Something's happened with Stringer. I don't know details, but it sounds like he's missing."

"Missing?"

"Maybe kidnapped."

Dread descended over Sam. "*Kidnapped?* What are you talking about?"

Cindy put up her hands. "Like I said, I don't know much, but something about Francis and a train robbery. And Stringer may be out on a boat. It doesn't make any sense."

Mouth pursed, Sam took in a sharp breath through her nose. "The Rhode Island guy that stabbed their door—"

Cindy looked confused. "What Rhode Island guy?"

"Never mind. I need a ride home—now."

"That's what I was going to offer."

"Come on, then. Let's go." Sam grabbed her crutches and hurried back to her room. "I'll tell you what I know on the way."

While Sam waited impatiently in a wheelchair at the front of the hospital to get picked up, gusty winds blew dirt and litter about the parking lot. Dark clouds crowded in against the city, heralding the storm approaching from the south.

On the way north, Sam told Cindy what she knew about Rhode Island Jimmy and the ketchup-covered knife stabbed into the front door. When they reached the bungalow, it was unlocked, but no one was home. Sam wanted Cindy to take her down to the harbor in town, but she thought it would be too dangerous as Sam was still getting used to maneuvering on her crutches. Instead, Cindy convinced her to get comfortable on the couch in the parlor, where she helped Sam position her leg on the ottoman.

"Is it aching?"

"Doesn't matter."

Cindy's beeper went off and she checked it. "They want me back at the hospital, but I don't want to leave you here alone."

"I'm fine." Sam knew she didn't sound convincing.

"Do you know when they'll be back?"

"Probably soon."

Cindy's beeper went off again. "I'm sorry, I'm on call. I've got to go." She brought Sam the portable phone from the hallway. "Call 911 if you need help." She touched Sam's shoulder. "I'm sure they'll find Stringer."

"I'm glad your fiancé is helping out."

Cindy smiled, gave her a quick hug, and left.

Sam's heart raced. How the hell could Stringer have been kidnaped? She pushed her head against a pillow and tried to rest, but it was no use. A few minutes later she opened her eyes and saw Stringer's painting of her in the corner. She hobbled over to the unfinished portrait and, balancing on a crutch, reached up and touched the shock of blue hair. She liked how Stringer caught the lopsided way she always wore her sweatshirts.

Sam stared at Stringer's tubes of paints, brushes, and his multi-colored pallet. "Where *are* you? You get me to care about you then you disappear?" Knowing why he hadn't texted that morning, her anger was soon replaced with fear. She didn't want to lose the first guy she liked to be around, who might actually be able to understand her.

Sam was edgy, pissed the hospital wouldn't let her take home her pre-scription for pain pills, said she had to have someone else manage them for her. Craving a drink, or *anything* to take the edge off, she crutched into the kitchen and rifled through the cupboards and under the sink. She looked in the laundry room, behind the shelves of detergents and clean clothes, but couldn't find any booze. Frustrated, she went back to the kitchen, found a bottle of vanilla extract mixed in with the spices, and unscrewed the cap. She took a whiff of the alcohol-based liquid and, without giving it another thought, chugged half the bottle. Grimacing at the strong, astringent taste, she leaned over the sink and drank from the tap to wash it down.

Scared about what may have happened to Stringer, Sam went out-side, stood on the front stoop and leaned on her crutches. Strong winds carried cool sea spray up over the cliff, which felt good on her face. She struggled across the lawn to the bluff, her crutches sinking into the moist grass. The ocean looked dark as a cave, and with the fog, she couldn't see the lighthouse that marked the entrance to the bay. She heard waves crashing against the cliff, the strength of the surf building in front of the storm. Staring into the darkness, it scared her to think Stringer might be out there.

"Stringer!" She yelled in a hoarse scream. "Don't you fucking die on me!" Her voice faltered. "Don't you dare leave me," she whispered.

CHAPTER FIFTY-FIVE

NOT SURE WHERE THE EDGE OF THE CLIFF WAS, SAM BECAME DIZZY and started to lose her balance. A gust of wind pushed her off the path into the hedge roses. She was able to maneuver her crutches under her armpits, leaned toward the bungalow and made her way back inside. She landed on the couch, tired and distraught. Her life sucked. She had no way to get out there and help Stringer. At least not at the moment.

Sam became sleepy as sheets of rain raked against the windows. She was vaguely aware of thunder rumbling in the distance and intensifying flashes of light illuminating her portrait. Strong gusts of wind rattled the old shutters and windows and made high-pitched wails as they raced around the corner of the bungalow.

She had to have fallen asleep as her body jumped when she heard a car drive up, its headlights sweeping across the front of the house. She squinted at the clock; it was almost midnight. Her leg felt stiff as cement and it took a couple of tries to lift the fixator off the couch.

Through the drenched window, Sam saw a white sheriff's cruiser park near the front door. She squinted, saw Francis and Kate sitting in the front seat, the windshield wipers intermittently clearing the rain. Sam *so* hoped Stringer was with them, but in the glow of the new security lights, she saw only Francis and Kate, and they looked like people who'd run out of hope. Sam didn't want to scare them, so she got up and turned on the floor lamp.

Charlie came through the door with his gun drawn. "Who's in here?" he demanded, scanning the darkened foyer with his flashlight. He stopped when his light illuminated Sam, balancing on her crutches.

"It's me."

Charlie lowered his gun. "Anyone else?"

"Nope."

Charlie's uniform shirt was only partially tucked into his pants. One sleeve was torn, and he was soaked. He looked like he'd been dragged behind a boat.

Charlie stepped back outside. "It's okay, Sam's here." He helped Kate and Francis into the house. Their wet clothes dripped onto the red tile floor. Kate's eyes were swollen, her hair twisted about her head and neck. Francis' shoulders slumped, like his foul weather gear might just slide off of him. Charlie helped them shed their jackets then Kate saw Sam and hurried over to her.

Sam dropped her crutches to the floor, reached out and wrapped her arms around Kate. After a few seconds, Sam lifted her head and looked at Francis, who enclosed them all in a long embrace. Kate started softly crying. Sam, who had not shed a tear in many years, felt her tough resistance dissolve. "I *know* he's going to be okay."

Kate placed her palm against Sam's face as tears streamed down her cheeks.

Soon they changed into dry clothes and Francis explained to Sam what had happened. Though he sounded overwhelmed with sadness and exhaustion, there was a comforting steadiness about him. Sitting by the cold woodstove with a quilt wrapped loosely around her, Sam realized how much Francis truly loved Stringer and Kate.

Sam's spirits sank as Francis finished speaking. "We searched till the storm drove us in. Reg's boat got shot up pretty badly. All his lights were gone and there must be twenty bullet holes in the hull. The bilge couldn't keep up with the leaks, but somehow he still made it back to the harbor in the dark."

Sam searched Francis' face. "Do you think he's alive?"

Francis nodded. "I think there's a chance."

Kate lifted her head. "I do. I feel him, his courage, somewhere, struggling."

Sam felt a small surge of energy. "Me, too." She shifted across the couch toward Kate. They held each other for a long time.

For much of the night, Francis walked back and forth to the front door, looking out at the storm, which raged unabated. Sometime in the early morning, he finally passed out in the overstuffed chair next to Stringer's portrait of Sam.

The line of storms continued to pound the area well into the next day. After forcing themselves to eat some mac-and-cheese, they all went to the command center in town, which the state police had moved down to the wharf. Several boats had attempted to go out searching, but the surf was so strong they'd had to turn back. Several dozen people came out to stand with Kate and Francis and Sam as they watched and waited for some sign Stringer might still be alive. Sam sat in a wheelchair with a blue tarp covering her, except for a hole cut out for her head.

Even within the protection of the seawall, the town's fleet of boats pitched up and down, pulling hard on their moorings. Every little while Francis checked in with the command center then continued pacing along the wharf. With sharp winds buffeting Kate, Francis tried to get her to wait inside where it was warm, but she wouldn't budge or take her gaze off the sea. At one point Francis heard a tinny, creaking sound in the wind and watched as a piece of metal roofing tore off the old harbormaster's shack and flew across the water.

The *Sunset Baby* was tied off to the wharf with multiple lines, waiting to be repaired. Captain Tom had nicked a reef trying to get a good shot at the cigarette boat. Now his boat rose and fell with the surf against a row of large white fenders.

The Coast Guard had brought their largest boat up from Portland and launched several Zodiac missions from it, including sending search parties to Crescent Island. Well after dark one of the Coast Guard boats came into the harbor and tied up at the main wharf. The commander came off with two of his petty officers and walked over to Kate and Francis. He told them they had searched everywhere they could think of but to no avail. It was with sadness he had to acknowledge that Stringer had in all probability drowned. He was reluctantly calling off the search and declaring it a recovery operation.

"No!" Kate screamed. Forcing himself to hold it together, Francis took Kate in his arms and they sort of collapsed onto a stack of lobster traps. Her whole body shook with grief.

Sam pulled off the plastic tarp and rolled her wheelchair over to the commander. "Did you search on the island?"

"Yes, ma'am. The lighthouse, the keeper's house, even under an old overturned boat we found. Our divers checked the shoals all the way around the island." He paused for a few moments, his face showing the drain of deep fatigue and failure. "I'm very sorry. We didn't find anything except the cigarette boat that sank during the gunfight, and we even checked under that."

Sam looked crestfallen. "Shit…" she said, her head falling. "I thought he'd make it to the island."

The commander spoke in a kind voice. "We hoped he would, but those currents are wicked, and with the storm and all…"

Francis looked at the exhausted Coast Guard crew. "Thank you," he said quietly.

Kate raised her head. "For what? My baby's lost at sea 'cause you can't keep these damn criminals under control." She wiped her face, which was smudged with dirt and tears.

Francis tried to comfort Kate, but she brushed his hand off her shoulder. He knew she and everyone else were devastated. There were no words.

"He can't have just disappeared," Sam said, mostly to herself.

Kate got up, walked over to Sam, and knelt in front of her. They wrapped their arms around each other.

"Would you let me come home with you for the night?" Sam asked.

"Of course," Kate said, still holding her.

It was very late when they made it to the bungalow. Kate went upstairs to try to rest. Sam sat on the couch and didn't bother to elevate her leg, even though it looked quite swollen. When Francis spoke to her about it, she just stared out the window as if catatonic. He sat on a wooden stool in his studio, thought about his yearlong search for Rachael. He'd do anything to bring back Stringer, but he couldn't survive another relentless vigil, another obsessive search for someone he'd lost. But how could he let go of this gifted boy he had come to cherish?

An hour later a large car drove slowly up the drive and there was a knock on the door. Francis found Kasa standing there with a loaf of warm bread wrapped in a linen towel. She had a hard time looking at Francis. "I am so sorry."

Francis felt he would cry if he tried to speak.

"Anything. Anything you need, you call."

He nodded then Kasa turned and walked back to Buster's Oldsmobile.

After they left, Francis stepped outside, away from the others. The storms had moved north, and with most of the fog clearing, stars were coming into view. He watched the Crescent Island lighthouse flashing in the distance. He felt terribly sad, so empty. He couldn't bear to think about how awful the end must have been for Stringer, and how much he would miss him. Francis' body weakened as a wave of emotion overtook him. He crossed the lawn to the edge of the cliff.

Francis looked up through a break in the clouds. "If you're really up there, why did you let this happen? He was just a kid making a new life." His jaw tight, he shook his head in confusion and defiance. "And people call you a merciful God."

CHAPTER FIFTY–SIX

STANDING AT THE BLUFF IN THE WEE HOURS OF THE MORNING, Francis heard the front door close behind him, saw Sam crutching across the lawn. As she came up beside him, he put his arm around her shoulders to steady her. She stared at the white flash from the lighthouse for a long time then rubbed her eyes and stared again.

"Did you see that?" She grabbed Francis' arm.

"See what?"

"Something different in the flash."

Francis looked at the light and watched it flash several times. "I don't see anything different."

Sam looked at him. "Do you have a pair of binoculars?"

"Sure."

"Can you get them?"

"What are you looking at?"

"The light. It's a little off."

"What do you mean?"

"Just get them!"

"You okay out here alone?"

"Yeah. Just hurry."

Francis retrieved his binoculars and handed them to Sam.

"Let me lean on you so I can hold them steady."

Francis braced her leg and back.

Sam trained the binoculars on the lighthouse. They both watched for several minutes but nothing looked different. Sam put the binoculars down, and rested her arms. "Maybe I was hallucinating. The light will go out in a couple of hours anyway."

Francis squinted. "Let me see those." He looked through the glasses. "What did you think you saw?"

"The light was dimmer at times. Do you see it?"

Francis kept his eyes trained on the lighthouse. "Maybe…" He adjusted the focus slightly. "Yes, there it is again. It's too far away to see any detail, but the light seems to intermittently change. Maybe the wiring is loose or something like that."

Sam grabbed the binoculars from him and looked again. "That's it, the light gets dimmer, but it's because there's something in front of it." Sam looked at Francis, her eyes wide. "I think it's Stringer."

"I wish, but they searched the whole island twice. If he was there, all he had to do was yell."

"Maybe he was hiding." She handed Francis the glasses and headed toward the house. "Come on, we've got to go look."

"Wait." Francis reached for her arm. "You can't go in there and give Kate false hope. As much as I wish he was there, this sounds crazy."

Sam stopped in the middle of the lawn and looked at him. "You normal, trusting people don't know how Stringer and I think. We trust no one. Well, almost no one."

Francis frowned. "What are you talking about?"

"Look, I think Stringer was hiding out. There's a secret cave…" Sam hesitated, became more impatient. "We gotta go down to the harbor, get a boat and go out there. I'll explain on the way." She headed to the house again.

"This is crazy," Francis said, following after her.

"You want to trust somebody?" she said, stopping and staring at him. "Then trust me on this."

Inside, Sam convinced Francis to call Charlie and tell him what she thought. Charlie said he didn't believe in that old legend but he'd call Reg anyway.

Though groggy, Kate came downstairs, apparently having heard the commotion. She thought what Sam was saying was unlikely but she would try anything that might bring Stringer back.

On the way into town Sam talked excitedly about the legend of the old sea captain's shipwreck, his mistress and the secret cave. By the time they made it to Winter's Cove, she had started to convince both Kate and Francis that Stringer might be alive. When they arrived at the sheriff's office, Francis realized the incident command unit had left. Only Charlie's cruiser was in the lot. Francis helped Sam out of the Jeep as Kate ran inside. By the time they were all in Charlie's office, Kate was animatedly pushing Charlie to get them a boat.

"Kate, I told you the harbormaster's boat is out of commission. It's all shot up."

"Then find another one. This *is* a harbor."

"Look, I would do anything to bring Stringer back alive, but this is crazy."

Kate glared at him. "Don't stand there and say you'd do anything to bring him back and then do nothing!"

Sam crutched up to Charlie's desk. "It isn't crazy. Both Francis and I saw something change with the light."

Francis spoke up. "I saw it, Charlie, through my binoculars. It looked like someone was purposefully blocking the light."

Charlie looked at Francis. "You *saw* Stringer up in the lighthouse?"

"I saw a change in the light I'd never seen before."

"Maybe the Coast Guard needs to so some maintenance out there on the electrical system."

Kate leaned closer to Charlie's face. "Maybe the damn Coast Guard needs to get back out there and take another look."

Charlie hesitated but Kate was not going to back down. "All right, for Christ's sake. The seas have settled down some. I'll see if one of the boys with a launch will take us out. I'm not calling the Coast Guard back at this hour. They'd have my head examined."

Kate made a fist. "If you don't get us out to that island, you'll need your head examined."

Charlie almost grinned. "If we find Stringer out there, you can clobber me all you want."

"I'll kiss you instead. Now let's go."

Charlie made the call. It was clear it took some convincing, but Oscar, one of the men who gave sightseeing tours out of the harbor, said he would take them. His boat was equipped with spotlights and would be able to land at the dock on the island.

A deputy came out of the jail cells in the back where he had been checking on a local drunk spending the night. Charlie looked at him. "Listen, we're going back out to Crescent in Oscar's boat. I don't want you to tell anyone, but keep your ears open. If we run into any trouble, I'll call you on our frequency."

The deputy looked confused. "What're you doing?" Then he saw

Kate. "Oh, you're still looking for the kid."

"Yeah. You just keep an eye on things."

Unlike when all the people were down on the wharf during the search, the harbor was quiet. As they waited for Oscar to fire up his small tour boat, Francis knew that even a slim hope Stringer was still alive kept him, and he assumed everyone else, going.

Though Charlie didn't want Sam on the boat, Oscar said he took people out in wheelchairs all the time, so they helped her aboard. Francis knew a team of horses couldn't have kept her off. Kate stayed close to Francis as they left the wharf. He wholeheartedly embraced her for the first time since the condom incident. As the emptiness over losing Stringer grew, so did Francis' realization of how deeply he loved Kate. Over the last few days she'd shown her love for him, too. And he was also touched by Kate's tenderness toward Sam.

Crossing the harbor, Francis saw where sections of the old harbormaster's shack's roof had blown off. It was actually peaceful as they passed through the breakwater and headed across a calmed ocean. Everyone kept their gaze trained on the lighthouse. When they were about halfway there, all of them suddenly pointed and called out. Everyone saw the unmistakable change in the light.

Charlie nodded. "Yup, now I see what you mean."

Oscar wasn't convinced. "Don't get your hopes too high. Water gets into the electrical and causes shorts."

They watched as the island, and possibly Stringer, got closer and closer. As they approached, no one saw any further changes with the light, its beam clear and bright, just as it had been, in one form or another, since George Washington authorized construction of the light tower in the late 1700s.

As they made the passage between Sliver Cove and the island, Francis marveled at what a different sea it was: small, smooth waves rolled past the area where huge breakers had battered their boat less than two days before. As they skirted the shoals on the south end of the island, his pulse quickened when he saw the bow of the cigarette boat splintered on the ledges beneath the surface. He gently turned Kate away so she wouldn't see the wreckage. As they approached the tiny harbor once used by the lighthouse keepers, Francis saw that some of the planks had been torn from the dock by the storm. With a spotlight on, Oscar flipped a row of fenders over the port side of the launch as they slowly motored toward the dock.

As Charlie tied them off, Kate yelled for Stringer, but there was no response. Back on her crutches, it was difficult for Sam to navigate across the broken boards but she made it with Francis' help. At the keeper's house, they found everything locked and shuttered. Kate yanked on a padlock several times, but it did not give. She looked up at the tall light tower and yelled again. Francis prayed Stringer would appear up in the lantern room, but only the light appeared, every five seconds, strong and bright.

Charlie and Sam also checked the windows and pulled on the pad-locked door of the light keeper's house. "I know he's here, she said. "I can feel him."

Francis and Oscar walked around the tiny island with their flash-lights, checking every crevice and tidal pool, but found nothing. When they returned to the keeper's house, Kate was sitting on a rock, dejected and scared. Francis knelt and held her.

With a headlight mounted on her baseball cap, and Charlie watch-ing out for her, Sam crutched over to the base of the light tower, which was built into a rock promontory over a precipitous cliff. She banged on the tower and yelled for Stringer. Listening with her ear against the cold metal, she heard nothing but the fading echo of her own voice. She closed her eyes and tried to remember details from the sea captain's legend.

If Sam recalled correctly, the old man told her that the captain's mis-tress found her way to an underwater cave then climbed up through a secret passageway to the tower. But unless the passageway opened inside the tower, there had to have been some way she got in from the outside. Sam hadn't noticed any obvious doors in the tower, but she got her crutches underneath her and, shining her headlight, checked as much of the base of the tower as she could, finding nothing."

"What are you looking for?" Charlie asked.

"Just hang on, I'm trying to see something."

Still not satisfied, Sam went back and had Charlie shine his light down on the metal plates at the base of the tower. They extended about halfway down the twenty foot cliff.

"There's got to be a door or something," Sam said, straining to see.

Hanging onto Charlie's hand, she tried to get a good look over the edge.

"This is crazy," Charlie said, seeming a bit out of breath.

Thinking she saw something that broke up the smooth contour of the metal, Sam let go of Charlie's hand and tried to lower herself down onto the rocks, but her crutches and the fixator prevented it.

"Francis! Kate!" Sam yelled. "Over here!"

Francis came running up to Charlie. "What is it?"

"I'm not sure," he said, holding his light steady.

Kate and Oscar followed behind Francis.

Sam looked up at Francis. "I need your help to see where the tower is built into the cliff. The metal side goes down there towards the water. I think I might have seen something—like a door—you know, to get into the tower."

Francis stood at the edge of the cliff. "Down *there*?"

"Yeah. Get down here and shine your light on it."

Francis looked hesitant but did as she suggested. Kate and Charlie held his legs as he carefully leaned over the cliff. "Look at that," he said. "There is some sort of small door about halfway down."

He pulled back from the edge. "Oscar, can I use your light? It's brighter than mine."

Francis took Oscar's searchlight, pushed his other hand into a ridge in the rocks, and leaned farther out.

"Be careful," Kate said, putting most of her weight on his legs.

"Yes, sir. The door's ajar, and there's a long piece of driftwood lean-ing next to it, like someone placed it there." Francis pulled himself back. "We've got to get down there."

Kate took hold of Francis' coat. "Do you think Stringer might have gotten in that door?"

"Possibly. If he did, we need to hurry because he's not responding to us." He looked at Sam. "You're awesome. We never would've found this without you."

"Hurry!"

"Charlie, why don't you stay up here and Kate and I'll go down." Francis shone the light along the edge of the cliff and saw a way to climb down. "Come on," he said, leading Kate and Oscar over the rocks. "Sam, go back out front and keep an eye on the top of the tower."

"Be careful!" Charlie called out as they descended.

Though they slipped on several rocks, they made it to the bottom of the tower and there, next to the driftwood was a broken padlock. Francis picked it up. "Amazing. He has to be here."

Francis took hold of the waterlogged driftwood which felt unstable against the curved metal plates of the tower. "Can you hold this while I climb?"

Kate reached up with both hands and supported the wood. Francis climbed up to a heavy metal door. It squeaked as he pushed it further open, flakes of rust falling from its hinges. He shined his headlight inside, illuminating a cast iron spiral staircase, supported by a large metal pole running up through the middle, and heavy bolts that held each stair section to the inner wall of the tower. Looking upwards, he was startled to see on the stairs a plastic skeleton holding a pumpkin and a tall witch's hat all intertwined with spider webs. "What the hell...?"

"What is it?" Kate yelled up.

"Weird. There've been Halloween parties in here. Then he saw a recent hand print in the moist rust on the metal railing. And above that, a few spots that looked like dried blood.

Francis leaned out the opening. "I think Stringer got in here!" He steadied the driftwood. "Come on up."

Kate struggled a bit but climbed up and joined him.

"Oscar, you coming?" Francis said.

"Nope. I'll wait here. Too old for this stuff."

With his light, Francis showed Kate the hand print but not the blood. "He's got to be in here, probably up in the lantern room."

"The what?"

"Up top, where the light is."

Francis started up the iron stairs, which curved around the central pole like a spiral fan. "Hold onto the railings with both hands; there may be weak spots from all the rust." He swept away a batch of cobwebs caught in his hair.

They climbed up about ten steps before Kate recoiled from something on the railing and stopped. She held her hand up to her light. There was a blotch of deep red on her palm. "Shit, this is blood." She looked up into the tower and yelled, "Stringer!"

No response.

"Come on," Francis said, resuming the climb.

Though the stairs were slippery from a layer of mildew, they felt fairly sturdy until Francis and Kate were about three-quarters of the way up, where a couple of rusted bolts loosened from the inside of the tower. A section of stairs creaked and pulled away from the steel wall under their weight.

Francis froze as the staircase shifted. A bolt snapped and a piece of railing dislodged from its mounting. "Don't move."

Kate momentarily lost her footing and screamed.

Francis reached for her. "Take my hand!"

Kate grabbed his hand and he pulled her up over the loose steps. She quickly climbed ahead of him.

"Be careful, we're a long way up."

Kate continued climbing the creaky spiral. Francis picked his footholds carefully and followed after her. Though the metal railing was unstable, they were able to keep moving higher and were soon at the top landing. From there, a ladder led up to a small door in the ceiling. Brilliant shards of light shown through cracks in the floor of the lantern room.

Pale and out of breath, Kate looked like she might fall. Francis quickly slid his arm around her.

"Can you go first?" she asked, shaking.

"Of course, but stay here until you feel steady."

Francis helped her sit back against the wall then grasped the rungs of the ladder and climbed up through the door. It was blindingly bright inside the lamp room, forcing him to crouch down. He shielded his eyes with his hand and started to crawl around the large lamp apparatus then stopped abruptly.

On the floor in front of him was a bloody foot and a leg partially covered with the tattered remains of a pair of jeans. Stringer's jeans.

CHAPTER FIFTY-SEVEN

TRYING HARD TO FOCUS, AND WITH THE IMPOSING LIGHT ROTATING above him, Francis crawled toward the body. He was scared to see Stringer's face.

"What do you see?" Kate yelled up.

Francis' heart pounded in his ears. Stringer was lying on his side, the flesh over his chest gouged and caked with blood.

"Oh, my god," Francis whispered.

He crouched on the floor alongside Stringer, looked to see if he was breathing.

He wasn't sure.

He held his ear next to Stringer's face. Yes! He heard a little air moving, gurgling in his mouth.

"Kate..." Francis said, in a barely perceptible voice. "Kate!"

"What?"

He could hear her climbing the metal stairs.

"It's String—he's alive."

Kate hurried up the ladder into the lantern room. "Ahhh—" she said, as the light hit her. She dropped down and crawled to Stringer, cradled his face in her hands. "Oh, baby..."

Kate's face was wracked with pain. "Are you sure he's alive?"

"Yes, I heard him breathe."

Kate put her ear to Stringer's mouth then nodded. "Thank God."

Francis stood up in front of a large section of plate glass and waved his arms. The light was so bright he couldn't see Sam, Oscar, or Charlie. He felt along the next couple of sections and found one that was a window. He threw the stiff latch, and pushed hard to open the corroded hinges. "We found him!"

"Awesome!" Sam was waiting below. "He all right?"

"He's alive, but unconscious. Call for rescue."

"Okay!"

"That's great!" Charlie yelled up. "I'll get on the radio."

"Can you get him down?" Oscar yelled up. "We can get him to the hospital faster than waiting for the Coast Guard; they're back in South Portland b'now."

Francis looked around. It was a good thirty feet down to the roof of the keeper's house. There was no way. "The only way down is the stairway, which is falling apart. I don't know if it will hold us. Do you have a long rope?"

"Just some boat lines. Nothing that'll reach up there. Plus, got no litter basket or nothin'."

Francis wished there was a rescue chopper nearby.

"He's got a pulse," Kate said, pulling off her jacket. "It's weak, and he's really cold." She wrapped her jacket around him. "We gotta get him out of here or he's not going to make it."

The light intermittently illuminated Kate's face, and despite the terrible strain, Francis couldn't help but notice the depth of her beauty. A moment of peace in the middle of chaos.

He put his head out the window again. "We'll have to take him back down the stairway. Call Reg and tell him what's going on. Get the fire department's rescue boat headed out."

"You got it," Oscar responded.

Francis took off his jacket, knelt down and looked at Stringer. He hadn't moved but Francis didn't see signs of a spine or head injury, though it looked like the rest of his body had been badly beaten up. He was clearly hypothermic and dehydrated. "I think my jacket is large enough that we can zip it around him. I've got to get him on my back with his arms over my shoulder."

"Really?" Kate said.

"Yes. Sort of a fireman's carry. You'll need to tie his hands together in front of me because I've got to be able to use my arms."

Kate frowned. "But what if the stairs collapse?"

"What choice do we have? We've got to do it. As I carry him down you can help by bracing the staircase against the inside of the tower so the whole thing doesn't start shaking."

With Francis' coat wrapped around her son, Kate helped Francis pull Stringer up onto his back. He was surprised at how heavy Stringer felt and was worried his bound arms would choke him. Francis kept his chin down to keep the pressure off his throat.

Kate went down the ladder first and steadied it from below. Francis faced the ladder, carefully taking it rung-by-rung to the landing, where she immediately supported some of Stringer's weight to give Francis a rest.

"Should I go down the stairs first?" Kate asked.

"Why don't you stay above me? In case it collapses I don't want you under me."

Kate's eyes looked wild. "This is crazy."

"Yup." Francis lifted Stringer a little higher on his back, and stepped onto the first stair. He grabbed both railings but the outer one was too loose, so he reached back and held Stringer's butt with that hand and held tight to the inside railing with the other. With Kate following above him, Francis began his descent. Every few stairs, he stopped and leaned back, letting Stringer's feet take some of the weight off his shoulders. When Francis approached the section where the bolts had pulled out of the metal wall, the unsupported stairs shook under his weight. There was a creaking noise. Another bolt broke loose.

"Francis!" Kate cried out. Bracing herself, she pushed against the tower wall trying to steady the broken stairs, "I can't keep it from moving—it's too loose."

Francis tried to go back up a step, but in shifting his weight, another rusted bolt came loose and a section of staircase below twisted away from him. "Shit, we're going down…"

Kate screamed, reached down and grabbed hold of Stringer. She pulled him up as hard as she could. Losing his balance, Francis flailed backwards, his fingers catching the holes in the iron stair above him. Kate continued to pull up on Stringer, got his torso onto her stair, though by then his arms were choking Francis.

"Pull up!" Kate yelled. Francis' fingers were blanched and bleeding as the iron scrollwork cut into them.

There was a creaking sound then the section Francis was standing on bent away from him, broke off, and fell out of sight. His legs flailing, he grabbed hold of the railing above him and pulled mightily. Seeing that Francis was choking, Kate got Stringer's arms from around Francis' neck and steadied Stringer's body against the railing with her own. She took hold of Francis' armpits with both hands and gave a tremendous tug. Under their weight, the railing next to Kate's face started to loosen.

She grit her teeth, straining tremendously to pull Francis up a little further. "Don't you pull out of there, you sonofabitch!" she yelled at the railing.

As soon as the top half of Francis' body was on her stair, they rested for a few seconds. His arms burned as if on fire but his legs still dangled below him where the stairs had collapsed, and were getting heavier by the second. He looked around, saw the remnant of a broken-off bolt in the metal wall and swung his right leg over so he could rest his foot on it, which took some of the strain off.

"Okay. When you're ready, I'm going to push off with my foot and try to pull myself up to you."

Stringer stirred for the first time, said something unintelligible.

"You're okay, String," Kate said, in a remarkably calm voice. "We're getting you out of here."

Stringer started to twist his body, but Kate kept him pinned against the railing. With her pulling as hard as she could, Francis pushed off the bolt, pulled up with his arms and crawled onto the edge of the stair with them. He pulled his hand from the holes in the stairs. Bloody flesh hung from two fingers.

"What are we going to do now?" Kate sounded desperate.

Francis looked around as he worked to catch his breath. There was a good six foot gap below them where the damaged stairs had broken off. There was no way to bridge the gap, certainly not with Stringer on his back. And there was no way he was leaving him, or her, behind. He looked at the heavy metal pole that ran up through the middle of the tower to which all the stairs were attached.

"Got an idea. I'm going to shimmy down that pole in the middle. I should be able to get a foothold where each stair attaches, even where the broken ones were."

"*Really?*"

"Come on, get Stringer onto my back again, just the way he was. Then help support him and I'll climb over the railing and grab the pole."

As they maneuvered to get Stringer up onto Francis' back, Kate's face was right next to his. For the first time in a while, they looked into each other's eyes. Just for a moment. "I love you, Francis." She kissed him with dry, salty lips.

Francis tried to smile, but the crippling spasms in his back were too much. "Thank you," he whispered.

Above them in the lamp room, the light went out and the inside of the tower became dark save for a little daylight coming in the lower door.

"Sweet Jesus," Kate said. "I can't see a thing."

"Wait a minute and our eyes will adjust."

As soon as they could see at all, Kate helped Francis get first one, then his other leg over the iron railing so he could reach out and take hold of the ridges on the center pole. He realized they were going to have to descend mostly by feel. Though Stringer felt like a hundred bags of cement, Francis was able to hold onto the pole and start moving down, half-climbing, half-shimmying. With Stringer's body hanging off his back, Francis struggled to keep from choking. Ironically, it was a relief that Stringer didn't regain consciousness.

Though he wanted to tell Kate to wait for rescue to help her down, he heard her climb onto the pole and start to descend above him. He couldn't blame her for not waiting, and after her heartfelt words, he wanted her close to him and Stringer.

At one point, Francis' fingers could no longer hold on and he started to fall backwards. He curved his arm around the pole and slid down a few stair heights, finally stopping himself with his feet.

When he reached the lower platform, his arms were so tired and bruised he could barely move them. He collapsed with Stringer on top of him.

Soon, Kate made it to the platform and carefully rolled Stringer off of Francis, enabling him to breathe much needed cool air streaming in through the small door.

"Francis?"

It was Oscar, down on the ground.

Kate stuck her head out the opening. "Francis got him down! We're coming."

"I got a rope I'll throw up that you can tie to something sturdy to hold onto."

Kate caught the rope and tied it to the platform. She looked at Francis. "You're amazing, but you can't carry Stringer down that driftwood. Let's tie the rope around him and lower him down."

Francis nodded.

With the rope securely tied around Stringer's waist, they managed to slide him down the driftwood to Oscar. Kate, then Francis, followed. With them all supporting Stringer's injured body, and the help of Charlie, they worked to carry him up over the rocks to the top of the cliff where Sam waited.

They lowered Stringer to the ground. When Sam saw his face in her headlight beam, she let go of her crutches, and, without regard for her fixator, dropped down and wrapped her arms around him. She kissed his swollen face. "Is he okay?" she asked Kate.

Charlie quickly looked Stringer over. "Got to get him to the hospital. Fast."

Francis retrieved Sam's crutches and helped her up onto them.

Without saying anything else, they lifted Stringer again, and led by Sam's headlight, carried him around the light tower, past the keeper's house to Oscar's boat. They laid him on several seat cushions then Francis got on the radio and told dispatch they were on their way. He was told the fire department's rescue boat had just launched and was racing out of the harbor. They would intercept and at least be able to start some first aid.

Charlie threw the lines, and they left the dock. Sam stretched her legs out and lay down next to Stringer, who was still wrapped in Francis' jacket. She bunched up her coat and cautiously pushed it under his head. Kate knelt on the other side of him, holding his bruised cheek in her hand. She intermittently checked his breathing, which she said was weak and shallow.

Oscar drove his boat faster than he ever had, making good time as the lighthouse was left in the distance. About halfway to shore, they saw red strobe lights on the fire department boat, with which they quickly rendezvoused. Two EMTs jumped with their gear onto the tour boat, and Oscar headed straight for the red and green lights marking the opening in the breakwater. One EMT put an oxygen mask on Stringer's face while the other set up an IV then cut a slit in one sleeve of Francis' jacket. Due to Stringer's profound dehydration, it was difficult to cannulate a vein, but after several tries, the man was successful. Francis squeezed in an entire bag of saline before they passed through the breakwater. Along the wharf a collection of brightly flashing emergency vehicles, as well as a small crowd, waited for them.

As they were docking, Francis felt lightheaded. He tried to help carry Stringer off the boat, but he was too weak and had to lean against the gunwale. Charlie put his arm around Francis to steady him.

"Looks bad. Hope he makes it," a woman bystander said.

Francis felt nauseous, dizzy. He staggered to one side as he tried, unsuccessfully to step off the boat.

The last thing he remembered was Kate curving her arm around him and asking if he was all right.

CHAPTER FIFTY-EIGHT

SOME OF THE SPEAKERS IN THE SOUND SYSTEM MUST HAVE BLOWN because the music coming from the oceanside stage was garbled. What a bummer, but that happens sometimes at concerts on Muscle Beach. But with Tracy Chapman playing...come on!

"I love this song," Stringer murmured.

Chapman was awesome. And she was singing "The Promise," the song he'd been practicing for Sam while she was in ICU.

Stringer squinted against the large, fiery orange sun descending though a small grove of palms along the edge of the beach. There was barely any breeze coming off the Pacific, the hot, dry sand uncomfortable beneath his feet, which had become wimpy wearing sneakers most of the time in Maine.

Chapman sounded so much like Sam; he hadn't realized that before.

"Where *is* Sam?" Stringer wasn't sure if he was talking out loud or not.

Someone was trying to talk to him.

Stringer frowned. "Wait, be quiet, she's still singing."

"Gotta find Sam. She'd love this." He reached down for his skateboard, which was always under his foot or leaning against his leg waiting to flip up into his hand.

Alarmed that it wasn't there, he tried to look around but felt wicked stiff. "Where's my board?" Everything was fuzzy, out of focus. "My board—"

"String..." Sounded like his mother. "String, can you hear me?"

His eyes stung and his lids were swollen nearly shut.

The singing stopped. *Was the concert over?*

He felt warm hands take each of his. Straining against the sun, he saw something blue and flowing, like a mini waterfall. But there were no waterfalls at the beach.

"Stringer..." a face in front of him said. He tried hard to focus.

Short blond hair slowly came into view. The blue. A shock of hair. He started when the face came close and kissed him on the lips. "We're here, Stringer."

"Sam! Isn't Tracy awesome? I can't believe she's playing the beach."

"She's awesome, all right." Sam was smiling. She rested her guitar on her lap. "Never sounded better."

"Thank god, String, you're coming around." It was his mother again, from the other side. He looked to the right and watched Kate's face materialize. She looked older.

And there at the foot of the bed stood a guy in a long white coat with a stethoscope sticking out of his pocket. Charlie was next to him.

Stringer looked back at his mom. "You don't look so good," he said in a concerned voice.

"*I* don't look good?"

People started chuckling.

Stringer was puzzled. "What's so funny?"

They all laughed, each one in turn touching him, like they wanted to make sure he was real. Then Stringer started to laugh, though it made him wince. His chest and face hurt. He lifted up the sheet and saw lots of nasty gouges in his skin.

It all started flooding back. He closed his eyes for a few seconds. Those huge waves throwing him onto the rocks by the island. Banging his head in that cave. Skinning his fingertips pounding on that old padlock with a rock at the bottom of the lighthouse. The Halloween skeleton and that rat that scurried away from him when he climbed the spiral staircase. How dizzy that crazy bright light made him.

Stringer forced his swollen eyelids open again and looked at Sam. "Some crazy shit…"

Sam sat on the edge of the bed. "You're crazier than I am."

"Doubt it." Stringer sort of smiled. "You saved me, Sam, telling me that sea captain's story about the cave and the secret passageway. But it was so dark in there it wasn't easy to find. I had just one shard of light from a crack in the rocks, like where two layers met."

He reached for Sam's hand. "Otherwise I would have drowned or froze to death for sure."

Charlie spoke up. "We searched the whole island a couple of times and couldn't find a trace. Where were you?"

Stringer grinned. "Pretty tricky, huh?"

Charlie made a face. "You scared the hell out of us."

Kate shook her head, held his other arm with both hands. "I was terrified of losing you, but I never thought you were dead."

"That's nice."

Kate shook her head. "Though after McNeal shot you, it could've been over."

Stringer's eyes opened a bit wider. "Here's the thing…" He stopped. "Where's Francis?"

"Over here," Francis said from the other bed where he lay with bandaged hands on top of the sheet.

Stringer smiled. "What happened to you?"

"Long story…"

"Looks like it. You should be more careful."

Everyone laughed again.

Francis tried to sit up. "You don't remember?"

"Remember what?"

"Oh, boy," Kate said, sarcastically.

Charlie cleared his throat. "What were you saying about McNeal?"

"Oh, that McNeal didn't try to hit me. He looked me right in the eye and just shot close to me. He's a prick, but I knew he was giving me a way to get off the boat alive. He made it look like he shot me, so the other guy wouldn't shoot him for helping me. Some shit like that. I didn't have a lot of time to think."

Charlie stepped closer to the bed. "Can't be right, I saw that bastard fire his gun right at you."

"I know," Stringer said, calmly with conviction. "But as I went over the side, McNeal quickly said *buoys* to me twice. When I got away from the boats, I realized there were lobster buoys all over the place. That's how I made it to the island—swimming one buoy to the next."

Everyone looked puzzled.

"When I was tied up down below, I heard them talking up on the bridge. I think Pike was the mastermind of the whole drug-running thing. He'd somehow blackmailed McNeal—not sure how—into being part of their drug ring. Sounded like he'd been protecting their system, probably got a kick-back."

Charlie nodded. "No kidding. That's why McNeal always insisted on patrolling the harbor himself. Hardly ever let anyone else in his patrol boat."

"I think you're right," Stringer said. "That's what I saw when we were out on the lobster boat and they did that drop-off in a little cove with the cigarette boat, and Pike tried to get me drunk."

"Which thankfully is now at the bottom of the ocean, thanks to Captain Tom," Charlie chimed in. "We'd seen that cigarette boat around but didn't know what it was up to."

Stringer perked up. "Captain Tom was awesome, blowing that guy away."

Kate squeezed Stringer's hand. "Wait a minute. You mean McNeal ended up being a good guy—kind of?"

Stringer nodded. "Yeah. I'm a little foggy about it all, but when Pike shot at me, he wasn't trying to miss. He hit me in the leg then aimed right at my stomach. All I had was that fishing spear thing, so I shot him with it. Went right through his leg."

Sam grimaced.

"Then I saw Nelson come up out of the hold with a machine gun—he was going to kill me, maybe McNeal, too. That's when McNeal fired at me and let me jump overboard. He made it look like he was trying to kill me."

"Are you *sure*?" Charlie asked.

Stringer frowned. "I know what a guy looks like when he's trying to kill you." He nodded at the other bed. "So does Francis."

Francis looked over at the doorway, where someone was standing, casting a large shadow from the lights in the hallway. Captain Tom took a hesitant step into the room. "Don't mean to bother you," he said, looking uncomfortable.

"Captain Tom—" Stringer called out. "You rock!"

"Just wanted to check on you," he said, quietly. He took his weathered cap off and held it by the brim. "Didn't think I'd ever come in this place again, but I was worried for you."

From his bed, Francis introduced himself. "You made a huge difference out there. That guy could have killed everyone." Francis gestured with his bandaged hand. "And we're so sorry about your daughter."

Captain Tom looked at the floor. "Wish I could've made a difference for Kendra."

"Can't imagine," Charlie said, touching his shoulder.

Captain Tom took a step toward the bed. "Well, I gotta go. Glad you're doing good."

Stringer reached up and gave the Captain a hug. Obviously touched, and perhaps a bit embarrassed, he backed away toward the door. He slid his cap back onto this head, nodded to everyone then left.

"Poor guy," Stringer said. After a short silence, he turned to Francis. "So what happened to your hands?"

Francis glanced at Kate. "I hurt them on some stairs."

"You've got to watch yourself." Stringer smiled.

"I'll remember that."

Before Kate left for the night, she went out in the hall and came back with Francis' guitar case. "I thought you might want this so you two could play together."

Sam and Stringer brightened. "Cool," Sam said.

Stringer raised the head of his bed and strummed a chord, but his fingers were too sore to really play.

Francis smiled at Sam. "Pretty cool instrument, isn't it?"

"Yeah, sounds good. Nice old beater."

"What do you think of that signature? Been there a long time."

Sam looked puzzled. "What signature?"

"Stringer didn't show you?"

She shook her head.

"Let me see that thing." Francis took the guitar from Stringer. He fogged the rosewood with his breath then wiped it with his bandaged hand. "See that, right there? The signature under 'New York Central Park, 1992,' like I'd mentioned before."

Sam looked at the signature, seemed confused. "Who's that?"

"Look carefully. Someone you two really like."

Sam frowned then her eyes opened wide. "Oh, my God. "You're *kidding*!" She brought the guitar closer. "That's really Tracy Chapman's signature?"

Francis nodded. "Sure is."

"Wow," Sam said, admiringly. She turned to Stringer. "Why didn't you tell me?"

"Been a lot going on."

"I can't believe I called it an old beater. Sorry."

Francis chuckled. "You didn't know."

Sam admired the guitar. "I wish she'd come play at the summer festival."

"That'd be awesome," Stringer said, "but fat chance. I don't think she tours anymore. Which should be illegal."

Francis adjusted himself in bed. "I saw that my old friend Dave Mallett is the headliner this year. He's a great performer."

Sam looked a little dejected. "He's not Tracy Chapman, but he was cool to stop by and see me. Showed me a few licks."

"Wait till you hear him perform. He's one of the best folk singers around."

"We'll see," Sam said. "Chapman's the best. Her songs are what my feelings sound like."

Chapter Fifty-nine

After a couple days in the hospital, both Francis and Stringer went home. With Nelson dead and his old lady an out-of-control drunk, Judge Thornton said Sam could temporarily stay at the bungalow, which delighted her and Stringer. It took a week or so for everyone to share their different perspectives on all that had happened, but things began to settle down. Kate, though still waiting for another shoe to drop, seemed especially grateful they were all home together.

The Feds took over the hunt for Rhode Island Jimmy, and Charlie arrested his former boss, Larry McNeal, and charged him with kidnapping and extortion. He figured the state's attorney would add a few more charges. Stringer, to the amazement of Francis and Kate, wanted to visit McNeal in jail to thank him for not killing him and for giving him a head's up about the lobster buoys. Kate didn't think it was a great idea but understood his motivations were good, so she said she'd let Francis take him.

One warm evening before the town's Summer Festival, Kate and Francis were sitting on the lawn watching a pale red moon lift over the Atlantic. She slid her hand over his. "I owe you an apology," she said, quietly. "A *big* one."

Francis listened.

"I know I hurt you, almost threw all this away. My insecurities run deep and they're mixed up with fears and anxiety. It's weird, but the way I used to deal with it all was to do whatever I wanted, not care much about other people, except Stringer. But it's not the way a sober woman acts. I don't mean it as an excuse, but I can't get away from meetings again. They keep me sane."

"I've noticed," Francis said, with a grin.

"Alcoholism's strange. It's a disease that tells you you don't have a disease."

"Interesting way to put it."

Kate pulled his hand towards her. "And I want to clear the air about Richard. I know I…"

Francis looked at her. "I hope we're done with Richard."

"Yes, but I need to get something off my—"

Francis shook his head. "If you want to move forward together—and I do—I don't want to hear any more about him. Whatever happened is done."

Kate gently persisted. "It wasn't as bad as you think. I never had sex with him."

Francis looked like he was trying hard to keep his emotions under control. "Good."

Kate felt a light, soothing sea breeze against her face. They shared a long silence, which to her felt like they were quietly healing together.

After a while, Francis spoke. "I know Richard wants to come by the studio and talk to Stringer, and now I feel a little better about it. I think it will be good for his ego, but then that's got to be it. Richard's gone from our lives."

Kate nodded. "I totally get it. And thank you for letting me clear my conscience."

"I understand, and I guess I'm glad you told me."

Despite the uneasiness between them, Kate pulled Francis closer. "I'm glad you took me back."

He touched her arm affectionately. "I never let you go. You were just wandering off the reservation for a while."

"So to speak."

"Yes." Francis lifted his arm so Kate could curl against him. "It feels good holding you." He stroked her long dark hair, which fell smoothly over her shoulder. "And let's not lose sight of the fact I've got my own stuff to work on." Francis made a face. "I think I was becoming an old fuddy-duddy."

"No comment."

"Smart woman."

The next day, because it would have felt so awkward, Francis decided not to be at the gallery when Richard came by to see Stringer. However, as soon as Kate and Stringer left for town, Francis felt left out of something important. He also felt acutely insecure, like he needed to keep an eye on Kate, at least when she was around Richard. So Francis drove into town after them, parked across the street from the gallery and waited. Soon a ridiculously shiny blue Mustang pulled up across from him. A man with slicked-back hair got out, flicked a cigarette to the pavement, and walked up the steps into the gallery.

Francis felt himself bristle. "You're kidding me—"

As Francis imagined Kate with this asshole, he again felt anger rise inside. Then he reminded himself she had chosen to come back to him and seemed genuine about it. Still, he'd take a gander in the gallery anyway. He got out, crossed the street, and slowly climbed the stairs. He felt nervous as he peeked in the window. Kate and Richard were standing next to each other with their backs to him. Stringer looked like he was bored with the conversation. Soon he saw Francis in the window and ran toward him.

"You came!" Stringer said, pulling the door open. He gave Francis a hug then pulled him inside.

Kate and Richard stepped away from each other. For a few awkward moments no one said anything. Then Richard pushed his hair back, stepped forward, and extended his hand to Francis.

Francis stared at Richard's hand, imagined it had held Kate's breast and probably done other things. He hesitated, then offered Richard his left hand, the one without a bandage.

Without a formal introduction, Richard turned to a pair of paintings on easels in the middle of the floor. "This kid has real talent."

"Yes, he does," Francis said.

Richard motioned to Kate. "I gave her a card for a dealer in New York who would like to represent him. He has a chance to make it and…" He paused. "It would be better if I didn't represent him."

Francis looked at the card and was surprised to see the name of a longtime friend in the city, ironically one of the dealers he would have suggested to Kate and Stringer in the first place. "Yes, I know Paul. He's experienced, and reputable."

Richard nodded. "He holds you in high regard, has one of your seascapes over a mantel in his gallery."

Stringer nudged Francis. "This is great, huh?"

Francis looked at Kate, who was smiling at Stringer, paying no attention to Richard.

"Yes, Stringer, this is terrific." Francis turned to Kate. "What do you think?"

"Richard can leave, and we'll talk about it."

Francis was pleased with her response.

Richard nervously lifted his belt, smoothed his black pants. "Get in touch if you need anything," he said to Kate. "You have my number."

Kate looked away.

"I wouldn't wait too long. Dealers have short attention spans with rookies."

As Richard prepared to leave, Francis backed off the braided rug to give him room. He did not want to shake the guy's hand again.

"Good luck," Richard said then he stepped over to Francis. "Take good care of Kate. You're lucky to have her."

Francis' breathing quickened. He wanted to punch this guy in the face.

Richard turned away and walked to the door. He spoke to Francis over his shoulder. "Not many women turn me down." The door shut behind him.

When Francis heard the sound of the Mustang's powerful engine, he stepped to the front window. There was the shrill screech of rubber as Richard tore out of his parking place, puffs of blue smoke lingering above fresh tire marks.

CHAPTER SIXTY

STRINGER WAS MORE THAN DELIGHTED TO HAVE SAM LIVING AT THE bungalow. He made money working for Kasa in her garden, as well as doing odd jobs for her and for Francis. He waited on Sam whenever she'd let him, and they played their guitars together, often late into the night, so much so Kate and Francis were surprised their fingers didn't bleed. It seemed like they were planning to do something special, but neither said anything about it and Kate and Francis didn't ask.

Everyone seemed excited for the upcoming Summer Festival to be held downtown at the harbor. Kasa made her usual half-dozen strawberry-rhubarb pies for the benefit dinner, and Stringer entered two of his paintings in the art show. Francis was particularly psyched about the annual concert, as David Mallett was headlining an excellent bill featuring many local musicians. The night would be topped off with a great fireworks show out over the water.

People came from all around, and Ginny sold almost as many Down East souvenirs during Festival as she did the rest of the summer. This year's favorites were little lobsters made out of clothes pins with big eyes that rolled around when you shook them. The local Brownie troop had made hundreds of them as a fundraiser, but Ginny still couldn't keep them in stock. "Tourists will buy anything with a damn lobster on it," she said.

Charlie closed off Harbor Avenue early in the day and by late afternoon hundreds of people had arrived for the concert, setting up their brightly-colored beach chairs overlooking the stage which had been constructed on the main wharf. It was a clear day, making it a beautiful venue with its backdrop of boats in the harbor and the shimmering Atlantic beyond. The lawns of homes facing the water were covered with beach towels, blankets, and coolers. A number of families had gathered near the stage where they were playing instruments, their little kids dancing on blankets, while the older ones ran around trailing lit sparklers over their heads.

That morning before anyone else was up, Francis had spent a little time alone in his studio. He thought back over all that had happened, but mostly about how much he loved Kate. He didn't want to live his life without her or Stringer. When turmoil had struck and he wasn't sure what the future held, he'd hidden the engagement ring back behind an old bookcase. He retrieved it, admired its bright sparkle and placed it in his jacket pocket.

Francis arrived downtown early so he could put their chairs up front near Pike's old shack. Kate came later with Kasa and Buster. Nearby, Charlie and his deputies had set up a tiny command center complete with a golf cart sporting small American flags and a blue light on top. The local ambulance was parked at the bottom of Harbor Avenue, surrounded by lawn chairs making it hard to imagine how it would get out if it was needed.

Stringer and Sam sat on the ground close to the stage with a couple of his skateboarding friends. Francis noticed that their guitars were on the ground next to them, but that wasn't unusual as they didn't go many places without them. Sam was happily out of her fixator and in a fiberglass cast, which made it much easier for her to get around.

Horace Bagley, Winter Cove's Mayor was the master of ceremonies, and as always, spent too much time talking about himself during the introductions. The first warm-up act was a local country singer who frequented the Mill Pub, and was known for doing pretty decent Toby Keith impersonations. Much of the crowd, as well as fishermen listening on their boats hooted and hollered through his rowdy renditions of "As Good As I Once Was," and "How Do You Like Me Now?"

The second act was a local high school senior who'd recently won the state harp competition. To the surprise of many, the audience settled down and listened to her beautiful rendition of Pachelbel's Canon in D Major followed by a surprisingly robust version of the Beatle's "We Can Work It Out," which she dedicated to her apparently wayward boyfriend.

The next performer was a slightly off-key jazz singer from Portland, whose blistering runs could have caused ears to bleed. Relieved when she concluded her last number, the crowd gave her muted but polite applause.

There was a short intermission for free Beal's Ice Cream while the stage crew set up for the Maine Event, as it was called. David Mallett had his sons' band playing with him, and by the time everything was ready, the stage was full of amplifiers, instruments and artists.

The sun had set over the hills west of town and a purple hue illuminated the edges of a few cumulous clouds out by Crescent Island. As people settled into their seats, two tall light towers came to life, bathing the stage in yellow, red and blue light.

Horace, now wearing a cowboy hat, stepped to the microphone. "Ladies and gentlemen—and the rest of you, too—" He laughed into the mic at his own joke. "First off, this news just in: on a Big Papi homer, the Red Sox beat the damn Yankees at Fenway, nine-to-seven."

A cheer went up from the crowd, with a few scattered boos from heavily outnumbered Yankee fans.

"Now this is the part of the festivities we've all been waiting for, the Maine Event. Tonight, we are fortunate to have with us one of Maine's most famous folk singers, direct from Sebec, right here on this very stage. After seventeen albums, thousands of shows, writer of the iconic 'Garden Song,' please help me welcome North Road Records recording artist, David Mallett and the Mallett Brothers Band!"

Horace swept his large arm across the stage as a bunch of unassuming guys came around a makeshift curtain in the back. They waved to the cheering audience and strapped on their guitars. The drummer hit a riff and the boys broke into their fast-paced, original song, "There Are No Rules In This Game." Many in the audience knew the song and sang and clapped along with the band. A dozen people got up in front of the stage and danced barefoot. One little blond-haired girl in particular got the attention of the crowd as her hair was full of daisies that went flying as she was swung around in the air by her father.

After another couple of songs, including their high-strung bluegrass tune, "F-150," Luke Mallett stepped to a mic, held up his hand, and quieted the crowd. "Thank you. We appreciate the applause, but we know why you're *really* here."

The crowd started clapping and yelling. "We love you!" a woman yelled.

"We love you, too!" Luke yelled back, laughing.

"So, without further ado, I want to introduce a man who needs no introduction, one of America's greatest folk singers, our father, David Mallett!"

A surge of people rose to their feet as a man with a gray beard and a guitar walked to the front microphone. He pulled a harmonica from his pants pocket, popped it into the metal holder around his neck and blew a few notes that sounded like an old-style train whistle.

He looked up at the crowd. "Nice to see all you folks out there tonight." His voice was gravelly and soothing, sort of like what God would sound like if he were a folk singer. "We're going to sing a bunch of songs for you, and if you've got any requests, just yell 'em out."

Immediately, the crowd started calling out a host of his many folk songs, which made him and the audience laugh.

"Well, we can only sing one tune at a time, so we'll try this one for you." He nodded to his sons, the band kicked in, and Mallett and his boys sang "Celebration," a modern ballad about how we need to work to save the earth, and ourselves—now!

Mallett performed a collection of his well-known tunes, including "Fire," "Greenin' Up," "I Knew This Place," and "The Haying Song." Then he slowed things down and introduced a beautiful new ballad. "This next song is called, 'The Girl with the Golden Hair,' and I'd like to send it out to someone special in the audience tonight, a girl named Sam."

Totally surprised, Sam and Stringer looked at each other.

With a single spotlight on him, Mallett sang the song with just his guitar, the nearly full moon reflecting off gentle waves in the harbor behind him. When the song came to a close, Mallett slipped his harmonica into his pocket, took a drink then looked at the crowd. "We've got a special treat for you folks tonight, a Maine debut of sorts. A while back I met a young fella and his girl. She was teaching him how to play the guitar when she was in a terrible accident and almost died up at the old lookout off Route One."

Murmurs went through the crowd as people realized who he was talking about.

"A helluva lot of good people worked hard to save her and now she's here in Winter's Cove convalescing with her boyfriend's family, whose father is an old friend of mine, the great painter, Francis Monroe."

Mallett looked at Stringer and Sam down in front of the stage.

"I'm going to ask these two kids to come up and sing a song for you. They've been practicing, and I think they're pretty darn good." Mallett waved them toward the stage. "Come on up here, now, and sing for us."

Looking sheepish, Stringer stood and helped Sam get up on her crutches. She limped toward the stage stairs followed by Stringer, who carried their guitars.

Powerful emotions rose inside Francis as he watched Stringer and Sam climb onto the stage where they were welcomed by Mallett and the band, all of whom started clapping with the audience. Francis held Kate tightly. She stared at the stage, her eyes wet with tears.

Mallett helped them get situated on stools in the center of the stage then leaned into a microphone. "Help me welcome, Stringer and Sam!" Then he stepped back out of the spotlight.

Stringer looked intimidated, but once Sam got her casted leg comfortable, she pulled her microphone closer and motioned for Stringer to do the same.

"How you all doing tonight?" Sam asked in her confident stage voice. Many in the crowd yelled back.

Sam motioned to Mallett who was standing at the side of the stage. "Thank you, Mr. Mallett, for letting us come up here." She looked out at the audience. "He's been a real inspiration to me and Stringer. And what a great singer!" The crowd broke into applause.

As Sam tuned her guitar, she seemed to get more nervous, emotional even.

Stringer hadn't yet said a word, but as Sam faltered, he cleared his throat and leaned toward the mic. "Francis had gotten out this beautiful old guitar and let me learn to play on it. Sam's the one who was teaching me—before the accident, I mean. When she got hurt, I tried to teach myself, and Mr. Mallett helped me a lot." He adjusted his guitar strap. "I don't play very well, but this song saved my sanity when Sam was in a coma in ICU. Her nurse, Cindy, let me practice in her room a lot."

Francis felt Kate lean into him on one side. Kasa stood close and patted his arm on the other side.

Sam spoke into the mic again. "I want to thank everyone who helped me, especially the Monroes." She pulled one of the mics closer to her guitar. "So this is our favorite Tracy Chapman song."

Stringer leaned back into the mic, and pointed. "We're dedicating it to my mom and my dad, who are right out there tonight."

"Yeah, you guys rock!" Sam chimed in.

Francis just about melted when he heard Stringer call him "dad."

Kate reached up and took Francis' hand in hers. "We are so lucky."

"We are," he said, kissing her on the forehead. "Let's never forget it."

"I'm so grateful to you. After all my shit, I've found what I didn't even know was possible." She looked into his eyes. "It's because of you, your steadiness, your belief in Stringer and me. Nobody ever believed in me."

Francis wrapped his arms around Kate and held her as Stringer and Sam performed a remarkably beautiful version of "The Promise," which brought the crowd to their feet for a prolonged standing ovation, which included Mallett and his sons.

Feeling a swell of emotion, Francis reached into his jacket pocket and held the ring box for a moment before letting it settle into his pocket again. Later. This moment was for Stringer and Sam.

Acknowledgements

I want to express deep appreciation to my first readers, Angela Peck, Toby Sadkin, and my wife, Marietta. Your thoughtful comments and suggestions were essential in bringing the manuscript from a loose first draft to a book ready for the world. I am so fortunate that for many years you all have been a vital part of my writer's journey.

I want to thank the great American folk singer, David Mallett, who gave me permission to use lines from his song, "Fire," for the epigraph, and also allowed me to use him as a character in the story. Please support his music by visiting: www.davidmallett.com

I have also been fortunate to work with professional freelance editor Lesley Kellas Payne of Fresno, California for over twenty years. Her insights, guidance and support have dramatically raised the level of all of my manuscripts. You are a special gift.

Thank you to Winslow Colwell of Middlebury, Vermont for your painstaking work in designing this book, inside and out, and for your careful reading of the manuscript. Please visit: www.wrensongdesign.com

And thanks also to Ruth Sylvester, copy editor and proofreader extraordinaire.

Finally, heartfelt remembrance of my dear, departed friend and mentor, Howard Frank Mosher. His many years of generous support made all the difference.